D0019406

THE JUVENILIA OF
JANE AUSTEN AND CHARLOTTE BRONTË

Jane Austen (1775–1817) was the seventh child in a family of eight and lived with her family at Steventon until they moved to Bath in 1801. After her father's death in 1805, she and her mother went to live in Southampton until, in 1809, they settled in Chawton, Hampshire. As a child and young woman she read widely, including work by Fielding, Sterne and her favourite poet, Crabbe, and wrote *Love and Friendship* when she was fourteen. She also wrote *A History of England* ('by a partial, ignorant and prejudiced historian') at fifteen and *A Collection of Letters* at sixteen. *Lesley Castle* was also probably written during these years and *Lady Susan* between 1793 and 1794. Her later works were only published after much revision, four novels being published during her lifetime. These were *Sense and Sensibility* (1811), *Pride and Prejudice* (1813), *Mansfield Park* (1814) and *Emma* (1816). Two other novels, *Northanger Abbey* and *Persuasion*, were published posthumously in 1818. She also left an unfinished novel, *The Watsons*, and at the time of her death was working on *Sanditon*, a fragmentary draft of which survives.

•

Charlotte Brontë (1816–55) spent most of her life in Haworth, on the Yorkshire moors, where her father was curate. Her mother died in 1821 and, left to pursue their education mainly at home, all the surviving Brontë children became involved in a rich fantasy life. They read widely, including works by Byron and Sir W. Scott, and *The Arabian Nights*. They wrote tales, fantasies, poems and journals, and brought out a monthly magazine. Charlotte and Branwell, her only brother, collaborated in the invention of the imaginary kingdom of Angria and Emily and Anne in the invention of Gondal. Charlotte wrote four novels, *Jane Eyre* (1847), *Shirley* (1849), *Villette* (1853) and *The Professor* (her first novel, but published posthumously in 1857). *Emma*, a fragment, was published in 1860.

•

Frances Beer gained her BA and MA degrees in English from Radcliffe College and Columbia University respectively, and her PhD from the University of Toronto. She has worked as an editor in New York and is now an Associate Professor of English at York University, Toronto, where she has taught since 1971. Her previous publications include an edition of Julian of Norwich's *Revelations of Divine Love* (1978) and a translation of Pierre le Gentil's *La Chanson de Roland* (1969).

PENGUIN CLASSICS

THE JUVENILIA OF
JANE AUSTEN
AND
CHARLOTTE BRONTË

Edited by Frances Beer

PENGUIN BOOKS

Penguin Books Ltd, Harmondsworth, Middlesex, England
Viking Penguin Inc., 40 West 23rd Street, New York, New York 10010, U.S.A.
Penguin Books Australia Ltd, Ringwood, Victoria, Australia
Penguin Books Canada Limited, 2801 John Street, Markham, Ontario, Canada L3R 1B4
Penguin Books (N.Z.) Ltd, 182–190 Wairau Road, Auckland 10, New Zealand

This edition first published in Penguin Books 1986

Introduction and Notes copyright © Frances Beer, 1986
All rights reserved

Typeset, printed and bound in Great Britain by
Hazell Watson & Viney Limited,
Member of the BPCC Group,
Aylesbury, Bucks
Filmset in 9/11pt VIP Plantin

Except in the United States of America,
this book is sold subject to the condition
that it shall not, by way of trade or otherwise,
be lent, re-sold, hired out, or otherwise circulated
without the publisher's prior consent in any form of
binding or cover other than that in which it is
published and without a similar condition
including this condition being imposed
on the subsequent purchaser

Contents

❖

CHARLOTTE BRONTË

Introduction

Jane Austen might be said to epitomize neoclassical elegance and proportion; Charlotte Brontë, on the other hand, represents all the passion and extravagance of the romantic spirit: in most obvious ways these two authors would seem to be radical opposites. Austen was born and raised at Steventon in the soft, rolling country of Hampshire; Brontë lived for most of her life on the forbidding moors of Yorkshire. Austen's family circle, including five brothers, a sister, and numerous cousins, was 'affectionate, cheerful, untroubled', their social life 'a steady leisurely spaced-out round of morning calls, dinner parties and card parties'; outings, musicmaking and dancing were frequent activities.[1] The four Brontë children, 'grave and silent beyond their years', were bound together by the shadow of death – first of their mother, when Charlotte was five, then of the two eldest girls, Maria and Elizabeth, less than four years later – and by their absolute social isolation: literally, 'they knew no other children' in Haworth, '. . . they were all in all to each other'.[2] Though both fathers were clergymen, their tempers were opposite: George Austen, known as the 'handsome proctor', was good-natured and outgoing, Patrick Brontë stern and withdrawn. Miss Branwell, the aunt who looked after the household after Mrs Brontë's death, was morbid and repressive, so that even at home the children's only comfortable contact was the family servant, Tabby.[3] Homes more different than Haworth and Steventon are difficult to conceive.

Yet there are a few peculiar ways in which the lives of their

1. David Cecil, *A Portrait of Jane Austen* (Harmondsworth, 1980), pp. 25, 34.

2. Elizabeth Gaskell, *The Life of Charlotte Brontë* (Harmondsworth, 1975), pp. 87, 93, 95.

3. Winifred Gérin, *Charlotte Brontë: The Evolution of Genius* (Oxford, 1967), p. 33 ff.

young occupants were alike. When Jane was seven and Charlotte eight they both were sent to boarding school, and both came dangerously close to death. At Mrs Cawley's establishment, Jane and Cassandra became seriously ill with a putrid fever, but were fetched home in time to be saved. At Cowan Bridge, Charlotte and Emily themselves escaped infection, but their two sisters succumbed to the epidemic that devastated the school. Perhaps because of these narrow escapes their sisterly bonds were intensified – as adults Cassandra and Emily remained their best friends – and in their later work the immense value of this bond is reflected: Elinor and Marianne Dashwood, Elizabeth and Jane Bennet, Jane Eyre and the Rivers sisters, Caroline Helstone and Shirley Keeldar are among the more remarkable portraits of female loyalty and devotion in English literature.

Both Austen and Brontë had free access to their fathers' libraries, in an age when popular literature was commonly considered dangerous to the suggestible minds of young ladies, and the reading of the Scriptures and of sermons the only really safe female activity. Jane's early readings included the works of such writers as Richardson and Burney as well as Pope, Johnson, and Cowper. Charlotte's ranged from Shakespeare and Milton to Scott and Byron; to her list must be added a variety of periodicals, *Annuals*, Aesop's *Fables*, and the *Arabian Nights*.[4] The precocious erudition of both is surely extraordinary.

But perhaps the most dramatic similarity between the two was the production, and preservation of, copious juvenile writings. These juvenilia are, of course, sometimes crude and sometimes childish. But they also serve to demonstrate their authors' originality and freedom of spirit, their delight in the very process of creation, their changing attitudes towards character and style. The youthful work of both girls, taken as a whole, can in fact be seen to reveal a certain winnowing process: some experiments are tried and modified or abandoned, others are pursued and developed, to recur in their later novels. Over time we can see decisions, whether conscious or otherwise, taking form that will lead with astonishing

4. Neither list, of course, is inclusive. It is revealing that as a girl, Jane re-read *Sir Charles Grandison* so often as to know parts of it almost by heart, while Charlotte had memorized passages of Byron's *Cain* and *Manfred* by the time she was thirteen.

steadiness from the pure fun of their first outpourings towards their artistically and morally mature work. Both sets of juvenilia provide us with an extraordinary opportunity to watch the growth and coalescence of the creative consciousness.

I

Jane Austen's juvenilia were composed roughly between 1787 and 1793, when she was between the ages of twelve and eighteen. She herself sorted and divided her work into three volumes, not necessarily chronological: the second volume bears the earliest date (1790) but, according to Southam, a number of pieces in the first volume are 'evidently of earlier composition'.[5] She made fair copies of all three volumes, to which she made additions and corrections as late as 1809. These efforts, described by her nephew as 'transitory amusements' which 'Jane was continually supplying to the family party',[6] were almost certainly not meant for other eyes, but it is characteristic that what she left would nonetheless be carefully culled and well-ordered. How much she rejected cannot be known, but she has made sure, in the three volumes that she decided to keep, to dedicate at least one piece each to every member of her family, to her best friend, and to two of her favourite cousins.

Such gentle tact is not extended to the targets of Jane's wit in Volume the First. She gleefully turns her critical guns on the excesses of sentimentality so typical of the period's 'lachrymose novel'[7] and the attendant vices and virtues of its dramatis personae. What is perhaps even more striking about these early pieces than their outrageous humour is their toughness; at twelve the little assassin is eagerly at work, showing no mercy to her victims. Even as she parodies literary excess, she takes deadly aim at a range of real human foibles.

Some of her targets, predictably, reflect the influence of that neoclassical perspective which she so admired. Thus we encounter

5. B. C. Southam, *Volume the Second by Jane Austen* (Oxford, 1963), p. 213.

6. J. E. Austen-Leigh, 'A Memoir of Jane Austen', reprinted in *Persuasion* (Harmondsworth, 1965), p. 302.

7. The term is Marvin Mudrick's (*Jane Austen: Irony as Defense and Discovery*, Princeton, 1952, p. 5).

an early tendency to characterize, along with Pope, according to
Ruling Passion: 'This clue once found, unravels all the rest.'[8] In
Jack and Alice, the three Simpson sisters – Caroline, Sukey, and
Cecilia – are always seen to be, respectively, ambitious, envious,
and affected: the cause and explanation of all their actions can be
found in these three vices. Poor Alice, of the title, whose fault was
that she was 'a little addicted to the bottle', is invariably at one or
another stage of intoxication, preferably as advanced as possible.
Sir William Mountague, in his story, does nothing but fall in love,
serially, with every pretty girl he meets, thereby as regularly
abandoning the previous object of his affections. And the lovelorn
Emma, learning of her Edgar's absence, 'continued in tears the
remainder of her life'.

With Fielding, Jane sees affectation, that is vanity and hypocrisy,
as a key source of 'the true ridiculous'.[9] The splendid ego of *Jack
and Alice*'s Charles Adams, a youth of 'so dazzling a beauty that
none but eagles could look him in the face', is reflected in his
response to the father of one of his desperate female suitors, come
to ask for his hand:

'Sir, I may perhaps be expected to appear pleased at and grateful for the
offer you have made me: but let me tell you that I consider it as an affront.
I look upon myself to be, sir, a perfect beauty . . . I expect nothing more
in my wife than my wife will find in me – perfection.'

In *Frederic and Elfrida* the heroine, delicate creature that she is,
postpones the day of her wedding for something approaching
twenty years; but upon 'perceiving a growing passion' in the bosom
of her fiancé for a younger woman, she manufactures a series of fits
which serve to bring him promptly to heel.

Most of the portraits in these first short burlesques are too brief
to allow for analysis of character, but Austen does show signs of
looking beyond simple vanity and hypocrisy in her criticism of
human weakness. She holds up for repeated ridicule examples of
emotional superficiality, materialism, self-importance, mental
vacancy, gross impracticality. While some of her characters, such
as Mr Clifford or the beautiful Cassandra, seem to be portraits in

8. Alexander Pope, *Moral Essays*, Epistle I, iii, 178.
9. Henry Fielding, Author's Preface, *Joseph Andrews* (Oxford, 1926).

pure silliness, a few, particularly *Jack and Alice*'s Lady Williams, are studies in corruption which, if they do not qualify as complex, are something more than simplistic. Lady Williams takes Alice, and then Lucy, both of whom are hopelessly in love with the dazzling Charles Adams, under her apparently protective wing. She listens with affected sympathy to Alice's pathetic tale, but enjoys goading her into a rage by alluding to her alcoholic complexion or her predilection for the bottle; she privately tells Lucy how fond she is of Alice, but laces her account with enough damning bits of information to eradicate any vestige of respect; her slippery equivocation ensures that Lucy will go off to Bath with the Simpson girls (who are, of course, still ambitious, envious and affected) and heads her towards a union with a rich but unprincipled duke: her machinations effectively leave the field clear for – Lady Williams, who, in a denouement that is a surprise to everyone else, snares Charles Adams for herself!

But these attacks, no matter how pitiless, are always delivered with an irrepressible sense of mischief: the method Jane uses to ridicule her silly and affected characters is simple, and its effect is excruciatingly funny; she manipulates her figures so that their every action and response is predictable, they have no freedom to surprise. The ingredients of this kind of humour are usefully analysed by Henri Bergson in his essay 'Laughter':[10] it should be accompanied by the 'absence of feeling', 'anaesthesia of the heart'; its appeal is to the intelligence. Laughter's cause is 'mechanical inelasticity', and it can be provoked by any sort of reflex action – by a person slipping on a road, by a practical joke, by absent-mindedness; or by vice, which so controls the individual that he resembles a puppet. Bergson's ingredients, it will be seen, dovetail quite neatly with the notion of Ruling Passion, and are likewise to be encountered in Austen's burlesques. She admits, and allows her audience, no sympathetic reaction to these early characters; the nature of our response, when we can stop laughing, is cerebral rather than emotional; the cause of our laughter is the predictability of these characters, the thoroughness with which they are controlled by their special vice. Bergson notes, finally, that the greater a

10. Henri Bergson, 'Laughter', in *Comedy*, ed. W. Sypher (New York, 1956), pp. 63 ff.

character's ignorance of himself, the more comic he is: Jane's early studies in pretension are blissfully unconscious, thoroughly un-educable; the regular discrepancy between the characters' own view of themselves and what they really are underscores their absurdity.[11] While Alice, for example, perceives herself as a touching romantic figure, we know that though one hand may clutch her heart, the other will always be reaching for the nearest bottle.

Austen took to the technique of ridicule with evident ease and relish, and though she qualified it in her later work, she did not let it go. *Northanger Abbey*'s Mrs Allen can always be counted on to reveal her superficiality through her obsession with dress; *Sense and Sensibility*'s Mr Palmer will predictably be rude to his wife and immediately bury his nose in the newspaper; *Emma*'s Mr Wood-house will invariably fret over the likelihood of everyone taking cold, and then try to offset the imminent epidemic by ordering gruel all round. But in the novels Austen provides her puppets with a context, surrounds them with numbers of three-dimensional characters, most of whom are eminently capable of silliness at one point or another, but who are allowed by their creator to grow beyond the narrow confines of a single Ruling Passion.

It is in Volume the Second's *Love and Friendship* – which in its limited way reveals an undeniable brilliance – that we encounter the culmination of Austen's effort at sustained and unmitigated ridicule. Laura and Sophia both fancy themselves to be quintes-sential representatives of sensibility. As Laura says of herself:

. . . lovely as I was, the graces of my person were the least of my perfections . . . In my mind, every virtue that could adorn it was centered; it was the rendezvous of every good quality and of every noble sentiment.

Theirs epitomizes the sentimental ideal of spontaneous attachment:

We flew into each other's arms, and after having exchanged vows of mutual friendship for the rest of our lives, instantly unfolded to each other the most inward secrets of our hearts.

Together they hold in infinite scorn the notion of filial obedience,

11. Cf. Mudrick, op. cit., p. 1. He points to the incongruity between the 'large idea and the inadequate ego'.

and succeed in turning the affections of their benefactor's daughter from a trustworthy suitor, approved by her father, to an unscrupulous fortune-hunter. As one, they believe in their inalienable right to acquire funds by whatever means are available, with the result that they regularly steal from this same benefactor, 'having agreed together that it would be a proper treatment of so vile a wretch'. Perhaps their only discernible difference is in their response to the sequential deaths of their romantic husbands. Laura merely runs mad, while Sophia is so imprudent as to swoon after the evening dew has fallen – and the effect for her is fatal: 'beware of swoons, dear Laura,' she cautions on her deathbed. 'A frenzy fit is not one quarter so pernicious . . . Run mad as often as you choose; but do not faint.'

Delightful as Laura, Sophia, and their absurdities may be, they are not capable of variety; and hilarious as the effect of Austen's ridicule assuredly is, it does not allow for dimension, or the detailed study of character which was to be so central to her later work, and which she so admired, for example, in the novels of Richardson.[12] For all its polish and wit, *Love and Friendship* proved too narrow; and where we first see an interest in character asserting itself in a recognizably Austenesque way is in a piece entitled *The Three Sisters*. Although included at the end of Volume the First, it is followed by two entries dated June 1793, and seems very likely, then, to have been composed well after *Love and Friendship*'s 1790. Certainly the contents show their author to have gained something in literary sophistication, and to be experimenting with a wider range of techniques.

The Three Sisters's form is epistolary but, unlike *Love and Friendship*, Austen allows the letters to be from two correspondents; thus she can try out different voices and points of view, different versions of the same reality. The situation that emerges from the letters also represents the first really interesting plot kernel encountered so far: the eldest of the Stanhope sisters, Mary, has received an offer of marriage from the odious Mr Watts; she despises him but cannot bear losing him; her mother refuses to let him out of the family, and decrees that if Mary won't have him one of the younger girls shall; the younger sisters, Sophy and Georgiana,

12. Frank Bradbrook, *Jane Austen and Her Predecessors* (New York, 1966), p. 84.

conspire to fool Mary into believing that they will accept Watts; out of pride, and spite, she then accepts him, and they are spared.

The figures of Mary and of Watts are not far off the caricatures of the early burlesques. Mary we soon find to be compulsively avaricious and competitive; hating Watts she nonetheless determines to have him so that she can lord it over the neighbour girls and chaperone her sisters. 'He is extremely disagreable,' she writes to a friend,

and I hate him more than any body else in the world. He has a large fortune . . . but then he is very healthy . . . If I accept him I know I shall be miserable all the rest of my life . . . I believe I shall have him. It will be such a triumph to be married before Sophy, Georgiana, and the Duttons . . .

But she doesn't accept without a desperate fight to see just how much she can get out of him in the way of a marriage settlement:

'And remember, I am to have a new carriage . . ., a new saddle horse, a suit of fine lace, and an infinite number of the most valuable jewels . . . You must set up your phaeton . . .; you must buy four of the finest bays in the kingdom . . .; you must entirely new furnish your house after my taste [etc., . . .]'

Needless to say our sympathetic response to Mary is hardly forthcoming, and Mr Watts with his unalleviated arrogance is calculated to sustain, if not increase, the anaesthesia of our hearts. 'Pray madam,' he says to Mary's mother,

'do not lay any restraint on Miss Stanhope by obliging her to be civil. If she does not choose to accept my hand, I can offer it else where; for as I am by no means guided by a particular preference to you above your sisters, it is equally the same to me which I marry of the three.'

But Mary and her suitor are set in context with the introduction of Sophy and Georgiana: the delineation of the younger sisters and of their relationship points to a new level of engagement on their author's part, and puts the whole of this novel fragment solidly on to new ground. Q. D. Leavis remarks that 'the second sister (Sophy) is the candid Jane Bennet, the youngest (Georgiana) the lively and determined Elizabeth'.[13] This may seem a slight exag-

13. Q. D. Leavis, 'A Critical Theory of Jane Austen's Writings', *Scrutiny*, X, 1941, p. 74.

gcration, but the parallels are remarkable. The sharpness of Georgiana's tongue is very like that of Elizabeth: of her mother, for instance, she says, 'we neither of us attempted to alter [her] resolution, which I am sorry to say is generally more strictly kept than rationally formed'. With Elizabeth Georgiana shares an absolute moral repugnance at the idea of marrying for convenience: 'My determination is made. I would never marry Mr Watts were beggary the only alternative.' The spirited Georgiana concocts the scheme to fool Mary as much to protect the softer Sophy as herself:

> I should not expect her to sacrifice *her* happiness by becoming his wife from a motive of generosity to me, which I was afraid her good nature and sisterly affection might induce her to do.

But she must overcome Sophy's Jane-like scruples before they can proceed with their plan. The process by which she accomplishes this involves a display of cleverness that again recalls Elizabeth: 'he is rather plain to be sure, but then what is beauty in a man? . . . They say he is stingy: we'll call that prudence . . .'; so she runs through the worst of his defects, pretending that they only conceal hidden virtues, and by laughter eases Sophy into collaboration. Still, in the execution of their scheme Sophy must be cued by the mischievous Georgiana, and – again like Jane – recoils from telling an outright untruth.

With *The Three Sisters* Austen is moving firmly in the direction of *Pride and Prejudice*. She has not rejected outright the materials of burlesque – though Mary is perhaps not quite so wooden as her predecessors – but she has modified them, and integrated them into a larger structure in which the burlesque elements themselves are able to play a more sophisticated part. Mary is made fun of, but she is not *only* made fun of. *The Three Sisters* begins to undertake the business of serious moral criticism – hardly a surprising development if, as we might expect, Austen agrees with her favourite, Dr Johnson, that 'the end of poetry is to instruct by pleasing'.[14] In none of the early pieces was a set of virtues advanced to oppose the parade of vices. How severely can a Laura or Sophia be judged if they have no positive foils, and if the feelings of the

14. Samuel Johnson, 'Preface to Shakespeare' *The Works of Samuel Johnson* (Oxford, 1825).

audience are in a state of total suspension anyhow? But the extremes of Mary Stanhope's greed and hypocrisy are countered by Sophy's gentleness and Georgiana's wit and integrity; and our sympathetic response to the characters of the two younger girls, to their plight and to their mutual loyalty, follows naturally.

This emotional thawing, too, accords with the Johnsonian theory of the successful moral function of literature: for the fullest effect, the faculties of intellect and reason are essential, but not sufficient; the imagination and the emotions must also be engaged. Literature must connect with feeling for it to be capable of instruction.

Thus Austen admits the sympathetic response, and broadens her critical targets to include society as well as the individual; as she promotes herself to a new grade of humanism, she becomes a more effective moral presence. The problem of what to do with Mr Watts is deadly serious: *someone* is going to get stuck with him, and it is an appalling social reality that forces a family of girls with a widowed mother of slender means into this grotesque corner. So Mary is criticized for her vices; but, though herself beyond sympathy, she is also presented as a victim, the warped product of a warping system.

The movement away from a strict neoclassical reaction to a series of isolated foibles – and towards a romantic response to the individual as potential victim of a materialistic, claustrophobic society – is crucial to Austen's artistic development, and will be carried over and refined in her novels. Her romanticism, if such we can call it, will not take her so far as to abandon her toughness on the question of personal responsibility, or to justify the extremes of rebellion or despair. But in the straits faced by the Dashwood or the Bennet girls – the narrowness of their lives, the apparent obligation to marry, no matter whom, to survive – and even more in the melancholy and quiet desperation of Fanny Price, or Jane Fairfax, or Anne Elliott, we see a crystallization of a negative view of society that first begins to be articulated in *The Three Sisters*.

Austen's emerging moral maturity is more evident in Volume the Third's *Catharine*, a happy synthesis of mischief and sympathy, and the *pièce de résistance* of her juvenilia. The figure of Camilla, foolish, vain, and pretentious, looks back to the burlesques and to Austen's early appetite for simplistic ridicule. Her friend's toothache on the day of a longed-for ball provides the opportunity for her silliness to be displayed in all its glory:

> 'To be sure, there never was anything so shocking . . . I wish there were no such things as teeth in the world; they are nothing but plagues to one, and I dare say people might easily invent something to eat with instead of them.'

But Austen's ridicule is tempered by her allusion to the part Camilla's environment has played in producing this stunted being. Weak as her character is, she might have been salvaged by education, but this has of course been denied her by a system that saw women as decorative creatures whose limited intellectual powers were insufficient to withstand the threats of any serious contact with reality. What is true for Camilla could as easily be said of the junior Bennet sisters, of either of the Bertram girls, or of Louisa or Henrietta Musgrove:

> She was . . . naturally not deficient in abilities; but those years which ought to have been spent in the attainment of useful knowledge and mental improvement, had all been bestowed in learning drawing, Italian, and music . . . and she now united to these accomplishments, an understanding unimproved by reading and a mind totally devoid of either taste or judgement.[15]

Faced with a repressive external reality, the moral challenge is still to make the right choices, to survive with dignity; the question of character becomes one of vital importance. Kitty, in contrast to Camilla, is Austen's first fully drawn heroine, and she survives despite, rather then because of, her society. Her character reflects the same impulse which gave life to Georgiana and Sophy. Kitty is altogether isolated, an orphan; her girlhood friends have been, literally, disposed of, one in an unhappy marriage, the other as a 'companion' – and we are left in no doubt as to just how distasteful and humiliating their present lives are. Despite the oppressive boredom and loneliness of her situation, Kitty is shown to resist

15. Poor Camilla's crime has been to follow the educational path advocated by such respected contemporary authorities as Thomas Gisborne (*An Enquiry into the Duties of the Female Sex*, London, 1796). He argues that in place of intellectual faculties, God has endowed women with the power to amuse, soothe, and charm the stronger sex; their education should therefore concentrate on the 'ornamental acquisitions'.

the temptation of a hasty intimacy with her garrulous visitor, Camilla, until she has a chance to measure her character. Resolutely unsentimental, Kitty's response to stress is not to faint, or even to complain, but to retire to her bower, where 'she always wandered whenever anything disturbed her; . . . it possessed such a charm over her senses as constantly to tranquillize her mind and quiet her spirits'. Her response to the above-mentioned toothache is radically different than Camilla's – even though it is *her* tooth, and *she* must be the one to stay at home:

. . . she was not so totally void of philosophy as many girls of her age . . . She considered that there were misfortunes of a much greater magnitude than the loss of a ball experienced every day by some part of mortality . . . she soon reasoned herself into . . . resignation and patience . . .

In her self-reliance and loneliness, her 'resignation and patience', Kitty looks forward, a little, to Fanny Price. But she has a lively, audacious streak that is more like Elizabeth Bennet, and an irresistible naïveté that most directly recalls Catherine Morland. The union of attributes in her heroine seems to mirror those of Austen herself – her identification with Kitty is evident – and, as it happens, is the spring which serves to engage the reader.

In *Catharine*, Austen has come nearly the whole distance from *Frederic and Elfrida* to *First Impressions*. We are presented with an integrated artistic effort to instruct by pleasing; intellectually and emotionally we are engaged by Kitty; through her we experience the damaging limitations of her world. But Kitty is not perfect. She makes errors of judgement to do with a young stranger and with her maiden aunt. She allows herself to be taken in by Stanley because he is exciting; she gives no credence to Mrs Percival's admonitions because she does not want them to be true. Unfinished as it is, the question this novel asks is not 'Will Kitty marry Stanley?' but 'Will Kitty grow up?' Will she survive her environment? Will she learn to admit her mistakes and to make the right moral choices? So, as with the mature novels, *Catharine* strives for a balanced division of criticism, pointing to faults both social and personal, to the overriding responsibility of individuals to develop and abide by their own moral code.

The possibility of growth for the heroine increases, in Austen's work, with the distance from mechanical inelasticity. It is not an option, of course, for Sophia and Laura; neither is it remotely likely in the cases of Mary and Mr Watts, yet they are set in contrast to Sophy and Georgiana who do, most assuredly, possess the potential for growth. Finally, the sympathetic Kitty is eminently educable; her ability to inspire identification means that her lessons become accessible to her readers, who can vicariously partake of her moral development, and, escaping the ubiquitous quagmires of materialism, vanity, and vapidity, be rescued from the fate of Camilla.

II

Charlotte Brontë's juvenilia were composed over a ten-year period, from 1829 to 1839. While her sisters Anne and Emily were writing their tales of Gondal, she and Branwell created the kingdom of Angria, and along with it an elaborate cast of characters. The writings of the children were meant for themselves alone, and were kept a strict secret not only from their later friends and acquaintances, but even from the other members of their household: hence the tiny size of the books and their famous microscopic print. Most of the Gondal material has not survived; but the Angrian MSS were carefully preserved by Charlotte throughout her lifetime. In quantity the material is vast, and does not reflect the same process of selection and recopying that Austen's early work does: it is 'an immense amount of manuscript', as Mrs Gaskell says, 'in an inconceivably small space'.[16] So we have the advantage of the texts in an uncensored form, as they were originally written. On the other hand, we face a number of disadvantages – ranging from an absence of concern for such details as paragraphs and punctuation to what seems a baffling jumble of character and action – which make for what might tactfully be called uphill work on the part of the unsuspecting reader. The texts included here reflect only a portion of what Charlotte actually wrote; their selection has been governed by an attempt to make evident the unexpected continuity of both plot and character which can in fact be discovered betwixt and between the sprawl and complexity of the Angrian scene.

16. Gaskell, op. cit. p. 112.

While the unity of Austen's early juvenilia is one of technique
and tone, Brontë's are primarily bound by the recurrence of a
single set of actors. The central, dominant protagonist is, unquestionably, Arthur Wellesley, son of the Duke of Wellington, later
Duke of Zamorna and King of Angria. Initially portrayed as gentle
and romantic, Arthur changes by degrees to become fabulously
handsome, irresistible to women, an eloquent parliamentarian, a
mighty warrior. But his successes in love and war are marked by
growing arrogance and amorality; at last he becomes a demonic
figure of destruction and, finally, depravity.

A number of key characters surround Arthur, or Zamorna, as he
is later called. Throughout his adult life he is engaged in an intense
love-hate relationship with Alexander Percy, Earl of Northangerland and quite the demon himself; these two are at times bitter
political foes, at others fast allies, their fates and their passions
mysteriously intertwined. Then there are the women, who, different as they may be, share a consuming ardour for their hero.
Chief among the infatuated company are Marian Hume, Arthur's
first wife; Zenobia Ellrington, Marian's rival; Mary Percy, Arthur's
second wife; and Mina Laury, Arthur's 'permanent' mistress.[17]
Finally, there is *one* woman, Elizabeth Hastings, who is refreshingly
immune to Arthur's ultimately quite jaded charms.

Over a ten-year period what we encounter in Charlotte's writings
is a preoccupation with character in the psychological, rather than
the ethical, sense. She is slow, in comparison with Austen, to
pursue the question of moral assessment. She delights in the
intricacies of her characters' relations, however destructive; her
interest is so keen that she seems to postpone for as long as she can
the business of making judgements. Only in 1838 do we find a
consistent moral consciousness asserting itself in her work – and
the next year, in *Farewell to Angria*, she wistfully admits that the
time has come to renounce her fantasy world and move on to
reality:

Yet do not urge me too fast, reader: it is no easy theme to dismiss from
my imagination the images which have filled it so long . . . [Still the] mind

17. Caroline Vernon deserves mention too, as the last, and youngest, of Zamorna's
victims; Charlotte devotes an entire novelette to the story of her seduction, which
appears in Gérin's *Five Novelettes*.

would cease from excitement and turn now to a cooler region where the dawn breaks grey and sober, and the coming day for a time at least is subdued by clouds.

From Marian Hume to Elizabeth Hastings a progression is nonetheless evident, and the development of Charlotte's central female characters can in fact serve as an index of the more general maturation of her artistic and moral sense.

All of these women enjoy a share of her interest for a time; but Zenobia, Marian, and Mary sequentially fall from favour as they are abandoned by Arthur. His bond with Mina emerges as the single enduring one of his amours-ridden career; but in her obsessive self-abasement Mina ends by losing Charlotte's respect, and it is the independent Elizabeth who stands out as the final object of her creator's regard.

Notwithstanding their shared creative enthusiasm, the directions of Austen's and Brontë's earliest efforts were thus radically different. The Angrian pieces show none of Austen's gleeful iconoclasm, whereby herds of sacred literary and social cows are lampooned; instead the joy in Brontë's writing comes from the free expression of the imagination, a revelling in the exotic and fabulous world of her creation. Whether her acute pleasure in fantasy – shared by her siblings – was in part a response to the narrowness and joylessness of life at the parsonage, is impossible to say, but in any case it is as striking a feature of Brontë's early work as Austen's wit and toughness were of hers.

Not surprisingly, the chief of Charlotte's first influences are rich in romantic fodder – *The Arabian Nights*, *The Tales of the Genii*, the extravagant engravings of John Martin;[18] with these ingredients are mingled fabulous elements that were doubtless of her own invention. *The Twelve Adventurers* opens with a deadly sandstorm and the gruesome image of an 'immense skeleton . . . bound with a long chain of rusty iron' lying in the barren desert (shades of Ozymandias?); a shipwreck ensures that the company of the *Invincible* are marooned and immediately confronted by a band of bloodthirsty savages; soon after, the crew are subjected to a collective visionary experience in the person of the Genius of the

18. See Gérin, *Charlotte Brontë*, chapter IV.

Storm striding over the thunderclouds; subsequently a genie leads them on an exhausting march through the desert to a diamond palace in which are throned the princes of the genii; when they return to their base they are immediately met with a new attack from the savages . . .

The voraciousness of the Brontë appetite for exotic adventure is clear enough, but there's more than random excitement to this sequence. First, the shipwrecked men begin construction of a city which will flourish and become the capital of Angria, the permanent setting of all Charlotte and Branwell's stories; Glass Town, later Verdopolis, will eventually be populated by all manner of high society and is to be the scene of many a political and amorous intrigue. Second, perhaps more important, a leader emerges out of the company, the heroic Duke of Wellington, who becomes their first king. Although he is soon to be replaced as hero by his son Arthur, his natural confidence and authority, his abundance of masculine power, reflect what will be a continuing interest in these qualities in her male characters throughout Brontë's writing career.

Without abandoning her taste for the exotic, Charlotte's juvenile imagination was not long in discovering its real focus: the degrees and forms of human passion. And with this new focus another crucial influence is felt: the poetry, and personality, of Lord Byron. We know that the Brontë children had easy access to his work, and to the periodicals which were filled with elegies and tributes at the time of his death, in 1824, when Charlotte would have been eight.[19] Later, in 1830, Thomas Moore's idealized biography appeared, with which we also know Charlotte to have been familiar.[20] This kind of intense conditioning evidently conspired with her own romantic appetite to create an abiding fascination with the figure of the Byronic hero, in a variety of incarnations ranging from the angelic to the satanic. In *Characters of Celebrated Men* we encounter the splendid young Arthur-as-Byron at his most benign, his external beauty the reflection of his inner perfection. His tastes reveal an intensely romantic cast of mind: 'the lonely traveller', 'the mournful song of a solitary exile', are his favourite themes, but not surprisingly he is also moved by roaring oceans

19. See Samuel Chew, *Byron in England* (Toronto, 1924), p. 196 ff.
20. Gérin, *Charlotte Brontë*, p. 51.

and thunder.[21] This youth is surely a prime candidate for passion
– though in its first appearance it will be of the pure and
gentlemanly variety – and in October 1830 we first find Arthur
testing the amorous waters.

In the opening scene Albion and Marina (who are really Arthur
and Marian) meet and fall in love directly; their union being
postponed on the grounds of youth, Albion goes with his father to
Glass Town, where, because of his poetic achievements, he becomes
the toast of the town and the object of the glamorous Lady Zelzia's
interest. In this piece, the sexual mercury stays at a fairly low level:
Albion shows that he is in love by becoming first 'listless and
abstracted', then 'more gloomy than before'; Marian's response to
Albion's declaration and proposal is to blush; Zelzia's way of
vamping Albion is to 'converse with lively eloquence' and to sing
a song of his composition at an evening party.

Yet here we have the ingredients of a bitter love triangle that is
to explode by December of the same year. *The Rivals* focuses on
the frenzied jealousy of Zenobia (a new incarnation of Zelzia); she
emerges as a figure of some stature, debased only by her hopeless
passion for Arthur, who is now officially engaged to Marian.[22]
Marian is a lovely girl, but she is something of a sexual lightweight,
along the lines of *Villette*'s Paulina Home. Zenobia is the real
dynamo: Marian wears green and has a garland of flowers in her
hair; Zenobia wears crimson velvet and black plumes. And Arthur
recognizes Zenobia's more powerful sexuality. In the end he yields
to her the rose he had intended for Marian, and pacifies his fainting
fiancée with the hastily concocted argument that the ring he offers
instead is better because it is 'symbolical of constancy'.

The Bridal (August 1832) presents us with an idealized portrait
of the newly-weds' domestic bliss. Arthur is a youth of 'lofty

21. Lists of typical Byronic traits are provided by Edward Botstetter (in *Byron:
Selected Poetry and Letters*, New York, 1966, p. xi) and Winifred Gérin (*Charlotte
Brontë*, pp. 53, 89). According to the former, these should include 'melancholy and
ennui; misanthropy, pride, remorse'. Gérin lists 'treachery and courage, grace and
melancholy, mystery and cunning'; the Byronic hero should be 'saturnine, faithless,
proud, disillusioned, masterful, melancholy, abrupt'. Obviously Charlotte has drawn
only from the positive end of the spectrum for her hero's early portrait.

22. Zenobia's namesake was a warrior queen of Syria, who challenged the Romans,
and was finally defeated by them in AD 272.

stature' and 'magnificent proportions', Marian has 'cheeks tinted with a rich, soft crimson', 'hazel eyes', 'auburn ringlets'. Their scene is one of tender, playful flirtation; Marian again recalls *Villette*'s Paulina as, for example, the little Countess coaxes and reconciles her father and lover by making an amulet of their hair bound by a lock of her own.[23] Both girls are utterly charming, but a little too sweet.

At sixteen, Charlotte's view of passion, what actually interests her, is already far from simple, and the patter between Arthur and Marian turns out to be only a frame for the real action: Zenobia's desperate last efforts to win Arthur for herself. With her hair dishevelled and wild, her mantle tattered, her features 'emaciated and pale as death', Zenobia seems almost physically to have been battered and wasted by the strength of her unfulfilled desire. Although she is radically different in temperament from any of Brontë's later heroines, the intensity of Zenobia's passion seems to look forward to that of Jane Eyre or Lucy Snowe. Theirs is unexpressed, but is similarly violent, presented in terms of literal pain: Jane's heart 'plained of its gaping wounds, its inward bleeding, its riven chords'; Lucy asks, 'What bodily illness was ever like this pain?' As it develops, Zenobia, who absolutely lacks Jane and Lucy's self-discipline, takes the rather tacky route of trying to trick Arthur into renouncing Marian, and she fails in what is a distinctly weak conclusion to the piece. But Charlotte's fascination with the dark side is there; though she does not condemn Marian for her simplicity, her attention is wandering.

By the next year Charlotte evidently decided to move away from the Zenobia–Marian polarity, and so she gets rid of them both. Zenobia is married off, and moves into the background; and Marian succumbs to a broken heart and dies – thus disappearing entirely – replaced in Arthur's affections by Mary, daughter of Alexander Percy. Arthur's second wife is as beautiful as his first, with golden curls and, again, hazel eyes. That she is rather more red-blooded is made clear, for example, in the *Return of Zamorna*, when she dashes into a cold, deep river just for a glimpse of Arthur:

23. Charlotte Brontë, *Villette* (Harmondsworth, 1979), chapter 37.

dizzy with the tumultuous feelings, the wild pulsations, the burning and impatient wishes that smile and glance excited, she closed her eyes in momentary blindness.

Mary remains Arthur's favourite for a total of four years, but during this period she is severely tried. Arthur, it develops, is a habitual philanderer, and he punctuates their marriage with repeated absences. Further, his rivalry with Percy erupts, and he repudiates Mary, leaving her to die in an attempt to get revenge on her thick-skinned father. To suffer, in fact, seems to be Mary's chief occupation.

With this character, Brontë has moved decisively towards the creation of a heroine of greater depth and complexity than her first two models. And with her delicate beauty, her capacity for ardent attachment and for suffering, Mary brings to mind *Shirley*'s Caroline Helstone. But she is spirited and wilful too: when she has been separated from Arthur for longer than she can bear, she twice follows him in disguise, defying his command and braving his terrific wrath. Her position as Percy's daughter puts her – again like Caroline – in the midst of an intensely painful and apparently irreconcilable conflict between the two men she cares for: in *My Angria and the Angrians* Mary pleads eloquently on her father's behalf, only to see her intervention precipitate in her husband a seizure approaching madness in its intensity.

While Mary arouses sympathy and admiration, in the end she retains too much of the conventional romantic heroine:

there she lay, arrayed in rich satin, . . . the shadowy ray of a single lamp shining on her white face and lighting the tears on her eyelashes and on her soft pure cheeks.

And she becomes increasingly suspicious, whining, tedious – losing the interest of both her husband and her creator. A late portrait, in 1839, shows her to be arrogant and cold, thoroughly unpleasant. Perhaps she has been brought to this by the cruelty of her husband, but there is no further appeal to our sympathy on her behalf.

Instead, Charlotte moves on, and with Mina Laury we find her experimenting with a new sort of heroine. Mina has been Arthur's mistress since she was fifteen, and in her the concept of self-sacrifice is actively glorified. She is isolated, without family or friends – her position as camp-follower ensures her status as an outsider. Her only purpose in life is to serve her master, and she speaks of her servitude with something like religious fervour: 'I've nothing else to exist for; I've no other interest in life. Just to stand by his grace . . . is to fulfil the destiny I was born to.' Charlotte is evidently powerfully drawn to this ideal of fulfilment-through-submission, and with Mina's statement calls to mind the words of her later heroines: 'Master, I consent to pass my life with you,' says *The Professor*'s Frances as she accepts Crimsworth's proposal; 'My dear master,' exclaims Jane Eyre as she returns to Ferndean, 'I am come back to you'; 'I will be your faithful steward,' says Lucy Snowe to M. Paul, kissing his hand; and proud Shirley Keeldar surrenders happily to the rule of her Louis: 'vanquished and restricted, she pined, like any other chained denizen of deserts'.

But there is a crucial difference, for all of Brontë's later women have questioned and proved the worth of their lovers before they surrender. In Mina's case, her hero has become a far different creature than in his first innocent incarnation as Marian's husband, or even his later philandering one as Mary's. By 1838 Zamorna is actively the sadist, exulting in gratuitous, punitive manipulation, now recalling Byron's satanic extreme, his 'ruthless cruelty' towards Caroline Lamb and Claire Clairmont, his 'hysterical brutality' towards his wife.[24] This is seen most clearly when Zamorna decides to test Mina's idolatry by pretending that he has offered her to Lord Hartford. Mina's reaction is to fall at his feet in a dead faint, which produces in her master a feeling of 'intense gratification'. When she revives he announces that he was merely testing her devotion, that in fact he has shot, and nearly killed, Hartford, for his effrontery in even daring to make a proposal of marriage to Mina when it should be clear that she is Zamorna's possession.

Charlotte cannot resist allowing Mina her disturbing – and wholly characteristic – response: 'this bloody proof of her master's love brought to her heart more rapture than horror'. But fascinating as such pathology may be, Charlotte recognizes that Mina, in playing masochist to Zamorna's sadist, is also in collusion with

24. Botstetter, op. cit., p. viii.

him. 'Strong-minded beyond her sex . . . here she was weak as a child. She lost her identity.' No matter how powerful the obsession, how delicious the fruit, the loss of selfhood that Mina revels in evidently ceases, from this point on, to be acceptable to Charlotte, and this is the last we hear of her. The turning away from Mina marks a definitive coalescence in Charlotte's sense of morality which, as we find it in her 1839 composition, *Henry Hastings*, largely matches that of *Jane Eyre* some eight years later; or, as Gérin puts it, 'what would constitute the whole difference between Jane Eyre and . . . Mina Laury, would precisely lie in the later heroine's power of conscience to resist temptation'.[25]

Elizabeth Hastings is as significant a creation for Brontë as Catharine Percival was for Austen: both heroines show their authors to have reached the final stage of their youthful development, to have refined and integrated their moral and artistic sense, to be recognizably on the threshold of their first mature work. Elizabeth's physical likeness to Jane Eyre and Lucy Snowe, as well as to Brontë herself, is striking in itself; but as her character emerges the resemblance becomes still more remarkable. Her responses to the men in her story reveal the details of her nature, her loyalty and independence, the extremes of her passion and her self-control.

Significantly, she is perfectly indifferent as to Zamorna, and pleased to be so. But there *are* three men who are vitally important to her, the first of whom is her father. Much as she loves him, she defies him when he disowns his miscreant son Henry:

'I told him he had done wrong and unnaturally . . . He knocked me down . . . I got up and said the words over again.'

She leaves home, and has 'been earning my bread since by my own efforts'. Lonely and homesick, she longs to be with the old man again. 'But pride is a thing not easily subdued. She would not return to him.'

The second man of importance is her would-be seducer, Sir William Percy, with whom Elizabeth falls in love. Although he scorns her on their first meeting, his interest in her grows until he decides that he must add her to his list of conquests. After a long

25. Gérin, *Charlotte Brontë*, p. 135.

afternoon ramble in the country, during which he extracts a confession of her love, he leads her to a moonlit churchyard and, fully expecting her to consent, asks her to become his mistress. What is her reply? 'No.' Why? 'I could not, without incurring the miseries of self-hatred.' And when a cloud next covers the moon, Elizabeth slips away, leaving the thwarted Sir William to stew – much to our satisfaction – in his own juice. As with her father, Elizabeth's commitment to her moral stand is paramount, no matter how bitter the loss.

Finally, the last man, and the one closest to her: her brother. Henry is in disgrace, a fugitive on the run, and he seeks cover with her in the isolated country manor where she is staying alone as housekeeper. Though he is 'mutinous and selfish and accursedly malignant', shown to be a terrible drunkard and a worse coward, Elizabeth is steadfast in her devotion. When he is finally tracked down, her courage in trying to protect him is splendid – and brings to mind Jane dousing the flames in Mr Rochester's bed or tending the wounded Mason in Thornfield's attic. She coolly confronts the leaders of the search party, asserting that Henry is not there; when she has been forced aside, she rushes ahead and tries to bar the door of the room where he is hiding. She manages to hold it shut 'for a fraction of time', but they burst through and she is 'flung to the ground'. Henry leaps through the window and is captured below.

After his arrest she again shows her courage by going to the duchess and asking her to intercede on Henry's behalf – a tricky enterprise at best, since one of Henry's offences has been to try to assassinate the duchess's husband. At his trial, Henry informs on his friends, as might be expected, in order to save his neck, 'but his sister did not think a pin the worse of him'. On her own, her brother and her father lost to her, she does the opposite of collapse: she goes about to the city's better families, gathers together a number of students, and sets up a successful school:

. . . she was dependent on nobody, responsible to nobody . . . her class enlarged, and she was as prosperous as any little woman of five feet high and not twenty years old need wish to be.

Like Lucy Snowe, she treasures her self-reliance, regardless of the extremes of personal grief with which she must privately contend.

The degeneration of Zamorna, the emergence of two such thorough cads as Sir William and Henry Hastings, as well as the inevitably painful nature of all the human relations in Brontë's juvenilia, must raise the matter of the special and extreme kinds of difficulties Charlotte encountered in her youth. The death of her mother and elder sisters, the emotional reserve of her father and aunt, were followed by other kinds of hardships. In 1831, after a serious illness of her father's, she was sent off to school at Roe Head, an existence she experienced as exile, not only from her brother and sisters, but from her adored world of Angria. To Miss Wooler's school she returned as governess in 1835, grimly determined to fulfil her moral obligation: 'I am sad – very sad,' she wrote to her friend Ellen Nussey, 'at the thought of leaving home; but *duty – necessity* – these are stern mistresses who will not be disobeyed.'[26] Her frustration at having to deal with her students – she refers to 'the idleness, the apathy, and the hyperbolical and most asinine stupidity of those fat-headed oafs'[27] – was obviously exacerbated by the fact that she had neither the time nor the privacy to write, and had to postpone this vital activity until the holiday breaks. But worst of all must have been the first unmistakable signs of Branwell's deterioration. In 1835 he was sent to London, supposedly to study at the Royal Academy. This project – which the Reverend Mr Brontë could ill afford – was financed by family and friends, and he was provided with letters of introduction. The letters were never presented; Branwell drank away the funds and came home in disgrace, claiming that he had been robbed.[28] Although Charlotte argues, through Elizabeth Hastings, that a brother's failings will not alter the devotion of a faithful sister, we have to wonder whether even she was beginning to protest too much. Certainly as her mistrust of men is seen to increase in the later juvenilia, the quality of self-reliance in her women becomes steadily more crucial; and her commitment to the importance of female independence and integrity remains unqualified in the mature novels, though her view of the opposite sex

26. T. J. Wise and J. A. Symington, *The Brontës: Their Lives, Friendships and Correspondence* (Oxford, 1932), I, p. 129.

27. Gérin, *Charlotte Brontë*, p. 104.

28. See Winifred Gérin, *Branwell Brontë: A Biography* (London, 1961).

broadens to admit the possibility of tenderness and honour.

*

Despite the evident differences between the juvenile works of Brontë and Austen, they end up arriving at a surprising number of similar conclusions. Brontë rejects the simplicity of her early works – the appetite for adventure and the exotic, the idealization of innocent romantic love – as Austen abandons her facile inclination to ridicule and to present her characters as two-dimensional puppets. In *Catharine* and *Henry Hastings*, both struggle to achieve some kind of balance on the question of the conflict between individual and social morality, representing their solutions in the characters of fully realized heroines who are distinguished by the degree of their spirit and feeling, and also by their independence. Both contrast their autonomous heroines with conventional products of female conditioning – Camilla Stanley and Jane Moore[29] – implicitly attributing these girls' stunted intellectual and emotional states to the social expectations by which they have been formed; both authors recognize the danger of the temptation, as a woman, to annex oneself to an attractive and apparently more powerful male – whether Edward Stanley or Sir William Percy.

Although Austen and Brontë chafe at the narrowness of their heroines' prospects, they are clear that the challenge is to arrive at solutions that allow for dignity and integrity within existing social bounds; emotional choices must be modified by reason and self-control. The extra-societal – and narcissistic – options pursued by Lydia Bennet and Maria Bertram are as obviously unacceptable to Austen as they are to Brontë when she has Jane Eyre refuse to become Mr Rochester's mistress. The dilemma faced by Catharine and Elizabeth – as by all of Austen's and Brontë's later heroines – is to transcend, and yet not transgress, and in this elusive space between conformity and self-indulgence the arduous hewing out of their personal moral visions must take place.

29. The Angrian society belle, Jane Moore, can be seen as Camilla Stanley's counterpart in *Henry Hastings*: she is charming and very pretty, but without a spark of imagination or real intelligence.

Note on the Text

✳

Initially I relied on existing printed editions to establish both the Austen and Brontë texts: Chapman's *Volume the First* and *Third*, Southam's *Volume the Second*; Wise and Symington's *Miscellaneous and Unpublished Writings*, Gérin's *Five Novelettes*. Subsequently I was able in some, but not all, cases to compare my texts with microfilm of the MSS, or with the MSS themselves, and thus to verify the accuracy of the earlier editors' transcriptions. The Southam and Gérin editions are particularly thorough, recording every aspect of their MSS in minute detail.

My editorial decisions as to how to treat the two sets of juvenilia have been varied, as a result of the dissimilar nature of the original MSS. I have treated the Austen texts conservatively; with the Brontë texts I have sometimes felt obliged to take measures that are unquestionably extreme.

Jane Austen's MSS are fair copies, revised and corrected by her after their preparation. For this reason I have endeavoured to keep editorial interference to a minimum. I have modernized punctuation, capitalization and hyphenation, but have altered paragraphs only where clarity required it. Dashes are used with such frequency throughout the MSS that to eliminate them would be to lose an important element of Austen's style; on the other hand many are evidently superfluous. I have kept those which seemed intended to serve a special purpose – chiefly to indicate personal rhythms in direct speech. Where used to mark the conclusion of a paragraph I have deleted the dash and substituted the paragraph break.

The question of spelling was not easily resolved. Tradition has a sentimental attachment to Austen's archaic forms (notably *Love and Freindship*, whose *-ei-* she later corrected herself); yet she clearly did not intend her forms to be out-of-date, and was in fact a very good speller. Therefore I have, reluctantly, modernized her spellings if their forms are no longer current, but retained those few old forms which are still listed as alternate spellings in the *OED* (especially *agreable* and its variations, as she uses them with such frequency). I have also allowed some of her more characteristic word divisions to stand (e.g. *any body*, *to day*, *up stairs*) as their rhythms are significantly altered if, as in modern usage, they are treated as single words.

In Austen's subsequent perusals of her three volumes, she made numbers of alterations; sometimes single words are changed, sometimes whole phrases are deleted. It has not been obvious whether her first or her second version ought to be reproduced. Some of the tinkerings introduce changes that are minimal and yet help to clarify her own meaning; in other cases, for instance where she has deleted whole phrases, she seems to be doing too much retrospective smoothing. Usually I have accepted her second variant when only a word or two is involved, but where I have retained phrases that she crossed out – which I have generally done unless they interfere stylistically with what remains – I have marked them with square brackets in the text and mentioned the deletion in the notes, so as to make both the original and the later readings accessible.

I have included nearly everything from *Volume the First*; from *Volume the Second* because of space considerations I have excluded two major pieces, *Lesley Castle* and *The History of England*; and from *Volume the Third*, *Evelyn*. Dull as they are, *Lesley Castle* and *Evelyn* have been abandoned without regret; *The History of England* has been more of a sacrifice, but as it does not reflect, as the other entries do, on Austen's novelistic development, I ended by deciding against its inclusion.

With Brontë's extensive juvenilia, the first problem was to bring them down to manageable size. Here I adhered to a few fairly strict principles: I chose selections that covered, as nearly as possible, each year in the 1829–39 decade; that revealed her growing narrative skill; that showed each of her important female characters, as well as her changing attitude towards her hero, Arthur Wellesley; that presented a coherent rendering of the developing Angrian saga. This selection process, of course, involved leaving out much more than it was possible to include; and has ended by creating an impression of clear linearity which is far from evident when the Brontë juvenilia are first approached.[30]

I also found that it was necessary to abridge many of the individual entries, partly from space considerations, partly for the sake of narrative coherence. In some cases I have summarized the missing portions within the body of the text; my additions are marked by square brackets. Many other omissions have been made silently, including numbers of superfluous ampersands, confusing proper nouns (e.g. names of extraneous characters or of Angrian locales), and occasional instances of distracting verbosity whose only function seemed to be to impede the story's progress. I remain uneasy about many of these omissions, but have held to them in the interest of clarity: I am convinced that Brontë's juvenilia have been chronically undervalued because they have been so terribly difficult to read.

Brontë's MSS were not fair copies and so are marked by many minor errors (e.g. the omission of single letters or words) which are, however, easily repaired; despite the problems presented by the microscopic print there are few words that are actually illegible.

I have modernized punctuation, capitalization, and hyphenation, and introduced paragraphs; as with the Austen texts I have used current spellings but allowed old forms still admitted by the *OED* to stand (e.g. *ancle*, *waggon*). Brontë's use of dashes is even more lavish than Austen's, and I have generally replaced them with the commas, semicolons, and periods that their usage seemed intended to designate.

30. See Christine Alexander's Appendix B (*The Early Writings of Charlotte Brontë*, Oxford, 1983, pp. 250 ff.) for a complete list of Charlotte's early prose MSS.

Suggested Further Reading

AUSTEN

Jane Austen, *Letters to her Sister Cassandra and Others*, in two volumes, collected and edited by R. W. Chapman (Oxford, 1932).
  Volume the First, ed. R. W. Chapman (Oxford, 1933).
  Volume the Second, ed. B. C. Southam (Oxford, 1963).
  Volume the Third, ed. R. W. Chapman (Oxford, 1951).

Austen-Leigh, James Edward, *A Memoir of Jane Austen, by her Nephew* (London, 1886). Reprinted with *Persuasion* (Harmondsworth, 1965).
Frank Bradbrook, *Jane Austen and her Predecessors* (New York, 1966).
David Cecil, *A Portrait of Jane Austen* (Harmondsworth, 1980).
R. W. Chapman, *Jane Austen: Facts and Problems* (London, 1948).
David Gilson, *A Bibliography of Jane Austen* (Oxford, 1982).
Margaret Kirkham, *Jane Austen: Feminism and Fiction* (Brighton, Sussex, 1983).
Marvin Mudrick, *Jane Austen: Irony as Defense and Discovery* (Princeton, 1952).
LeRoy W. Smith, *Jane Austen and the Drama of Woman* (New York, 1983).
B. C. Southam, *Jane Austen's Literary Manuscripts* (London, 1964).
Brian Wilks, *Jane Austen* (London, 1978).

BRONTË

Charlotte Brontë, *Five Novelettes*, ed. Winifred Gérin (London, 1971).
  Legends of Angria, ed. Fannie Ratchford, (New Haven, 1933).
  The Poems of Charlotte Brontë, ed. Tom Winnifrith (New York, 1984).
  'The Secret' and 'Lily Hart', ed. William Holtz (London, 1978).
  Something about Arthur, ed. Christine Alexander (Austin, Texas, 1981).
  The Spell: An Extravaganza, ed. George E. Maclean (London, 1931).
  The Twelve Adventurers, ed. C. W. Hatfield (London, 1925).
Charlotte, Emily and Anne Brontë, *Poems by Currer, Ellis and Acton Bell* (London, 1846). Reprinted in *Life and Works of the Sisters Brontë*, vol. IV (New York and London, 1900).

Charlotte and Patrick Branwell Brontë, *Miscellaneous and Unpublished Writings of Charlotte and Patrick Branwell Brontë*, ed. T. J. Wise and J. A. Symington, in two volumes (Oxford, 1938).

Christine Alexander, *A Bibliography of the Manuscripts of Charlotte Brontë* (Westport, Connecticut, 1983).

   The Early Writings of Charlotte Brontë (Oxford, 1983).

Phyllis Bentley, *The Brontës and Their World* (London, 1969).

Margaret Blom, *Charlotte Brontë* (Boston, 1977).

Elizabeth Gaskell, *The Life of Charlotte Brontë* (Harmondsworth, 1975).

Winifred Gérin, *Charlotte Brontë: The Evolution of Genius* (Oxford, 1967).

   The Brontës I: The Formative Years (Harlow, Essex, 1973).

Helene Moglen, *Charlotte Brontë: The Self Conceived* (New York, 1976).

Anne Passel, *Charlotte and Emily Brontë: An Annotated Bibliography* (New York, 1979).

Fannie Ratchford, *The Brontës' Web of Childhood* (New York, 1941).

Clement Shorter, *Charlotte Brontë and her Circle* (London, 1896).

Tom Winnifrith, *The Brontës* (London, 1977).

JANE AUSTEN

Volume the First

To Miss Lloyd [1]

My dear Martha,
As a small testimony of the gratitude I feel for your late generosity to me in finishing my muslin cloak, I beg leave to offer you this little production of your sincere friend,

the Author.

Frederic and Elfrida

A Novel

CHAPTER THE FIRST

The uncle of Elfrida was the father of Frederic; in other words, they were first cousins by the father's side.

Being both born in one day and both brought up at one school, it was not wonderful that they should look on each other with something more than bare politeness. They loved with mutual sincerity but were both determined not to transgress the rules of propriety by owning their attachment, either to the object beloved, or to any one else.

They were exceedingly handsome and so much alike that it was not every one who knew them apart. Nay, even their most intimate friends had nothing to distinguish them by but the shape of the face, the colour of the eye, the length of the nose, and the difference of the complexion.

Elfrida had an intimate friend to whom, being on a visit to an aunt, she wrote the following letter.

To Miss Drummond

'Dear Charlotte,

I should be obliged to you if you would buy me, during your stay with Mrs Williamson, a new and fashionable bonnet, to suit the complexion of your

E. Falknor'

Charlotte, whose character was a willingness to oblige every one, when she returned into the country, brought her friend the wished-for bonnet, and so ended this little adventure, much to the satisfaction of all parties.

On her return to Crankhumdunberry (of which sweet village her father was rector), Charlotte was received with the greatest joy by Frederic and Elfrida, who, after pressing her alternately to their bosoms, proposed to her to take a walk in a grove of poplars, which led from the parsonage to a verdant lawn, enamelled with a variety of variegated flowers, and watered by a purling stream, brought from the Valley of Tempé by a passage under ground.[2]

In this grove they had scarcely remained above nine hours, when they were suddenly agreably surprised by hearing a most delightful voice warble the following stanza.

Song

> That Damon was in love with me
> I once thought and believ'd;
> But now that he is not I see,
> I fear I was deceiv'd.

No sooner were the lines finished than they beheld by a turning in the grove two elegant young women leaning on each other's arm, who, immediately on perceiving them, took a different path and disappeared from their sight.

CHAPTER THE SECOND

As Elfrida and her companions had seen enough of them to know
that they were neither the two Miss Greens, nor Mrs Jackson and
her daughter, they could not help expressing their surprise at their
appearance; till at length recollecting that a new family had lately
taken a house not far from the grove, they hastened home,
determined to lose no time in forming an acquaintance with two
such amiable and worthy girls, of which family they rightly
imagined them to be a part.

Agreable to such a determination, they went that very evening
to pay their respects to Mrs Fitzroy and her two daughters. On
being shewn into an elegant dressing room, ornamented with
festoons of artificial flowers, they were struck with the engaging
exterior and beautiful outside of Jezalinda, the eldest of the young
ladies; but ere they had been many minutes seated, the wit and
charms which shone resplendent in the conversation of the amiable
Rebecca enchanted them so much that they all with one accord
jumped up and exclaimed,

'Lovely and too charming fair one, notwithstanding your forbidding squint, your greasy tresses, and your swelling back, which are
more frightful than imagination can paint or pen describe, I cannot
refrain from expressing my raptures at the engaging qualities of
your mind, which so amply atone for the horror with which your
first appearance must ever inspire the unwary visitor.

'Your sentiments so nobly expressed on the different excellencies
of Indian and English muslins, and the judicious preference you
give the former, have excited in me an admiration of which I can
alone give an adequate idea by assuring you it is nearly equal to
what I feel for myself.'

Then, making a profound curtesy to the amiable and abashed
Rebecca, they left the room and hurried home.

From this period, the intimacy between the families of Fitzroy,
Drummond, and Falknor daily increased, till at length it grew to
such a pitch that they did not scruple to kick one another out of the
window on the slightest provocation.

During this happy state of harmony, the eldest Miss Fitzroy ran off with the coachman and the amiable Rebecca was asked in marriage by Captain Roger of Buckinghamshire.

Mrs Fitzroy did not approve of the match on account of the tender years of the young couple, Rebecca being but 36 and Captain Roger little more than 63. To remedy this objection, it was agreed that they should wait a little while till they were a good deal older.

CHAPTER THE THIRD

In the mean time, the parents of Frederic proposed to those of Elfrida an union between them, which being accepted with pleasure, the wedding clothes were bought, and nothing remained to be settled but the naming of the day.

As to the lovely Charlotte, being importuned with eagerness to pay another visit to her aunt, she determined to accept the invitation, and in consequence of it walked to Mrs Fitzroy's to take leave of the amiable Rebecca, whom she found surrounded by patches, powder, pomatum, and paint, with which she was vainly endeavouring to remedy the natural plainness of her face.

'I am come, my amiable Rebecca, to take my leave of you for the fortnight I am destined to spend with my aunt. Believe me, this separation is painful to me, but it is as necessary as the labour which now engages you.'

'Why to tell you the truth, my love,' replied Rebecca, 'I have lately taken it into my head to think (perhaps with little reason) that my complexion is by no means equal to the rest of my face, and have therefore taken, as you see, to white and red paint, which I would scorn to use on any other occasion, as I hate art.'

Charlotte, who perfectly understood the meaning of her friend's speech, was too good-tempered and obliging to refuse her what she knew she wished – a compliment; and they parted the best friends in the world.

With a heavy heart and streaming eyes did she ascend the lovely vehicle which bore her from her friends and home; but grieved as she was, she little thought in what a strange and different manner she should return to it.

On her entrance into the city of London, which was the place of

Mrs Williamson's abode, the postilion, whose stupidity was amazing, declared, and declared even without the least shame or compunction, that having never been informed, he was totally ignorant of what part of the town he was to drive to.

Charlotte, whose nature we have before intimated was an earnest desire to oblige every one, with the greatest condescension and good humour informed him that he was to drive to Portland Place, which he accordingly did; and Charlotte soon found herself in the arms of a fond aunt.

Scarcely were they seated as usual in the most affectionate manner in one chair, than the door suddenly opened and an aged gentleman with a sallow face and old pink coat, partly by intention and partly through weakness was at the feet of the lovely Charlotte, declaring his attachment to her, and beseeching her pity in the most moving manner.

Not being able to resolve to make any one miserable, she consented to become his wife; where upon the gentleman left the room and all was quiet.

Their quiet, however, continued but a short time, for on a second opening of the door, a young and handsome gentleman with a new blue coat entered and entreated from the lovely Charlotte permission to pay to her his addresses.

There was a something in the appearance of the second stranger that influenced Charlotte in his favour, to the full as much as the appearance of the first: she could not account for it, but so it was.

Having therefore (agreable to that, and the natural turn of her mind to make every one happy), promised to become his wife the next morning, he took his leave, and the two ladies sat down to supper on a young leveret, a brace of partridges, a leash of pheasants, and a dozen of pigeons.[3]

CHAPTER THE FOURTH

It was not till the next morning that Charlotte recollected the double engagement she had entered into; but when she did, the reflection of her past folly operated so strongly on her mind, that she resolved to be guilty of a greater, and to that end threw herself into a deep stream which ran through her aunt's pleasure grounds in Portland Place.

She floated to Crankhumdunberry, where she was picked up and buried; the following epitaph, composed by Frederic, Elfrida, and Rebecca, was placed on her tomb.

Epitaph

Here lies our friend who having promis-ed
That unto two she would be marri-ed
Threw her sweet body and her lovely face
Into the stream that runs through Portland Place.

These sweet lines, as pathetic as beautiful, were never read by any one who passed that way without a shower of tears, which, if they should fail of exciting in you, reader, your mind must be unworthy to peruse them.

Having performed the last sad office to their departed friend, Frederic and Elfrida, together with Captain Roger and Rebecca, returned to Mrs Fitzroy's, at whose feet they threw themselves with one accord, and addressed her in the following manner.

'Madam: when the sweet Captain Roger first addressed the amiable Rebecca, you alone objected to their union on account of the tender years of the parties. That plea can be no more, seven days being now expired, together with the lovely Charlotte, since the captain first spoke to you on the subject.

'Consent then, madam, to their union, and as a reward, this smelling bottle which I enclose in my right hand shall be yours and yours forever; I never will claim it again. But if you refuse to join their hands in three days' time, this dagger which I enclose in my left shall be steeped in your heart's blood.

'Speak then, madam, and decide their fate and yours.'

Such gentle and sweet persuasion could not fail of having the desired effect. The answer they received was this.

'My dear young friends: the arguments you have used are too just and too eloquent to be withstood; Rebecca, in three days' time you shall be united to the captain.'

This speech, than which nothing could be more satisfactory, was received with joy by all; and peace being once more restored on all sides, Captain Roger entreated Rebecca to favour them with a song, in compliance with which request, having first assured them that she had a terrible cold, she sung as follows.

Song

When Corydon went to the fair
    He bought a red ribbon for Bess,
With which she encircled her hair
    And made herself look very fess.[4]

CHAPTER THE FIFTH

At the end of three days Captain Roger and Rebecca were united, and immediately after the ceremony set off in the stage waggon for the captain's seat in Buckinghamshire.

The parents of Elfrida, although they earnestly wished to see her married to Frederic before they died, yet knowing the delicate frame of her mind could ill bear the least exertion, and rightly judging that naming her wedding day would be too great a one, forbore to press her on the subject.

Weeks and fortnights flew away without gaining the least ground; the clothes grew out of fashion; and at length Captain Roger and his lady arrived, to pay a visit to their mother and introduce to her their beautiful daughter of eighteen.

Elfrida, who had found her former acquaintance were growing too old and too ugly to be any longer agreable, was rejoiced to hear of the arrival of so pretty a girl as Eleanor, with whom she determined to form the strictest friendship.

But the happiness she had expected from an acquaintance with Eleanor she soon found was not to be received, for she had not only the mortification of finding herself treated by her as little less than an old woman, but had actually the horror of perceiving a growing passion in the bosom of Frederic for the daughter of the amiable Rebecca.

The instant she had the first idea of such an attachment, she flew to Frederic, and in a manner truly heroic, spluttered out to him her intention of being married the next day.

To one in his predicament who possessed less personal courage than Frederic was master of, such a speech would have been death; but he, not being the least terrified, boldly replied,

'Damme, Elfrida, *you* may be married tomorrow but *I* won't.'

This answer distressed her too much for her delicate constitution. She accordingly fainted, and was in such a hurry to have a succession of fainting fits, that she had scarcely patience enough to recover from one before she fell into another.

Though in any threatening danger to his life or liberty, Frederic was as bold as brass, yet in other respects his heart was as soft as cotton, and immediately on hearing of the dangerous way Elfrida was in, he flew to her; and finding her better than he had been taught to expect, was united to her forever –.

Finis

Jack and Alice,

A Novel,
is respectfully inscribed to Francis William Austen Esq.,[5]
midshipman on board his majesty's ship the Perseverance,
by his obedient humble servant,

the Author.

CHAPTER THE FIRST

Mr Johnson was once upon a time about 53; in a twelvemonth afterwards he was 54, which so much delighted him that he was determined to celebrate his next birthday by giving a masquerade to his children and friends. Accordingly, on the day he attained his 55th year, tickets were dispatched to all his neighbours to that purpose. His acquaintance indeed in that part of the world were not very numerous, as they consisted only of Lady Williams, Mr and Mrs Jones, Charles Adams, and the three Miss Simpsons, who composed the neighbourhood of Pammydiddle and formed the masquerade.

Before I proceed to give an account of the evening, it will be proper to describe to my reader the persons and characters of the party introduced to his acquaintance.

Mr and Mrs Jones were both rather tall and very passionate, but were in other respects good-tempered, well-behaved people. Charles Adams was an amiable, accomplished, and bewitching young man, of so dazzling a beauty that none but eagles could look him in the face.

Miss Simpson was pleasing in her person, in her manners, and in her disposition; an unbounded ambition was her only fault. Her second sister Sukey was envious, spiteful, and malicious. Her person was short, fat, and disagreable. Cecilia (the youngest) was perfectly handsome, but too affected to be pleasing.

In Lady Williams every virtue met. She was a widow with a handsome jointure and the remains of a very handsome face. Though benevolent and candid, she was generous and sincere; though pious and good, she was religious and amiable; and though elegant and agreable, she was polished and entertaining.

The Johnsons were a family of love, and though a little addicted to the bottle and the dice, had many good qualities.

Such was the party assembled in the elegant drawing room of Johnson Court, amongst which the pleasing figure of a sultana was the most remarkable of the female masks. Of the males a mask representing the sun was the most universally admired. The beams that darted from his eyes were like those of that glorious luminary, though infinitely superior. So strong were they that no one dared venture within half a mile of them; he had therefore the best part of the room to himself, its size not amounting to more than three quarters of a mile in length and half a one in breadth. The gentleman, at last finding the fierceness of his beams to be very inconvenient to the concourse by obliging them to crowd together in one corner of the room, half shut his eyes, by which means the company discovered him to be Charles Adams in his plain green coat, without any mask at all.

When their astonishment was a little subsided, their attention was attracted by two dominos who advanced in a horrible passion;

they were both very tall, but seemed in other respects to have many good qualities.

'These,' said the witty Charles, 'these are Mr and Mrs Jones.' And so indeed they were.

No one could imagine who was the sultana! Till at length on her addressing a beautiful Flora who was reclining in a studied attitude on a couch, with 'Oh Cecilia, I wish I was really what I pretended to be,' she was discovered by the never failing genius of Charles Adams to be the elegant but ambitious Caroline Simpson; and the person to whom she addressed herself he rightly imagined to be her lovely but affected sister Cecilia.

The company now advanced to a gaming table where sat three dominos (each with a bottle in their hand) deeply engaged: but a female in the character of Virtue fled with hasty footsteps from the shocking scene, whilst a little fat woman representing Envy sat alternately on the foreheads of the three gamesters. Charles Adams was still as bright as ever; he soon discovered the party at play to be the three Johnsons, Envy to be Sukey Simpson, and Virtue to be Lady Williams.

The masks were then all removed, and the company retired to another room to partake of an elegant and well-managed entertainment; after which, the bottle being pretty briskly pushed about by the three Johnsons, the whole party, not excepting even Virtue, were carried home, Dead Drunk.

CHAPTER THE SECOND

For three months did the masquerade afford ample subject for conversation to the inhabitants of Pammydiddle; but no character at it was so fully expatiated on as Charles Adams. The singularity of his appearance, the beams which darted from his eyes, the brightness of his wit, and the whole tout ensemble of his person had subdued the hearts of so many of the young ladies, that of the six present at the masquerade but five had returned uncaptivated. Alice Johnson was the unhappy sixth whose heart had not been able to withstand the power of his charms. But as it may appear strange to my readers that so much worth and excellence as he possessed should have conquered only hers, it will be necessary to inform them that the Miss Simpsons were defended from his power by ambition, envy, and self-admiration.

Every wish of Caroline was centered in a titled husband; whilst in Sukey such superior excellence could only raise her envy, not her love; and Cecilia was too tenderly attached to herself to be pleased with any one besides. As for Lady Williams and Mrs Jones, the former of them was too sensible to fall in love with one so much her junior, and the latter, though very tall and very passionate, was too fond of her husband to think of such a thing.

Yet in spite of every endeavour on the part of Miss Johnson to discover any attachment to her in him, the cold and indifferent heart of Charles Adams still to all appearance preserved its native freedom; polite to all but partial to none, he still remained the lovely, the lively, but insensible Charles Adams.

One evening, Alice, finding herself somewhat heated by wine (no very uncommon case), determined to seek a relief for her disordered head and love-sick heart in the conversation of the intelligent Lady Williams.

She found her ladyship at home, as was in general the case, for she was not fond of going out; and like the great Sir Charles Grandison,[6] scorned to deny herself when at home, as she looked on that fashionable method of shutting out disagreable visitors as little less than downright bigamy.

In spite of the wine she had been drinking, poor Alice was uncommonly out of spirits; she could think of nothing but Charles Adams, she could talk of nothing but him, and in short spoke so openly that Lady Williams soon discovered the unreturned affection she bore him, which excited her pity and compassion so strongly that she addressed her in the following manner.

'I perceive but too plainly, my dear Miss Johnson, that your heart has not been able to withstand the fascinating charms of this young man, and I pity you sincerely. Is it a first love?'

'It is.'

'I am still more grieved to hear *that*; I am myself a sad example of the miseries in general attendant on a first love, and I am determined for the future to avoid the like misfortune. I wish it may not be too late for you to do the same; if it is not, endeavour, my dear girl, to secure yourself from so great a danger. A second attachment is seldom attended with any serious consequences; against *that* therefore I have nothing to say. Preserve yourself from a first love and you need not fear a second.'

'You mentioned, madam, something of your having yourself been a sufferer by the misfortune you are so good as to wish me to avoid. Will you favour me with your life and adventures?'

'Willingly, my love.'

CHAPTER THE THIRD

'My father was a gentleman of considerable fortune in Berkshire; myself and a few more his only children. I was but six years old when I had the misfortune of losing my mother, and being at that time young and tender, my father, instead of sending me to school, procured an able-handed governess to superintend my education at home. My brothers were placed at schools suitable to their ages, and my sisters, being all younger than myself, remained still under the care of their nurse.

'Miss Dickins was an excellent governess. She instructed me in the paths of virtue; under her tuition I daily became more amiable, and might perhaps by this time have nearly attained perfection, had not my worthy preceptoress been torn from my arms ere I had attained my seventeenth year. I never shall forget her last words. "My dear Kitty," she said, "Good night t'ye." I never saw her afterwards,' continued Lady Williams, wiping her eyes. 'She eloped with the butler the same night.

'I was invited the following year by a distant relation of my father's to spend the winter with her in town. Mrs Watkins was a lady of fashion, family, and fortune; she was in general esteemed a pretty woman, but I never thought her very handsome, for my part. She had too high a forehead, her eyes were too small, and she had too much colour.'

'How can *that* be?' interrupted Miss Johnson, reddening with anger. 'Do you think that any one can have too much colour?'

'Indeed I do, and I'll tell you why I do, my dear Alice; when a person has too great a degree of red in their complexion, it gives their face, in my opinion, too red a look!'

'But can a face, my lady, have too red a look?'

'Certainly, my dear Miss Johnson, and I'll tell you why. When a face has too red a look it does not appear to so much advantage as it would were it paler.'

'Pray, ma'am, proceed in your story.'

'Well, as I said before, I was invited by this lady to spend some weeks with her in town. Many gentlemen thought her handsome, but in my opinion, her forehead was too high, her eyes too small, and she had too much colour.'

'In that, madam, as I said before, your ladyship must have been mistaken. Mrs Watkins could not have too much colour, since no one can have too much.'

'Excuse me, my love, if I do not agree with you in that particular. Let me explain myself clearly; my idea of the case is this. When a woman has too great a proportion of red in her cheeks, she must have too much colour.'

'But madam, I deny that it is possible for any one to have too great a proportion of red in their cheeks.'

'What, my love, not if they have too much colour?'

Miss Johnson was now out of all patience, the more so perhaps as Lady Williams still remained so inflexibly cool. It must be remembered, however, that her ladyship had in one respect by far the advantage of Alice; I mean in not being drunk, for heated with wine and raised by passion, she could have little command of her temper.

The dispute at length grew so hot on the part of Alice that from words she almost came to blows, when Mr Johnson luckily entered and with some difficulty forced her away from Lady Williams, Mrs Watkins, and her red cheeks.

CHAPTER THE FOURTH

My readers may perhaps imagine that after such a fracas, no intimacy could longer subsist between the Johnsons and Lady Williams, but in that they are mistaken; for her ladyship was too sensible to be angry at a conduct which she could not help perceiving to be the natural consequence of her inebriety, and Alice had too sincere a respect for Lady Williams, and too great a relish for her claret, not to make every concession in her power.

A few days after their reconciliation, Lady Williams called on Miss Johnson to propose a walk in a citron grove which led from her ladyship's pigsty to Charles Adams' horsepond. Alice was too sensible of Lady Williams' kindness in proposing such a walk, and too much pleased with the prospect of seeing at the end of it a horsepond of Charles's, not to accept it with visible delight. They had not proceeded far before she was roused from the reflection of the happiness she was going to enjoy by Lady Williams thus addressing her.

'I have as yet forborn, my dear Alice, to continue the narrative of my life from an unwillingness of recalling to your memory a scene which (since it reflects on you rather disgrace than credit) had better be forgot than remembered.'

Alice had already begun to colour up and was beginning to speak, when her ladyship, perceiving her displeasure, continued thus.

'I am afraid, my dear girl, that I have offended you by what I have just said; I assure you I do not mean to distress you by a retrospection of what cannot now be helped; considering all things I do not think you so much to blame as many people do; for when a person is in liquor, there is no answering for what they may do. [A woman in such a situation is particularly off her guard because her head is not strong enough to support intoxication.]'[7]

'Madam, this is not to be borne; I insist –'

'My dear girl, don't vex yourself about the matter; I assure you I have entirely forgiven every thing respecting it; indeed I was not angry at the time, because as I saw all along, you were nearly dead drunk. I knew you could not help saying the strange things you did. But I see I distress you; so I will change the subject and desire it may never again be mentioned; remember it is all forgot – I will now pursue my story; but I must insist upon not giving you any description of Mrs Watkins: it would only be reviving old stories, and as you never saw her, it can be nothing to you if her forehead *was* too high, her eyes *were* too small, or if she *had* too much colour.'

'Again! Lady Williams: this is too much –'

So provoked was poor Alice at this renewal of the old story, that I know not what might have been the consequence of it, had not their attention been engaged by another object. A lovely young woman, lying apparently in great pain beneath a citron tree, was an object too interesting not to attract their notice. Forgetting their own dispute, they both with sympathizing tenderness advanced towards her and accosted her in these terms.

'You seem, fair nymph, to be labouring under some misfortune which we shall be happy to relieve if you will inform us what it is. Will you favour us with your life and adventures?'

'Willingly, ladies, if you will be so kind as to be seated.' They took their places and she thus began.

CHAPTER THE FIFTH

'I am a native of North Wales and my father is one of the most capital tailors in it. Having a numerous family, he was easily prevailed on by a sister of my mother's, who is a widow in good circumstances and keeps an alehouse in the next village to ours, to let her take me and breed me up at her own expense. Accordingly, I have lived with her for the last eight years of my life, during which time she provided me with some of the first-rate masters, who taught me all the accomplishments requisite for one of my sex and rank. Under their instructions I learned dancing, music, drawing, and various languages, by which means I became more accomplished than any other tailor's daughter in Wales. Never was there a happier creature than I was, till within the last half year – but I should have told you before that the principal estate in our neighbourhood belongs to Charles Adams, the owner of the brick house you see yonder.'

'Charles Adams!' exclaimed the astonished Alice. 'Are you acquainted with Charles Adams?'

'To my sorrow, madam, I am. He came about half a year ago to receive the rents of the estate I have just mentioned. At that time I first saw him; as you seem, ma'am, acquainted with him, I need not describe to you how charming he is. I could not resist his attractions.'

'Ah! who can?' said Alice with a deep sigh.

'My aunt, being in terms of the greatest intimacy with his cook, determined, at my request, to try whether she could discover by means of her friend if there were any chance of his returning my affection. For this purpose she went one evening to drink tea with Mrs Susan, who in the course of conversation mentioned the goodness of her place and the goodness of her master; upon which my aunt began pumping her with so much dexterity that in a short time Susan owned that she did not think her master would ever marry; "for," said she, "he has often and often declared to me that his wife, whoever she might be, must possess youth, beauty, birth, wit, merit, and money. I have many a time," she continued, "endeavoured to reason him out of his resolution and to convince him of the improbability of his ever meeting with such a lady; but my arguments have had no effect and he continues as firm in his determination as ever."[8] You may imagine, ladies, my distress on hearing this; for I was fearful that, though possessed of youth, beauty, wit, and merit, and though the probable heiress of my aunt's house and business, he might think me deficient in rank, and in being so, unworthy of his hand.

'However, I was determined to make a bold push, and therefore wrote him a very kind letter, offering him with great tenderness my hand and heart. To this I received an angry and peremptory refusal, but thinking it might be rather the effect of his modesty than any thing else, I pressed him again on the subject. But he never answered any more of my letters and very soon afterwards left the country. As soon as I heard of his departure I wrote to him here, informing him that I should shortly do myself the honour of waiting on him at Pammydiddle, to which I received no answer; therefore, choosing to take silence for consent, I left Wales, unknown to my aunt, and arrived here after a tedious journey this morning. On enquiring for his house, I was directed through this wood, to the one you there see. With a heart elated by the expected happiness of beholding him, I entered it and had proceeded thus far in my progress through it, when I found myself suddenly seized by the leg, and on examining the cause of it, found that I was caught in one of the steel traps so common in gentlemen's grounds.'[9]

'Ah!' cried Lady Williams, 'how fortunate we are to meet with you; since we might otherwise perhaps have shared the like misfortune.'

'It is indeed happy for you, ladies, that I should have been a short time before you. I screamed, as you may easily imagine, till the woods resounded again and till one of the inhuman wretch's servants came to my assistance and released me from my dreadful prison; but not before one of my legs was entirely broken.'

CHAPTER THE SIXTH

At this melancholy recital the fair eyes of Lady Williams were suffused in tears, and Alice could not help exclaiming,

'Oh! cruel Charles to wound the hearts and legs of all the fair.'

Lady Williams now interposed and observed that the young lady's leg ought to be set without farther delay. After examining the fracture, therefore, she immediately began and performed the operation with great skill, which was the more wonderful on account of her having never performed such a one before. Lucy then arose from the ground, and finding that she could walk with the greatest ease, accompanied them to Lady Williams' house at her ladyship's particular request.

The perfect form, the beautiful face, and elegant manners of Lucy so won on the affections of Alice that when they parted, which was not till after supper, she assured her that except her father, brother, uncles, aunts, cousins and other relations, Lady Williams, Charles Adams, and a few dozen more of particular friends, she loved her better than almost any other person in the world.

Such a flattering assurance of her regard would justly have given much pleasure to the object of it, had she not plainly perceived that the amiable Alice had partaken too freely of Lady Williams' claret.

Her ladyship (whose discernment was great) read in the intelligent countenance of Lucy her thoughts on the subject, and as soon as Miss Johnson had taken her leave, thus addressed her.

'When you are more intimately acquainted with my Alice, you will not be surprised, Lucy, to see the dear creature drink a little too much; for such things happen every day. She has many rare and charming qualities, but sobriety is not one of them. The whole family are indeed a sad, drunken set. I am sorry to say, too, that I never knew three such thorough gamesters as they are, more particularly Alice. But she is a charming girl. I fancy not one of the sweetest tempers in the world; to be sure I have seen her in such passions! However she is a sweet young woman. I am sure you'll like her. I scarcely know any one so amiable – Oh! that you could but have seen her the other evening! How she raved! And on such a trifle too! She is indeed a most pleasing girl! I shall always love her!'

'She appears by your ladyship's account to have many good qualities,' replied Lucy.

'Oh! a thousand,' answered Lady Williams, 'though I am very partial to her, and perhaps am blinded by my affection to her real defects.'

CHAPTER THE SEVENTH

The next morning brought the three Miss Simpsons to wait on Lady Williams, who received them with the utmost politeness and introduced to their acquaintance Lucy, with whom the eldest was so much pleased that at parting she declared her sole *ambition* was to have her accompany them the next morning to Bath, whither they were going for some weeks.

'Lucy,' said Lady Williams, 'is quite at her own disposal, and if she chooses to accept so kind an invitation, I hope she will not hesitate from any motives of delicacy on my account. I know not indeed how I shall ever be able to part with her. She never was at Bath, and I should think that it would be a most agreable jaunt to her. Speak, my love,' continued she, turning to Lucy. 'What say you to accompanying these ladies? I shall be miserable without you – t'will be a most pleasant tour to you – I hope you'll go; if you do I am sure t'will be the death of me – pray be persuaded –'

Lucy begged leave to decline the honour of accompanying them, with many expressions of gratitude for the extreme politeness of Miss Simpson in inviting her.

Miss Simpson appeared much disappointed by her refusal. Lady Williams insisted on her going – declared that she would never forgive her if she did not, and that she should never survive it if she did, and in short used such persuasive arguments that it was at length resolved she was to go. The Miss Simpsons called for her at ten o'clock the next morning, and Lady Williams had soon the satisfaction of receiving from her young friend the pleasing intelligence of their safe arrival in Bath.

It may now be proper to return to the hero of this novel, the brother of Alice, of whom I believe I have scarcely ever had occasion to speak; which may perhaps be partly owing to his unfortunate propensity to liquor, which so completely deprived him of the use of those faculties nature had endowed him with, that he never did anything worth mentioning. His death happened a short time after Lucy's departure and was the natural consequence of this pernicious practice. By his decease, his sister became the sole inheritress of a very large fortune, which, as it gave her fresh hopes of rendering herself acceptable as a wife to Charles Adams, could not fail of being most pleasing to her – and as the effect was joyful, the cause could scarcely be lamented.

Finding the violence of her attachment to him daily augment, she at length disclosed it to her father and desired him to propose a union between them to Charles. Her father consented and set out one morning to open the affair to the young man. Mr Johnson being a man of few words, his part was soon performed, and the answer he received was as follows.

'Sir, I may perhaps be expected to appear pleased at and grateful for the offer you have made me: but let me tell you that I consider it as an affront. I look upon myself to be, sir, a perfect beauty – where would you see a finer figure or a more charming face? Then, sir, I imagine my manners and address to be of the most polished kind; there is a certain elegance, a peculiar sweetness in them that I never saw equalled and cannot describe –. Partiality aside, I am certainly more accomplished in every language, every science, every art, and every thing than any other person in Europe. My temper is even, my virtues innumerable, my self unparalleled. Since such, sir, is my character, what do you mean by wishing me to marry your daughter? Let me give you a short sketch of yourself and of her. I look upon you, sir, to be a very good sort of man in the main; a drunken old dog to be sure, but that's nothing to me. Your daughter, sir, is neither sufficiently beautiful, sufficiently amiable, sufficiently witty, nor sufficiently rich for me. I expect nothing more in my wife than my wife will find in me – perfection. These, sir, are my sentiments and I honour myself for having such.

One friend I have, and glory in having but one –. She is at present preparing my dinner, but if you choose to see her, she shall come and she will inform you that these have ever been my sentiments.'

Mr Johnson was satisfied: and expressing himself to be much obliged to Mr Adams for the characters he had favoured him with of himself and his daughter, took his leave.

The unfortunate Alice, on receiving from her father the sad account of the ill success his visit had been attended with, could scarcely support the disappointment. She flew to her bottle and it was soon forgot.

CHAPTER THE EIGHTH

While these affairs were transacting at Pammydiddle, Lucy was conquering every heart at Bath. A fortnight's residence there had nearly effaced from her remembrance the captivating form of Charles. The recollection of what her heart had formerly suffered by his charms and her leg by his trap enabled her to forget him with tolerable ease, which was what she determined to do; and for that purpose dedicated five minutes in every day to the employment of driving him from her remembrance.

Her second letter to Lady Williams contained the pleasing intelligence of her having accomplished her undertaking to her entire satisfaction; she mentioned in it also an offer of marriage she had received from the Duke of ——, an elderly man of noble fortune whose ill health was the chief inducement of his journey to Bath.

'I am distressed,' she continued, 'to know whether I mean to accept him or not. There are a thousand advantages to be derived from a marriage with the duke, for besides those more inferior ones of rank and fortune, it will procure me a home, which of all other things is what I most desire. Your ladyship's kind wish of my always remaining with you is noble and generous, but I cannot think of becoming so great a burden on one I so much love and esteem. That one should receive obligations only from those we despise is a sentiment instilled into my mind by my worthy aunt in my early years, and cannot, in my opinion, be too strictly adhered to. The excellent woman of whom I now speak is, I hear, too much incensed by my imprudent departure from Wales to receive me again.

'I most earnestly wish to leave the ladies I am now with. Miss Simpson is indeed (setting aside ambition) very amiable, but her second sister, the envious and malevolent Sukey, is too disagreeable to live with. I have reason to think that the admiration I have met with, in the circles of the great at this place, has raised her hatred and envy; for often has she threatened, and sometimes endeavoured, to cut my throat.

'Your ladyship will therefore allow that I am not wrong in wishing to leave Bath, and in wishing to have a home to receive me, when I do. I shall expect with impatience your advice concerning the duke and am your most obliged etc.

Lucy'

Lady Williams sent her her opinion on the subject in the following manner.

'Why do you hesitate, my dearest Lucy, a moment with respect to the duke? I have enquired into his character and find him to be an unprincipled, illiterate man. Never shall my Lucy be united to such a one! He has a princely fortune, which is every day increasing. How nobly will you spend it! What credit will you give him in the eyes of all! How much will he be respected on his wife's account! But why, my dearest Lucy, why will you not at once decide this affair by returning to me and never leaving me again? Although I admire your noble sentiments with respect to obligations, yet let me beg that they may not prevent your making me happy. It will, to be sure, be a great expense to me to have you always with me – I shall not be able to support it – but what is that in comparison with the happiness I shall enjoy in your society? 'Twill ruin me I know – you will not therefore, surely, withstand these arguments, or refuse to return to yours most affectionately etc. etc.

C. Williams'

CHAPTER THE NINTH

What might have been the effect of her ladyship's advice, had it ever been received by Lucy, is uncertain, as it reached Bath a few hours after she had breathed her last. She fell a sacrifice to the envy and malice of Sukey, who, jealous of her superior charms, took her by poison from an admiring world at the age of seventeen.

Thus fell the amiable and lovely Lucy, whose life had been marked by no crime, and stained by no blemish but her imprudent departure from her aunt's, and whose death was sincerely lamented by every one who knew her. Among the most afflicted of her friends were Lady Williams, Miss Johnson, and the duke; the two first of whom had a most sincere regard for her, more particularly Alice, who had spent a whole evening in her company and had never thought of her since. His grace's affliction may likewise be easily accounted for, since he lost one for whom he had experienced, during the last ten days, a tender affection and sincere regard. He mourned her loss with unshaken constancy for the next fortnight, at the end of which time he gratified the ambition of Caroline Simpson by raising her to the rank of a duchess. Thus was she at length rendered completely happy in the gratification of her favourite passion. Her sister, the perfidious Sukey, was likewise shortly after exalted in a manner she truly deserved, and by her actions appeared to have always desired. Her barbarous murder was discovered and in spite of every interceding friend she was speedily raised to the gallows. The beautiful but affected Cecilia was too sensible of her own superior charms not to imagine that if Caroline could engage a duke, she might, without censure, aspire to the affections of some prince – and knowing that those of her native country were chiefly engaged, she left England and, I have since heard, is at present the favourite sultana of the great mogul.

In the mean time the inhabitants of Pammydiddle were in a state of the greatest astonishment and wonder, a report being circulated of the intended marriage of Charles Adams. The lady's name was still a secret. Mr and Mrs Jones imagined it to be Miss Johnson; but she knew better; all her fears were centered on his cook, when to the astonishment of every one, he was publicly united to Lady Williams –

Finis

Edgar and Emma

A Tale

CHAPTER THE FIRST

'I cannot imagine,' said Sir Godfrey to his lady, 'why we continue in such deplorable lodgings as these, in a paltry market town, while we have three good houses of our own situated in some of the finest parts of England, and perfectly ready to receive us!'

'I'm sure, Sir Godfrey,' replied Lady Marlow, 'it has been much against my inclination that we have stayed here so long; or why we should ever have come at all, indeed, has been to me a wonder, as none of our houses have been in the least want of repair.'

'Nay, my dear,' answered Sir Godfrey, 'you are the last person who ought to be displeased with what was always meant as a compliment to you; for you cannot but be sensible of the very great inconvenience your daughters and I have been put to, during the two years we have remained crowded in these lodgings in order to give you pleasure.'

'My dear,' replied Lady Marlow, 'how can you stand and tell such lies, when you very well know that it was merely to oblige the girls and you that I left a most commodious house, situated in a most delightful country, and surrounded by a most agreable neighbourhood, to live two years cramped up in lodgings three pair of stairs high, in a smoky and unwholesome town, which has given me a continual fever and almost thrown me into a consumption.'

As, after a few more speeches on both sides, they could not determine which was the most to blame, they prudently laid aside the debate, and having packed up their clothes and paid their rent, they set out the next morning with their two daughters for their seat in Sussex.

Sir Godfrey and Lady Marlow were indeed very sensible people, and though (as in this instance), like many other sensible people, they sometimes did a foolish thing, yet in general their actions were guided by prudence and regulated by discretion.

After a journey of two days and a half, they arrived at Marlhurst in good health and high spirits; so overjoyed were they all to inhabit again a place they had left with mutual regret for two years, that they ordered the bells to be rung and distributed ninepence among the ringers.

CHAPTER THE SECOND

The news of their arrival being quickly spread throughout the country brought them, in a few days, visits of congratulation from every family in it.

Amongst the rest came the inhabitants of Willmot Lodge, a beautiful villa not far from Marlhurst. Mr Willmot was the representative of a very ancient family, and possessed, besides his paternal estate, a considerable share in a lead mine and a ticket in the lottery. His lady was an agreable woman. Their children were too numerous to be particularly described; it is sufficient to say that in general they were virtuously inclined and not given to any wicked ways. Their family being too large to accompany them in every visit, they took nine with them alternately.

When their coach stopped at Sir Godfrey's door, the Miss Marlows' hearts throbbed in the eager expectation of once more beholding a family so dear to them. Emma, the youngest (who was more particularly interested in their arrival, being attached to their eldest son), continued at her dressing-room window in anxious hopes of seeing young Edgar descend from the carriage.

Mr and Mrs Willmot, with their three eldest daughters, first appeared – Emma began to tremble. Robert, Richard, Ralph, and Rodolphus followed – Emma turned pale. Their two youngest girls were lifted from the coach – Emma sunk breathless on a sofa. A footman came to announce to her the arrival of company; her heart was too full to contain its afflictions. A confidante was necessary. In Thomas she hoped to experience a faithful one – for one she must have and Thomas was the only one at hand. To him she unbosomed herself without restraint, and after owning her passion for young Willmot, requested his advice in what manner she should conduct herself in the melancholy disappointment under which she laboured.

Thomas, who would gladly have been excused from listening to her complaint, begged leave to decline giving any advice concerning it; which, much against her will, she was obliged to comply with.

Having dispatched him therefore with many injunctions of secrecy, she descended with a heavy heart into the parlour, where she found the good party seated in a social manner round a blazing fire.

CHAPTER THE THIRD

Emma had continued in the parlour some time before she could summon up sufficient courage to ask Mrs Willmot after the rest of her family; and when she did, it was in so low, so faltering a voice that no one knew she spoke. Dejected by the ill success of her first attempt, she made no other, till on Mrs Willmot's desiring one of the little girls to ring the bell for their carriage, she stepped across the room, and seizing the string, said in a resolute manner,

'Mrs Willmot, you do not stir from this house till you let me know how all the rest of your family do, particularly your eldest son.'

They were all greatly surprised by such an unexpected address, and the more so on account of the manner in which it was spoken; but Emma, who would not be again disappointed, requesting an answer, Mrs Willmot made the following eloquent oration.

'Our children are all extremely well, but at present most of them from home. Amy is with my sister Clayton. Sam at Eton. David with his Uncle John. Jem and Will at Winchester. Kitty at Queen's Square. Ned with his grandmother. Hetty and Patty in a convent at Brussels. Edgar at college, Peter at nurse, and all the rest (except the nine here) at home.'

It was with difficulty that Emma could refrain from tears on hearing of the absence of Edgar; she remained, however, tolerably composed till the Willmots were gone, when having no check to the overflowings of her grief, she gave free vent to them, and retiring to her own room, continued in tears the remainder of her life.

Finis

Henry and Eliza,

A Novel,
is humbly dedicated to Miss Cooper[10] by her obedient
humble servant,

the Author.

As Sir George and Lady Harcourt were superintending the labours
of their haymakers, rewarding the industry of some by smiles of
approbation, and punishing the idleness of others by a cudgel, they
perceived, lying closely concealed beneath the thick foliage of a
haycock, a beautiful little girl not more than three months old.

Touched with the enchanting graces of her face, and delighted
with the infantine though sprightly answers she returned to their
many questions, they resolved to take her home, and having no
children of their own, to educate her with care and cost.

Being good people themselves, their first and principal care was
to incite in her a love of virtue and a hatred of vice, in which they
so well succeeded (Eliza having a natural turn that way herself),
that when she grew up she was the delight of all who knew her.

Beloved by Lady Harcourt, adored by Sir George, and admired
by all the world, she lived in a continued course of uninterrupted
happiness till she had attained her eighteenth year, when, happening one day to be detected in stealing a banknote of 50£, she was
turned out of doors by her inhuman benefactors. Such a transition
to one who did not possess so noble and exalted a mind as Eliza
would have been death, but she, happy in the conscious knowledge
of her own excellence, amused herself, as she sat beneath a tree,
with making and singing the following lines.

Song

Though misfortune my footsteps may ever attend
     I hope I shall never have need of a friend
As an innocent heart I will ever preserve
     And will never from virtue's dear boundaries swerve.

Having amused herself some hours with this song and her own
pleasing reflections, she arose and took the road to M., a small

market town of which place her most intimate friend kept the Red Lion.

To this friend she immediately went, to whom having recounted her late misfortune, she communicated her wish of getting into some family in the capacity of humble companion.

Mrs Wilson, who was the most amiable creature on earth, was no sooner acquainted with her desire, than she sat down in the bar and wrote the following letter to the Duchess of F., the woman whom of all others she most esteemed.

'To the Duchess of F.: Receive into your family at my request a young woman of unexceptionable character, who is so good as to choose your society in preference to going to service. Hasten, and take her from the arms of your

Sarah Wilson.'

The duchess, whose friendship for Mrs Wilson would have carried her any lengths, was overjoyed at such an opportunity of obliging her, and accordingly set out immediately on the receipt of her letter for the Red Lion, which she reached the same evening. The Duchess of F. was about forty-five and a half; her passions were strong, her friendships firm, and her enmities unconquerable. She was a widow, and had only one daughter, who was on the point of marriage with a young man of considerable fortune.

The duchess no sooner beheld our heroine, than throwing her arms around her neck, she declared herself so much pleased with her, that she was resolved they never more should part. Eliza was delighted with such a protestation of friendship, and after taking a most affecting leave of her dear Mrs Wilson, accompanied her grace the next morning to her seat in Surrey.

With every expression of regard did the duchess introduce her to Lady Harriet, who was so much pleased with her appearance that she besought her to consider her as her sister; which Eliza, with the greatest condescension, promised to do.

Mr Cecil, the lover of Lady Harriet, being often with the family, was often with Eliza. A mutual love took place; and Cecil, having declared his first, prevailed on Eliza to consent to a private union, which was easy to be effected, as the duchess' chaplain, being very much in love with Eliza himself, would, they were certain, do anything to oblige her.

The duchess and Lady Harriet being engaged one evening to an assembly, they took the opportunity of their absence and were united by the enamoured chaplain. When the ladies returned, their amazement was great at finding instead of Eliza the following note.

'Madam:
    We are married and gone.
                            Henry and Eliza Cecil.'

Her grace, as soon as she had read the letter – which sufficiently explained the whole affair – flew into the most violent passion, and after having spent an agreable half hour in calling them by all the shocking names her rage could suggest to her, sent out after them 300 armed men, with orders not to return without their bodies, dead or alive; intending that, if they should be brought to her in the latter condition, to have them put to death in some torturelike manner, after a few years' confinement.

In the mean time Cecil and Eliza continued their flight to the continent, which they judged to be more secure than their native land from the dreadful effects of the duchess' vengeance, which they had so much reason to apprehend.

In France they remained three years, during which time they became the parents of two boys, and at the end of it Eliza became a widow without any thing to support either her or her children. They had lived since their marriage at the rate of 18,000£ a year, of which Mr Cecil's estate being rather less than the twentieth part, they had been able to save but a trifle, having lived to the utmost extent of their income.

Eliza, being perfectly conscious of the derangement in their affairs, immediately on her husband's death set sail for England in a man-of-war of fifty-five guns, which they had built in their more prosperous days. But no sooner had she stepped on shore at Dover, with a child in each hand, than she was seized by the officers of the duchess, and conducted by them to a snug little Newgate of their lady's, which she had erected for the reception of her own private prisoners.

No sooner had Eliza entered her dungeon, than the first thought which occurred to her was how to get out of it again.

She went to the door; but it was locked. She looked at the window; but it was barred with iron. Disappointed in both her expectations, she despaired of effecting her escape, when she fortunately perceived in a corner of her cell a small saw and ladder of ropes. With the saw she instantly went to work, and in a few weeks had displaced every bar but one, to which she fastened the ladder.

A difficulty then occurred which for some time she knew not how to obviate. Her children were too small to get down the ladder by themselves, nor would it be possible for her to take them in her arms when *she* did. At last she determined to fling down all her clothes, of which she had a large quantity, and then, having given them strict charge not to hurt themselves, threw her children after them. She herself with ease descended by the ladder, at the bottom of which she had the pleasure of finding her little boys in perfect health and fast asleep.

Her wardrobe she now saw a fatal necessity of selling, both for the preservation of her children and herself. With tears in her eyes, she parted with these last relics of her former glory, and with the money she got for them, bought others more useful: some playthings for her boys and a gold watch for herself.

But scarcely was she provided with the above-mentioned necessaries, than she began to find herself rather hungry, and had reason to think, by their biting off two of her fingers, that her children were much in the same situation.

To remedy these unavoidable misfortunes, she determined to return to her old friends, Sir George and Lady Harcourt, whose generosity she had so often experienced, and hoped to experience as often again.

She had about forty miles to travel before she could reach their hospitable mansion, of which having walked thirty without stopping, she found herself at the entrance of a town, where often, in happier times, she had accompanied Sir George and Lady Harcourt to regale themselves with a cold collation at one of the inns.

The reflections that her adventures, since the last time she had

partaken of these happy junketings, afforded her occupied her
mind for some time as she sat on the steps at the door of a
gentleman's house. As soon as these reflections were ended, she
arose and determined to take her station at the very inn she
remembered with so much delight, from the company of which, as
they went in and out, she hoped to receive some charitable gratuity.

She had but just taken her post at the innyard before a carriage
drove out of it, and on turning the corner at which she was
stationed, stopped to give the postilion an opportunity of admiring
the beauty of the prospect. Eliza then advanced to the carriage and
was going to request their charity, when, on fixing her eyes on the
lady within it, she exclaimed,

'Lady Harcourt!'

To which the lady replied,

'Eliza!'

'Yes, madam, it is the wretched Eliza herself.'

Sir George, who was also in the carriage, but too much amazed
to speak, was proceeding to demand an explanation from Eliza of
the situation she was then in, when Lady Harcourt, in transports
of joy, exclaimed,

'Sir George, Sir George, she is not only Eliza our adopted
daughter, but our real child.'

'Our real child! What, Lady Harcourt, do you mean? You know
you never even was with child. Explain yourself, I beseech you.'

'You must remember, Sir George, that when you sailed for
America, you left me breeding.'

'I do, I do; go on, dear Polly.'

'Four months after you were gone, I was delivered of this girl,
but dreading your just resentment at her not proving the boy you
wished, I took her to a haycock and laid her down. A few weeks
afterwards, you returned, and fortunately for me, made no
enquiries on the subject. Satisfied within myself of the welfare of
my child, I soon forgot I had one, insomuch that when we shortly
after found her in the very haycock I had placed her, I had no more
idea of her being my own than you had, and nothing, I will venture
to say, would have recalled the circumstance to my remembrance
but my thus accidentally hearing her voice, which now strikes me
as being the very counterpart of my own child's.'

'The rational and convincing account you have given of the whole affair,' said Sir George, 'leaves no doubt of her being our daughter, and as such I freely forgive the robbery she was guilty of.'

A mutual reconciliation then took place, and Eliza, ascending the carriage with her two children, returned to that home from which she had been absent nearly four years.

No sooner was she reinstated in her accustomed power at Harcourt Hall, than she raised an army, with which she entirely demolished the duchess's Newgate, snug as it was; and by that act gained the blessings of thousands and the applause of her own heart.

Finis

The Adventures of Mr Harley,

a short but interesting tale, is with all imaginable respect inscribed to Mr Francis William Austen, midshipman on board his majesty's ship the Perseverance, by his obedient servant,

the Author.

Mr Harley was one of many children. Destined by his father for the Church and by his mother for the sea, desirous of pleasing both, he prevailed on Sir John to obtain for him a chaplaincy on board a man of war. He accordingly cut his hair and sailed.

In half a year he returned and set off in the stage coach for Hogsworth Green, the seat of Emma. His fellow travellers were a man without a hat, another with two, an old maid, and a young wife.

This last appeared about seventeen, with fine, dark eyes and an elegant shape; in short, Mr Harley soon found out that she was his Emma and recollected he had married her a few weeks before he left England.

Finis

Sir William Mountague,

an unfinished performance,
is humbly dedicated to Charles John
Austen Esq.,[11] by his most obedient humble
servant,

the Author.

Sir William Mountague was the son of Sir Henry Mountague, who was the son of Sir John Mountague, a descendant of Sir Christopher Mountague, who was the nephew of Sir Edward Mountague, whose ancestor was Sir James Mountague, a near relation of Sir Robert Mountague, who inherited the title and estate from Sir Frederic Mountague.

Sir William was about seventeen when his father died and left him a handsome fortune, an ancient house, and a park well-stocked with deer. Sir William had not been long in the possession of his estate before he fell in love with the three Miss Cliftons of Kilhoobery Park. These young ladies were all equally young, equally handsome, equally rich, and equally amiable – Sir William was equally in love with them all, and knowing not which to prefer, he left the country and took lodgings in a small village near Dover.

In his retreat, to which he had retired in the hope of finding a shelter from the pangs of love, he became enamoured of a young widow of quality, who came for change of air to the same village, after the death of a husband whom she had always tenderly loved and now sincerely lamented.

Lady Percival was young, accomplished, and lovely. Sir William adored her and she consented to become his wife. Vehemently pressed by Sir William to name the day in which he might conduct her to the altar, she at length fixed on the following Monday, which was the first of September. Sir William was a shot and could not support the idea of losing such a day, even for such a cause. He begged her to delay the wedding a short time. Lady Percival was enraged and returned to London the next morning.

Sir William was sorry to lose her, but as he knew that he should have been much more grieved by the loss of the first of September, his sorrow was not without a mixture of happiness, and his affliction was considerably lessened by his joy.

After staying at the village a few weeks longer, he left it and went to a friend's house in Surrey. Mr Brudenell was a sensible man, and had a beautiful niece with whom Sir William soon fell in love. But Miss Arundel was cruel; she preferred a Mr Stanhope. Sir William shot Mr Stanhope: the lady had then no reason to refuse him; she accepted him, and they were to be married on the twenty-seventh of October. But on the twenty-fifth Sir William received a visit from Emma Stanhope, the sister of the unfortunate victim of his rage. She begged some recompense, some atonement for the cruel murder of her brother. Sir William bade her name her price. She fixed on 14s. Sir William offered her himself and fortune. They went to London the next day and were there privately married. For a fortnight Sir William was completely happy, but chancing one day to see a charming young woman entering a chariot in Brook Street, he became again most violently in love. On enquiring the name of this fair unknown, he found that she was the sister of his old friend Lady Percival, at which he was much rejoiced, as he hoped to have, by his acquaintance with her ladyship, free access to Miss Wentworth . . .

Finis

Memoirs of Mr Clifford

An Unfinished Tale

To Charles John Austen Esq.

Sir,

 Your generous patronage of the unfinished tale I have already taken the liberty of dedicating to you, encourages me to dedicate to you a second, as unfinished as the first.

I am, sir, with every expression
of regard for you and your noble
family, your most obedient
etc. etc . . .
the Author.

Mr Clifford lived at Bath; and having never seen London, set off one Monday morning, determined to feast his eyes with a sight of that great metropolis. He travelled in his coach and four, for he was a very rich young man and kept a great many carriages, of which I do not recollect half. I can only remember that he had a coach, a chariot, a chaise, a landeau, a landeaulet, a phaeton, a gig, a whisky, an Italian chair, a buggy, a curricle, and a wheelbarrow. He had likewise an amazing fine stud of horses. To my knowledge he had six greys, four bays, eight blacks, and a pony.

In his coach and four bays Mr Clifford set forward about five o'clock on Monday morning, the first of May, for London. He always travelled remarkably expeditiously and contrived therefore to get to Devizes from Bath, which is no less than nineteen miles, the first day.[12] To be sure, he did not get in till eleven at night, and pretty tight work it was, as you may imagine.

However, when he was once got to Devizes, he was determined to comfort himself with a good hot supper, and therefore ordered a whole egg to be boiled for him and his servants. The next morning he pursued his journey and in the course of three days' hard labour reached Overton, where he was seized with a dangerous fever, the consequence of too violent exercise.

Five months did our hero remain in this celebrated city under the care of its no less celebrated physician, who at length completely cured him of his troublesome disease.

As Mr Clifford still continued very weak, his first day's journey carried him only to Dean Gate, where he remained a few days and found himself much benefited by the change of air.

In easy stages, he proceeded to Basingstoke, one day carrying him to Clarkengreen, the next to Worting, the third to the bottom of Basingstoke Hill, and the fourth to Mr Robins' . . .[13]

Finis

The Beautiful Cassandra,

A Novel in Twelve Chapters,
dedicated by permission to Miss Austen.[14]

Dedication

Madam:
   You are a phoenix. Your taste is refined, your sentiments
are noble, and your virtues innumerable. Your person is
lovely, your figure elegant, and your form majestic. Your
manners are polished, your conversation is rational, and
your appearance singular. If, therefore, the following tale
will afford one moment's amusement to you, every wish will
be gratified of

> Your most obedient
> humble servant,
> the Author.

CHAPTER THE FIRST

Cassandra was the daughter and the only daughter of a celebrated
milliner in Bond Street. Her father was of noble birth, being the
near relation of the Duchess of —'s butler.

CHAPTER THE SECOND

When Cassandra had attained her sixteenth year, she was lovely
and amiable, and chancing to fall in love with an elegant bonnet
her mother had just completed, bespoke by the Countess of —, she
placed it on her gentle head and walked from her mother's shop to
make her fortune.

CHAPTER THE THIRD

The first person she met was the Viscount of —, a young man no less celebrated for his accomplishments and virtues than for his elegance and beauty. She curtseyed and walked on.

CHAPTER THE FOURTH

She then proceeded to a pastry-cook's, where she devoured six ices, refused to pay for them, knocked down the pastry cook, and walked away.

CHAPTER THE FIFTH

She next ascended a hackney coach and ordered it to Hampstead, where she was no sooner arrived than she ordered the coachman to turn round and drive her back again.

CHAPTER THE SIXTH

Being returned to the same spot of the same street she had set out from, the coachman demanded his pay.

CHAPTER THE SEVENTH

She searched her pockets over again and again; but every search was unsuccessful. No money could she find. The man grew peremptory. She placed her bonnet on his head and ran away.

CHAPTER THE EIGHTH

Through many a street she then proceeded and met in none the least adventure, till on turning a corner of Bloomsbury Square, she met Maria.

CHAPTER THE NINTH

Cassandra started and Maria seemed surprised; they trembled, blushed, turned pale, and passed each other in a mutual silence.

CHAPTER THE TENTH

Cassandra was next accosted by her friend the widow, who, squeezing out her little head through her less window, asked her how she did? Cassandra curtseyed and went on.

CHAPTER THE ELEVENTH

A quarter of a mile brought her to her paternal roof in Bond Street, from which she had now been absent nearly seven hours.

CHAPTER THE TWELFTH

She entered it and was pressed to her mother's bosom by that worthy woman. Cassandra smiled and whispered to herself, 'This is a day well spent.'

Finis

Amelia Webster,

an interesting and well-written tale,
is dedicated by permission
to
Mrs Austen[15]
by
her humble servant,
the Author.

LETTER THE FIRST

To Miss Webster

My dear Amelia,

You will rejoice to hear of the return of my amiable brother from abroad. He arrived on Thursday, and never did I see a finer form, save that of your sincere friend

Matilda Hervey

LETTER THE SECOND

To H. Beverley Esq.

Dear Beverley,

I arrived here last Thursday and met with a hearty reception from my father, mother, and sisters. The latter are both fine girls – particularly Maud, who I think would suit you as a wife well enough. What say you to this? She will have two thousand pounds and as much more as you can get. If you don't marry her you will mortally offend

George Hervey

LETTER THE THIRD

To Miss Hervey

Dear Maud,

Believe me I'm happy to hear of your brother's arrival. I have a thousand things to tell you, but my paper will only permit me to add that I am your affectionate friend

Amelia Webster

LETTER THE FOURTH

To Miss S. Hervey

Dear Sally,

I have found a very convenient old hollow oak to put our letters in; for you know we have long maintained a private correspondence. It is about a mile from my house and seven from yours. You may perhaps imagine that I might have made choice of a tree which would have divided the distance more equally – I was sensible of this at the time, but as I considered that the walk would be of benefit to you in your weak and uncertain state of health, I preferred it to one nearer your house, and am your faithful

Benjamin Bar

LETTER THE FIFTH

To Miss Hervey

Dear Maud,

I write now to inform you that I did not stop at your house in my way to Bath last Monday. I have many things to inform you of besides, but my paper reminds me of concluding; and believe me yours ever etc.

Amelia Webster

LETTER THE SIXTH

To Miss Webster

Saturday

Madam,

An humble admirer now addresses you. I saw you, lovely fair one, as you passed on Monday last before our house in your way to Bath. I saw you through a telescope, and was so struck by your charms that from that time to this I have not tasted human food.

George Hervey

LETTER THE SEVENTH

To Jack

As I was this morning at breakfast the newspaper was brought to me, and in the list of marriages I read the following:

George Hervey Esq. to Miss Amelia Webster;
Henry Beverley Esq. to Miss Hervey;
            and
Benjamin Bar Esq. to Miss Sarah Hervey.

                                        Yours, Tom

Finis

The Visit

A Comedy in Two Acts

Dedication

To the Rev. James Austen[16]

Sir,

   The following drama, which I humbly recommend to your protection and patronage, though inferior to those celebrated comedies called The School for Jealousy and The Travelled Man,[17] will, I hope, afford some amusement to so respectable a curate as yourself; which was the end in view when it was first composed by your humble servant,

                                        the Author.

Dramatis Personae

Sir Arthur Hampton	Lady Hampton
Lord Fitzgerald	Miss Fitzgerald
Stanly	Sophy Hampton
Willoughby, Sir Arthur's nephew	Cloe Willoughby

The scenes are laid in Lord Fitzgerald's house.

ACT THE FIRST

Scene the first. A parlour.

Enter LORD FITZGERALD *and* STANLY.

STANLY. Cousin, your servant.

FITZGERALD. Stanly, good morning to you. I hope you slept well last night.

STANLY. Remarkably well, I thank you.

FITZGERALD. I am afraid you found your bed too short. It was bought in my grandmother's time, who was herself a very short woman and made a point of suiting all her beds to her own length, as she never wished to have any company in the house, on account of an unfortunate impediment in her speech, which she was sensible of being very disagreable to her inmates.

STANLY. Make no more excuses, dear Fitzgerald.

FITZGERALD. I will not distress you by too much civility – I only beg you will consider yourself as much at home as in your father's house. Remember, 'The more free, the more welcome.'

    [*Exit* FITZGERALD.]

STANLY. Amiable youth!

        Your virtues could he imitate
        How happy would be Stanly's fate!

    [*Exit* STANLY.]

Scene the second.

STANLY *and* MISS FITZGERALD, *discovered.*

STANLY. What company is it you expect to dine with you today, cousin?

MISS F. Sir Arthur and Lady Hampton; their daughters, nephew and niece.

STANLY. Miss Hampton and her cousin are both handsome, are they not?

MISS F. Miss Willoughby is extremely so. Miss Hampton is a fine girl, but not equal to her.

STANLY. Is not your brother attached to the latter?

MISS F. He admires her I know, but I believe nothing more. Indeed

I have heard him say that she was the most beautiful, pleasing, and amiable girl in the world, and that of all others he should prefer her for his wife. But it never went any farther, I'm certain.

STANLY. And yet my cousin never says a thing he does not mean.

MISS F. Never. From his cradle he has always been a strict adherent to truth. [He never told a lie but once, and that was merely to oblige me. Indeed I may truly say there never was such a brother!][18]

[*Exeunt severally.*]

End of the First Act.

ACT THE SECOND

Scene the first. The drawing room.

Chairs set round in a row. LORD FITZGERALD,
MISS FITZGERALD, *and* STANLY, *seated.*
Enter a Servant.

SERVANT. Sir Arthur and Lady Hampton. Miss Hampton, Mr and Miss Willoughby.

[*Exit* SERVANT. *Enter the Company.*]

MISS F. I hope I have the pleasure of seeing your ladyship well. Sir Arthur, your servant. Yours, Mr Willoughby. Dear Sophy, dear Cloe, –

[*They pay their compliments alternately.*]

MISS F. Pray be seated. [*They sit.*] Bless me! there ought to be eight chairs and there are but six. However, if your ladyship will but take Sir Arthur in your lap, and Sophy my brother in hers, I believe we shall do pretty well.

LADY H. Oh! with pleasure . . .

SOPHY. I beg his lordship would be seated.

MISS F. I am really shocked at crowding you in such a manner, but my grandmother (who bought all the furniture of this room), as she had never a very large party, did not think it necessary to buy more chairs than were sufficient for her own family and two of her particular friends.

SOPHY. I beg you will make no apologies. Your brother is very light.

STANLY [*aside*]. What a cherub is Cloe!

CLOE [*aside*]. What a seraph is Stanly.

[*Enter a Servant.*]

SERVANT. Dinner is on table.

[*They all rise.*]

MISS F. Lady Hampton, Miss Hampton, Miss Willoughby.

[STANLY *hands* CLOE; LORD FITZGERALD, SOPHY; WIL-
LOUGHBY, MISS FITZGERALD; *and* SIR ARTHUR, LADY
HAMPTON. *Exeunt.*]

Scene the second. The dining parlour.

MISS FITZGERALD *at top.* LORD FITZGERALD *at bottom.*
Company ranged on each side. Servants waiting.

CLOE. I shall trouble Mr Stanly for a little of the fried cow heel and
onion.

STANLY. Oh, madam, there is a secret pleasure in helping so
amiable a lady.

LADY H. I assure you, my lord, Sir Arthur never touches wine; but
Sophy will toss off a bumper I am sure, to oblige your lordship.

LORD F. Elder wine or mead, Miss Hampton?

SOPHY. If it is equal to you, sir, I should prefer some warm ale
with a toast and nutmeg.

LORD F. Two glasses of warmed ale with a toast and nutmeg.

MISS F. I am afraid, Mr Willoughby, you take no care of yourself.
I fear you don't meet with any thing to your liking.

WILLOUGHBY. Oh! madam, I can want for nothing while there are
red herrings on table.

LORD F. Sir Arthur, taste that tripe. I think you will not find it
amiss.

LADY H. Sir Arthur never eats tripe; 'tis too savoury for him you
know, my lord.

MISS F. Take away the liver and crow and bring in the suet
pudding.

[*A short pause.*]

MISS F. Sir Arthur, shan't I send you a bit of pudding?

LADY H. Sir Arthur never eats suet pudding, ma'am. It is too high
a dish for him.

MISS F. Will no one allow me the honour of helping them? Then, John, take away the pudding, and bring the wine.

[SERVANTS *take away the things and bring in the bottles and glasses.*]

LORD F. I wish we had any dessert to offer you. But my grandmother, in her lifetime, destroyed the hothouse in order to build a receptacle for the turkeys with its materials; and we have never been able to raise another tolerable one.

LADY H. I beg you will make no apologies, my lord.

WILLOUGHBY. Come, girls, let us circulate the bottle.

SOPHY. A very good notion, cousin; and I will second it with all my heart. Stanly, you don't drink.

STANLY. Madam, I am drinking draughts of love from Cloe's eyes.

SOPHY. That's poor nourishment, truly. Come, drink to her better acquaintance.

[MISS FITZGERALD *goes to a closet and brings out a bottle.*]

MISS F. This, ladies and gentlemen, is some of my dear grandmother's own manufacture. She excelled in gooseberry wine. Pray taste it, Lady Hampton?

LADY H. How refreshing it is!

MISS F. I should think, with your ladyship's permission, that Sir Arthur might taste a little of it.

LADY H. Not for worlds. Sir Arthur never drinks any thing so high.

LORD F. And now, my amiable Sophia, condescend to marry me.

[*He takes her hand and leads her to the front.*]

STANLY. Oh! Cloe could I but hope you would make me blessed –

CLOE. I will.

[*They advance.*]

MISS F. Since you, Willoughby, are the only one left, I cannot refuse your earnest solicitations – there is my hand.

LADY H. And may you all be happy!

Finis

The Mystery

An Unfinished Comedy

Dedication

To the Rev. George Austen.[19]

Sir,

I humbly solicit your patronage to the following comedy, which though an unfinished one, is, I flatter myself, as complete a mystery as any of its kind.

I am, sir, your most humble servant,

the Author.

Dramatis Personae

Colonel Elliott	Fanny Elliott
Sir Edward Spangle	Mrs Humbug
Old Humbug	Daphne
Young Humbug	
Corydon	

ACT THE FIRST

Scene the first. A garden.

Enter CORYDON.

CORY. But hush! I am interrupted.

[*Exit* CORYDON. *Enter* OLD HUMBUG *and his* SON, *talking.*]

OLD HUM. It is for that reason I wish you to follow my advice. Are you convinced of its propriety?

YOUNG HUM. I am, sir, and will certainly act in the manner you have pointed out to me.

OLD HUM. Then let us return to the house.

[*Exeunt.*]

Scene the second. A parlour in HUMBUG's *house.*

MRS HUMBUG *and* FANNY, *discovered at work.*

MRS HUM. You understand me, my love?

FANNY. Perfectly, ma'am. Pray, continue your narration.

MRS HUM. Alas! it is nearly concluded, for I have nothing more to say on the subject.

FANNY. Ah! here's Daphne.
    [*Enter* DAPHNE.]

DAPHNE. My dear Mrs Humbug, how d'ye do? Oh! Fanny 'tis all over.

FANNY. Is it indeed!

MRS HUM. I'm very sorry to hear it.

FANNY. Then 'twas to no purpose that I . . .

DAPHNE. None upon earth.

MRS HUM. And what is to become of? . . .

DAPHNE. Oh! that's all settled. [*Whispers* MRS HUMBUG.]

FANNY. And how is it determined?

DAPHNE. I'll tell you. [*Whispers* FANNY.]

MRS HUM. And is he to? . . .

DAPHNE. I'll tell you all I know of the matter.
    [*Whispers* MRS HUMBUG *and* FANNY.]

FANNY. Well! now I know everything about it, I'll go away [and dress][20].

MRS HUM., DAPHNE. And so will I.
    [*Exeunt.*]

Scene the third.

The curtain rises and discovers SIR EDWARD SPANGLE *reclined in an elegant attitude on a sofa, fast asleep.*
Enter COLONEL ELLIOTT.

COLONEL. My daughter is not here I see . . . there lies Sir Edward . . . Shall I tell him the secret? . . . No, he'll certainly blab it . . . But he is asleep and won't hear me . . . So I'll e'en venture.
    [*Goes up to* SIR EDWARD, *whispers him, and exit.*]
    End of the first Act.
    Finis

To Edward Austen Esq.[21]
The following unfinished novel
is respectfully inscribed
by
his obedient humble servant,
the Author.

The Three Sisters[22]

A Novel

Miss Stanhope to Mrs —

My dear Fanny,

I am the happiest creature in the world, for I have received an offer of marriage from Mr Watts. It is the first I have ever had and I hardly know how to value it enough. How I will triumph over the Duttons! I do not intend to accept it, at least I believe not, but as I am not quite certain, I gave him an equivocal answer and left him. And now my dear Fanny I want your advice whether I should accept his offer or not, but that you may be able to judge of his merits and the situation of affairs I will give you an account of them. He is quite an old man, about two and thirty, very plain, *so* plain that I cannot bear to look at him. He is extremely disagreable and I hate him more than any body else in the world. He has a large fortune and will make great settlements on me; but then he is very healthy. In short I do not know what to do. If I refuse him he as good as told me that he should offer himself to Sophia and if she refused him to Georgiana, and I could not bear to have either of them married before me. If I accept him I know I shall be miserable all the rest of my life, for he is very ill-tempered and peevish, extremely jealous, and so stingy that there is no living in the house with him. He told me he should mention the affair to Mama, but I insisted upon it that he did not, for very likely she would make me marry him whether I would or no; however probably he *has* before now, for he never does anything he is desired to do. I believe I shall have him. It will be such a triumph to be married before Sophy, Georgiana, and the Duttons; and he promised to have a new carriage on the occasion, but we almost quarrelled about the colour, for I insisted upon its being blue spotted with silver, and he declared it should be plain chocolate; and to provoke me more said it should be just as low as his old one. I won't have him, I declare. He said he should come again tomorrow and take my final answer, so I believe I must get him while I can. I know the Duttons will envy me and I shall be able to chaperone Sophy and Georgiana to all the winter balls. But then what will be the use of that when very likely he won't let me go myself, for I know he hates dancing and [has a great idea of women's never going from home].[23] What he hates himself he has no idea of any other person's liking; and besides he talks a great deal of women's always staying at home and such stuff. I believe I shan't have him; I would refuse him at once if I were certain that neither of my sisters would accept him, and that if they did not, he would not offer to the Duttons. I cannot run such a risk, so, if he will promise to have the carriage ordered as I like, I will have him; if not he may ride in it by himself for me. I hope you like my determination; I can think of nothing better; and am your ever affectionate

                                                    Mary Stanhope

From the same to the same

Dear Fanny,

I had but just sealed my last letter to you when my mother came up and told me she wanted to speak to me on a very particular subject.

'Ah! I know what you mean,' said I. 'That old fool Mr Watts has told you all about it, though I bid him not. However you shan't force me to have him if I don't like it.'

'I am not going to force you, child, but only want to know what your resolution is with regard to his proposals, and to insist upon your making up your mind one way or t'other, that if *you* don't accept him, *Sophy* may.'

'Indeed,' replied I hastily, 'Sophy need not trouble herself for I shall certainly marry him myself.'

'If that is your resolution,' said my mother, 'why should you be afraid of my forcing your inclinations?'

'Why! because I have not settled whether I shall have him or not.'

'You are the strangest girl in the world, Mary. What you say one moment, you unsay the next. Do tell me once for all, whether you intend to marry Mr Watts or not?'

'Law, Mama, how can I tell you what I don't know myself?'

'Then I desire you will know, and quickly too, for Mr Watts says he won't be kept in suspense.'

'That depends upon me.'

'No it does not, for if you do not give him your final answer tomorrow when he drinks tea with us, he intends to pay his addresses to Sophy.'

'Then I shall tell all the world that he behaved very ill to me.'

'What good will that do? Mr Watts has been too long abused by all the world to mind it now.'

'I wish I had a father or a brother because then they should fight him.'

'They would be cunning if they did, for Mr Watts would run away first; and therefore you must and shall resolve either to accept or refuse him before tomorrow evening.'

'But why, if I don't have him, must he offer to my sisters?'

'Why! because he wishes to be allied to the family and because they are as pretty as you are.'

'But will Sophy marry him, Mama, if he offers to her?'

'Most likely; why should not she? If, however, she does not choose it, then Georgiana must, for I am determined not to let such an opportunity escape of settling one of my daughters so advantageously. So, make the most of your time; I leave you to settle the matter with yourself.' And then she went away. The only thing I can think of my dear Fanny is to ask Sophy and Georgiana whether they would have him were he to make proposals to them, and if they say they would not I am resolved to refuse him too, for I hate him more than you can imagine. As for the Duttons, if he marries one of *them* I shall still have the triumph of having refused him first. So, adieu my dear friend –

Yours ever, M.S.

Miss Georgiana Stanhope to Miss —

Wednesday

My dear Anne,

Sophy and I have just been practising a little deceit on our eldest sister, to which we are not perfectly reconciled, and yet the circumstances were such that if any thing will excuse it, they must. Our neighbour Mr Watts has made proposals to Mary: proposals which she knew not how to receive, for though she has a particular dislike to him (in which she is not singular), yet she would willingly marry him sooner than risk his offering to Sophy or me, which in case of a refusal from herself, he told her he should do; for you must know the poor girl considers our marrying before her as one of the greatest misfortunes that can possibly befall her, and to prevent it would willingly ensure herself everlasting misery by a marriage with Mr Watts. An hour ago she came to us to sound our inclinations respecting the affair, which were to determine hers. A little before she came my mother had given us an account of it, telling us that she certainly would not let him go farther than our own family for a wife. 'And therefore,' said she, 'If Mary won't have him Sophy must, and if Sophy won't Georgiana *shall*.' Poor Georgiana! – We neither of us attempted to alter my mother's resolution, which I am sorry to say is generally more strictly kept than rationally formed. As soon as she was gone, however, I broke silence to assure Sophy that if Mary should refuse Mr Watts I should not expect her to sacrifice *her* happiness by becoming his wife from a motive of generosity to me, which I was afraid her good nature and sisterly affection might induce her to do.

'Let us flatter ourselves', replied she, 'that Mary will not refuse him. Yet how can I hope that my sister may accept a man who cannot make her happy?'

'*He* cannot, it is true, but his fortune, his name, his house, his carriage will, and I have no doubt that Mary will marry him; indeed why should she not? He is not more than two and thirty; a very proper age for a man to marry at; he is rather plain to be sure, but then what is beauty in a man? If he has but a genteel figure and a sensible looking face it is quite sufficient.'

'This is all very true, Georgiana, but Mr Watts's figure is unfortunately extremely vulgar and his countenance is very heavy.'

'And then, as to his temper, it has been reckoned bad, but may not the world be deceived in their judgement of it? There is an open frankness in his disposition which becomes a man. They say he is stingy; we'll call that prudence. They say he is suspicious; that proceeds from a warmth of heart always excusable in youth: and in short I see no reason why he should not make a very good husband, or why Mary should not be very happy with him.'

Sophy laughed; I continued,

'However, whether Mary accepts him or not I am resolved. My determination is made. I never would marry Mr Watts were beggary the only alternative. So deficient in every respect! Hideous in his person and without one good quality to make amends for it. His fortune to be sure is good. Yet not so very large! Three thousand a year. What is three thousand a year? It is but six times as much as my mother's income. It will not tempt me.'

'Yet it will be a noble fortune for Mary,' said Sophy, laughing again.

'For Mary! Yes indeed, it will give me pleasure to see *her* in such affluence.'

Thus I ran on to the great entertainment of my sister till Mary came into the room to appearance in great agitation. She sat down. We made room for her at the fire. She seemed at a loss how to begin and at last said in some confusion,

'Pray Sophy, have you any mind to be married?'

'To be married! None in the least. But why do you ask me? Are you acquainted with any one who means to make me proposals?'

'I – no, how should I? But mayn't I ask a common question?'

'Not a very common one Mary, surely,' said I. She paused and after some moments' silence went on –

'How should you like to marry Mr Watts, Sophy?'

I winked at Sophy and replied for her. 'Who is there but must rejoice to marry a man of three thousand a year [who keeps a postchaise and pair, with silver harness, a boot before, and a window to look out at behind]?'[24]

'Very true,' she replied. 'That's very true. So you would have him if he would offer, Georgiana; and would *you* Sophy?'

Sophy did not like the idea of telling a lie and deceiving her sister; she prevented the first and saved half her conscience by equivocation.

'I should certainly act just as Georgiana would do.'

'Well then,' said Mary with triumph in her eyes, '*I* have had an offer from Mr Watts.'

We were of course very much surprised;

'Oh! do not accept him,' said I, 'and then perhaps he may have me.'

In short my scheme took and Mary is resolved to do that to prevent our supposed happiness which she would not have done to ensure it in reality. Yet, after all, my heart cannot acquit me, and Sophy is even more scrupulous. Quiet our minds, my dear Anne, by writing and telling us you approve our conduct. Consider it well over. Mary will have real pleasure in being a married woman, and able to chaperone us, which she certainly shall do, for I think myself bound to contribute as much as possible to her happiness in a state I have made her choose. They will probably have a new carriage, which will be paradise to her, and if we can prevail on Mr Watts to set up his phaeton she will be too happy. These things however would be no consolation to Sophy or me for domestic misery. Remember all this and do not condemn us.

Friday

Last night Mr Watts, by appointment, drank tea with us. As soon as his carriage stopped at the door, Mary went to the window.

'Would you believe it, Sophy,' said she, 'the old fool wants to have his new chaise just the colour of the old one, and hung as low too. But it shan't be – I *will* carry my point. And if he won't let it be as high as the Duttons', and blue spotted with silver, I won't have him. Yes I will too. Here he comes. I know he'll be rude; I know he'll be ill-tempered and won't say one civil thing to me! Nor behave at all like a lover.' She then sat down and Mr Watts entered.

'Ladies, your most obedient.' We paid our compliments and he seated himself.

'Fine weather, ladies.' Then, turning to Mary, 'Well, Miss Stanhope, I hope you have *at last* settled the matter in your own mind; and will be so good as to let me know whether you will *condescend* to marry me or not.'

'I think, sir,' said Mary, 'you might have asked in a genteeler way than that. I do not know whether I *shall* have you if you behave so odd.'

'Mary!' said my mother.

'Well, Mama, if he will be so cross . . .'

'Hush, hush, Mary, you shall not be rude to Mr Watts.'

'Pray, madam, do not lay any restraint on Miss Stanhope by obliging her to be civil. If she does not choose to accept my hand, I can offer it else where; for as I am by no means guided by a particular preference to you above your sisters, it is equally the same to me which I marry of the three.' Was there ever such a wretch! Sophy reddened with anger, and I felt *so* spiteful!

'Well then,' said Mary in a peevish accent, 'I *will* have you if I *must.*'

'I should have thought, Miss Stanhope, that when such settlements are offered as I have offered to you there can be no great violence done to the inclinations in accepting of them.'

Mary mumbled out something, which I who sat close to her could just distinguish to be 'What's the use of a great jointure if men live forever?' And then audibly, 'Remember the pinmoney; two hundred a year.'

'A hundred and seventy-five, madam.'

'Two hundred indeed, sir,' said my mother.

'And remember, I am to have a new carriage hung as high as the Duttons', and blue spotted with silver; and I shall expect a new saddle horse, a suit of fine lace, and an infinite number of the most valuable jewels. Diamonds such as never were seen[25] and pearls, rubies, emeralds and beads out of number. You must set up your phaeton which must be cream coloured with a wreath of silver flowers round it; you must buy four of the finest bays in the kingdom and you must drive me in it every day. This is not all; you must entirely new furnish your house after my taste, you must hire two more footmen to attend me, two women to wait on me, must always let me do just as I please, and make a very good husband.'

Here she stopped, I believe rather out of breath.

'This is all very reasonable, Mr Watts, for my daughter to expect.'

'And it is very reasonable, Mrs Stanhope, that your daughter should be disappointed.' He was going on but Mary interrupted him.

'You must build me an elegant greenhouse and stock it with plants. You must let me spend every winter in Bath, every spring in town, every summer in taking some tour, and every autumn at a watering place, and if we are at home the rest of the year (Sophy and I laughed) you must do nothing but give balls and masquerades. You must build a room on purpose and a theatre to act plays in. The first play we have shall be Which is the Man,[26] and I will do Lady Bell Bloomer.'

'And pray, Miss Stanhope,' said Mr Watts, 'what am I to expect from you in return for all this?'

'Expect? Why you may expect to have me pleased.'

'It would be odd if I did not. Your expectations, madam, are too high for me, and I must apply to Miss Sophy, who perhaps may not have raised hers so much.'

'You are mistaken, sir, in supposing so,' said Sophy, 'for though they may not be exactly in the same line, yet my expectations are to the full as high as my sister's; for I expect my husband to be good-tempered and cheerful; to consult my happiness in all his actions; and to love me with constancy and sincerity.'

Mr Watts stared. 'These are very odd ideas, truly, young lady. You had better discard them before you marry, or you will be obliged to do it afterwards.'

My mother in the meantime was lecturing Mary, who was sensible that she had gone too far, and when Mr Watts was just turning towards me in order, I believe, to address me, she spoke to him in a voice half humble, half sulky.

'You are mistaken, Mr Watts, if you think I was in earnest when I said I expected so much. However I must have a new chaise.'

'Yes, sir, you must allow that Mary has a right to expect that.'

'Mrs Stanhope, I *mean* and have always meant to have a new one on my marriage. But it shall be the colour of my present one.'

'I think, Mr Watts, you should pay my girl the compliment of consulting her taste on such matters.'

Mr Watts would not agree to this, and for some time insisted upon its being a chocolate colour, while Mary was as eager for having it blue with silver spots. At length, however, Sophy proposed that to please Mr Watts it should be dark brown and to please Mary it should be hung rather high and have a silver border. This was at length agreed to, though reluctantly on both sides, as each had intended to carry their point entire. We then proceeded to other matters, and it was settled that they should be married as soon as the writings could be completed. Mary was very eager for a special licence and Mr Watts talked of banns. A common licence was at last agreed on. Mary is to have all the family jewels, which are very inconsiderable, I believe, and Mr Watts promised to buy her a saddle horse; but in return she is not to expect to go to town or any other public place for these three years. She is to have neither greenhouse, theatre or phaeton; to be contented with one maid without an additional footman.

It engrossed the whole evening to settle these affairs; Mr Watts supped with us and did not go till twelve. As soon as he was gone Mary exclaimed,

'Thank heaven! he's off at last; how I do hate him!' It was in vain that Mama represented to her the impropriety she was guilty of in disliking him who was to be her husband, for she persisted in declaring her aversion to him and hoping she might never see him again. What a wedding will this be! Adieu my dear Anne. Your faithfully sincere

Georgiana Stanhope

From the same to the same

Saturday

Dear Anne,

Mary, eager to have every one know of her approaching wedding, and more particularly desirous of triumphing as she called it over the Duttons, desired us to walk with her this morning to Stoneham.

As we had nothing else to do we readily agreed, and had as pleasant a walk as we could have with Mary, whose conversation entirely consisted in abusing the man she is so soon to marry and in longing for a blue chaise spotted with silver. When we reached the Duttons' we found the two girls in the dressing room with a very handsome young man, who was of course introduced to us. He is the son of Sir Henry Brudenell of Leicestershire – [not related to the family and even but distantly connected with it. His sister is married to John Dutton's wife's brother. When you have puzzled over this account a little you will understand it.]²⁷ Mr Brudenell is the handsomest man I ever saw in my life; we are all three very much pleased with him. Mary, who from the moment of our reaching the dressing room had been swelling with the knowledge of her own importance and with the desire of making it known, could not remain long silent on the subject after we were seated, and soon addressing herself to Kitty said,

'Don't you think it will be necessary to have all the jewels new set?'

'Necessary for what?'

'For what! why for my appearance.'

'I beg your pardon, but I really do not understand you. What jewels do you speak of, and where is your appearance to be made?'

'At the next ball to be sure, after I am married.'

You may imagine their surprise. They were at first incredulous, but on our joining in the story they at last believed it. 'And who is it to' was of course the first question. Mary pretended bashfulness, and answered in confusion, her eyes cast down, 'to Mr Watts.' This also required confirmation from us, for that anyone who had the beauty and fortune (though small, yet a provision) of Mary would willingly marry Mr Watts, could by them scarcely be credited. The subject being now fairly introduced, and she found herself the object of every one's attention in company, she lost all her confusion and became perfectly unreserved and communicative.

'I wonder you should never have heard of it before, for in general things of this nature are very well known in the neighbourhood.'

'I assure you,' said Jemima, 'I never had the least suspicion of such an affair. Has it been in agitation long?'

'Oh! yes, ever since Wednesday.'

They all smiled, particularly Mr Brudenell.

'You must know Mr Watts is very much in love with me, so that it is quite a match of affection on his side.'

'Not on his only, I suppose,' said Kitty.

'Oh! when there is so much love on one side there is no occasion for it on the other. However I do not much dislike him, though he is very plain to be sure.'

Mr Brudenell stared, the Miss Duttons laughed, and Sophy and I were heartily ashamed of our sister. She went on.

'We are to have a new postchaise and very likely may set up our phaeton.'

This we knew to be false but the poor girl was pleased at the idea of persuading the company that such a thing was to be and I would not deprive her of so harmless an enjoyment. She continued.

'Mr Watts is to present me with the family jewels, which I fancy are very considerable.' I could not help whispering Sophy, 'I fancy not.' 'These jewels are what I suppose must be new set before they can be worn. I shall not wear them till the first ball I go to after my marriage. If Mrs Dutton should not go to it, I hope you will let me chaperone you; I shall certainly take Sophy and Georgiana.'

'You are very good,' said Kitty, 'and since you are inclined to undertake the care of young ladies, I should advise you to prevail on Mrs Edgecumbe to let you chaperone her six daughters which, with your two sisters and ourselves, will make your entrée very respectable.'

Kitty made us all smile except Mary who did not understand her meaning and coolly said that she should not like to chaperone so many. Sophy and I now endeavoured to change the conversation but succeeded only for a few minutes, for Mary took care to bring back their attention to her and her approaching wedding. I was sorry for my sister's sake to see that Mr Brudenell seemed to take pleasure in listening to her account of it, and even encouraged her by his questions and remarks, for it was evident that his only aim was to laugh at her. I am afraid he found her very ridiculous. He kept his countenance extremely well, yet it was easy to see that it was with difficulty he kept it. At length, however, he seemed fatigued and disgusted with her ridiculous conversation, as he turned from her to us, and spoke but little to her for about half an hour before we left Stoneham. As soon as we were out of the house we all joined in praising the person and manners of Mr Brudenell.

We found Mr Watts at home.

'So, Miss Stanhope,' said he, 'you see I am come a-courting in a true lover-like manner.'

'Well, you need not have *told* me that. I knew why you came very well.'

Sophy and I then left the room, imagining of course that we must be in the way, if a scene of courtship were to begin. We were surprised at being followed almost immediately by Mary.

'And is your courting so soon over?' said Sophy.

'Courting!' replied Mary, 'we have been quarrelling. Watts is such a fool! I hope I shall never see him again.'

'I am afraid you will,' said I, 'as he dines here today. But what has been your dispute?'

'Why only because I told him that I had seen a man much handsomer than he was this morning, he flew into a great passion and called me a vixen, so I only stayed to tell him I thought him a blackguard and came away.'

'Short and sweet,' said Sophy, 'but pray, Mary, how will this be made up?'

'He ought to ask my pardon; but if he did, I would not forgive him.'

'His submission then would not be very useful.'

When we were dressed we returned to the parlour where Mama and Mr Watts were in close conversation. It seems that he had been complaining to her of her daughter's behaviour, and she had persuaded him to think no more of it. He therefore met Mary with all his accustomed civility, and except one touch at the phaeton and another at the greenhouse, the evening went off with great harmony and cordiality. Watts is going to town to hasten the preparations for the wedding.

I am your affectionate friend,

G.S.

[*A Fragment*

written to inculcate the practice of virtue

We all know that many are unfortunate in their progress through the world, but we do not know all that are so. To seek them out, to study their wants, and to leave them supplied is the duty, and ought to be the business, of man. But few have time, fewer still have inclination, and no one has either the one or the other for such employments. Who, amidst those that perspire away their evenings in crowded assemblies, can have leisure to bestow a thought on such as sweat under the fatigue of their daily labour?][28]

To Miss Austen, the following Ode to Pity is dedicated, from a thorough knowledge of her pitiful nature, by her obedient humble servant,

the Author.

Ode to Pity

I

Ever musing I delight to tread
  The paths of honour and the myrtle grove
Whilst the pale moon her beams doth shed
  On disappointed love;
While Philomel on airy hawthorn bush
  Sings sweet and melancholy, and the thrush
Converses with the dove.

2

Gently brawling down the turnpike road,
  Sweetly noisy falls the silent stream –
The moon emerges from behind a cloud
  And darts upon the myrtle grove her beam.
Ah! then what lovely scenes appear,
  The hut, the cot, the grot, and chapel queer,

And eke the abbey too, a mouldering heap,
   Conceal'd by aged pines her head doth rear
And quite invisible doth take a peep.

                      June 3rd, 1793

Volume the Second

*

To Madame La Comtesse De Feuillide this
novel is inscribed by her obliged humble
servant, the Author.

Love and Friendship[1]

a novel in a series of letters.
'Deceived in Friendship and Betrayed in Love'

LETTER THE FIRST

From Isabel to Laura

How often, in answer to my repeated entreaties that you would
give my daughter a regular detail of the misfortunes and adventures
of your life,[2] have you said 'No, my friend, never will I comply
with your request till I may be no longer in danger of again
experiencing such dreadful ones.' Surely that time is now at hand.
You are this day fifty-five. If a woman may ever be said to be in
safety from the determined perseverance of disagreeable lovers and
the cruel persecutions of obstinate fathers, surely it must be at
such a time of life.

Isabel

LETTER 2ND

Laura to Isabel

Although I cannot agree with you in supposing that I shall never again be exposed to misfortunes as unmerited as those I have already experienced, yet to avoid the imputation of obstinacy or ill-nature I will gratify the curiosity of your daughter; and may the fortitude with which I have suffered the many afflictions of my past life prove to her a useful lesson for the support of those which may befall her in her own.

Laura

LETTER 3RD

Laura to Marianne

As the daughter of my most intimate friend I think you entitled to that knowledge of my unhappy story, which your mother has so often solicited me to give you.

My father was a native of Ireland and an inhabitant of Wales; my mother was the natural daughter of a Scotch peer by an Italian opera-girl – I was born in Spain and received my education at a convent in France.

When I had reached my eighteenth year I was recalled by my parents to my paternal roof in Wales. Our mansion was situated in one of the most romantic parts of the Vale of Usk. Though my charms are now considerably softened and somewhat impaired by the misfortunes I have undergone, I was once beautiful. But lovely as I was, the graces of my person were the least of my perfections. Of every accomplishment accustomary to my sex, I was mistress. When in the convent, my progress had always exceeded my instructions, my acquirements had been wonderful for my age, and I had shortly surpassed my masters.

In my mind, every virtue that could adorn it was centered; it was the rendezvous of every good quality and of every noble sentiment.

A sensibility too tremblingly alive to every affliction of my friends, my acquaintance, and particularly to every affliction of my own, was my only fault, if a fault it could be called. Alas! how altered now! Though indeed my own misfortunes do not make less impression on me than they ever did, yet now I never feel for those of an other. My accomplishments too, begin to fade – I can neither sing so well nor dance so gracefully as I once did – and I have entirely forgot the Minuet Dela Cour.

Adieu,

Laura

LETTER 4TH

Laura to Marianne

Our neighbourhood was small, for it consisted only of your mother. She may probably have already told you that, being left by her parents in indigent circumstances, she had retired into Wales on economical motives. There it was our friendship first commenced. Isabel was then one and twenty. Though pleasing both in her person and manners, between ourselves she never possessed the hundredth part of my beauty or accomplishments. Isabel had seen the world. She had passed two years at one of the first boarding schools in London, had spent a fortnight in Bath, and had supped one night in Southampton.

'Beware, my Laura,' she would often say, 'beware of the insipid vanities and idle dissipations of the Metropolis of England; beware of the unmeaning luxuries of Bath and of the stinking fish of Southampton.'

'Alas!' exclaimed I, 'how am I to avoid those evils I shall never be exposed to? What probability is there of my ever tasting the dissipations of London, the luxuries of Bath, or the stinking fish of Southampton? I, who am doomed to waste my days of youth and beauty in an humble cottage in the Vale of Usk.'

Ah! little did I then think I was ordained so soon to quit that humble cottage for the deceitful pleasures of the world.

Adieu,

Laura

LETTER 5TH

Laura to Marianne

One evening in December, as my father, my mother, and myself
were arranged in social converse round our fireside, we were on a
sudden greatly astonished by hearing a violent knocking on the
outward door of our rustic cot.

My father started – 'What noise is that?' said he. 'It sounds like
a loud rapping at the door,' replied my mother. 'It does indeed,'
cried I. 'I am of your opinion,' said my father, 'it certainly does
appear to proceed from some uncommon violence exerted against
our unoffending door.' 'Yes,' exclaimed I, 'I cannot help thinking
it must be somebody who knocks for admittance.'

'That is another point,' replied he. 'We must not pretend to
determine on what motive the person may knock – though that
someone *does* rap at the door, I am partly convinced.'[3]

Here, a second tremendous rap interrupted my father in his
speech and somewhat alarmed my mother and me.

'Had we not better go and see who it is?' said she. 'The servants
are out.' 'I think we had,' replied I. 'Certainly,' added my father,
'by all means.' 'Shall we go now?' said my mother. 'The sooner the
better,' answered he. 'Oh! let no time be lost,' cried I.

A third more violent rap than ever again assaulted our ears. 'I am
certain there is somebody knocking at the door,' said my mother. 'I
think there must,' replied my father. 'I fancy the servants are
returned,' said I; 'I think I hear Mary going to the door.' 'I'm glad of
it,' cried my father, 'for I long to know who it is.'

I was right in my conjecture; for Mary instantly entering the
room, informed us that a young gentleman and his servant were at
the door, who had lost their way, were very cold, and begged leave
to warm themselves by our fire.

'Won't you admit them?' said I. 'You have no objection, my
dear?' said my father. 'None in the world,' replied my mother.

Mary, without waiting for any further commands, immediately
left the room and quickly returned, introducing the most beauteous
and amiable youth I had ever beheld. The servant she kept to
herself.

My natural sensibility had already been greatly affected by the sufferings of the unfortunate stranger, and no sooner did I first behold him, than I felt that on him the happiness or misery of my future life must depend.

Adieu,
Laura

LETTER 6TH

Laura to Marianne

The noble youth informed us that his name was Lindsay – for particular reasons however I shall conceal it under that of Talbot. He told us that he was the son of an English baronet, that his mother had been many years no more and that he had a sister of the middle size. 'My father,' he continued, 'is a mean and mercenary wretch – it is only to such particular friends as this dear party that I would thus betray his failings. Your virtues, my amiable Polydore (addressing himself to my father), yours, dear Claudia, and yours, my charming Laura, call on me to repose in you my confidence.' We bowed. 'My father, seduced by the false glare of fortune and the deluding pomp of title, insisted on my giving my hand to Lady Dorothea. "No, never!" exclaimed I. "Lady Dorothea is lovely and engaging; I prefer no woman to her; but know, sir, that I scorn to marry her in compliance with your wishes. No! never shall it be said that I obliged my father." '

We all admired the noble manliness of his reply. He continued.

'Sir Edward was surprised; he had perhaps little expected to meet with so spirited an opposition to his will. "Where, Edward, in the name of wonder," said he, "did you pick up this unmeaning gibberish? You have been studying novels, I suspect." I scorned to answer: it would have been beneath my dignity. I mounted my horse, and followed by my faithful William set forwards for my aunt's.

'My father's house is situated in Bedfordshire, my aunt's in Middlesex, and though I flatter myself with being a tolerable proficient in geography, I know not how it happened,[4] but I found myself entering this beautiful vale which I find is in South Wales, when I had expected to have reached my aunt's.

'After having wandered some time on the banks of the Usk without knowing which way to go, I began to lament my cruel destiny in the bitterest and most pathetic manner. It was now perfectly dark, not a single star was there to direct my steps, and I know not what might have befallen me had I not at length discerned, through the solemn gloom that surrounded me, a distant light, which, as I approached it, I discovered to be the cheerful blaze of your fire. Impelled by the combination of misfortunes under which I laboured, namely fear, cold, and hunger, I hesitated not to ask admittance, which at length I have gained; and now, my adorable Laura,' continued he, taking my hand, 'when may I hope to receive that reward of all the painful sufferings I have undergone during the course of my attachment to you, to which I have ever aspired? Oh! when will you reward me with yourself?'

'This instant, dear and amiable Edward,' replied I. We were immediately united by my father, who, though he had never taken orders, had been bred to the church.

Adieu,
Laura

LETTER 7TH

Laura to Marianne

We remained but a few days after our marriage in the Vale of Usk. After taking an affecting farewell of my father, my mother, and my Isabel, I accompanied Edward to his aunt's in Middlesex. Philippa received us both with every expression of affectionate love. My arrival was indeed a most agreable surprise to her as she had not only been totally ignorant of my marriage with her nephew, but had never even had the slightest idea of there being such a person in the world.

Augusta, the sister of Edward, was on a visit to her when we arrived. I found her exactly what her brother had described her to be – of the middle size. She received me with equal surprise, though not with equal cordiality, as Philippa. There was a disagreable coldness and forbidding reserve in her reception of me which was equally distressing and unexpected: none of that interesting sensibility or amiable sympathy in her manners and address to me which should have distinguished our introduction to each other. Her language was neither warm, nor affectionate, her expressions of regard were neither animated nor cordial; her arms were not opened to receive me to her heart, though my own were extended to press her to mine.

A short conversation between Augusta and her brother, which I accidentally overheard, increased my dislike to her, and convinced me that her heart was no more formed for the soft ties of love than for the endearing intercourse of friendship.

'But do you think that my father will ever be reconciled to this imprudent connection?' said Augusta.

'Augusta,' replied the noble youth, 'I thought you had a better opinion of me than to imagine I would so abjectly degrade myself as to consider my father's concurrence in any of my affairs either of consequence or concern to me. Tell me, Augusta, tell me with sincerity; did you ever know me consult his inclinations or follow his advice in the least trifling particular since the age of fifteen?'

'Edward,' replied she, 'you are surely too diffident in your own praise. Since you were fifteen only! – My dear brother, since you were five years old, I entirely acquit you of ever having willingly contributed to the satisfaction of your father. But still I am not without apprehensions of your being shortly obliged to degrade yourself in your own eyes by seeking a support for your wife in the generosity of Sir Edward.'

'Never, never, Augusta, will I so demean myself,' said Edward. 'Support! what support will Laura want which she can receive from him?'

'Only those very insignificant ones of victuals and drink,' answered she.

'Victuals and drink!' replied my husband in a most nobly contemptuous manner, 'and dost thou then imagine that there is no other support for an exalted mind such as is my Laura's than the mean and indelicate employment of eating and drinking?'

'None that I know of so efficacious,' returned Augusta.

'And did you then never feel the pleasing pangs of love, Augusta?' replied my Edward. 'Does it appear impossible to your vile and corrupted palate to exist on love? Can you not conceive the luxury of living in every distress that poverty can inflict, with the object of your tenderest affection?'

'You are too ridiculous,' said Augusta, 'to argue with; perhaps, however, you may in time be convinced that . . .'

Here I was prevented from hearing the remainder of her speech by the appearance of a very handsome young woman, who was ushered into the room at the door of which I had been listening. On hearing her announced by the name of Lady Dorothea, I instantly quitted my post and followed her into the parlour, for I well remembered that she was the lady proposed as a wife for my Edward by the cruel and unrelenting baronet.

Although Lady Dorothea's visit was nominally to Philippa and Augusta, yet I have some reason to imagine that (acquainted with the marriage and arrival of Edward) to see me was a principal motive to it.

I soon perceived that, though lovely and elegant in her person, and though easy and polite in her address, she was of that inferior order of beings with regard to delicate feelings, tender sentiments, and refined sensibility, of which Augusta was one.

She stayed but half an hour, and neither in the course of her visit confided to me any of her secret thoughts, nor requested me to confide in her any of mine. You will easily imagine therefore, my dear Marianne, that I could not feel any ardent affection or very sincere attachment for Lady Dorothea.

Adieu,

Laura

LETTER 8TH

Laura to Marianne, in continuation

Lady Dorothea had not left us long before another visitor, as unexpected a one as her ladyship, was announced. It was Sir Edward, who, informed by Augusta of her brother's marriage, came doubtless to reproach him for having dared to unite himself to me without his knowledge. But Edward, foreseeing his design, approached him with heroic fortitude as soon as he entered the room, and addressed him in the following manner.

'Sir Edward, I know the motive of your journey here. You come with the base design of reproaching me for having entered into an indissoluble engagement with my Laura without your consent. But sir, I glory in the act –. It is my greatest boast that I have incurred the displeasure of my father!'

So saying, he took my hand, and whilst Sir Edward, Philippa, and Augusta were doubtless reflecting with admiration on his undaunted bravery, led me from the parlour to his father's carriage, which yet remained at the door and in which we were instantly conveyed from the pursuit of Sir Edward.

The postilions had at first received orders only to take the London road; as soon as we had sufficiently reflected, however, we ordered them to drive to M—, the seat of Edward's most particular friend, which was but a few miles distant.

At M—, we arrived in a few hours; and on sending in our names, were immediately admitted to Sophia, the wife of Edward's friend. After having been deprived during the course of three weeks of a real friend (for such I term your mother), imagine my transports at beholding one most truly worthy of the name. Sophia was rather above the middle size; most elegantly formed. A soft languor spread over her lovely features, but increased their beauty. It was the characteristic of her mind: she was all sensibility and feeling. We flew into each other's arms, and after having exchanged vows of mutual friendship for the rest of our lives, instantly unfolded to each other the most inward secrets of our hearts –. We were interrupted in this delightful employment by the entrance of Augustus (Edward's friend), who was just returned from a solitary ramble.

Never did I see such an affecting scene as was the meeting of Edward and Augustus.

'My life! My soul!' exclaimed the former. 'My adorable angel!' replied the latter, as they flew into each other's arms. It was too pathetic for the feelings of Sophia and myself. We fainted alternately on a sofa.[5]

Adieu,
Laura

LETTER THE 9TH

From the Same to the Same

Towards the close of the day we received the following letter from Philippa.[6]

'Sir Edward is greatly incensed by your abrupt departure; he has taken back Augusta with him to Bedfordshire. Much as I wish to enjoy again your charming society, I cannot determine to snatch you from that of such dear and deserving friends. When your visit to them is terminated, I trust you will return to the arms of your Philippa.'

We returned a suitable answer to this affectionate note, and after thanking her for her kind invitation, assured her that we would certainly avail ourselves of it whenever we might have no other place to go to. Though certainly nothing could to any reasonable being have appeared more satisfactory than so grateful a reply to her invitation, yet I know not how it was, but she was certainly capricious enough to be displeased with our behaviour, and in a few weeks after, either to revenge our conduct, or relieve her own solitude, married a young and illiterate fortune hunter. This imprudent step (though we were sensible that it would probably deprive us of that fortune which Philippa had ever taught us to expect) could not on our own accounts excite from our exalted minds a single sigh; yet fearful lest it might prove a source of endless misery to the deluded bride, our trembling sensibility was greatly affected when we were first informed of the event. The affectionate entreaties of Augustus and Sophia, that we would for ever consider their house as our home, easily prevailed on us to determine never more to leave them.

In the society of my Edward and this amiable pair I passed the happiest moments of my life: our time was most delightfully spent in mutual protestations of friendship, and in vows of unalterable love, in which we were secure from being interrupted by intruding and disagreeable visitors, as Augusta and Sophia had, on their first entrance in the neighbourhood, taken due care to inform the surrounding families that, as their happiness centered wholly in themselves, they wished for no other society. But alas! my dear Marianne, such happiness as I then enjoyed was too perfect to be lasting. A most severe and unexpected blow at once destroyed every sensation of pleasure. Convinced as you must be, from what I have already told you concerning Augustus and Sophia, that there never were a happier couple, I need not, I imagine, inform you that their union had been contrary to the inclinations of their cruel and mercenary parents, who had vainly endeavoured with obstinate perseverance to force them into a marriage with those whom they had ever abhorred; but with an heroic fortitude worthy to be related and admired, they had both constantly refused to submit to such despotic power.

After having so nobly disentangled themselves from the shackles of parental authority by a clandestine marriage, they were determined never to forfeit the good opinion they had gained in the world in so doing by accepting any proposals of reconciliation that might be offered them by their fathers. To this farther trial of their noble independence, however, they never were exposed.

They had been married but a few months when our visit to them commenced, during which time they had been amply supported by a considerable sum of money which Augustus had gracefully purloined from his unworthy father's escritoire a few days before his union with Sophia.

By our arrival their expenses were considerably increased, though their means for supplying them were then nearly exhausted. But they, exalted creatures! scorned to reflect a moment on their pecuniary distresses and would have blushed at the idea of paying their debts. – Alas! what was their reward for such disinterested behaviour! The beautiful Augustus was arrested and we were all undone. Such perfidious treachery in the merciless perpetrators of the deed will shock your gentle nature, dearest Marianne, as much as it then affected the delicate sensibility of Edward, Sophia, your Laura, and of Augustus himself. To complete such unparalleled barbarity we were informed that an execution in the house would shortly take place. Ah! what could we do but what we did! We sighed and fainted on the sofa.

Adieu,

Laura

LETTER IOTH

Laura, in continuation

When we were somewhat recovered from the overpowering effusions of our grief, Edward desired that we would consider what
was the most prudent step to be taken in our unhappy situation,
while he repaired to his imprisoned friend to lament over his
misfortunes. We promised that we would, and he set forwards on
his journey to town. During his absence we faithfully complied
with his desire, and after the most mature deliberation, at length
agreed that the best thing we could do was to leave the house, of
which we every moment expected the officers of justice to take
possession. We waited, therefore, with the greatest impatience, for
the return of Edward, in order to impart to him the result of our
deliberations –. But no Edward appeared –. In vain did we count
the tedious moments of his absence – in vain did we weep – in vain
even did we sigh – no Edward returned –. This was too cruel, too
unexpected a blow to our gentle sensibility –. We could not support
it – we could only faint –. At length, collecting all the resolution I
was mistress of, I arose, and after packing up some necessary
apparel for Sophia and myself, I dragged her to a carriage I had
ordered and instantly we set out for London. As the habitation of
Augustus was within twelve miles of town, it was not long ere we
arrived there, and no sooner had we entered Holbourn, than letting
down one of the front glasses, I enquired of every decent-looking
person that we passed 'If they had seen my Edward?'

But as we drove too rapidly to allow them to answer my repeated
enquiries, I gained little, or indeed, no information concerning
him. 'Where am I to drive?' said the postilion. 'To Newgate, gentle
youth,' replied I, 'to see Augustus.' 'Oh! no, no,' exclaimed
Sophia, 'I cannot go to Newgate; I shall not be able to support the
sight of my Augustus in so cruel a confinement – my feelings are
sufficiently shocked by the *recital* of his distress, but to behold it
will overpower my sensibility.' As I perfectly agreed with her in
the justice of her sentiments, the postilion was instantly directed
to return into the country.

You may perhaps have been somewhat surprised, my dearest

Marianne, that in the distress I then endured, destitute of any support, and unprovided with any habitation, I should never once have remembered my father and mother or my paternal cottage in the Vale of Usk. To account for this seeming forgetfulness I must inform you of a trifling circumstance concerning them which I have as yet never mentioned –. The death of my parents, a few weeks after my departure, is the circumstance I allude to. By their decease I became the lawful inheritress of their house and fortune. But alas! the house had never been their own and their fortune had only been an annuity on their own lives. Such is the depravity of the world! To your mother I should have returned with pleasure, should have been happy to have introduced to her my charming Sophia, and should with cheerfulness have passed the remainder of my life in their dear society in the Vale of Usk, had not one obstacle to the execution of so agreable a scheme intervened: which was the marriage and removal of your mother to a distant part of Ireland.

Adieu,
Laura

LETTER 11TH

Laura, in continuation

'I have a relation in Scotland,' said Sophia to me as we left London, 'who I am certain would not hesitate in receiving me.' 'Shall I order the boy to drive there?' said I – but instantly recollecting myself, exclaimed, 'Alas, I fear it will be too long a journey for the horses.' Unwilling, however, to act only from my own inadequate knowledge of the strength and abilities of horses, I consulted the postilion, who was entirely of my opinion concerning the affair. We therefore determined to change horses at the next town and to travel post the remainder of the journey.

When we arrived at the last inn we were to stop at, which was but a few miles from the house of Sophia's relation, unwilling to intrude our society on him unexpected and unthought of, we wrote a very elegant and well-penned note to him containing an account of our destitute and melancholy situation, and of our intention of spending some months with him in Scotland. As soon as we had dispatched this letter, we immediately prepared to follow it in person and were stepping into the carriage for that purpose when our attention was attracted by the entrance of a coroneted coach and four into the inn yard. A gentleman considerably advanced in years descended from it. At his first appearance my sensibility was wonderfully affected and ere I had gazed at him a second time, an instinctive sympathy whispered to my heart that he was my grandfather.

Convinced that I could not be mistaken in my conjecture, I instantly sprang from the carriage I had just entered, and following the venerable stranger into the room he had been shewn to, I threw myself on my knees before him and besought him to acknowledge me as his grandchild. – He started, and after having attentively examined my features, raised me from the ground, and throwing his grandfatherly arms around my neck, exclaimed; 'Acknowledge thee! Yes, dear resemblance of my Laurina and my Laurina's daughter, sweet image of my Claudia and my Claudia's mother, I do acknowledge thee as the daughter of the one and the grand-daughter of the other.' While he was thus tenderly embracing me, Sophia, astonished at my precipitate departure, entered the room in search of me –. No sooner had she caught the eye of the venerable peer, than he exclaimed with every mark of astonishment – 'Another granddaughter! Yes, yes, I see you are the daughter of my Laurina's eldest girl; your resemblance to the beauteous Matilda sufficiently proclaims it.' 'Oh!' replied Sophia, 'when I first beheld you the instinct of nature whispered me that we were in some degrees related –. But whether grandfathers, or grand-mothers, I could not pretend to determine.' He folded her in his arms, and whilst they were tenderly embracing, the door of the apartment opened and a most beautiful young man appeared. On perceiving him, Lord St Clair started, and retreating back a few paces with uplifted hands, said, 'Another grandchild! What an unexpected happiness is this! To discover in the space of three minutes as many of my descendants! This, I am certain is Philander, the son of my Laurina's third girl, the amiable Bertha; there wants now but the presence of Gustavus to complete the union of my Laurina's grandchildren.'

'And here he is,' said a graceful youth, who that instant entered the room, 'here is the Gustavus you desire to see. I am the son of Agatha, your Laurina's fourth and youngest daughter.' 'I see you are indeed,' replied Lord St Clair. 'But tell me,' continued he, looking fearfully towards the door, 'tell me, have I any other grandchildren in the house?' 'None, my lord.' 'Then I will provide for you all without further delay –. Here are four banknotes of 50£ each – take them and remember I have done the duty of a grandfather –.' He instantly left the room, and immediately afterwards the house.

Adieu,

Laura

LETTER THE 12TH

Laura, in continuation

You may imagine how greatly we were suprised by the sudden departure of Lord St Clair. 'Ignoble grandsire!' exclaimed Sophia. 'Unworthy grandfather!' said I, and instantly fainted in each other's arms. How long we remained in this situation I know not; but when we recovered we found ourselves alone, without either Gustavus, Philander, or the banknotes. As we were deploring our unhappy fate, the door of the apartment opened and 'Macdonald' was announced. He was Sophia's cousin. The haste with which he came to our relief so soon after the receipt of our note spoke so greatly in his favour, that I hesitated not to pronounce him, at first sight, a tender and sympathetic friend. Alas! he little deserved the name – for though he told us that he was much concerned at our misfortunes, yet by his own account it appeared that the perusal of them had neither drawn from him a single sigh, nor induced him to bestow one curse on our vindictive stars.

He told Sophia that his daughter depended on her returning with him to Macdonald Hall, and that as his cousin's friend he should be happy to see me there also. To Macdonald Hall, therefore, we went, and were received with great kindness by Janetta, the daughter of Macdonald and the mistress of the mansion. Janetta was then only fifteen, naturally well-disposed; endowed with a susceptible heart and a sympathetic disposition, she might, had these amiable qualities been properly encouraged, have been an ornament to human nature. But unfortunately her father possessed not a soul sufficiently exalted to admire so promising a disposition, and had endeavoured by every means in his power to prevent its increasing with her years. He had actually so far extinguished the natural noble sensibility of her heart, as to prevail on her to accept an offer from a young man of his recommendation. They were to be married in a few months, and Graham was in the house when we arrived. *We* soon saw through his character.

He was just such a man as one might have expected to be the choice of Macdonald. They said he was sensible, well-informed, and agreable; we did not pretend to judge of such trifles;[7] but as we were convinced he had no soul, that he had never read the Sorrows of Werter, and that his hair bore not the slightest resemblance to auburn, we were certain that Janetta could feel no affection for him, or at least that she ought to feel none. The very circumstance of his being her father's choice, too, was so much in his disfavour, that had he been deserving her in every other respect, yet *that* of itself ought to have been a sufficient reason in the eyes of Janetta for rejecting him. These considerations we were determined to represent to her in their proper light, and doubted not of meeting with the desired success from one naturally so well-disposed, whose errors in the affair had only arisen from a want of proper confidence in her own opinion, and a suitable contempt of her father's. We found her indeed all that our warmest wishes could have hoped for; we had no difficulty to convince her that it was impossible she could love Graham, or that it was her duty to disobey her father; the only thing at which she rather seemed to hesitate was our assertion that she must be attached to some other person. For some time, she persevered in declaring that she knew no other young man for whom she had the smallest affection; but upon explaining the impossibility of such a thing, she said that she believed she *did like* Captain M'Kenzie better than any one she knew besides. This confession satisfied us, and after having enumerated the good qualities of M'Kenzie and assured her that she was violently in love with him, we desired to know whether he had ever in any wise declared his affection to her.

'So far from having ever declared it, I have no reason to imagine that he has ever felt any for me,' said Janetta. 'That he certainly adores you,' replied Sophia, 'there can be no doubt –. The attachment must be reciprocal –. Did he never gaze on you with admiration – tenderly press your hand – drop an involuntary tear – and leave the room abruptly?' 'Never,' replied she, 'that I remember – he has always left the room, indeed, when his visit has been ended, but has never gone away particularly abruptly, or without making a bow.' 'Indeed, my love,' said I, 'you must be mistaken –: for it is absolutely impossible that he should ever have left you but with confusion, despair, and precipitation –. Consider but for a moment, Janetta, and you must be convinced how absurd it is to suppose that he could ever make a bow, or behave like any other person.' Having settled this point to our satisfaction, the next we took into consideration was to determine in what manner we should inform M'Kenzie of the favourable opinion Janetta entertained of him –. We at length agreed to acquaint him with it by an anonymous letter, which Sophia drew up in the following manner.

'Oh! happy lover of the beautiful Janetta; oh! enviable possessor of her heart whose hand is destined to another; why do you thus delay a confession of your attachment to the amiable object of it? Oh! consider that a few weeks will at once put an end to every flattering hope that you may now entertain, by uniting the unfortunate victim of her father's cruelty to the execrable and detested Graham.

'Alas! why do you thus so cruelly connive at the projected misery of her and of yourself by delaying to communicate that scheme which had doubtless long possessed your imagination? A secret union will at once secure the felicity of both.'

The amiable M'Kenzie, whose modesty, as he afterwards assured us, had been the only reason of his having so long concealed the violence of his affection for Janetta, on receiving this billet, flew on the wings of love to Macdonald Hall; and so powerfully pleaded his attachment to her who inspired it, that after a few more private interviews, Sophia and I experienced the satisfaction of seeing them depart for Gretna Green, which they chose for the celebration of their nuptials, in preference to any other place, although it was at a considerable distance from Macdonald Hall.[8]

Adieu,

Laura

LETTER THE 13TH

Laura, in continuation

They had been gone nearly a couple of hours, before either Macdonald or Graham had entertained any suspicion of the affair –. And they might not even then have suspected it, but for the following little accident. Sophia, happening one day to open a private drawer in Macdonald's library with one of her own keys, discovered that it was the place where he kept his papers of consequence, and amongst them some banknotes of considerable amount. This discovery she imparted to me; and having agreed together that it would be a proper treatment of so vile a wretch as Macdonald to deprive him of money, perhaps dishonestly gained, it was determined that the next time we should either of us happen to go that way, we would take one or more of the banknotes from the drawer. This well-meant plan we had often successfully put in execution; but alas! on the very day of Janetta's escape, as Sophia was majestically removing the fifth banknote from the drawer to her own purse, she was suddenly most impertinently interrupted in her employment by the entrance of Macdonald himself, in a most abrupt and precipitate manner. Sophia (who, though naturally all winning sweetness, could, when occasions demanded it, call forth the dignity of her sex) instantly put on a most forbidding look, and darting an angry frown on the undaunted culprit, demanded in a haughty tone of voice, 'Wherefore her retirement was thus insolently broken in on?' The unblushing Macdonald, without even endeavouring to exculpate himself from the crime he was charged with, meanly endeavoured to reproach Sophia with ignobly defrauding him of his money. The dignity of Sophia was wounded; 'Wretch!' exclaimed she, hastily replacing the banknote in the drawer, 'how darest thou to accuse me of an act of which the bare idea makes me blush?' The base wretch was still unconvinced, and continued to upbraid the justly-offended Sophia in such opprobrious language, that at length he so greatly provoked the gentle sweetness of her nature as to induce her to revenge herself on him by informing him of Janetta's elopement, and of the active part we had both taken in the affair. At this period of their quarrel I entered the library, and was, as you may imagine, equally offended as Sophia at the ill-grounded accusations of the malevolent and contemptible Macdonald. 'Base miscreant,' cried I, 'how can'st thou thus undauntedly endeavour to sully the spotless reputation of such bright excellence? Why do'st thou not suspect *my* innocence as soon?' 'Be satisfied, madam,' replied he, 'I *do* suspect it, and therefore must desire that you will both leave this house in less than half an hour.'

'We shall go, willingly,' answered Sophia. 'Our hearts have long detested thee, and nothing but our friendship for thy daughter could have induced us to remain so long beneath thy roof.'

'Your friendship for my daughter has indeed been most power-fully exerted by throwing her into the arms of an unprincipled fortune hunter,' replied he.

'Yes,' exclaimed I, 'amidst every misfortune, it will afford us some consolation to reflect that by this one act of friendship to Janetta, we have amply discharged every obligation that we have received from her father.'

'It must indeed be a most grateful reflection to your exalted minds,' said he.

As soon as we had picked up our wardrobe and valuables, we left Macdonald Hall, and after having walked about a mile and a half, we sat down by the side of a clear, limpid stream to refresh our exhausted limbs. The place was suited to meditation.

A grove of full-grown elms sheltered us from the east. A bed of full-grown nettles from the west. Before us ran the murmuring brook and behind us ran the turnpike road. We were in a mood for contemplation and in a disposition to enjoy so beautiful a spot. A mutual silence, which had for some time reigned between us, was at length broke by my exclaiming, 'What a lovely scene! Alas, why are not Edward and Augustus here to enjoy its beauties with us?'

'Ah! my beloved Laura,' cried Sophia, 'for pity's sake forbear recalling to my remembrance the unhappy situation of my imprisoned husband. Alas, what would I not give to learn the fate of my Augustus! To know if he is still in Newgate, or if he is yet hung. But never shall I be able so far to conquer my tender sensibility as to enquire after him. Oh! do not, I beseech you, ever let me again hear you repeat his beloved name –. It affects me too deeply –. I cannot bear to hear him mentioned; it wounds my feelings.'

'Excuse me, my Sophia, for having thus unwillingly offended you –' replied I, and then changing the conversation, desired her to admire the noble grandeur of the elms which sheltered us from the eastern zephyr. 'Alas! my Laura,' returned she, 'avoid so melancholy a subject, I entreat you. Do not again wound my sensibility by observations on those elms. They remind me of Augustus –. He was like them, tall, majestic – he possessed that noble grandeur which you admire in them.'[9]

I was silent, fearful lest I might any more unwillingly distress her by fixing on any other subject of conversation which might again remind her of Augustus.

'Why do you not speak, my Laura?' said she after a short pause. 'I cannot support this silence – you must not leave me to my own reflections; they ever recur to Augustus.'

'What a beautiful sky!' said I. 'How charmingly is the azure varied by those delicate streaks of white!'

'Oh! my Laura,' replied she, hastily withdrawing her eyes from a momentary glance at the sky. 'Do not thus distress me by calling my attention to an object which so cruelly reminds me of my Augustus' blue satin waistcoat striped with white! In pity to your unhappy friend avoid a subject so distressing.' What could I do? The feelings of Sophia were at that time so exquisite, and the tenderness she felt for Augustus so poignant, that I had not the power to start any other topic, justly fearing that it might in some unforeseen manner again awaken all her sensibility by directing her thoughts to her husband –. Yet to be silent would be cruel; she had entreated me to talk.

From this dilemma I was most fortunately relieved by an accident truly à propos; it was the lucky overturning of a gentleman's phaeton, on the road which ran murmuring behind us. It was a most fortunate accident as it diverted the attention of Sophia from the melancholy reflections which she had been before indulging. We instantly quitted our seats and ran to the rescue of those who but a few moments before had been in so elevated a situation as a fashionably high phaeton, but who were now laid low and sprawling in the dust.

'What an ample subject for reflection on the uncertain enjoyments of this world, would not that phaeton and the life of Cardinal Wolsey[10] afford a thinking mind!' said I to Sophia, as we were hastening to the field of action.

She had not time to answer me, for every thought was now engaged by the horrid spectacle before us. Two gentlemen most elegantly attired, but weltering in their blood, was what first struck our eyes – we approached – they were Edward and Augustus. Yes, dearest Marianne, they were our husbands. Sophia shrieked and fainted on the ground – I screamed and instantly ran mad –. We remained thus mutually deprived of our senses some minutes, and on regaining them were deprived of them again.

For an hour and a quarter did we continue in this unfortunate situation – Sophia fainting every moment and I running mad as often. At length a groan from the hapless Edward (who alone retained any share of life) restored us to ourselves. Had we indeed before imagined that either of them lived, we should have been more sparing of our grief – but as we had supposed when we first beheld them that they were no more, we knew that nothing could remain to be done but what we were about.

No sooner, therefore, did we hear my Edward's groan, than postponing our lamentations for the present, we hastily ran to the dear youth, and kneeling on each side of him, implored him not to die.

'Laura,' said he, fixing his now languid eyes on me. 'I fear I have been overturned.'

I was overjoyed to find him yet sensible.

'Oh! tell me, Edward,' said I, 'tell me, I beseech you, before you die, what has befallen you since that unhappy day in which Augustus was arrested and we were separated –'

'I will,' said he, and instantly fetching a deep sigh, expired.

Sophia immediately sunk again into a swoon –. *My* grief was more audible. My voice faltered, my eyes assumed a vacant stare, my face became as pale as death, and my senses were considerably impaired.

'Talk not to me of phaetons,' said I, raving in a frantic, incoherent manner. 'Give me a violin –. I'll play to him and soothe him in his melancholy hours –. Beware, ye gentle nymphs, of Cupid's thunderbolts, avoid the piercing shafts of Jupiter – look at that grove of firs – I see a leg of mutton –. They told me Edward was not dead; but they deceived me – they took him for a cucumber.'[11] Thus I continued wildly exclaiming on my Edward's death.

For two hours did I rave thus madly, and should not then have left off, as I was not in the least fatigued, had not Sophia, who was just recovered from her swoon, entreated me to consider that night was now approaching and that the damps began to fall.

'And whither shall we go,' said I, 'to shelter us from either?'

'To that white cottage,' replied she, pointing to a neat building which rose up amidst the grove of elms and which I had not before observed. I agreed and we instantly walked to it. We knocked at the door; it was opened by an old woman. On being requested to afford us a night's lodging, she informed us that her house was but small, that she had only two bedrooms, but that however we should be welcome to one of them. We were satisfied and followed the good woman into the house where we were greatly cheered by the sight of a comfortable fire –. She was a widow and had only one daughter, who was then just seventeen – one of the best of ages.[12] But alas! she was very plain and her name was Bridget . . . Nothing therefore could be expected from her – she could not be supposed to possess either exalted ideas, delicate feelings, or refined sensibilities. She was nothing more than a mere good-tempered, civil, and obliging young woman; as such we could scarcely dislike her – she was only an object of contempt.

Adieu,
Laura

LETTER THE 14TH

Laura, in continuation

Arm yourself, my amiable young friend, with all the philosophy you are mistress of; summon up all the fortitude you possess, for alas! in the perusal of the following pages your sensibility will be most severely tried. Ah! what were the misfortunes I had before experienced and which I have already related to you, to the one I am now going to inform you of. The death of my father, my mother, and my husband, though almost more than my gentle nature could support, were trifles in comparison to the misfortune I am now proceeding to relate. The morning after our arrival at the cottage, Sophia complained of a violent pain in her delicate limbs, accompanied with a disagreable headache. She attributed it to a cold caught by her continued faintings in the open air as the dew was falling the evening before. This I feared was but too probably the case; since how could it be otherwise accounted for that I should have escaped the same indisposition, but by supposing that the bodily exertions I had undergone, in my repeated fits of frenzy, had so effectually circulated and warmed my blood as to make me proof against the chilling damps of night; whereas Sophia, lying totally inactive on the ground, must have been exposed to all their severity. I was most seriously alarmed by her illness, which, trifling as it may appear to you, a certain instinctive sensibility whispered me would in the end be fatal to her.

Alas! my fears were but too fully justified; she grew gradually worse and I daily became more alarmed for her. At length she was obliged to confine herself solely to the bed allotted us by our worthy landlady.

Her disorder turned to a galloping consumption, and in a few days carried her off. Amidst all my lamentations for her (and violent you may suppose they were), I yet received some consolation in the reflection of my having paid every attention to her that could be offered in her illness. I had wept over her every day – had bathed her sweet face with my tears and had pressed her fair hands continually in mine.

'My beloved Laura,' said she to me a few hours before she died, 'take warning from my unhappy end and avoid the imprudent conduct which has occasioned it: beware of fainting-fits . . . Though at the time they may be refreshing and agreable, yet believe me they will, in the end, if too often repeated and at improper seasons, prove destructive to your constitution . . . My fate will teach you this . . . I die a martyr to my grief for the loss of Augustus . . . One fatal swoon has cost me my life . . . Beware of swoons, dear Laura . . . A frenzy fit is not one quarter so pernicious; it is an exercise to the body and if not too violent, is, I dare say, conducive to health in its consequences. Run mad as often as you choose; but do not faint.'

These were the last words she ever addressed to me. It was her dying advice to her afflicted Laura, who has ever most faithfully adhered to it.

After having attended my lamented friend to her early grave, I immediately (though late at night) left the detested village in which she died, and near which had expired my husband and Augustus. I had not walked many yards from it before I was overtaken by a stagecoach, in which I instantly took a place, determined to proceed in it to Edinburgh, where I hoped to find some kind, pitying friend who would receive and comfort me in my afflictions.

It was so dark when I entered the coach that I could not distinguish the number of my fellow-travellers; I could only perceive that they were many. Regardless, however, of any thing concerning them, I gave myself up to my own sad reflections. A general silence prevailed – a silence, which was by nothing interrupted but by the loud and repeated snores of one of the party.

'What an illiterate villain must that man be!' thought I to myself. 'What a total want of delicate refinement must he have who can thus shock our senses by such a brutal noise! He must, I am certain, be capable of every bad action! There is no crime too black for such a character!'[13] Thus reasoned I within myself, and doubtless such were the reflections of my fellow travellers.

At length, returning day enabled me to behold the unprincipled scoundrel who had so violently disturbed my feelings. It was Sir Edward, the father of my deceased husband. By his side sat Augusta, and on the same seat with me were your mother and Lady Dorothea. Imagine my surprise at finding myself thus seated amongst my old acquaintance. Great as was my astonishment, it was yet increased, when on looking out of windows, I beheld the husband of Philippa, with Philippa by his side, on the coach-box; and when on looking behind, I beheld Philander and Gustavus in the basket.[14] 'Oh! heavens,' exclaimed I, 'is it possible that I should so unexpectedly be surrounded by my nearest relations and connections?' These words roused the rest of the party, and every eye was directed to the corner in which I sat. 'Oh! my Isabel,' continued I, throwing myself across Lady Dorothea into her arms, 'receive once more to your bosom the unfortunate Laura. Alas! when we last parted in the Vale of Usk, I was happy in being united to the best of Edwards; I had then a father and a mother, and had never known misfortunes. But now, deprived of every friend but you –'

'What!' interrupted Augusta, 'is my brother dead then? Tell us, I entreat you, what is become of him?'

'Yes, cold and insensible nymph,' replied I, 'that luckless swain, your brother, is no more, and you may now glory in being the heiress of Sir Edward's fortune.'

Although I had always despised her from the day I had overheard her conversation with my Edward, yet in civility I complied with hers and Sir Edward's entreaties that I would inform them of the whole melancholy affair. They were greatly shocked – even the obdurate heart of Sir Edward and the insensible one of Augusta were touched with sorrow by the unhappy tale. At the request of your mother I related to them every other misfortune which had befallen me since we parted. Of the imprisonment of Augustus and the absence of Edward; of our arrival in Scotland; of our unexpected meeting with our grandfather and our cousins; of our visit to Macdonald Hall; of the singular service we there performed towards Janetta; of her father's ingratitude for it; of his inhuman behaviour, unaccountable suspicions, and barbarous treatment of us, in obliging us to leave the house; of our lamentations on the loss of Edward and Augustus; and finally of the melancholy death of my beloved companion.

Pity and surprise were strongly depictured in your mother's countenance during the whole of my narration, but I am sorry to say, that to the eternal reproach of her sensibility, the latter infinitely predominated. Nay, faultless as my conduct had certainly been during the whole course of my late misfortunes and adventures, she pretended to find fault with my behaviour in many of the situations in which I had been placed. As I was sensible myself that I had always behaved in a manner which reflected honour on my feelings and refinement, I paid little attention to what she said, and desired her to satisfy my curiosity by informing me how she came there, instead of wounding my spotless reputation with unjustifiable reproaches. As soon as she had complied with my wishes in this particular, and had given me an accurate detail of every thing that had befallen her since our separation (the particulars of which, if you are not already acquainted with, your mother will give you) I applied to Augusta for the same information respecting herself, Sir Edward, and Lady Dorothea.

She told me that, having a considerable taste for the beauties of nature, her curiosity to behold the delightful scenes it exhibited in that part of the world had been so much raised by Gilpin's Tour to the Highlands,[15] that she had prevailed on her father to undertake a tour of Scotland and had persuaded Lady Dorothea to accompany them; that they had arrived at Edinburgh a few days before, and from thence had made daily excursions into the country around in the stagecoach they were then in, from one of which excursions they were at that time returning. My next enquiries were concerning Philippa and her husband, the latter of whom I learned, having spent all her fortune, had recourse for subsistence to the talent in which he had always most excelled, namely, driving; and that, having sold every thing which belonged to them except their coach, had converted it into a stage, and in order to be removed from any of his former acquaintance, had driven it to Edinburgh, from whence he went to Sterling every other day; that Philippa, still retaining her affection for her ungrateful husband, had followed him to Scotland, and generally accompanied him in his little excursions to Sterling.

'It has only been to throw a little money into their pockets,' continued Augusta, 'that my father has always travelled in their coach to view the beauties of the country since our arrival in Scotland; for it would certainly have been much more agreable to us to visit the Highlands in a postchaise than merely to travel from

Edinburgh to Sterling and from Sterling to Edinburgh every other day in a crowded and uncomfortable stage.'[16] I perfectly agreed with her in her sentiments on the affair, and secretly blamed Sir Edward for thus sacrificing his daughter's pleasure for the sake of a ridiculous old woman whose folly in marrying so young a man ought to be punished. His behaviour, however, was entirely of a piece with his general character; for what could be expected from a man who possessed not the smallest atom of sensibility, who scarcely knew the meaning of sympathy, and who actually snored –.

Adieu,

Laura

LETTER THE 15TH

Laura, in continuation

When we arrived at the town where we were to breakfast, I was determined to speak with Philander and Gustavus, and to that purpose, as soon as I left the carriage, I went to the basket and tenderly enquired after their health, expressing my fears of the uneasiness of their situation. At first they seemed rather confused at my appearance, dreading no doubt that I might call them to account for the money which our grandfather had left me, and which they had unjustly deprived me of; but finding that I mentioned nothing of the matter, they desired me to step into the basket, as we might there converse with greater ease. Accordingly, I entered, and whilst the rest of the party were devouring green tea and buttered toast,[17] we feasted ourselves in a more refined and sentimental manner by a confidential conversation. I informed them of every thing which had befallen me during the course of my life, and at my request they related to me every incident of theirs.

'We are the sons, as you already know, of the two youngest daughters which Lord St Clair had by Laurina, an Italian opera girl. Our mothers could neither of them exactly ascertain who were our fathers; though it is generally believed that Philander is the son of one Philip Jones, a bricklayer, and that my father was Gregory Staves, a staymaker of Edinburgh. This is, however, of little consequence, for as our mothers were certainly never married to either of them, it reflects no dishonour on our blood, which is of a most ancient and unpolluted kind.

'Bertha (the mother of Philander) and Agatha (my own mother) always lived together. They were neither of them very rich; their united fortunes had originally amounted to nine thousand pounds, but as they had always lived upon the principal of it, when we were fifteen it was diminished to nine hundred. This nine hundred they always kept in a drawer in one of the tables which stood in our common sitting parlour, for the convenience of having it always at hand. Whether it was from this circumstance of its being easily taken, or from a wish of being independent, or from an excess of sensibility (for which we were always remarkable), I cannot now determine, but certain it is that when we had reached our fifteenth year, we took the nine hundred pounds and ran away. Having obtained this prize, we were determined to manage it with economy and not to spend it either with folly or extravagance. To this purpose we therefore divided it into nine parcels, one of which we devoted to victuals, the second to drink, the third to housekeeping, the fourth to carriages, the fifth to horses, the sixth to servants, the seventh to amusements, the eighth to clothes, and the ninth to silver buckles.

'Having thus arranged our expenses for two months (for we expected to make the nine hundred pounds last as long), we hastened to London and had the good luck to spend it in seven weeks and a day, which was six days sooner than we had intended. As soon as we had thus happily disencumbered ourselves from the weight of so much money, we began to think of returning to our mothers; but accidentally hearing that they were both starved to death, we gave over the design and determined to engage ourselves to some strolling company of players, as we had always a turn for the stage. Accordingly, we offered our services to one, and were accepted; our company was indeed rather small, as it consisted only of the manager, his wife, and ourselves, but there were fewer to pay and the only inconvenience attending it was the scarcity of plays which, for want of people to fill the characters, we could perform.[18]

'We did not mind trifles, however –. One of our most admired performances was Macbeth, in which we were truly great. The manager always played Banquo himself, his wife my Lady Macbeth. I did the Three Witches and Philander acted all the rest. To say the truth this tragedy was not only the best, but the only play we ever performed; and after having acted it all over England and Wales, we came to Scotland to exhibit it over the remainder of Great Britain. We happened to be quartered in that very town where you came and met your grandfather.

'We were in the inn yard when his carriage entered, and perceiving by the arms to whom it belonged, and knowing that Lord St Clair was our grandfather, we agreed to endeavour to get something from him by discovering the relationship. You know how well it succeeded. Having obtained the two hundred pounds, we instantly left the town, leaving our manager and his wife to act Macbeth by themselves, and took the road to Sterling, where we spent our little fortune with great éclat. We are now returning to Edinburgh to get some preferment in the acting way; and such, my dear cousin, is our history.'

I thanked the amiable youth for his entertaining narration; and after expressing my wishes for their welfare and happiness, left them in their little habitation and returned to my other friends, who impatiently expected me.

My adventures are now drawing to a close, my dearest Marianne; at least for the present.

When we arrived at Edinburgh, Sir Edward told me that as the widow of his son, he desired I would accept from his hands of four hundred a year. I graciously promised that I would, but could not help observing that the unsympathetic baronet offered it more on account of my being the widow of Edward than in being the refined and amiable Laura.

I took up my residence in a romantic village in the Highlands of Scotland, where I have ever since continued, and where I can, uninterrupted by unmeaning visits, indulge, in a melancholy solitude, my unceasing lamentations for the death of my father, my mother, my husband, and my friend.

Augusta has been, for several years, united to Graham, the man of all others most suited to her; she became acquainted with him during her stay in Scotland.

Sir Edward, in hopes of gaining an heir to his title and estate, at the same time married Lady Dorothea. His wishes have been answered.

Philander and Gustavus, after having raised their reputation by their performances in the theatrical line at Edinburgh, removed to Covent Garden, where they still exhibit under the assumed names of Lewis and Quick.

Philippa has long paid the debt of nature. Her husband, however, still continues to drive the stagecoach from Edinburgh to Sterling.

Adieu, my dearest Marianne,

Laura—

Finis

June 13th, 1790

A Collection of Letters[19]

FROM A MOTHER TO HER FRIEND

My children begin now to claim all my attention in a different manner from that in which they have been used to receive it, as they are now arrived at that age when it is necessary for them in some measure to become conversant with the world. My Augusta is seventeen and her sister scarcely a twelvemonth younger. I flatter myself that their education has been such as will not disgrace their appearance in the world; and that _they_ will not disgrace their education I have every reason to believe. Indeed they are sweet girls. Sensible yet unaffected – accomplished yet easy – lively yet gentle.

As their progress in every thing they have learnt has been always the same, I am willing to forget the difference of age, and to introduce them together into public. This very evening is fixed on as their first entrée into life, as we are to drink tea with Mrs Cope and her daughter. I am glad that we are to meet no one for my girls' sake, as it would be awkward for them to enter too wide a circle on the very first day. But we shall proceed by degrees –. Tomorrow Mr Stanly's family will drink tea with us, and perhaps the Miss Phillips will meet them. On Tuesday we shall pay morning visits; on Wednesday we are to dine at Westbrook. On Thursday we have company at home. On Friday we are to be at a private concert at Sir John Wynne's; and on Saturday we expect Miss Dawson to call in the morning, which will complete my daughters' introduction into life. How they will bear so much dissipation I cannot imagine; of their spirits I have no fear, I only dread their health.

This mighty affair is now happily over, and my girls *are out*. As the moment approached for our departure, you can have no idea how the sweet creatures trembled with fear and expectation. Before the carriage drove to the door, I called them into my dressing room, and as soon as they were seated, thus addressed them.

'My dear girls, the moment is now arrived when I am to reap the rewards of all my anxieties and labours towards you during your education. You are this evening to enter a world in which you will meet with many wonderful things. Yet let me warn you against suffering yourselves to be meanly swayed by the follies and vices of others, for believe me, my beloved children, that if you do – I shall be very sorry for it.' They both assured me that they would ever remember my advice with gratitude, and follow it with attention; that they were prepared to find a world full of things to amaze and shock them; but that they trusted their behaviour would never give me reason to repent the watchful care with which I had presided over their infancy and formed their minds.

'With such expectations and such intentions,' cried I, 'I can have nothing to fear from you – and can cheerfully conduct you to Mrs Cope's without a fear of your being seduced by her example or contaminated by her follies. Come, then, my children,' added I, 'the carriage is driving to the door, and I will not a moment delay the happiness you are so impatient to enjoy.' When we arrived at Warleigh, poor Augusta could hardly breathe, while Margaret was all life and rapture. 'The long-expected moment is now arrived,' said she, 'and we shall soon be in the world.'

In a few moments we were in Mrs Cope's parlour, where with her daughter she sat ready to receive us. I observed with delight the impression my children made on them –. They were indeed two sweet, elegant-looking girls, and though somewhat abashed from the peculiarity of their situation, yet there was an ease in their manners and address which could not fail of pleasing. Imagine, my dear madam, how delighted I must have been in beholding as I did how attentively they observed every object they saw, how disgusted with some things, how enchanted with others, how astonished at all! On the whole, however, they returned in raptures with the world, its inhabitants, and manners.

Yours ever,
A— F—

FROM A YOUNG LADY
IN DISTRESSED CIRCUMSTANCES TO HER FRIEND

A few days ago I was at a private ball given by Mr Ashburnham. As my mother never goes out, she entrusted me to the care of Lady Greville, who did me the honour of calling for me in her way[20] and of allowing me to sit forwards, which is a favour about which I am very indifferent, especially as I know it is considered as conferring a great obligation on me.

'So, Miss Maria,' said her ladyship, as she saw me advancing to the door of the carriage, 'you seem very smart tonight. My poor girls will appear quite to disadvantage by you –. I only hope your mother may not have distressed herself to set *you* off. Have you got a new gown on?'

'Yes, ma'am,' replied I, with as much indifference as I could assume.

'Aye, and a fine one too, I think,' feeling it, as by her permission I seated myself by her. 'I dare say it is all very smart – but I must own, for you know I always speak my mind, that I think it was quite a needless piece of expense. Why could not you have worn your old striped one? It is not my way to find fault with people because they are poor, for I always think that they are more to be despised and pitied than blamed for it, especially if they cannot help it. But at the same time I must say that, in my opinion, your old striped gown would have been quite fine enough for its wearer; for to tell you the truth – I always speak my mind – I am very much afraid that one half of the people in the room will not know whether you have a gown on or not –. But I suppose you intend to make your fortune tonight – well, the sooner the better; and I wish you success.'[21]

'Indeed, ma'am I have no such intention –'

'Who ever heard a young lady own that she was a fortune hunter?' Miss Greville laughed, but I am sure Ellen felt for me.

'Was your mother gone to bed before you left her?' said her ladyship.

'Dear ma'am,' said Ellen, 'it is but nine o'clock.'

'True, Ellen, but candles cost money, and Mrs Williams is too wise to be extravagant.'

'She was just sitting down to supper, ma'am.'

'And what had she got for supper?'

'I did not observe.'

'Bread and cheese, I suppose.'

'I should never wish for a better supper,' said Ellen. 'You have never any reason,' replied her mother, 'as a better is always provided for you.' Miss Greville laughed excessively, as she constantly does at her mother's wit.

Such is the humiliating situation in which I am forced to appear while riding in her ladyship's coach – I dare not be impertinent, as my mother is always admonishing me to be humble and patient if I wish to make my way in the world. She insists on my accepting every invitation of Lady Greville, or you may be certain that I would never enter either her house, or her coach, with the disagreable certainty I always have of being abused for my poverty while I am in them.

When we arrived at Ashburnham, it was nearly ten o'clock, which was an hour and a half later than we were desired to be there; but Lady Greville is too fashionable (or fancies herself to be so) to be punctual. The dancing, however, was not begun, as they waited for Miss Greville. I had not been long in the room before I was engaged to dance by Mr Bernard, but just as we were going to stand up, he recollected that his servant had got his white gloves, and immediately ran out to fetch them. In the mean time the dancing began, and Lady Greville, in passing to another room, went exactly before me. She saw me, and instantly stopping, said to me, though there were several people close to us,

'Hey day, Miss Maria! What, cannot you get a partner? Poor young lady! I am afraid your new gown was put on for nothing. But do not despair; perhaps you may get a hop before the evening is over.' So saying, she passed on without hearing my repeated assurance of being engaged, and leaving me very provoked at being so exposed before every one.

Mr Bernard, however, soon returned, and by coming to me the moment he entered the room, and leading me to the dancers, my character, I hope, was cleared from the imputation Lady Greville had thrown on it in the eyes of all the old ladies who had heard her speech. I soon forgot all my vexations in the pleasure of dancing and of having the most agreable partner in the room. As he is, moreover, heir to a very large estate, I could see that Lady Greville did not look very well pleased when she found who had been his choice.

She was determined to mortify me, and accordingly, when we were sitting down between the dances, she came to me with *more* than her usual insulting importance, attended by Miss Mason, and said, loud enough to be heard by half the people in the room,

'Pray, Miss Maria, in what way of business was your grandfather? For Miss Mason and I cannot agree whether he was a grocer or a bookbinder.' I saw that she wanted to mortify me and was resolved if I possibly could to prevent her seeing that her scheme succeeded.

'Neither, madam; he was a wine merchant.'

'Aye, I knew he was in some such low way – he broke[22] did not he?'

'I believe not, ma'am.'

'Did not he abscond?'

'I never heard that he did.'

'At least he died insolvent?'

'I was never told so before.'

'Why, was not your father as poor as a rat?'

'I fancy not.'

'Was not he in the King's Bench once?'[23]

'I never saw him there.'[24] She gave me *such* a look, and turned away in a great passion; while I was half delighted with myself for my impertinence, and half afraid of being thought too saucy. As Lady Greville was extremely angry with me, she took no further notice of me all the evening; and indeed, had I been in favour I should have been equally neglected, as she was got into a party of great folks and she never speaks to me when she can to any one else. Miss Greville was with her mother's party at supper, but Ellen preferred staying with the Bernards and me. We had a very pleasant dance, and as Lady G. slept all the way home, I had a very comfortable ride.

The next day, while we were at dinner, Lady Greville's coach stopped at the door, for that is the time of day she generally contrives it should. She sent in a message by the servant to say that 'she should not get out, but that Miss Maria must come to the coach door, as she wanted to speak to her, and that she must make haste and come immediately.'

'What an impertinent message, mama!' said I. 'Go, Maria –' replied she. Accordingly, I went and was obliged to stand there at her ladyship's pleasure, though the wind was extremely high and very cold.[25]

'Why I think, Miss Maria, you are not quite so smart as you were last night. But I did not come to examine your dress, but to tell you that you may dine with us the day after tomorrow. Not tomorrow, remember, do not come tomorrow, for we expect Lord and Lady Clermont and Sir Thomas Stanley's family. There will be no occasion for your being very fine for I shan't send the carriage – if it rains you may take an umbrella' – I could hardly help laughing at hearing her give me leave to keep myself dry – 'and pray remember to be in time, but I shan't wait – I hate my victuals over-done. But you need not come *before* the time –. How does your mother do –? She is at dinner is not she?'

'Yes, ma'am, we were in the middle of dinner when your ladyship came.'

'I am afraid you find it very cold, Maria,' said Ellen.

'Yes, it is an horrible east wind,' said her mother. 'I assure you I can hardly bear the window down. But you are used to be blown about the wind, Miss Maria, and that is what has made your complexion so ruddy and coarse. You young ladies who cannot often ride in a carriage never mind what weather you trudge in, or how the wind shews your legs.[26] I would not have *my* girls stand out of doors as you do in such a day as this. But some sort of people have no feelings either of cold or delicacy –. Well, remember that we shall expect you on Thursday at five o'clock. You must tell your maid to come for you at night –. There will be no moon, and you will have an horrid walk home.

'My compliments to your mother – I am afraid your dinner will be cold – drive on.' And away she went, leaving me in a great passion with her as she always does.

Maria Williams

THE FEMALE PHILOSOPHER[27]

My dear Louisa,

Your friend Mr Millar called upon us yesterday in his way to Bath, whither he is going for his health; two of his daughters were with him, but the oldest and the three boys are with their mother in Sussex. Though you have often told me that Miss Millar was remarkably handsome, you never mentioned anything of her sisters' beauty; yet they are certainly extremely pretty. I'll give you their description. Julia is eighteen, with a countenance in which modesty, sense, and dignity are happily blended; she has a form which at once presents you with grace, elegance, and symmetry. Charlotte, who is just sixteen, is shorter than her sister, and though her figure cannot boast the easy dignity of Julia's, yet it has a pleasing plumpness which is in a different way as estimable. She is fair, and her face is expressive sometimes of softness the most bewitching, and at others of vivacity the most striking. She appears to have infinite wit and a good humour unalterable; her conversation during the half hour they set with us was replete with humorous sallies, bonmots, and repartees; while the sensible, the amiable Julia uttered sentiments of morality worthy of a heart like her own. Mr Millar appeared to answer the character I had always received of him. My father met him with that look of love, that social shake, and cordial kiss which marked his gladness at beholding an old and valued friend from whom, through various circumstances, he had been separated nearly twenty years. Mr Millar observed (and very justly too) that many events had befallen each during that interval of time, which gave occasion to the lovely Julia for making most sensible reflections on the many changes in their situation which so long a period had occasioned, on the advantages of some, and the disadvantages of others. From this subject she made a short digression to the instability of human pleasures and the uncertainty of their duration, which led her to observe that all earthly joys must be imperfect. She was proceeding to illustrate this doctrine by examples from the lives of great men when the carriage came to the door and the amiable moralist, with her father and sister, was obliged to depart; but not without a promise of spending five or six months with us on their return. We of course mentioned you, and I assure you that ample justice was done to your merits by all. 'Louisa Clarke,' said I, 'is in general a very pleasant girl, yet sometimes her good humour is clouded by peevishness, envy, and spite. She neither wants understanding nor is without some pretentions to beauty, but these are so very trifling, that the value she sets on her personal charms, and the adoration she expects them to be offered, are at once a striking example of her vanity, her pride, and her folly.' So said I, and to my opinion everyone added weight by the concurrence of their own.

Your affectionate
Arabella Smythe

Volume the Third

To Miss Austen

Madam,

Encouraged by your warm patronage of 'The Beautiful Cassandra' and 'The History of England,' which, through your generous support, have obtained a place in every library in the kingdom, and run through threescore editions, I take the liberty of begging the same exertions in favour of the following novel, which, I humbly flatter myself, possesses merit beyond any already published, or any that will ever in future appear, except such as may proceed from the pen of your most grateful humble servant,

the Author.

Steventon, August 1792

Catharine,[1] or The Bower

Catharine had the misfortune, as many heroines have had before her, of losing her parents when she was very young, and of being brought up under the care of a maiden aunt, who, while she tenderly loved her, watched over her conduct with so scrutinizing a severity as to make it very doubtful to many people, and to Catharine amongst the rest, whether she loved her or not. She had frequently been deprived of a real pleasure through this jealous caution, had been sometimes obliged to relinquish a ball because an officer was to be there, or to dance with a partner of her aunt's introduction in preference to one of her own choice. But her spirits were naturally good, and not easily depressed, and she possessed such a fund of vivacity and good humour as could only be damped by some very serious vexation.

Besides these antidotes against every disappointment, and consolations under them, she had another, which afforded her constant relief in all her misfortunes, and that was a fine shady bower, the work of her own infantine labours, assisted by those of two young companions who had resided in the same village. To this bower, which terminated a very pleasant and retired walk in her aunt's garden, she always wandered whenever anything disturbed her, and it possessed such a charm over her senses as constantly to tranquillize her mind and quiet her spirits. Solitude and reflection might perhaps have had the same effect in her bed chamber, yet habit had so strengthened the idea which fancy had first suggested, that such a thought never occurred to Kitty, who was firmly persuaded that her bower alone could restore her to herself.

Her imagination was warm, and in her friendships, as well as in the whole tenure of her mind, she was enthusiastic. This beloved bower had been the united work of herself and two amiable girls, for whom, since her earliest years, she had felt the tenderest regard. They were the daughters of the clergyman of the parish, with whose family, while it had continued there, her aunt had been on the most intimate terms; and the little girls, though separated for the greatest part of the year by the different modes of their education, were constantly together during the holidays of the Miss Wynnes; [they were companions in their walks, their schemes and amusements, and while the sweetness of their dispositions had prevented any serious quarrels, the trifling disputes which it was impossible wholly to avoid had been far from lessening their affection][2]. In those days of happy childhood, now so often regretted by Kitty, this arbour had been formed; and separated perhaps for ever from these dear friends, it encouraged more than any other place the tender and melancholy recollections of hours rendered pleasant by them, at once so sorrowful, yet so soothing!

It was now two years since the death of Mr Wynne and the consequent dispersion of his family, who had been left by it in great distress. They had been reduced to a state of absolute dependance on some relations, who though very opulent, and very nearly connected with them, had with difficulty been prevailed on to contribute anything towards their support. Mrs Wynne was fortunately spared the knowledge and participation of their distress by her release from a painful illness a few months before the death of her husband. The eldest daughter had been obliged to accept the offer of one of her cousins to equip her for the East Indies, and though infinitely against her inclinations, had been necessitated to embrace the only possibility that was offered to her of a maintenance. Yet it was one so opposite to all her ideas of propriety, so contrary to her wishes, so repugnant to her feelings, that she would almost have preferred servitude to it, had choice been allowed her.[3] Her personal attractions had gained her a husband as soon as she had arrived at Bengal, and she had now been married nearly a twelvemonth. Splendidly, yet unhappily married; united to a man of double her own age, whose disposition was not amiable, and whose manners were unpleasing, though his character was respectable. Kitty had heard twice from her friend since her marriage, but her letters were always unsatisfactory, and though she did not openly avow her feelings, yet every line proved her to be unhappy. She spoke with pleasure of nothing but of those amusements which they had shared together and which could return no more, and seemed to have no happiness in view but that of returning to England again.[4]

Her sister had been taken by another relation, the Dowager Lady Halifax, as a companion to her daughters, and had accompanied her family into Scotland about the same time of Cecilia's leaving England. From Mary, therefore, Kitty had the power of hearing more frequently, but her letters were scarcely more comfortable. There was not indeed that hopelessness of sorrow in her situation as in her sister's; she was not married, and could yet look forward to a change in her circumstances. But situated for the present without any immediate hope of it, in a family where, though all were her relations she had no friend, she wrote usually in depressed spirits, which her separation from her sister, and her sister's marriage, had greatly contributed to make so.

Divided thus from the two she loved best on earth, while Cecilia and Mary were still more endeared to her by their loss, everything that brought a remembrance of them was doubly cherished; and the shrubs they had planted and the keepsakes they had given were rendered sacred. The living of Chetwynde was now in the possession of a Mr Dudley,[5] whose family, unlike the Wynnes, were productive only of vexation and trouble to Mrs Percival[6] and her niece. Mr Dudley, who was the younger son of a very noble family – of a family more famed for their pride than their opulence – tenacious of his dignity, and jealous of his rights, was forever quarrelling, if not with Mrs Percival herself, with her steward and tenants concerning tithes, and with the principal neighbours themselves concerning the respect and parade he exacted. His wife, an ill-educated, untaught woman of ancient family, was proud of that family almost without knowing why, and like him too was haughty and quarrelsome, without considering for what. Their only daughter, who inherited the ignorance, the insolence, and pride of her parents, was, from that beauty of which she was unreasonably vain, considered by them as an irresistible creature, and looked up to as the future restorer, by a splendid marriage, of the dignity which their reduced situation, and Mr Dudley's being obliged to take orders for a country living, had so much lessened. They at once despised the Percivals as people of mean family, and envied them as people of fortune. They were jealous of their being more respected than themselves, and while they affected to consider them as of no consequence, were continually seeking to lessen them in the opinion of the neighbourhood by scandalous and malicious reports.

Such a family as this was ill-calculated to console Kitty for the loss of the Wynnes, or to fill up, by their society, those occasionally irksome hours which in so retired a situation would sometimes occur for want of a companion. Her aunt was most excessively fond of her, and miserable if she saw her for a moment out of spirits. Yet she lived in such constant apprehension of her marrying imprudently if she were allowed the opportunity of choosing, and was so dissatisfied with her behaviour when she saw her with young men – for it was, from her natural disposition, remarkably open and unreserved – that though she frequently wished for her niece's sake that the neighbourhood were larger, and that she had used herself to mix more with it, yet the recollection of there being young men in almost every family in it always conquered the wish.

The same fears that prevented Mrs Percival's joining much in the society of her neighbours led her equally to avoid inviting her relations to spend any time in her house. She had therefore constantly regretted the annual attempt of a distant relation to visit her at Chetwynde, as there was a young man in the family of whom she had heard many traits that alarmed her. This son was, however, now on his travels; and the repeated solicitations of Kitty, joined to a consciousness of having declined with too little ceremony the frequent overtures of her friends to be admitted, and a real wish to see them herself, easily prevailed on her to press with great earnestness the pleasure of a visit from them during the summer.

Mr and Mrs Stanley were accordingly to come, and Catharine, in having an object to look forward to, a something to expect that must inevitably relieve the dullness of a constant tête-à-tête with her aunt, was so delighted, and her spirits so elevated, that for the three or four days immediately preceding their arrival, she could scarcely fix herself to any employment. In this point Mrs Percival always thought her defective, and frequently complained of a want of steadiness and perseverance in her occupations, which were by no means congenial to the eagerness of Kitty's disposition, and perhaps not often met with in any young person. The tediousness too of her aunt's conversation, and the want of agreable companions, greatly increased this desire of change in her employments; for Kitty found herself much sooner tired of reading, working, or drawing in Mrs Percival's parlour than in her own arbour, where Mrs Percival, for fear of its being damp, never accompanied her.

As her aunt prided herself on the exact propriety and neatness with which everything in her family was conducted, and had no higher satisfaction than that of knowing her house to be always in complete order; as her fortune was good, and her establishment ample, few were the preparations necessary for the reception of her visitors. The day of their arrival, so long expected, at length came, and the noise of the coach and four as it drove round the sweep was to Catharine a more interesting sound than the music of an Italian opera, which to most heroines is the height of enjoyment.[7] Mr and Mrs Stanley were people of large fortune and high fashion. He was a member of the House of Commons, and they were therefore most agreably necessitated to reside half the year in town, where Miss

Stanley had been attended by the most capital masters from the time of her being six years old to the last spring; which, comprehending a period of twelve years, had been dedicated to the acquirement of accomplishments which were now to be displayed and in a few years entirely neglected.[8]

She was not inelegant in her appearance, rather handsome, and naturally not deficient in abilities; but those years which ought to have been spent in the attainment of useful knowledge and mental improvement, had been all bestowed in learning drawing, Italian, and music, more especially the latter, and she now united to these accomplishments, an understanding unimproved by reading and a mind totally devoid either of taste or judgement. Her temper was by nature good, but unassisted by reflection, she had neither patience under disappointment, nor could sacrifice her own inclinations to promote the happiness of others. All her ideas were towards the elegance of her appearance, the fashion of her dress, and the admiration she wished them to excite. She professed a love of books without reading, was lively without wit, and generally good humoured without merit.[9]

Such was Camilla Stanley; and Catharine, who was prejudiced by her appearance, and who from her solitary situation was ready to like anyone, though her understanding and judgement would not otherwise have been easily satisfied, felt almost convinced when she saw her that Miss Stanley would be the very companion she wanted, and in some degree make amends for the loss of Cecilia and Mary Wynne. She therefore attached herself to Camilla from the first day of her arrival, and from being the only young people in the house they were by inclination constant companions. Kitty was herself a great reader, though perhaps not a very deep one, and felt therefore highly delighted to find that Miss Stanley was equally fond of it. Eager to know that their sentiments as to books were similar, she very soon began questioning her new acquaintance on the subject; but though she was well read in modern history herself, she chose rather to speak first of books of a lighter kind, of books universally read and admired, [and that have given rise perhaps to more frequent arguments than any other of the same sort].[10]

'You have read Mrs Smith's novels,[11] I suppose?' said she to her companion.

'Oh! yes,' replied the other, 'and I am quite delighted with them – they are the sweetest things in the world –'

'And which do you prefer of them?'

'Oh! dear, I think there is no comparison between them – Emmeline is *so much* better than any of the others –'

'Many people think so, I know; but there does not appear so great a disproportion in their merits to *me*; do you think it is better written?'

'Oh! I do not know anything about *that* – but it is better in *everything* –. Besides, Ethelinde is so long –'

'That is a very common objection, I believe,' said Kitty, 'but for my own part, if a book is well-written, I always find it too short.'

'So do I, only I get tired of it before it is finished.'

'But did not you find the story of Ethelinde very interesting? And the descriptions of Grasmere,[12] are not they beautiful?'

'Oh! I missed them all, because I was in such a hurry to know the end of it.'[13] Then from an easy transition she added, 'We are going to the Lakes this autumn, and I am quite mad with joy; Sir Henry Devereux has promised to go with us, and that will make it so pleasant, you know –'

'I dare say it will; but I think it is a pity that Sir Henry's powers of pleasing were not reserved for an occasion where they might be more wanted. However I quite envy you the pleasure of such a scheme.'

'Oh! I am quite delighted with the thoughts of it; I can think of nothing else. I assure you I have done nothing for this last month but plan what clothes I should take with me, and I have at last determined to take very few indeed besides my travelling dress, and so I advise you to do, when ever you go; for I intend in case we should fall in with any races, or stop at Matlock or Scarborough, to have some things made for the occasion.'

'You intend then to go into Yorkshire?'

'I believe not – indeed I know nothing of the route, for I never trouble myself about such things –. I only know that we are to go from Derbyshire to Matlock and Scarborough,[14] but to which of them first, I neither know nor care – I am in hopes of meeting some particular friends of mine at Scarborough – Augusta told me in her last letter that Sir Peter talked of going; but then you know that is so uncertain. I cannot bear Sir Peter, he is such a horrid creature –'

'He *is*, is he?' said Kitty, not knowing what else to say.

'Oh! he is quite shocking.'

Here the conversation was interrupted, and Kitty was left in a painful uncertainty as to the particulars of Sir Peter's character; she knew only that he was horrid and shocking, but why, and in what, yet remained to be discovered. She could scarcely resolve what to think of her new acquaintance; she appeared to be shamefully ignorant as to the geography of England, if she had understood her right, and equally devoid of taste and information. Kitty was however unwilling to decide hastily; she was at once desirous of doing Miss Stanley justice, and of having her own wishes in her answered; she determined therefore to suspend all judgement for some time.

After supper, the conversation turning on the state of affairs in the political world, Mrs Percival, who was firmly of the opinion that the whole race of mankind were degenerating, said that, for her part, everything she believed was going to rack and ruin, all order was destroyed over the face of the world, the House of Commons she heard did not break up sometimes till five in the morning, and depravity never was so general before; concluding with a wish that she might live to see the manners of the people in Queen Elizabeth's reign restored again.

'Well, ma'am,' said her niece, '[I believe you have as good a chance of it as any one else,]¹⁵ but I hope you do not mean with the times to restore Queen Elizabeth herself.'

'Queen Elizabeth,' said Mrs Stanley, who never hazarded a remark on history that was not well-founded, 'lived to a good old age, and was a very clever woman.'

'True, ma'am,' said Kitty, 'but I do not consider either of those circumstances as meritorious in herself, and they are very far from making me wish her return, for if she were to come again with the same abilities and the same good constitution, she might do as much mischief and last as long as she did before –.' Then turning to Camilla, who had been sitting very silent for some time, she added, 'What do *you* think of Elizabeth, Miss Stanley? I hope you will not defend her.'¹⁶

'Oh! dear,' said Miss Stanley, 'I know nothing of politics, and cannot bear to hear them mentioned.' Kitty started at this repulse, but made no answer; that Miss Stanley must be ignorant of what she could not distinguish from politics she felt perfectly convinced. She retired to her own room, perplexed in her opinion about her new acquaintance, and fearful of her being very unlike Cecilia and Mary.

She arose the next morning to experience a fuller conviction of this, and every future day increased it. She found no variety in her conversation; she received no information from her but in fashions, and no amusement but in her performance on the harpsichord; and after repeated endeavours to find her what she wished, she was obliged to give up the attempt and to consider it as fruitless. There had occasionally appeared a something like humour in Camilla which had inspired her with hopes that she might at least have a natural genius, though not an improved one; but these sparklings of wit happened so seldom, and were so ill-supported, that she was at last convinced of their being merely accidental. All her stock of knowledge was exhausted in a very few days; and when Kitty had learnt from her how large their house in town was, when the fashionable amusements began, who were the celebrated beauties, and who the best milliner, Camilla had nothing further to teach, except the characters of any of her acquaintance as they occurred in conversation, which was done with equal ease and brevity, by saying that the person was either the sweetest creature in the world, and one of whom she was doatingly fond, or horrid, shocking, and not fit to be seen.

As Catharine was very desirous of gaining every possible information as to the characters of the Halifax family, and concluded that Miss Stanley must be acquainted with them, as she seemed to be so with every one of any consequence, she took an opportunity, as Camilla was one day enumerating all the people of rank that her mother visited, of asking her whether Lady Halifax were among the number.

'Oh! thank you for reminding me of her. She is the sweetest woman in the world, and one of our most intimate acquaintances; I do not suppose there is a day passes during the six months that we are in town, but what we see each other in the course of it –. And I correspond with all the girls.'

'They *are* then a very pleasant family?' said Kitty. 'They ought to be so indeed, to allow of such frequent meetings, or all conversation must be at end.'

'Oh! dear, not at all,' said Miss Stanley, 'for sometimes we do not speak to each other for a month together. We meet perhaps only in public, and then you know we are often not able to get near enough; but in that case we always nod and smile.'

'Which does just as well –. But I was going to ask you whether you have ever seen a Miss Wynne with them?'

'I know who you mean perfectly – she wears a blue hat –. I have frequently seen her in Brook Street, when I have been at Lady Halifax's balls – she gives one every month during the winter –. But only think how good it is in her to take care of Miss Wynne, for she is a very distant relation, and so poor that, as Miss Halifax told me, her mother was obliged to find her in clothes.[17] Is not it shameful?'

'That she should be so poor? It is indeed, with such wealthy connexions as the family have.'

'Oh! no; I mean, was not it shameful in Mr Wynne to leave his children so distressed, when he had actually the living of Chetwynde and two or three curacies, and only four children to provide for –. What would he have done if he had had ten, as many people have?'

'He would have given them all a good education and have left them all equally poor.'

'Well, I do think there never was so lucky a family. Sir George Fitzgibbon you know sent the eldest girl to India entirely at his own expense, where they say she is most nobly married and the happiest creature in the world –. Lady Halifax you see has taken care of the youngest and treats her as if she were her daughter. She does not go out into public with her to be sure; but then she is always present when her ladyship gives her balls, and nothing can be kinder to her than Lady Halifax is; she would have taken her to Cheltenham last year, if there had been room enough at the lodgings, and therefore I don't think that *she* can have anything to complain of. Then there are the two sons; one of them the Bishop of M— has got into the army as a lieutenant I suppose; and the other is extremely well off I know, for I have a notion that somebody puts him to school somewhere in Wales. Perhaps you knew them when they lived here?'

'Very well. We met as often as your family and the Halifaxes do in town, but as we seldom had any difficulty in getting near enough to speak, we seldom parted with merely a nod and a smile. They were indeed a most charming family, and I believe have scarcely their equals in the world. The neighbours we now have at the parsonage appear to more disadvantage in coming after them.'

'Oh! horrid wretches! I wonder you can endure them.'

'Why, what would you have one do?'

'Oh! Lord, if I were in your place, I should abuse them all day long.'

'So I do, but it does no good.'

'Well, I declare it is quite a pity that they should be suffered to live. I wish my father would propose knocking all their brains out some day or other when he is in the house. So abominably proud of their family! And I dare say after all, that there is nothing particular in it.'

'Why yes, I believe they have reason to value themselves on it, if any body has; for you know he is Lord Amyatt's brother.'

'Oh! I know all that very well, but it is no reason for their being so horrid. I remember I met Miss Dudley last spring with Lady Amyatt at Ranelagh, and she had such a frightful cap on, that I have never been able to bear any of them since.[18] – And so you used to think the Wynnes very pleasant?'

'You speak as if their being so were doubtful! Pleasant! Oh! they were every thing that could interest and attach. It is not in my power to do justice to their merits, though not to feel them I think must be impossible. They have unfitted me for any society but their own!'

'Well, that is just what I think of the Miss Halifaxes; by the by, I must write to Caroline tomorrow, and I do not know what to say to her. The Barlows too are just such other sweet girls; but I wish Augusta's hair was not so dark. I cannot bear Sir Peter – horrid wretch! He is *always* laid up with the gout, which is exceedingly disagreable to the family.'

'And perhaps not very pleasant to himself –. But as to the Wynnes: do you really think them very fortunate?'

'Do I? Why, does not every body? Miss Halifax and Caroline and Maria all say that they are the luckiest creatures in the world. So does Sir George Fitzgibbon and so do every body.'

'That is, every body who have themselves conferred an obligation on them. But do you call it lucky, for a girl of genius and feeling to be sent in quest of a husband to Bengal, to be married there to a man of whose disposition she has no opportunity of judging till her judgement is of no use to her, who may be a tyrant, or a fool, or both, for what she knows to the contrary. Do you call *that* fortunate?'

'I know nothing of all that; I only know that it was extremely good in Sir George to fit her out and pay her passage, and that she would not have found many who would have done the same.'

'I wish she had not found *one*,' said Kitty with great eagerness. 'She might then have remained in England and been happy.'

'Well, I cannot conceive the hardship of going out in a very agreable manner with two or three sweet girls for companions, having a delightful voyage to Bengal or Barbadoes or wherever it is, and being married soon after one's arrival to a very charming man immensely rich –. I see no hardship in all that.'

'Your representation of the affair,' said Kitty laughing, 'certainly gives a very different idea of it from mine. But supposing all this to be true; still, as it was by no means certain that she would be so fortunate either in her voyage, her companions, or her husband, in being obliged to run the risk of their proving very different, she undoubtedly experienced a great hardship –. Besides, to a girl of any delicacy, the voyage in itself, since the object of it is so universally known, is a punishment that needs no other to make it very severe.'

'I do not see that at all. She is not the first girl who has gone to the East Indies for a husband, and I declare I should think it very good fun if I were as poor.'

'I believe you would think very differently *then*. But at least you will not defend her sister's situation? Dependant even for her clothes on the bounty of others, who of course do not pity her, as by your own account, they consider her as very fortunate.'

'You are extremely nice,[19] upon my word; Lady Halifax is a delightful woman, and one of the sweetest-tempered creatures in the world; I am sure I have every reason to speak well of her, for we are under most amazing obligations to her. She has frequently chaperoned me when my mother has been indisposed, and last spring she lent me her own horse three times, which was a prodigious favour, for it is the most beautiful creature that ever was seen, and I am the only person she ever lent it to.'

['If so, *Mary Wynne* can receive very little advantage from her having it.'][20]

'And then,' continued she, 'the Miss Halifaxes are quite delightful. Maria is one of the cleverest girls that ever were known – draws in oils, and plays anything by sight. She promised me one of her drawings before I left town, but I entirely forgot to ask her for it. I would give anything to have one.'

['Why, indeed, if Maria will give my friend a drawing, she can have nothing to complain of; but as she does not write in spirits, I suppose she has not yet been fortunate enough to be so distinguished.'][21]

'But was not it very odd,' said Kitty, 'that the bishop should send Charles Wynne to sea, when he must have had a much better chance of providing for him in the Church, which was the profession that Charles liked best, and the one for which his father had intended him? The bishop I know had often promised Mr Wynne a living, and as he never gave him one, I think it was incumbent on him to transfer the promise to his son.'

'I believe you think he ought to have resigned his bishopric to him; you seem determined to be dissatisfied with every thing that has been done for them.'

'Well,' said Kitty, 'this is a subject on which we shall never agree, and therefore it will be useless to continue it farther, or to mention it again –'

She then left the room; and running out of the house, was soon in her dear bower, where she could indulge in peace all her affectionate anger against the relations of the Wynnes, which was greatly heightened by finding from Camilla that they were in general considered as having acted particularly well by them –. She amused herself for some time in abusing and hating them all with great spirit; and when this tribute to her regard for the Wynnes was paid, and the bower began to have its usual influence over her spirits, she contributed towards settling them by taking out a book, for she had always one about her, and reading.

She had been so employed for nearly an hour, when Camilla came running towards her with great eagerness, and apparently great pleasure. 'Oh! my dear Catharine,' said she, half out of breath, 'I have such delightful news for you – but you shall guess what it is –. We are all the happiest creatures in the world; would you believe it, the Dudleys have sent us an invitation to a ball at their own house –. What charming people they are! I had no idea of there being so much sense in the whole family – I declare I quite doat upon them –. And it happens so fortunately too, for I expect a new cap from town tomorrow which will just do for a ball – gold net – it will be a most angelic thing – every body will be longing for the pattern –'

The expectation of a ball was indeed very agreable intelligence to Kitty, who, fond of dancing and seldom able to enjoy it, had reason to feel even greater pleasure in it than her friend; for to *her*, it was now no novelty. Camilla's delight however was by no means inferior to Kitty's, and she rather expressed the most of the two. The cap came and every other preparation was soon completed; while these were in agitation the days passed gaily away, but when directions were no longer necessary, taste could no longer be displayed, and difficulties no longer overcome, the short period that intervened before the day of the ball hung heavily on their hands, and every hour was too long. The very few times that Kitty had ever enjoyed the amusement of dancing was an excuse for *her* impatience, and an apology for the idleness it occasioned to a mind naturally very active; but her friend without such a plea was infinitely worse than herself. She could do nothing but wander from the house to the garden, and from the garden to the avenue, wondering when Thursday would come, which she might easily have ascertained, and counting the hours as they passed, which served only to lengthen them.

They retired to their rooms in high spirits on Wednesday night, but Kitty awoke the next morning with a violent toothache. It was in vain that she endeavoured at first to deceive herself; her feelings were witnesses too acute of its reality; with as little success did she try to sleep it off, for the pain she suffered prevented her closing her eyes.

She then summoned her maid, and with the assistance of the housekeeper, every remedy that the receipt book or the head of the latter contained, was tried, but ineffectually; for though for a short time relieved by them, the pain still returned. She was now obliged to give up the endeavour, and to reconcile herself not only to the pain of a toothache, but to the loss of a ball; and though she had with so much eagerness looked forward to the day of its arrival, had received such pleasure in the necessary preparations, and promised herself so much delight in it, yet she was not so totally void of philosophy as many girls of her age might have been in her situation. She considered that there were misfortunes of a much greater magnitude than the loss of a ball experienced every day by some part of mortality, and that the time might come when she would herself look back with wonder and perhaps with envy on her having known no greater vexation. By such reflections as these, she soon reasoned herself into as much resignation and patience as the pain she suffered would allow of, which after all was the greatest misfortune of the two, and told the sad story when she entered the breakfast room with tolerable composure.

Mrs Percival – more grieved for her toothache than her disappointment, as she feared that it would not be possible to prevent her dancing with a man if she *went* – was eager to try everything that had already been applied to alleviate the pain, while at the same time she declared it was impossible for her to leave the house. Miss Stanley, who, joined to her concern for her friend, felt a mixture of dread lest her mother's proposal that they should all remain at home might be accepted, was very violent in her sorrow on the occasion; and though her apprehensions on the subject were soon quieted by Kitty's protesting that sooner than allow any one to stay with her, she would herself go, she continued to lament it with such unceasing vehemence as at last drove Kitty to her own room. Her fears for herself being now entirely dissipated left her more than ever at leisure to pity and persecute her friend, who, though safe when in her own room, was frequently removing from it to some other in hopes of being more free from pain, and then had no opportunity of escaping her.

'To be sure, there never was anything so shocking,' said Camilla. 'To come on such a day too! For one would not have minded it you know had it been at *any other* time. But it always is so. I never was at a ball in my life but what something happened to prevent somebody from going! I wish there were no such things as teeth in the world; they are nothing but plagues to one, and I dare say that people might easily invent something to eat with instead of them. Poor thing! What pain you are in! I declare it is quite shocking to look at you. But you won't have it out, will you? For heaven's sake don't; for there is nothing I dread so much. I declare I had rather undergo the greatest tortures in the world than have a tooth drawn. Well! how patiently you do bear it! How can you be so quiet? Lord, if I were in your place I should make such a fuss, there would be no bearing me. I should torment you to death.'

'So you do, as it is,' thought Kitty.

'For my own part, Catharine,' said Mrs Percival, 'I have not a doubt but that you caught this toothache by sitting so much in that arbour, for it is always damp. I know it has ruined your constitution entirely; and indeed I do not believe it has been of much service to mine; I sat down in it last May to rest myself, and I have never been quite well since –. I shall order John to pull it all down, I assure you.'

'I know you will not do that, ma'am,' said Kitty, 'as you must be convinced how unhappy it would make me.'

'You talk very ridiculously, child; it is all whim and nonsense. Why cannot you fancy this room an arbour?'

'Had this room been built by Cecilia and Mary, I should have valued it equally, ma'am, for it is not merely the name of an arbour which charms me.'

'Why, indeed, Mrs Percival,' said Mrs Stanley, 'I must think that Catharine's affection for her bower is the effect of a sensibility that does her credit. I love to see a friendship between young persons, and always consider it as a sure mark of an amiable, affectionate disposition.[22] I have, from Camilla's infancy, taught her to think the same, and have taken great pains to introduce her to young people of her own age who were likely to be worthy of her regard. [There is something mighty pretty, I think, in young ladies corresponding with each other, and]²³ nothing forms the taste more than sensible and elegant letters –. Lady Halifax thinks just like me –. Camilla corresponds with her daughters, and I believe I may venture to say that they are none of them the *worse* for it.'²⁴ These ideas were too modern to suit Mrs Percival, who considered a correspondence between girls as productive of no good, and as the frequent origin of imprudence and error by the effect of pernicious advice and bad example. She could not therefore refrain from saying that for her part, she had lived fifty years in the world without having ever had a correspondent, and did not find herself at all the less respectable for it.

Mrs Stanley could say nothing in answer to this, but her daughter, who was less governed by propriety, said in her thoughtless way,

'But who knows what you might have been, ma'am, if you *had* had a correspondent; perhaps it would have made you quite a different creature. I declare I would not be without those I have for all the world. It is the greatest delight of my life, and you cannot think how much their letters have formed my taste, as mama says, for I hear from them generally every week.'

'You received a letter from Augusta Barlow to day, did you not, my love?' said her mother. 'She writes remarkably well, I know.'

'Oh! yes, ma'am, the most delightful letter you ever heard of. She sends me a long account of the new Regency walking dress²⁵ Lady Susan has given her, and it is so beautiful that I am quite dying with envy for it.'

'Well, I am prodigiously happy to hear such pleasing news of my young friend; I have a high regard for Augusta, and most sincerely partake in the general joy on the occasion. But does she say nothing else? It seemed to be a long letter – are they to be at Scarborough?'

'Oh! Lord, she never once mentions it, now I recollect it; and I entirely forgot to ask her when I wrote last. She says nothing indeed except about the Regency.'

'She *must* write well,' thought Kitty, 'to make a long letter upon a bonnet and pelisse.' She then left the room, tired of listening to a conversation which, though it might have diverted her had she been well, served only to fatigue and depress her while in pain.

Happy was it for *her* when the hour of dressing came; for Camilla, satisfied with being surrounded by her mother and half the maids in the house, did not want her assistance, and was too agreably employed to want her society. She remained, therefore, alone in the parlour, till joined by Mr Stanley and her aunt, who, however, after a few enquiries, allowed her to continue undisturbed, and began their usual conversation on politics. This was a subject on which they could never agree, for Mr Stanley, who considered himself as perfectly qualified, by his seat in the house, to decide on it without hesitation, resolutely maintained that the kingdom had not for ages been in so flourishing and prosperous a state; and Mrs Percival, with equal warmth, though perhaps less argument, as vehemently asserted that the whole nation would speedily be ruined, and everything, as she expressed herself, be at sixes and sevens.

It was not, however, unamusing to Kitty to listen to the dispute, especially as she began then to be more free from pain; and without taking any share in it herself, she found it very entertaining to observe the eagerness with which they both defended their opinions, and could not help thinking that Mr Stanley would not feel more disappointed if her aunt's expectations were fulfilled, than her aunt would be mortified by their failure. After waiting a considerable time, Mrs Stanley and her daughter appeared, and Camilla, in high spirits and perfect good humour with her own looks, was more violent than ever in her lamentations over her friend as she practised her Scotch steps about the room.

At length they departed, and Kitty, better able to amuse herself than she had been the whole day before, wrote a long account of her misfortunes to Mary Wynne. When her letter was concluded, she had an opportunity of witnessing the truth of that assertion which says that sorrows are lightened by communication, for her toothache was then so much relieved that she began to entertain an idea of following her friends to Mr Dudley's. They had been gone an hour, and as every thing relative to her dress was in complete readiness, she considered that in another hour, since there was so little a way to go, she might be there.[26]

They were gone in Mr Stanley's carriage, and therefore she might follow in her aunt's. As the plan seemed so very easy to be executed, and promising so much pleasure, it was after a few minutes' deliberation finally adopted; and running up stairs, she rang in great haste for her maid. The bustle and hurry which then ensued for nearly an hour was at last happily concluded by her finding herself very well-dressed and in high beauty. Anne was then dispatched in the same haste to order the carriage, while her mistress was putting on her gloves, and arranging the folds of her dress, [and providing herself with lavender water].[27]

In a few minutes, she heard the carriage drive up to the door, and though at first surprised at the expedition with which it had been got ready, she concluded after a little reflection that the men had received some hint of her intentions beforehand, and was hastening out of the room, when Anne came running into it in the greatest hurry and agitation, exclaiming,

'Lord, ma'am! here's a gentleman in a chaise and four come, and I cannot for my life conceive who it is! I happened to be crossing the hall when the carriage drove up, and I knew nobody would be in the way to let him in but Tom, and he looks so awkward you know, ma'am, now his hair is just done up, that I was not willing the gentleman should see him, and so I went to the door myself. And he is one of the handsomest young men you would wish to see; I was almost ashamed of being seen in my apron, ma'am, [for because you know, ma'am, I am all over powder,][28] but however he is vastly handsome and did not seem to mind it at all. – And he asked me whether the family were at home; and so I said everybody was gone out but you, ma'am, for I would not deny you because I was sure you would like to see him. And then he asked me whether Mr and Mrs Stanley were not here, and so I said Yes, and then –'

'Good heavens!' said Kitty, 'what can all this mean? And who can it possibly be? Did you never see him before? And did not he tell you his name?'

'No, ma'am, he never said anything about it – so then I asked him to walk into the parlour, and he was prodigious agreable, and –'

'Whoever he is,' said her mistress, 'he has made a great

impression upon you, Nanny – but where did he come from? And what does he want here?'

'Oh! ma'am, I was going to tell you, that I fancy his business is with you; for he asked me whether you were at leisure to see any body, and desired I would give his compliments to you, and say he should be very happy to wait on you. However I thought he had better not come up into your dressing room, especially as everything is in such a litter, so I told him if he would be so obliging as to stay in the parlour, I would run upstairs and tell you he was come, and I dared to say that you would wait upon *him*. Lord, ma'am, I'd lay anything that he is come to ask you to dance with him tonight, and has got his chaise ready to take you to Mr Dudley's.'[29]

Kitty could not help laughing at this idea, and only wished it might be true, as it was very likely that she would be too late for any other partner.

'But what, in the name of wonder, can he have to say to me? Perhaps he is come to rob the house – he comes in style at least; and it will be some consolation for our losses to be robbed by a gentleman in a chaise and four –. What livery has his servants?'

'Why that is the most wonderful thing about him, ma'am, for he has not a single servant with him, and came back with hack horses;[30] but he is as handsome as a prince, for all that, and has quite the look of one. Do, dear ma'am, go down, for I am sure you will be delighted with him –'

'Well, I believe I must go; but it is very odd! What can he have to say to me?' Then giving one look at herself in the glass, she walked with great impatience, though trembling all the while from not knowing what to expect, down stairs; and after pausing a moment at the door to gather courage for opening it, she resolutely entered the room. The stranger, whose appearance did not disgrace the account she had received of it from her maid, rose up on her entrance, and laying aside the newspaper he had been reading, advanced towards her with an air of the most perfect ease and vivacity, and said to her,

'It is certainly a very awkward circumstance to be thus obliged to introduce myself, but I trust that the necessity of the case will plead my excuse, and prevent your being prejudiced by it against me –. *Your* name, I need not ask, ma'am –. Miss Percival is too well

known to me by description to need any information of that.'
Kitty, who had been expecting him to tell his own name instead of
hers, and who from having been little in company, and never
before in such a situation, felt herself unable to ask it, though she
had been planning her speech all the way down stairs, was so
confused and distressed by this unexpected address that she could
only return a slight curtsy[31] to it, and accepted the chair he
reached her, without knowing what she did.

The gentleman then continued. 'You are, I dare say, surprised
to see me returned from France so soon, and nothing indeed but
business could have brought me to England; a very melancholy
affair has now occasioned it, and I was unwilling to leave it without
paying my respects to the family in Devonshire whom I have so
long wished to be acquainted with –'

Kitty, who felt much more surprised at his supposing her to *be*
so, than at seeing a person in England whose having ever left it was
perfectly unknown to her, still continued silent from wonder and
perplexity, and her visitor still continued to talk.

'You will suppose, madam, that I was not the *less* desirous of
waiting on you, from your having Mr and Mrs Stanley with you
–. I hope they are well? And Mrs Percival; how does *she* do?' Then,
without waiting for an answer, he gaily added, 'But my dear Miss
Percival, you are going out I am sure; and I am detaining you from
your appointment. How can I ever expect to be forgiven for such
injustice! Yet how can I, so circumstanced, forbear to offend! You
seem dressed for a ball? But this is the land of gaiety, I know; I
have for many years been desirous of visiting it. You have dances,
I suppose, at least every week – but where are the rest of your party
gone, and what kind angel, in compassion to me, has excluded *you*
from it?'

'Perhaps, sir,' said Kitty, extremely confused by his manner of
speaking to her, and highly displeased with the freedom of his
conversation towards one who had never seen him before and did
not *now* know his name, 'perhaps, sir, you are acquainted with Mr
and Mrs Stanley; and your business may be with *them*?'

'You do me too much honour, ma'am,' replied he laughing, 'in
supposing me to be acquainted with Mr and Mrs Stanley; I merely

know them by sight; very distant relations; only my mother and father. Nothing more, I assure you.'[32]

'Gracious heaven!' said Kitty, 'are you Mr Stanley then? – I beg a thousand pardons – though really upon recollection I do not know for what – for you never told me your name –'

'I beg your pardon – I made a very fine speech when you entered the room, all about introducing myself; I assure you it was very great for *me*.'

'The speech had certainly great merit,' said Kitty smiling. 'I thought so at the time; but since you never mentioned your name in it, as an *introductory* one it might have **been** better.'

There was such an air of good humour and gaiety in Stanley, that Kitty, though perhaps not authorized to address him with so much familiarity on so short an acquaintance, could not forbear indulging the natural unreserve and vivacity of her own disposition in speaking to him as he spoke to her. She was intimately acquainted too with his family, who were her relations, and she chose to consider herself entitled by the connexion to forget how little a while they had known each other.

'Mr and Mrs Stanley and your sister are extremely well,' said she, 'and will, I dare say, be very much surprised to see you – but I am sorry to hear that your return to England has been occasioned by any unpleasant circumstance.'

'Oh! don't talk of it,' said he, 'it is a most confounded shocking affair, and makes me miserable to think of it; but where are my father and mother, and your aunt gone? Oh! do you know that I met the prettiest little waiting maid in the world when I came here; she let me into the house; I took her for you at first.'[33]

'You did me a great deal of honour, and give me more credit for good nature than I deserve, for I *never* go to the door when any one comes.'

'Nay, do not be angry; I mean no offence. But tell me, where are you going to so smart? Your carriage is just coming round.'

'I am going to a dance at a neighbour's, where your family and my aunt are already gone.'

'Gone, without you! What's the meaning of *that*? But I suppose you are like myself, rather long in dressing.'

'I must have been so indeed, if that were the case, for they have been gone nearly these two hours; the reason, however, was not what you suppose – I was prevented going by a pain –'

'By a pain!' interrupted Stanley, 'Oh! heavens, that is dreadful indeed! No matter where the pain was. But my dear Miss Percival, what do you say to my accompanying you? And suppose you were to dance with me too? *I* think it would be very pleasant.'

'I can have no objection to either, I am sure,' said Kitty, laughing to find how near the truth her maid's conjecture had been; 'on the contrary, I shall be highly honoured by both, and I can answer for your being extremely welcome to the family who give the ball.'

'Oh! hang them; who cares for that; they cannot turn me out of the house. But I am afraid I shall cut a sad figure among all your Devonshire beaux in this dusty travelling apparel, and I have not wherewithal to change it. You can procure me some powder, perhaps, and I must get a pair of shoes from one of the men, for I was in such a devil of a hurry to leave Lyons that I had not time to have anything pack'd up but some linen.'

Kitty very readily undertook to procure for him everything he wanted, and telling the footman to shew him into Mr Stanley's dressing room, gave Nanny orders to send in some powder and pomatum, which orders Nanny chose to execute in person. As Stanley's preparations in dressing were confined to such very trifling articles, Kitty of course expected him in about ten minutes; but she found that it had not been merely a boast of vanity in saying that he was dilatory in that respect, as he kept her waiting for him above half an hour, so that the clock had struck ten before he entered the room, and the rest of the party had gone by eight.

'Well,' said he as he came in, 'have not I been very quick? I never hurried so much in my life before.'

'In that case you certainly have,' said Kitty, 'for all merit, you know, is comparative.'

'Oh! I knew you would be delighted with me for making so much haste –. But come, the carriage is ready; so, do not keep me waiting.' And so saying, he took her by the hand and led her out of the room. 'Why, my dear cousin,' said he when they were seated, 'this will be a most agreable surprise to everybody to see you enter the room with such a smart young fellow as I am – I hope your aunt won't be alarmed.'

'To tell you the truth,' replied Kitty, 'I think the best way to prevent it will be to send for her or your mother before we go into the room, especially as you are a perfect stranger, and must of course be introduced to Mr and Mrs Dudley –'

'Oh! nonsense,' said he; 'I did not expect *you* to stand upon such ceremony; our acquaintance with each other renders all such prudery ridiculous; besides, if we go in together, we shall be the whole talk of the country –'

'To *me*,' replied Kitty, 'that would certainly be a most powerful inducement; but I scarcely know whether my aunt would consider it as such –. Women at her time of life have odd ideas of propriety, you know.'

'Which is the very thing that you ought to break them of; and why should you object to entering a room with me where all our relations are, when you have done me the honour to admit me without any chaperone into your carriage? Do not you think your aunt will be as much offended with you for one, as for the other of these mighty crimes?'

'Why really,' said Catharine, 'I do not know but that she may; however, it is no reason that I should offend against decorum a second time, because I have already done it once.'

'On the contrary, that is the very reason which makes it impossible for you to prevent it, since you cannot offend for the *first time* again.'

'You are very ridiculous,' said she laughing, 'but I am afraid your arguments divert me too much to convince me.'

'At least they will convince you that I am very agreable, which after all, is the happiest conviction for me; and as to the affair of propriety, we will let that rest till we arrive at our journey's end –. This is a monthly ball I suppose. Nothing but dancing here –.'

'I thought I had told you that it was given by a Mr Dudley –.'

'Oh! aye so you did; but why should not Mr Dudley give one every month? By the by, who *is* that man? Every body gives balls now, I think; I believe I must give one myself soon –. Well, but how do you like my father and mother? And poor little Camilla, too, has not she plagued you to death with the Halifaxes?' Here the carriage fortunately stopped at Mr Dudley's, and Stanley was too much engaged in handing her out of it to wait for an answer, or to remember that what he had said required one.

They entered the small vestibule which Mr Dudley had raised to the dignity of a Hall, and Kitty immediately desired the footman, who was leading the way up stairs, to inform either Mrs Percival or Mrs Stanley of her arrival, and beg them to come to her. But Stanley, unused to any contradiction, and impatient to be amongst them, would neither allow her to wait, or listen to what she said, and forcibly seizing her arm within his, overpowered her voice with the rapidity of his own; Kitty, half angry and half laughing, was obliged to go with him up stairs, and could even with difficulty prevail on him to relinquish her hand before they entered the room.

Mrs Percival was at that very moment engaged in conversation with a lady at the upper end of the room, to whom she had been giving a long account of her niece's unlucky disappointment, and the dreadful pain that she had with so much fortitude endured the whole day.

'I left her, however,' said she, 'thank heaven! a little better, and I hope she has been able to amuse herself with a book, poor thing! For she must otherwise be very dull. She is probably in bed by this time, which, while she is so poorly, is the best place for her, you know, ma'am.'

The lady was going to give her assent to this opinion, when the noise of voices on the stairs, and the footman's opening the door as if for the entrance of company, attracted the attention of every body in the room; and as it was in one of those intervals between the dances when every one seemed glad to sit down, Mrs Percival had a most unfortunate opportunity of seeing her niece, whom she had supposed in bed or amusing herself as the height of gaiety with a book, enter the room most elegantly dressed, with a smile on her countenance, and a glow of mingled cheerfulness and confusion on her cheeks, attended by a young man uncommonly handsome, and who, without any of her confusion, appeared to have all her vivacity.

Mrs Percival, colouring with anger and astonishment, rose from her seat, and Kitty walked eagerly towards her, impatient to account for what she saw appeared wonderful to every body, and extremely offensive to *her*; while Camilla, on seeing her brother, ran instantly towards him, and very soon explained who he was by her words and her actions. Mr Stanley, who so fondly doated on his son that the pleasure of seeing him again after an absence of three months prevented his feeling for the time any anger against him for returning to England without his knowledge, received him with equal surprise and delight; and soon comprehending the cause of his journey, forbore any further conversation with him, as he was eager to see his mother, and it was necessary that he should be introduced to Mr Dudley's family.

This introduction, to any one but Stanley, would have been highly unpleasant, for they considered their dignity injured by his coming uninvited to their house, and received him with more than their usual haughtiness: but Stanley, who with a vivacity of temper seldom subdued, and a contempt of 'censure not to be overcome, possessed an opinion of his own consequence and a perseverance in his own schemes which were not to be damped by the conduct of others, appeared not to perceive it. The civilities therefore which they coldly offered, he received with a gaiety and ease peculiar to himself; and then, attended by his father and sister, walked into another room where his mother was playing at cards, to experience another meeting, and undergo a repetition of pleasure, surprise, and explanations.

While these were passing, Camilla, eager to communicate all she felt to some one who would attend to her, returned to Catharine, and seating herself by her, immediately began.

'Well, did you ever know anything so delightful as this? But it always is so; I never go to a ball in my life but what something or other happens unexpectedly that is quite charming!'

'A ball,' replied Kitty, 'seems to be a most eventful thing to you –'

'Oh! Lord, it is indeed – but only think of my brother's returning so suddenly – and how shocking a thing it is that has brought him over! I never heard anything so dreadful –!'

'What is it, pray, that has occasioned his leaving France? I am sorry to find that it is a melancholy event.'

'Oh! it is beyond anything you can conceive! His favourite hunter, who was turned out in the park on his going abroad, somehow or other fell ill – no, I believe it was an accident; but however it was something or other, or else it was something else, and so they sent an express immediately to Lyons where my brother was, for they knew that he valued this mare more than anything else in the world besides; and so my brother set off directly for England, and without packing up another coat; I am quite angry with him about it; it was so shocking you know to come away without a change of clothes –'

'Why indeed,' said Kitty, 'it seems to have been a very shocking affair from beginning to end.'

'Oh! it is beyond anything you can conceive! I would rather have had *anything* happen than that he should have lost that mare.'

'Except his coming away without another coat.'

'Oh! yes, that has vexed me more than you can imagine –. Well, and so Edward got to Brampton just as the poor thing was dead; but as he could not bear to remain there *then*, he came off directly to Chetwynde on purpose to see us –. I hope he may not go abroad again.'

'Do you think he will not?'

'Oh! dear, to be sure he must, but I wish he may not with all my heart –. You cannot think how fond I am of him! By the by, are not you in love with him yourself?'

'To be sure I am,' replied Kitty laughing, 'I am in love with every handsome man I see.'

'That is just like me – *I* am always in love with every handsome man in the world.'

'There you outdo me,' replied Catharine, 'for I am only in love with those I *do* see.'

Mrs Percival, who was sitting on the other side of her, and who began now to distinguish the words, *love* and *handsome man*, turned hastily towards them, and said,

'What are you talking of, Catharine?' To which Catharine immediately answered, with the simple artifice of a child,

'Nothing, ma'am.' She had already received a very severe lecture from her aunt on the imprudence of her behaviour during the whole evening. She blamed her for coming to the ball, for coming in the same carriage with Edward Stanley, and still more for entering the room with him. For the last-mentioned offence

Catharine knew not what apology to give; and though she longed in answer to the second to say that she had not thought it would be civil to make Mr Stanley *walk*, she dared not so to trifle with her aunt, who would have been but the more offended by it. The first accusation, however, she considered as very unreasonable, as she thought herself perfectly justified in coming.

This conversation continued till Edward Stanley, entering the room, came instantly towards her, and telling her that every one waited for *her* to begin the next dance, led her to the top of the room; for Kitty, impatient to escape from so unpleasant a companion, without the least hesitation or one civil scruple at being so distinguished, immediately gave him her hand, and joyfully left her seat. This conduct, however, was highly resented by several ladies present, and among the rest by Miss Stanley, whose regard for her brother, though *excessive*, and whose affection for Kitty, though *prodigious*, were not proof against such an injury to her importance and her peace.

Edward had, however, only consulted his own inclinations in desiring Miss Percival to begin the dance, nor had he any reason to know that it was either wished or expected by anyone else in the party. As an heiress she was certainly of consequence, but her birth gave her no other claim to it, for her father had been a merchant. It was this very circumstance which rendered this unfortunate affair so offensive to Camilla, for though she would sometimes boast, in the pride of her heart and her eagerness to be admired, that she did not know who her grandfather had been, and was as ignorant of everything relative to genealogy as to astronomy (and, she might have added, geography), yet she was really proud of her family and connexions, and easily offended if they were treated with neglect.

'I should not have minded it,' said she to her mother, 'if she had been *anybody* else's daughter; but to see her pretend to be above *me*, when her father was only a tradesman, is too bad! It is such an affront to our whole family! I declare I think papa ought to interfere in it, but he never cares about anything but politics. If I were Mr Pitt[34] or the Lord Chancellor, he would take care I should not be insulted, but he never thinks about *me*; and it is so provoking that *Edward* should let her stand there. I wish with all my heart that he had never come to England! I hope she may fall down and break her neck, or sprain her ancle.'

Mrs Stanley perfectly agreed with her daughter concerning the affair, and though with less violence, expressed almost equal resentment at the indignity.

Kitty in the mean time remained insensible of having given any one offence, and therefore unable either to offer an apology, or make a reparation; her whole attention was occupied by the happiness she enjoyed in dancing with the most elegant young man in the room, and every one else was equally unregarded. The evening indeed to *her* passed off delightfully; he was her partner during the greatest part of it, and the united attractions that he possessed of person, address, and vivacity, had easily gained that preference from Kitty which they seldom fail of obtaining from every one. She was too happy to care either for her aunt's ill humour, which she could not help remarking, or for the alteration in Camilla's behaviour, which forced itself at last on her observation. Her spirits were elevated above the influence of displeasure in any one, and she was equally indifferent as to the cause of Camilla's or the continuance of her aunt's.

Though Mr Stanley could never be really offended by any imprudence or folly in his son that had given him the pleasure of seeing him, he was yet perfectly convinced that Edward ought not to remain in England, and was resolved to hasten his leaving it as soon as possible. But when he talked to Edward about it, he found him much less disposed towards returning to France than to accompany them in their projected tour, which, he assured his father, would be infinitely more pleasant to him; and that as to the affair of travelling, he considered it of no importance, and what might be pursued at any little odd time, when he had nothing better to do. He advanced these objections in a manner which plainly shewed that he had scarcely a doubt of their being complied with, and appeared to consider his father's arguments in opposition to them as merely given with a view to keep up his authority, and such as he should find little difficulty in combating. He concluded at last by saying, as the chaise in which they returned together from Mr Dudley's reached Mrs Percival's,

'Well, sir, we will settle this point some other time; and

fortunately it is of so little consequence that an immediate discussion of it is unnecessary.' He then got out of the chaise and entered the house without waiting for his father's reply.

It was not till their return that Kitty could account for that coldness in Camilla's behaviour to her, which had been so pointed as to render it impossible to be entirely unnoticed. When, however, they were seated in the coach with two other ladies, Miss Stanley's indignation was no longer to be suppressed from breaking out into words, and found the following vent.

'Well, I must say *this*, that I never was at a stupider ball in my life! But it always is so; I am always disappointed in them for some reason or other. I wish there were no such things.'

'I am sorry, Miss Stanley,' said Mrs Percival, drawing herself up, 'that you have not been amused; every thing was meant for the best I am sure, and it is a poor encouragement for your mama to take you to another if you are so hard to be satisfied.'

'I do not know what you mean, ma'am, about mama's *taking* me to another. You know I am come out.'

'Oh! dear Mrs Percival,' said Mrs Stanley, 'you must not believe everything that my lively Camilla says, for her spirits are prodigiously high sometimes, and she frequently speaks without thinking. I am sure it is impossible for any one to have been at a more elegant or agreable dance, and so she wishes to express herself, I am certain.'

'To be sure I do,' said Camilla very sulkily, 'only I must say that it is not very pleasant to have any body behave so rude to me as to be quite shocking! I am sure I am not at all offended, and should not care if all the world were to stand above me, but still it is extremely abominable, and what I cannot put up with. It is not that I mind it in the least, for I had just as soon stand at the bottom as at the top all night long, if it was not so very disagreable –. But to have a person come in the middle of the evening and take everybody's place is what I am not used to, and though I do not care a pin about it myself, I assure you I shall not easily forgive or forget it.'

This speech, which perfectly explained the whole affair to Kitty, was shortly followed on her side by a very submissive apology, for she had too much good sense to be proud of her family, and too much good nature to live at variance with any one. The excuses she made were delivered with so much real concern for the offence, and such unaffected sweetness, that it was almost impossible for Camilla to retain that anger which had occasioned them. She felt indeed most highly gratified to find that no insult had been intended and that Catharine was very far from forgetting the difference in their birth for which she could *now* only pity her; and her good humour being restored with the same ease in which it had been affected, she spoke with the highest delight of the evening, and declared that she had never before been at so pleasant a ball.

The same endeavours that had procured the forgiveness of Miss Stanley ensured to her the cordiality of her mother, and nothing was wanting but Mrs Percival's good humour to render the happiness of the others complete; but she, offended with Camilla for her affected superiority, still more so with her brother for coming to Chetwynde, and dissatisfied with the whole evening, continued silent and gloomy, and was a restraint on the vivacity of her companions.

She eagerly seized the very first opportunity which the next morning offered to her of speaking to Mr Stanley on the subject of his son's return, and after having expressed her opinion of its being a very silly affair that he came at all, concluded with desiring him to inform Mr Edward Stanley that it was a rule with her never to admit a young man into her house as a visitor for any length of time.

'I do not speak, sir,' she continued, 'out of any disrespect to you, but I could not answer it to myself to allow of his stay; there is no knowing what might be the consequence of it if he were to continue here, for girls nowadays will always give a handsome young man the preference before any other, though for why, I never could discover – for what, after all, is youth and beauty? It[35] is but a poor substitute for real worth and merit. Believe me, cousin, that what ever people may say to the contrary, there is certainly nothing like virtue for making us what we ought to be, and as to a young man's being young and handsome and having an agreable person, it is nothing at all to the purpose, for he had much better be respectable. I always *did* think so, and I always *shall*, and therefore you will oblige me very much by desiring your son to leave Chetwynde, or

I cannot be answerable for what may happen between him and my niece. You will be surprised to hear *me* say it,' she continued, lowering her voice, 'but truth will out, and I must own that Kitty is one of the most impudent[36] girls that ever existed. [Her intimacies with young men are abominable, and it is all the same to her who it is, no one comes amiss to her.][37] I assure you sir, that I have seen her sit and laugh and whisper with a young man whom she has not seen above half a dozen times. Her behaviour indeed is scandalous, and therefore I beg you will send your son away immediately, or everything will be at sixes and sevens.'

Mr Stanley, who from one part of her speech had scarcely known to what length her insinuations of Kitty's impudence were meant to extend, now endeavoured to quiet her fears on the occasion by assuring her that on every account he meant to allow only of his son's continuing that day with them, and that she might depend on his being more earnest in the affair from a wish of obliging her. He added also that he knew Edward to be very desirous himself of returning to France, as he wisely considered all time lost that did not forward the plans in which he was at present engaged – though he was but too well convinced of the contrary himself.

His assurance in some degree quieted Mrs Percival, and left her tolerably relieved of her cares and alarms, and better disposed to behave with civility towards his son during the short remainder of his stay at Chetwynde. Mr Stanley went immediately to Edward, to whom he repeated the conversation that had passed between Mrs Percival and himself, and strongly pointed out the necessity of his leaving Chetwynde the next day, since his word was already engaged for it. His son, however, appeared struck only by the ridiculous apprehensions of Mrs Percival; and highly delighted at having occasioned them himself, seemed engrossed alone in thinking how he might increase them, without attending to any other part of his father's conversation. Mr Stanley could get no determinate answer from him, and though he still hoped for the best, they parted almost in anger on his side.

His son, though by no means disposed to marry, or any otherwise attached to Miss Percival than as a good-natured, lively girl who seemed pleased with him, took infinite pleasure in alarming the jealous fears of her aunt by his attentions to her, without considering what effect they might have on the lady herself. He would always sit by her when she was in the room, appeared dissatisfied if she left it, and was the first to enquire whether she meant soon to return. He was delighted with her drawings, and enchanted with her performance on the harpsichord; everything that she said appeared to interest him. His conversation was addressed to her alone, and she seemed to be the sole object of his attention.

That such efforts should succeed, with one so tremblingly alive to every alarm of the kind as Mrs Percival, is by no means unnatural; and that they should have equal influence with her niece, whose imagination was lively and whose disposition romantic, who was already extremely pleased with him and of course desirous that he might be so with her, is as little to be wondered at. Every moment, as it added to the conviction of his liking her, made him still more pleasing, and strengthened in her mind a wish of knowing him better.

As for Mrs Percival, she was in tortures the whole day. Nothing that she had ever felt before on a similar occasion was to be compared to the sensations which then distracted her; her fears had never been so strongly, or indeed so reasonably, excited. Her dislike of Stanley, her anger at her niece, her impatience to have them separated, conquered every idea of propriety and good breeding; and though he had never mentioned any intention of leaving them the next day, she could not help asking him after dinner, in her eagerness to have him gone, at what time he meant to set out.

'Oh! ma'am,' replied he, 'if I am off by twelve at night, you may think yourself lucky; and if I am not, you can only blame yourself for having left so much as the *hour* of my departure to my own disposal.'

Mrs Percival coloured very highly at this speech; and without addressing herself to any one in particular, immediately began a long harangue on the shocking behaviour of modern young men, and the wonderful alteration that had taken place in them since her time, which she illustrated with many instructive anecdotes of the decorum and modesty which had marked the characters of those whom she had known when she had been young. This, however, did not prevent his walking in the garden with her niece, without any other companion, for nearly an hour in the course of the evening. They had left the room for that purpose with Camilla at a time when Mrs Percival had been out of it, nor was it for some time after her return to it that she could discover where they were.

Camilla had taken two or three turns with them in the walk which led to the arbour; but soon growing tired of listening to a conversation in which she was seldom invited to join, and from its turning occasionally on books, very little able to do it, she left them together in the arbour to wander alone to some other part of the garden, to eat the fruit, and examine Mrs Percival's greenhouse. Her absence was so far from being regretted, that it was scarcely noticed by them; and they continued conversing together on almost every subject, for Stanley seldom dwelt long on any, and had something to say on all, till they were interrupted by her aunt.

Kitty was by this time perfectly convinced that, both in natural abilities and acquired information, Edward Stanley was infinitely superior to his sister. Her desire of knowing that he was so had induced her to take every opportunity of turning the conversation on history, and they were very soon engaged in an historical dispute, for which no one was more calculated[38] than Stanley, who was so far from being really of any party that he had scarcely a fixed opinion on the subject. He could therefore always take either side, and always argue with temper. In his indifference on all such topics he was very unlike his companion, whose judgement being guided by her feelings, which were eager and warm, was easily decided; and though it was not always infallible, she defended it with a spirit and enthusiasm which marked her own reliance on it.

They had continued therefore for sometime conversing in this manner on the character of Richard the Third,[39] which he was warmly defending, when he suddenly seized hold of her hand, and exclaiming with great emotion, 'Upon my honour you are entirely mistaken,' pressed it passionately to his lips, and ran out of the arbour. Astonished at this behaviour, for which she was wholly unable to account, she continued for a few moments motionless on the seat where he had left her, and was then on the point of following him up the narrow walk through which he had passed, when on looking up the one that lay immediately before the arbour, she saw her aunt walking towards her with more than her usual quickness. This explained at once the reason of his leaving her, but his leaving her in such manner was rendered still more inexplicable by it. She felt a considerable degree of confusion at having been seen by her in such a place with Edward, and at having that part of his conduct for which she could not herself account witnessed by one to whom all gallantry was odious. She remained therefore confused, distressed, and irresolute, and suffered her aunt to approach her, without leaving the arbour.

Mrs Percival's looks were by no means calculated to animate the spirits of her niece, who in silence awaited her accusation, and in silence meditated her defence. After a few moments' suspense, for Mrs Percival was too much fatigued to speak immediately, she began with great anger and asperity the following harangue.

'Well; *this* is beyond anything I could have supposed. *Profligate* as I *knew* you to be, I was not prepared for such a sight. This is beyond anything you ever did before; beyond anything I ever heard of in my life! Such impudence I never witnessed before in such a girl! And this is the reward for all the cares I have taken in your education; for all my troubles and anxieties; and heaven knows how many they have been! All I wished for was to breed you up virtuously; I never wanted you to play upon the harpsichord, or draw better than any one else; but I had hoped to see you respectable and good; to see you able and willing to give an example of modesty and virtue to the young people here abouts. I bought you Blair's Sermons, and Cœlebs in Search of a Wife,[40] I gave you the key to my own library, and borrowed a great many good books of my neighbours for you, all to this purpose. But I might have spared myself the trouble. Oh! Catharine, you are an abandoned creature, and I do not know what will become of you.

'I am glad, however,' she continued, softening into some degree of mildness, 'to see that you have some shame for what you have done, and if you are really sorry for it, and your future life is a life of penitence and reformation, perhaps you may be forgiven. But I plainly see that everything is going to sixes and sevens and all order will soon be at an end throughout the kingdom.'

'Not however, ma'am, the sooner, I hope, from any conduct of mine,' said Catharine in a tone of great humility, 'for upon my honour I have done nothing this evening that can contribute to overthrow the establishment of the kingdom.'

'You are mistaken, child,' replied she; 'the welfare of every nation depends upon the virtue of its individuals, and any one who offends in so gross a manner against decorum and propriety is certainly hastening its ruin. You have been giving a bad example to the world, and the world is but too well disposed to receive such.'

'Pardon me, madam,' said her niece; 'but I *can* have given an example only to *you*, for you alone have seen the offence. Upon my word, however, there is no danger to fear from what I have done; Mr Stanley's behaviour has given me as much surprise as it has done to you, and I can only suppose that it was the effect of his high spirits, authorized in his opinion by our relationship. But do you consider, madam, that it is growing very late? Indeed, you had better return to the house.' This speech, as she well knew, would be unanswerable with her aunt, who instantly rose, and hurried away under so many apprehensions for her own health as banished for the time all anxiety about her niece, who walked quietly by her side, revolving within her own mind the occurrence that had given her aunt so much alarm.

'I am astonished at my own imprudence,' said Mrs Percival; 'how could I be so forgetful as to sit down out of doors at such a time of night? I shall certainly have a return of my rheumatism after it – I begin to feel very chill already. I must have caught a dreadful cold by this time – I am sure of being lain up all the winter after it –'

Then reckoning with her fingers, 'Let me see; this is July; the cold weather will soon be coming in – August – September – October – November – December – January – February – March – April – very likely I may not be tolerable again before May. I must and will have that arbour pulled down – it will be the death of me; who knows *now*, but what I may never recover – Such things *have* happened – my particular friend Miss Sarah Hutchinson's death was occasioned by nothing more – she stayed out late one evening in April, and got wet through, for it rained very hard, and never changed her clothes when she came home. It is unknown how many people have died in consequence of catching cold! I do not believe there is a disorder in the world except the smallpox which does not spring from it.'

It was in vain that Kitty endeavoured to convince her that her fears on the occasion were groundless; that it was not yet late enough to catch cold, and that even if it were, she might hope to escape any other complaint, and to recover in less than ten months. Mrs Percival only replied that she hoped she knew more of ill health than to be convinced in such a point by a girl who had always been perfectly well, and hurried up stairs leaving Kitty to make her apologies to Mr and Mrs Stanley for going to bed –. Though Mrs Percival seemed perfectly satisfied with the goodness of the apology herself, yet Kitty felt somewhat embarrassed to find that the only one she could offer to their visitors was that her aunt had *perhaps* caught cold, for Mrs Percival charged her to make light of it for fear of alarming them.

Mr and Mrs Stanley, however, who well knew that their cousin was easily terrified on that score, received the account of it with very little surprise, and all proper concern. Edward and his sister soon came in, and Kitty had no difficulty in gaining an explanation of his conduct from him, for he was too warm on the subject himself, and too eager to learn its success, to refrain from making immediate enquiries about it; and she could not help feeling both surprised and offended at the ease and indifference with which he owned that all his intentions had been to frighten her aunt by pretending an affection for *her*, a design so very incompatible with that partiality which she had at one time been almost convinced of his feeling for her.

It is true that she had not yet seen enough of him to be actually in love with him, yet she felt greatly disappointed that so handsome, so elegant, so lively a young man should be so perfectly free from any such sentiment as to make it his principal sport. There was a novelty in his character which to *her* was extremely pleasing; his person was uncommonly fine, his spirits and vivacity suited to her own; and his manners at once so animated and insinuating, that she thought it must be impossible for him to be otherwise than amiable, and was ready to give him credit for being perfectly so. He knew the powers of them himself; to them he had often been indebted for his father's forgiveness of faults which, had he been awkward and inelegant, would have appeared very serious; to them, even more than to his person or his fortune, he owed the regard which almost every one was disposed to feel for him, and which young women in particular were inclined to entertain. Their influence was acknowledged on the present occasion by Kitty, whose anger they entirely dispelled, and whose cheerfulness they had power not only to restore, but to raise –.

The evening passed off as agreably as the one that had preceded it; they continued talking to each other during the chief part of it, and such was the power of his address, and the brilliancy of his eyes, that when they parted for the night, though Catharine had but a few hours before totally given up the idea, yet she felt almost convinced again that he was really in love with her. She reflected on their past conversation, and though it had been on various and indifferent subjects, and she could not exactly recollect any speech on his side expressive of such a partiality, she was still, however, nearly certain of its being so. But fearful of being vain enough to suppose such a thing without sufficient reason, she resolved to suspend her final determination on it till the next day, and more especially till their parting, which she thought would infallibly explain his regard, if any he had.

The more she had seen of him, the more inclined was she to like him, and the more desirous that he should like *her*. She was convinced of his being naturally very clever and very well disposed; and that his thoughtlessness and negligence – which though they appeared to *her* as very becoming in *him*, she was aware would by many people be considered as defects in his character – merely proceeded from a vivacity always pleasing in young men, and were far from testifying a weak or vacant understanding.

Having settled this point within herself, and being perfectly convinced by her own arguments of its truth, she went to bed in high spirits, determined to study his character and watch his behaviour still more the next day. She got up with the same good resolutions and would probably have put them in execution, had not Anne informed her as soon as she entered the room that Mr Edward Stanley was already gone. At first she refused to credit the information, but when her maid assured her that he had ordered a carriage the evening before to be there at seven o'clock in the morning, and that she herself had actually seen him depart in it a little after eight, she could no longer deny her belief to it.

'And this,' thought she to herself, blushing with anger at her own folly, 'this is the affection for me of which I was so certain. Oh! what a silly thing is woman! How vain, how unreasonable! To suppose that a young man would be seriously attached in the course of four and twenty hours to a girl who has nothing to recommend her but a good pair of eyes! And he is really gone! Gone perhaps without bestowing a thought on me! Oh! why was not I up by eight o'clock? But it is a proper punishment for my laziness and folly, and I am heartily glad of it. I deserve it all, and ten times more, for such insufferable vanity. It will at least be of service to me in that respect; it will teach me in future *not* to think every body is in love with me.[41]

'Yet I should like to have seen him before he went, for perhaps it may be many years before we meet again. By his manner of leaving us, however, he seems to have been perfectly indifferent about it. How very odd, that he should go without giving us notice of it, or taking leave of any one! But it is just like a young man, governed by the whim of the moment, or actuated merely by the love of doing anything oddly! Unaccountable beings indeed! And young women are equally ridiculous! I shall soon begin to think, like my aunt, that everything is going to sixes and sevens, and that the whole race of mankind are degenerating.'

She was just dressed, and on the point of leaving her room to make her personal enquiries after Mrs Percival, when Miss Stanley knocked at her door, and on her being admitted, began in her usual strain a long harangue upon her father's being so shocking as to make Edward go at all, and upon Edward's being so horrid as to leave them at such an hour in the morning.

'You have no idea,' said she, 'how surprised I was, when he came into my room to bid me good-bye –'

'Have you seen him then, this morning?' said Kitty.

'Oh yes! and I was so sleepy that I could not open my eyes. And so he said, "Camilla, good-bye to you, for I am going away –. I have not time to take leave of any body else, and I dare not trust myself to see Kitty, for then you know I should never get away –" '

'Nonsense,' said Kitty; 'he did not say that, or he was in joke, if he did.'

'Oh! no I assure you he was as much in earnest as he ever was in his life; he was too much out of spirits to joke then. And he desired me, when we all met at breakfast, to give his compliments to your aunt, and his love to you, for you was a nice girl, he said, and he only wished it were in his power to be more with you. You were just the girl to suit him, because you were so lively and good-natured, and he wished with all his heart that you might not be married before he came back, for there was nothing he liked better than being here. Oh! you have no idea what fine things he said about you, till at last I fell asleep and he went away. But he certainly is in love with you – I am sure he is – I have thought so a great while, I assure you.'

'How can you be so ridiculous?' said Kitty, smiling with pleasure. 'I do not believe him to be so easily affected. But he did desire his love to me then? And wished I might not be married before his return? And said I was a nice girl, did he?'

'Oh! dear, yes, and I assure you it is the greatest praise in his opinion, that he can bestow on any body; I can hardly ever persuade him to call me one, though I beg him sometimes for an hour together.'

'And do you really think that he was sorry to go?'

'Oh! you can have no idea how wretched it made him. He would not have gone this month, if my father had not insisted on it; Edward told me so himself yesterday. He said that he wished with all his heart he had never promised to go abroad, for that he repented it more and more every day; that it interfered with all his other schemes, and that since papa had spoken to him about it, he was more unwilling to leave Chetwynde than ever.'

'Did he really say all this? And why would your father insist upon his going? – "His leaving England interfered with all his other plans, and his conversation with Mr Stanley had made him still more averse to it" – what can this mean?'

'Why that he is excessively in love with you to be sure; what other plans can he have? And I suppose my father said that if he had not been going abroad, he should have wished him to marry you immediately. – But I must go and see your aunt's plants –.

There is one of them that I quite doat on – and two or three more besides –'

'Can Camilla's explanation be true?' said Catharine to herself, when her friend had left the room. 'And after all my doubts and uncertainties, can Stanley really be averse to leaving England for my sake only? – His plans interrupted – and what indeed can his plans be, but towards marriage? Yet so soon to be in love with me! – But it is the effect perhaps only of a warmth of heart, which to me is the highest recommendation in any one. A heart disposed to love – and such under the appearance of so much gaiety and inattention – is Stanley's! Oh! how much does it endear him to me! But he is gone – gone perhaps for years. Obliged to tear himself from what he most loves, his happiness is sacrificed to the vanity of his father! In what anguish he must have left the house! Unable to see me, or to bid me adieu, while I, senseless wretch, was daring to sleep. This, then, explained his leaving us at such a time of day –. He could not trust himself to see me –. Charming young man! How much must you have suffered! I knew that it was impossible for one so elegant, and so well bred, to leave any family in such a manner, but for a motive like this unanswerable.' Satisfied beyond the power of change of this, she went in high spirits to her aunt's apartment, without giving a moment's recollection on the vanity of young women, or the unaccountable conduct of young men.[42]

Kitty continued in this state of satisfaction during the remainder of the Stanleys' visit, who took their leave with many pressing invitations to visit them in London, when, as Camilla said, she might have an opportunity of becoming acquainted with that sweet girl Augusta Halifax – or rather, thought Kitty, of seeing my dear Mary Wynne again. Mrs Percival, in answer to Mrs Stanley's invitation, replied that she looked upon London as the hothouse of vice, where virtue had long been banished from society, and wickedness of every description was daily gaining ground; that Kitty was of herself sufficiently inclined to give way to, and indulge in, vicious inclinations, and therefore was the last girl in the world to be trusted in London, as she would be totally unable to withstand temptation –.

After the departure of the Stanleys Kitty returned to her usual occupations, but alas! they had lost their power of pleasing. Her bower alone retained its interest in her feelings, and perhaps that was owing to the particular remembrance it brought to her mind of Edward Stanley.

The summer passed away unmarked by any incident worth narrating, or any pleasure to Catharine, save one, which arose from the receipt of a letter from her friend Cecilia, now Mrs Lascelles, announcing the speedy return of herself and husband to England.

A correspondence productive indeed of little pleasure to either party had been established between Camilla and Catharine. The latter had now lost the only satisfaction she had ever received from the letters of Miss Stanley, as that young lady, having informed her friend of the departure of her brother to Lyons, now never mentioned his name. Her letters seldom contained any intelligence except a description of some new article of dress, an enumeration of various engagements, a panegyric on Augusta Halifax, and perhaps a little abuse of the unfortunate Sir Peter.

The Grove, for so was the mansion of Mrs Percival at Chetwynde denominated, was situated within five miles from Exeter, but though that lady possessed a carriage and horses of her own, it was seldom that Catharine could prevail on her to visit that town for the purpose of shopping, on account of the many officers perpetually quartered there, and infesting the principal streets.

A company of strolling players, in their way from some neighbouring races, having opened a temporary theatre there, Mrs Percival was prevailed on by her niece to indulge her by attending the performance once during their stay. Mrs Percival insisted on paying Miss Dudley the compliment of inviting her to join the party, when a new difficulty arose, from the necessity of having some gentleman to attend them –

CHARLOTTE BRONTË

PART I

Origins of Angria

❋

The History of the Year[1]

Once papa lent my sister Maria a book. It was an old geography book. She wrote on its blank leaf, 'Papa lent me this book.' This book is a hundred and twenty years old; it is at this moment lying before me. While I write this I am in the kitchen of the parsonage, Haworth. Tabby, the servant, is washing up the breakfast things, and Anne, my younger sister (Maria was my eldest), is kneeling on a chair, looking at some cakes which Tabby had been baking for us. Emily is in the parlour, brushing the carpet. Papa and Branwell are gone to Keighley. Aunt is upstairs in her room, and I am sitting by the table writing this in the kitchen.

Keighley is a small town four miles from here. Papa and Branwell are gone for the newspaper, the *Leeds Intelligencer*, a most excellent Tory newspaper, edited by Mr Wood, and the proprietor, Mr Henneman. We take two and see three newspapers a week. We take the *Leeds Intelligencer*, Tory, and the *Leeds Mercury*, Whig, edited by Mr Baines, and his brother, son-in-law, and his two sons, Edward and Talbot. We see the *John Bull*. It is high Tory, very violent. Dr Driver lends us it, as likewise *Blackwood's Magazine*, the most able periodical there is. The editor is Mr Christopher North, an old man seventy-four years of age; the 1st of April is his birthday; his company are Timothy Tickler, Morgan O'Doherty, Macrabin Mordecai, Mullion, Warnell, and James Hogg, a man of most extraordinary genius, a Scottish shepherd.

Our plays were established: *Young Men*, June 1826; *Our Fellows*, July 1827; *Islanders*, December 1827. These are our three great plays that are not kept secret. Emily's and my bed plays were established December 1, 1827; the others March 1828. Bed plays mean secret plays; they are very nice ones. All our plays are very strange ones. Their nature I need not write on paper, for I think I shall always remember them. The *Young Men*'s play took its rise from some wooden soldiers Branwell had; *Our Fellows* from *Aesop's Fables*; and the *Islanders* from several events which happened.

I will sketch out the origin of our plays more explicitly if I can. First, *Young Men*. Papa bought Branwell some wooden soldiers at Leeds. When Papa came home it was night, and we were in bed, so next morning Branwell came to our door with a box of soldiers. Emily and I jumped out of bed, and I snatched up one and exclaimed, 'This is the Duke of Wellington! This shall be the duke!' When I had said this Emily likewise took up one and said it should be hers; when Anne came down she said one should be hers. Mine was the prettiest of the whole, and the tallest, and the most perfect in every part. Emily's was a grave-looking fellow, and we called him 'Gravey'. Anne's was a queer little thing, much like herself, and we called him 'Waiting-boy'. Branwell chose his and called him 'Buonaparte.'

March, 1829

Two Romantic Tales

1. THE TWELVE ADVENTURERS

There is a tradition that some thousands of years ago twelve men from Britain, of a most gigantic size, and twelve men from Gaul, came over to the country of the genii; while there they were continually at war with each other, and, after remaining many years, returned again to Britain and Gaul. And in the inhabited parts of the genii country there are now no vestiges of them, though it is said there have been found some colossal skeletons in that wild, barren land, the evil desert.

But I have read a book called *The Travels of Captain Parnell*, out of which the following is an extract:

'About four in the afternoon I saw a dark red cloud arise in the east, which gradually grew larger till it covered the whole sky. As the cloud spread, the wind rose, and blew a tremendous hurricane. The sand of the desert began to move and rolled like the waves of the sea. As soon as I saw this I threw myself on my face and stopped my breath, for I knew that this was the tornado, or whirlwind. I remained in this situation for three minutes, for at the end of that time I ventured to look up. The whirlwind had passed over and had not hurt *me*, but close by lay my poor camel, quite dead. At this sight I could not forbear weeping, but my attention was soon diverted by another object. About one hundred yards further off lay an immense skeleton. I immediately ran up to it, and examined it closely. While I was gazing at the long, ghastly figure which lay stretched upon the sand before me, the thought came into my mind that it might be the skeleton of one of those ancient Britons who, tradition tells us, came from their own country to this evil land, and here miserably perished.

'While I was pursuing this train of meditation, I observed that it was bound with a long chain of rusty iron. Suddenly the iron clanked and the bones strove to rise, but a huge mountain of sand overwhelmed the skeleton with a tremendous crash, and when the dust which had hid the sun and enveloped everything in darkness cleared away, not a mark could be distinguished to show the future traveller where the bones had lain.'

Now, if this account be true – and I see no reason why we should suppose it is not – I think we may fairly conclude that these skeletons are evil genii chained in these deserts by the fairy Maimoune.[3]

There are several other traditions, but they are all so obscure that no reliance is to be placed on them.

*

In the year 1793 the *Invincible*, 74 guns, set sail with a fair wind from England, her crew, twelve men, every one healthy and stout and in the best temper.[4] Their names as follows:

Marcus O'Donell,	Ronald Traquair,
Ferdinand Cortez,	Ernest Fortescue,
Felix de Rothesay,	Gustavus Dunally,
Eugene Cameron,	Frederick Brunswick
Harold FitzGeorge,	and
Henry Clinton,	Arthur Wellesley.
Francis Stewart,	

Well, as I said before, we set sail with a fair wind from England on the 1st of March 1793. On the 15th we came in sight of Spain. On the 16th we landed, bought a supply of provisions, and set sail again on the 20th. On the 25th, about noon, Henry Clinton, who was in the shrouds, cried out that he saw the oxeye.[5]

In a minute we were all on deck and all eyes gazing eagerly and fearfully towards the mountain over which we saw hanging in the sky the ominous speck. Instantly the sails were furled, the ship tacked about, and the boat was made ready for launching in our last extremity.

Thus having made everything ready we retired to the cabin; everyone looked as sheepish as possible, and no way inclined to meet our fate like men. Some of us began to cry, but we waited a long time and heard no sound of the wind, and the cloud did not increase in size. At last Marcus O'Donell exclaimed,

'I wish it would either go backward or forward.'

At this Stewart reproved him, and Ferdinand gave him a box on the ear. O'Donell returned the compliment; but just then we heard the sound of the wind, and Ronald bawled out:

'The cloud is as big as me!'

We were all silenced by a fierce flash of lightning and a loud peal of thunder. The wind rose and the planks of our ship creaked. Another flash of lightning, brighter and more terrible than the first, split our mainmast and carried away our fore topsail. And now the flashes of lightning grew terrific, and the thunder roared tremendously. The rain poured down in torrents, and the gusts of wind were most loud and terrible. The hearts of the stoutest men in our company now quailed, and even the chief doctor was afraid.

At last the storm ceased, but we found it had driven us quite out of our course, and we knew not where we were. On the 30th, G. Dunally, who was on deck, cried out,

'Land!'

We sailed along the coast for some time to find a good landing place. We at last found one, and landed on the 2nd of June, 1793. We moored our battered ship in a small harbour and advanced up into the country. To our great surprise we found it cultivated. Grain of a peculiar sort grew in great abundance, and there were large plantations of palm trees, and likewise an immense number of almond trees. There were also many olives, and large enclosures of rice. We were greatly surprised at these marks of the land being inhabited. It seemed to be a part of an immense continent.

After we had travelled about two miles, we saw at a distance twenty men, well-armed. We immediately prepared for battle, having each of us a pistol, sword, and bayonet. We stood still and they came near. When they had come close up to us, they likewise stopped. They seemed greatly surprised at us, and we heard one of them say,

'What strange people!' The chief then said,

'Who are you?' Wellesley answered,

'We were cast up on your shores by a storm, and request shelter.'

They said, 'You shall not have any.'

W.: 'We will take it, then!' We prepared for battle; they did the same.

It was a very fierce encounter, but we conquered: killed ten, took the chief prisoner, wounded five, and the remaining four retreated. The chief was quite black, very tall. He had a fierce countenance, and the finest eyes I ever saw. We asked him what his name was, but he would not speak. We asked him the name of his country, and he said,

'Ashantee.'

Next morning a party of twelve men came to our tents bringing with them a ransom for their chief, and likewise a proposition of peace from their king. This we accepted, as it was on terms the most advantageous to ourselves.

Immediately after the treaty of peace was concluded, we set about building a city. The situation was in the middle of a large plain, bounded on the north by high mountains, on the south by the sea, on the east by gloomy forests, and on the west by evil deserts.

About a month after we had begun our city the following adventures happened to us.

One evening, when all were assembled in the great tent, most of us sitting round the fire which blazed in the middle of the pavilion, listening to the storm which raged without our camp, a dead silence prevailed. None of us felt inclined to speak, still less to laugh, and the wine cups stood upon the round table filled to the brim. In the midst of this silence we heard the sound of a trumpet which seemed to come from the desert. The next moment, a peal of thunder rolled through the sky, which seemed to shake the earth to its centre.

By this time we were all on our legs, and filled with terror which was changed to desperation by another blast of the terrible trumpet. We all rushed out of the tent with a shout, not of courage, but fear; and then we saw a sight so terribly grand that even now when I think of it, at the distance of forty years from that dismal night when I saw it, my limbs tremble and my blood is chilled with fear. High in the clouds was a tall and terrible giant. In his right hand he held a trumpet; in his left, two darts pointed with fire. On a thunder cloud, which rolled before him, his shield rested. On his forehead was written: 'The Genius[6] of the Storm.' On he strode, over the black clouds which rolled beneath his feet, regardless of the fierce lightning which flashed around him. But soon the thunder ceased and the lightning no longer glared so terribly.

The hoarse voice of the storm was hushed, and a gentler light than the fire of the elements spread itself over the face of the now cloudless sky. The calm moon shone forth in the midst of the firmament, and the little stars seemed rejoicing in their brightness. The giant had descended to the earth, and approaching the place where we stood trembling, he made three circles in the air with his flaming scimitar, then lifted his hand to strike. Just then we heard a loud voice saying,

'Genius, I command thee to forbear!'

We looked round and saw a figure so tall that the genius seemed to it but a diminutive dwarf. It cast one joyful glance on us and disappeared.

[The building of the new city proceeds so expeditiously that all are convinced they are receiving supernatural assistance from the genii. At a meeting in the Grand Hall Arthur Wellesley suggests that reinforcements from England be sent for before the Ashantees renew their hostilities. But the proceedings are interrupted by an imperious genie who orders them to undertake an arduous desert journey, the purpose of which is that Arthur's predestined dukedom, and subsequent conflict with Napoleon, shall be revealed.]

We reached the desert about 4 a.m. There we stopped. Far off to the east the long black line of gloomy forests skirted the horizon. To the north the Mountains of the Moon seemed a misty girdle to the plain; to the south the ocean guarded the coasts of Africa; before us to the west lay the desert.

In a few minutes we saw a dense vapour arise from the sands, which, gradually collecting, took the form of a genius larger than any of the giants. It advanced towards us and cried with a loud voice;

'Follow me!' We obeyed and entered the desert.

After we had travelled a long time, about noon, the genius told us to look around. We were now about the middle of the desert. Nothing was to be seen far or near but vast plains of sand under a burning sun and cloudless sky. We were dreadfully fatigued and begged the genius to allow us to stop a little, but he immediately ordered us to proceed. We therefore began our march again and travelled a long way, till the sun went down and the pale moon was rising in the east. Also a few stars might now be dimly seen, but still the sands were burning hot, and our feet were very much swollen.

At last the genius ordered us to halt and lie down. We soon fell asleep. We had slept about an hour when the genius awoke us and ordered us to proceed.

The moon had now risen and shone brightly in the midst of the sky – brighter far than it ever does in our country. The night wind had somewhat cooled the sands of the desert, so that we walked with more ease than before; but soon a mist arose which covered the whole plain. Through it we thought we could discern a dim light. We now likewise heard sounds of music at a great distance.

As the mist cleared away, the light grew more distinct till it burst upon us in almost insufferable splendour. Out of the barren desert arose a palace of diamond, the pillars of which were ruby and emerald illuminated with lamps too bright to look upon. The genius led us into a hall of sapphire in which were thrones of gold. On the thrones sat the princes of the genii. In the midst of the hall hung a lamp like the sun. Around it stood genii and fairies, whose robes were of beaten gold, sparkling with diamonds.[7]

As soon as their chiefs saw us they sprang up from their thrones, and one of them, seizing Arthur Wellesley, exclaimed,

'This is the Duke of Wellington!'[8] Arthur Wellesley asked her why she called him the Duke of Wellington. The genius answered,

'A prince will arise who shall be as a thorn in the side of England, and the desolator of Europe. Terrible shall be the struggle between that chieftain and you! It will last many years, and the conqueror shall gain eternal honour and glory. So likewise shall the vanquished; and though he shall die in exile his name shall never be remembered by his countrymen but with feelings of enthusiasm. The renown of the victor shall reach to the ends of the earth; kings and emperors shall honour him; and Europe shall rejoice in its deliverer; though in his lifetime fools will envy him, he shall overcome. At his death renown shall cover him, and his name shall be everlasting!'

When the genius finished speaking, we heard the sound of music far off, which drew nearer and nearer till it seemed within the hall. Then all the fairies and genii joined in one grand chorus which rose rolling to the mighty dome and stately pillars of the genii palace, and reached among the vaults and dungeons beneath; then, gradually dying away, it at last ceased entirely.

As the music went off the palace slowly disappeared, till it vanished and we found ourselves alone in the midst of the desert. The sun had just begun to enlighten the world, and the moon might be dimly seen; but all below them was sand as far as our eyes could reach. We knew not which way to go, and we were ready to faint with hunger; but on once more looking round we saw, lying on the sands, some dates and palm wine. Of this we made our breakfast, and then began again to think of our journey; suddenly there appeared a beaten track in the desert, which we followed.

About noon, when the sun was at its meridian, and we felt weary and faint with the heat, a grove of palm trees appeared in sight towards which we ran; and after we had reposed awhile under its shade, and refreshed ourselves with its fruit, we resumed our march; that same night, to our inexpressible joy, we entered the gates of our beautiful city and slept beneath the shadow of its roofs.

The next morning we awoke to the sound of trumpets and great war drums, and on looking towards the mountains, we saw descending on the plain an immense army of Ashantees. We were all thrown into the utmost consternation except Arthur Wellesley, who advised us to look to the great guns and to man the walls, never doubting that the genii would come to our help if we of ourselves could not beat them off by the help of the cannon and rockets.

This advice we immediately followed, while the Ashantees came on like a torrent, sweeping everything, burning the palm trees, and laying waste the rice fields.

When they came up to the walls of our city they set up a terrible yell, the meaning of which was that we should be consumed from the face of the earth, and that our city should vanish away; for as it came by magic it should go by the same. Our answer to this insolent speech was a peal of thunder from the mouths of our cannon. Two fell dead, and the rest gave us leg bail, setting off towards the mountains with inconceivable swiftness, followed by a triumphant shout from their conquerors.

They came back in the afternoon, and in the most submissive terms asked for their dead. We granted their request, and in return, they allowed us to witness the funeral a few days after.

On the 21st of September, Ronald came running into the Hall of Justice where we all were, shouting out that there was a ship from England. The Duke of York immediately sent Arthur Wellesley to ascertain the truth of this.

When he arrived at the seashore he found all the crew, consisting of fifty men, had landed. He then examined the state of the ship, and found it was almost a complete wreck. He asked the men a few questions and they seemed greatly surprised to find him here, and asked him how he contrived to live in such a country. He told them to follow him.

When he brought them to the Hall of Justice, the Duke of York ordered them to relate their story. They cried,

'We were driven on your shore by a storm, and request shelter.' The Duke of York answered,

'Fellow-English, we rejoice that you were driven on our part of the coast, and you shall have shelter if we can give it.'

Accordingly they remained with us about a fortnight, for at the end of that time the genii had fitted out their ship again, when they set sail for England accompanied by Arthur Wellesley.

For about ten years after this we continued at war with the blacks, and then made peace; after which, for about ten years more, nothing happened worth mentioning. On the 16th of May 1816, a voice passed through the city saying,

'Set a watch on the tower which looks towards the south, for tomorrow a conqueror shall enter your gates!' The Duke of York immediately despatched Henry Clinton to the highest tower in the city. About noon Clinton cried out,

'I see something at a great distance upon the Atlantic.'

We all of us ran to the watchtower; on looking toward the ocean, we could discern a dark object upon the verge of the horizon, which, as it neared the shore, we saw plainly was a fleet. At last it anchored and the crew began to land.

First came 12 regiments of horsemen; next, three of infantry; then several high officers, who seemed to be the staff of some great general. Last of all came the general himself, whom several of us asserted had the bearing of Arthur Wellesley.

After he had marshalled the regiments, he ordered them to march, and we saw them enter the gates of the city. When they arrived at the tower they stopped, and we heard the general, in the tone of Wellesley, say,

'Hill, you may stop here with the army while I go to the Palace of Justice, as I suppose they are all there if they be yet in the land of the living. And, Beresford, you must come with me.'

'No, no, we are here, Arthur, almost terrified out of our wits for fear you shall burn the tower and sack the city!' exclaimed the Duke of York as we descended from our hiding place.

'What! Are you all here, and not one of you slain in battle or dead in the hospital?' said his grace. He sprang from his war horse, and we shook hands with him one at a time.

'But come, my brave fellows, let us go to the Grand Inn, and in

Ferdinando Hall we will talk of what we have done and suffered since we last met.'

'The army are to follow His Grace the Duke of Wellington,' said one of the staff.

'His Grace the Duke of Wellington!' we all exclaimed at once in surprise.

'Yes – His Grace the Duke of Wellington,' said another of the staff. 'I don't know who you are, but our most noble general is the conqueror of Bonaparte and the deliverer of Europe.'

'Then the genii don't always tell lies,' said Marcus O'Donell; 'and I am very glad of it, for I always thought, duke, you would return to us with more glory than you had when you went away from us.'

'Indeed,' said Murray with a sneer.

'Murray,' said his grace sternly, 'I shall call you to account for this insolence and punish by martial law if you don't make a handsome apology to this gentleman.'

Murray immediately advanced to O'Donell and said, 'Sir, I am very sorry for my foolish insolence and I promise you I will never offend you so again.'

'Very well, Murray, very well indeed,' said the duke. 'Now shake hands and be friends. I hate civil war.'9

By this time we had arrived at the Grand Inn, which was large enough to accommodate 20,000 men. We were soon seated in the hall and listening to Beresford, as he related to us how Europe had been set free from the iron chain of a despot, and how the mighty victory had been achieved with which all the civilized world had rung; of the splendid triumphs which had taken place on that glorious occasion; and how all the high sovereigns of Europe had honoured England with their presence on that grand occasion. Longer could we have listened and more could he have told had we not heard the sound of the midnight bell, which reminded us that it was time to retire to rest.

Some days after this, the Duke of York expressed a wish to return to his own country, and one of the ships with about twenty men were appointed to convey him there.

There were now in the city fifteen thousand men,10 and we determined to elect a king. Accordingly a council of the whole

nation was summoned for the 14th of June 1827.[11] On that day
they all assembled in the Palace of Justice. Around the throne sat
Marcus O'Donell, F. Cortez, H. Clinton, G. Dunally, Harold
FitzGeorge and the Duke of Wellington and his staff.

An intense anxiety pervaded the council to know who would be
proposed as king, for not a man of us knew, and no hints had been
thrown out. At length the great entrance was closed, and Cortez
proclaimed the whole nation to be present. Stewart then rose and
said,

'I propose the most noble field marshal Arthur, Duke of
Wellington, as a fit and proper person to sit on the throne of these
realms.'

Immediately a loud shout burst forth from the multitude, and
the hall rang. 'Long live our most noble duke!' Wellington now
rose. Immediately a profound silence pervaded the house. He said
as follows,

'Soldiers, I will defend what you have committed to my care.'
Then, bowing to the council, he retired amidst thundering sounds
of enthusiastic joy.

2. AN ADVENTURE IN IRELAND

During my travels in the south of Ireland, the following adventure
happened to me. One evening in the month of August, after a long
walk, I was ascending the mountain which overlooks the village of
Cahin, when I suddenly came in sight of a fine old castle. It was
built upon a rock, and behind it was a large wood, and before it
was a river. Over the river there was a bridge, which formed the
approach to the castle.

When I arrived at the bridge, I stood still awhile to enjoy the
prospect around me. Far below was the wide sheet of still water in
which the reflection of the pale moon was not disturbed by the
smallest wave. In the valley was the cluster of cabins which is
known by the appellation of Cahin, and beyond these were the
mountains of Killala. Over all the grey robe of twilight was now
stealing with silent and scarcely perceptible advances. No sound
except the distant village and the sweet song of the nightingales in
the wood behind me broke upon the stillness of the scene.

While I was contemplating this beautiful prospect, a gentleman, whom I had not before observed, accosted me with,

'Good evening, sir, are you a stranger in these parts?'

[The speaker turns out to be Mr O'Callaghan, owner of the castle, who invites him to be his guest for the night.]

After supper, Mr O'Callaghan asked me if I should like to retire for the night. I answered in the affirmative, and a little boy was commissioned to show me to my apartment. It was a snug, clean, and comfortable little old-fashioned room at the top of the castle.[12] As soon as we had entered, the boy, who appeared to be a shrewd, good-tempered little fellow, said with a shrug of his shoulder,

'If it was going to bed I was, it shouldn't be here that you'd catch me.'

'Why?' said I.

'Because,' replied the boy, 'they say that the ould masther's ghost has been seen sitting on that there chair.'

'And have you seen him?'

'No, but I've heard him washing his hands in that basin often and often.'

'What is your name, my little fellow?'

'Dennis Mulready, please your honour.'

'Well, good night to you.'

'Good night, masther. And may the saints keep you from all fairies and brownies,' said Dennis as he left the room.

As soon as I had laid down I began to think of what the boy had been telling me, and I confess I felt a strange kind of fear, and once or twice I thought I could discern something white in the darkness which surrounded me. At length, by the help of reason, I succeeded in mastering these (what some would call idle) fancies, and fell asleep.

I had slept about an hour when a strange sound awoke me, and I saw, looking through my curtains, a skeleton wrapped in a white sheet. I was overcome with terror and tried to scream, but my tongue was paralysed and my whole frame shook with fear. In a deep, hollow voice it said to me,

'Arise, that I may show you the world's wonders,' and in an instant I found myself encompassed with clouds and darkness. But

soon the roar of mighty waters fell upon my ear, and I saw some
clouds of spray arising from high falls that rolled in awful majesty
down tremendous precipices, and then foamed and thundered in
the gulf beneath. The scene changed, and I found myself in the
mines of Cracone. There were high pillars and stately arches,
whose glittering splendour was never excelled by the brightest fairy
palaces. But in the midst of all this magnificence I felt an
indescribable sense of fear and terror, for the sea raged above us,
and by the awful and tumultuous noises of roaring winds and
dashing waves, it seemed as if the storm was violent. And now the
mossy pillars groaned beneath the pressure of the ocean, and the
glittering arches seemed about to be overwhelmed. When I heard
the rushing waters, and saw a mighty flood rolling towards me, I
gave a loud shriek of terror.

The scene vanished and I found myself in a wide desert full of
barren rocks and high mountains. As I was approaching one of the
rocks, my foot stumbled, and I fell. Just then I heard a deep growl,
and saw by the unearthly light of his own fiery eyes a royal lion
rousing himself; he sprang towards me . . .

'Well, masther, it's been a windy night, though it's fine now,'
said Dennis as he drew the window curtain and let the bright rays
of the morning sun into the little old-fashioned room at the top of
O'Callaghan Castle.

April, 1829

PART II

Marian v. Zenobia

✻

Characters of Celebrated Men

[The Duke of Wellington's elder son, Arthur Adrian Augustus, Marquis of Douro, is to become the central male figure of Charlotte's early work, increasingly sinister as the years pass, though at first a beautiful, poetic youth. An early, benign portrait follows, contrasted with one of Branwell's hero, Alexander Percy, or Rogue, with whom Arthur will develop an intricate love-hate relationship.]

CHARACTER OF THE MARQUIS OF DOURO

The eldest of these young noblemen, the Marquis of Douro, is now in the 22nd year of his age.[1] In appearance he strongly resembles his noble mother. He has the same tall, slender shape, the same fine and slightly Roman nose. His eyes, however, are large and brown like his father's, and his hair is dark auburn, curly and glossy, much like what his father's was when he was young. His character also resembles the duchess's: mild and humane, but very courageous; grateful for any favour that is done, and ready to forgive injuries; kind to others and disinterested in himself.

His mind is of the highest order, elegant and cultivated. His genius is lofty and soaring, but he delights to dwell among pensive thoughts and ideas rather than to roam in the bright regions of fancy. In short, the Marquis of Douro's strains are like the soft reverberations of an Æolian harp which, as its notes alternately die and swell, raise the soul to a pitch of wild sublimity or lead it to mournful and solemn thought. And when you rise from the perusal of his works, you are prone to meditate, without knowing the cause; only you can think of nothing else but the years of your childhood, and bright days now fled for ever. The meditations of a lonely traveller in the wilderness, or the mournful song of a solitary exile, are the themes in which he most delights and which he chiefly indulges in, though often his songs consist of grand and vivid descriptions of storms and tempests: of the wild roaring of the ocean mingling with the tremendous voice of thunder, when the flashing lightning gleams in unison with the bright lamp of some wicked spirit striding over the face of the troubled waters, or sending forth his cry from the bosom of a black and terrible cloud. Such is the Marquis of Douro.

CHARACTER OF ROGUE

Rogue is about 47 years of age. He is very tall, rather spare. His countenance is handsome, except that there is something very startling in his fierce grey eyes and formidable forehead. His manner is rather polished and gentlemanly, but his mind is deceitful, bloody, and cruel. His walk (in which he much prides himself) is stately and soldierlike, and he fancies that it greatly resembles that of the Duke of Wellington. He dances well and plays cards admirably, being skilled in all the sleight-of-hand blackleg tricks of the gaming table. And to crown all he is excessively vain of this (what he terms) accomplishment.

December, 1829

Albion and Marina[2]

[This tale initiates the theme of the love triangle which remains Charlotte's subject in the next few pieces: Arthur and Marian are young lovers, who eventually marry; Zenobia is Marian's passionate rival.]

I

There is a certain sweet little pastoral village in the south of England with which I am better acquainted than most men. The scenery around it possesses no distinguished characteristic of romantic grandeur or wildness that might figure to advantage in a novel, to which high title this brief narrative sets up no pretensions.

Neither rugged lofty rocks, nor mountains dimly huge, mark with frowns the undisturbed face of nature; but little peaceful valleys, low hills crowned with wood, murmuring cascades and streamlets, richly cultivated fields, farmhouses, cottages, and a wide river, form all the scenic features. And every hamlet has one or more great men.

This had one and he was 'na sheepshank'.[3] Every ear in the world had heard of his fame, and every tongue could bear testimony to it. I shall name him the Duke of Strathelleraye, and by that name the village was likewise denominated.

For more than thirty miles around every inch of ground belonged to him and every man was his retainer.

The magnificent villa, or rather palace, of this noble, stood on an eminence, surrounded by a vast park and the embowering shade of an ancient wood, proudly seeming to claim the allegiance of all the countryside.

The mind, achievements, and character of its great possessor, must not, *can* not, be depicted by a pen so feeble as mine; for though I could call filial love and devoted admiration to my aid, yet both would be utterly ineffective.

Though the duke seldom himself came among his attached vassals, being detained elsewhere by important avocations, yet his lady the duchess resided in the castle constantly. Of her I can only say that she was like an earthly angel. Her mind was composed of charity, beneficence, gentleness, and sweetness. All, both old and young, loved her; and the blessings of those that were ready to perish came upon her evermore.

His grace had also two sons, who often visited Strathelleraye. Of the youngest, Lord Cornelius, everything is said when I inform the reader that he was seventeen years of age, grave, sententious, stoical, rather haughty and sarcastic, of a fine countenance, though somewhat swarthy; that he had long thick hair black as the hoody's wing;[4] and liked nothing so well as to sit in moody silence musing over the vanity of human affairs, or improving and expanding his mind by the abstruse study of the higher branches of mathematics, and that sublime science, astronomy.

The eldest son, Albion,[5] Marquis of Tagus, is the hero of my present tale. He had entered his nineteenth year, his stature was lofty, his form equal in the magnificence of its proportions to that of Apollo Belvedere.[6] The bright wealth and curls of his rich brown hair waved over a forehead of the purest marble in the placidity of its unveined whiteness. His nose and mouth were cast in the most perfect mould. But saw I never anything to equal his eye! Oh! I could have stood riveted with the chains of admiration gazing for hours upon it! What clearness, depth, and lucid transparency in those large orbs of radiant brown! And the fascination of his smile was irresistible, though seldom did that sunshine of the mind break through the thoughtful and almost melancholy expression of his noble features. He was a soldier, captain in the Royal Regiment of Horse Guards, and all his attitudes and actions were full of martial grace. His mental faculties were in exact keeping with such an exterior, being of the highest order; and though not like his younger brother, wholly given up to study, yet he was well versed in the ancient languages, and deeply read in the Greek and Roman classics, in addition to the best works in the British, German, and Italian tongues.

Such was my hero. The only blot I was ever able to discover in his character was that of a slight fierceness or impetuosity of temper which sometimes carried him beyond bounds, though at the slightest look or word of command from his father he instantly bridled his passion and became perfectly calm.

No wonder the duke should be, as he was, proud of such a son.

II

About two miles from the castle there stood a pretty house, entirely hid from view by a thick forest, in a glade of which it was situated.

Behind it was a smooth lawn fringed with odoriferous shrubs, and before it a tasteful flower garden.

This was the abode of Sir Alured Angus, a Scotchman, who was physician to his grace, and though of gentlemanly manners and demeanour, yet harsh, stern, and somewhat querulous in countenance and disposition.

He was a widower, and had but one child, a daughter, whom I shall call Marina, which nearly resembles her true name.

No wild rose blooming in solitude, or bluebell peering from an old wall, ever equalled in loveliness this flower of the forest. The hue of her cheek would excel the most delicate tint of the former, even when its bud is just opening to the breath of summer, and the clear azure of her eyes would cause the latter to appear dull as a dusky hyacinth. Also, the silken tresses of her hazel hair, straying in light ringlets down a neck and forehead of snow, seemed more elegant than the young tendrils of a vine. Her dress was almost Quaker-like in its simplicity. Pure white or vernal green were the colours she constantly wore, without any jewels save one row of pearls round her neck. She never stirred beyond the precincts of the wooded and pleasant green lane which skirted a long cornfield near the house. There, on warm summer evenings, she would ramble and linger, listening to the woodlark's song, and occasionally join her own more harmonious voice to its delightful warblings.

When the gloomy days and regrets of autumn and winter did not permit these walks, she amused herself with drawing (for which she had an exact taste), playing on the harp, reading the best English, French, and Italian works (all which languages she understood) in her father's extensive library, and sometimes a little light needlework.

Thus, in a state of almost perfect seclusion (for seldom had she even Sir Alured's company, as he generally resided in London), she was quite happy, and reflected with innocent wonder on those who could find pleasure in the noisy delights of what is called 'fashionable society'.

One day, as Lady Strathelleraye was walking in the wood, she met Marina, and on learning who she was, being charmed with her beauty and sweet manners, invited her to go on the morrow to the castle. She did so, and there met the Marquis of Tagus. He was even more surprised and pleased with her than the duchess, and when she was gone he asked his mother many questions about her, all of which she answered to his satisfaction.

For some time afterwards he appeared listless and abstracted. The reader will readily perceive that he had, to use a cant phrase, fallen in love.

Lord Cornelius, his brother, warned him of the folly of doing so; but instead of listening to his sage admonitions he first strove to laugh, and then, frowning at him, commanded silence.

In a few days he paid a visit to Oakwood House (Sir Alured's mansion), and after that became more gloomy than before.

His father observed this; and one day, as they were sitting alone, remarked it to Albion, adding that he was fully acquainted with the reason.

Albion reddened but made no answer.

'I am not, my son,' continued the duke, 'opposed to your wishes, though certainly there is a considerable difference of rank between yourself and Marina Angus. But that difference is compensated by the many admirable qualities she possesses.'

On hearing these words, Arthur – Albion I mean – started up, and throwing himself at his father's feet, poured forth his thanks in terms of glowing gratitude, while his fine features, flushed with excitation, spoke even more eloquently than his eloquent words.

'Rise, Albion!' said the duke; 'you are worthy of her and she of you; but both are yet too young.[7] Some years must elapse before your union takes place. Therefore exert your patience, my son.'

Albion's joy was slightly damped by this news, but his thankfulness and filial obedience, as well as love, forced him to acquiesce; immediately after, he quitted the room and took his way to Oakwood House.

There he related the circumstance to Marina, who, though she blushed incredulously, yet in truth felt as much gladness and as great a relief from doubt – almost amounting to despair – as himself.

III

A few months afterwards, the Duke of Strathelleraye determined to visit that wonder of the world, the great city of Africa, the Glass Town – of whose splendour, magnificence, and extent, strength, and riches, occasional tidings came from afar, wafted by breezes of the ocean to Merry England.[8]

But to most of the inhabitants of that little isle it bore the character of a dream or gorgeous fiction. They were unable to comprehend how mere human beings could construct fabrics of such marvellous size and grandeur as many of the public buildings were represented to be; and as to the Tower of all the Nations, few believed in its existence. It seemed as the cities of old: Nineveh or Babylon[9] with the temples of their gods, Ninus or Jupiter Belus,[10] and their halls of Astarte and Semele.[11] These most people believe to be magnified by the dim haze of intervening ages, and the exaggerating page of history through which medium we behold them.

The duke, as he had received many invitations from the Glass Townians, who were impatient to behold one whose renown had spread so far, and who likewise possessed vast dominions near the African coast, informed his lady, the Marquis of Tagus, and Lord Cornelius, that in a month's time he should take his departure with them, and that he should expect them all to be prepared at that period, adding that when they returned Marina Angus should be created Marchioness of Tagus.

Though it was a bitter trial to Albion to part with one to whom he was now so entirely devoted, yet, comforted by the last part of his father's speech, he obeyed without murmuring.

On the last evening of his stay in Strathelleraye, he took a sad farewell of Marina, who wept as if hopeless. But suddenly restraining her griefs she looked up, with her beautiful eyes irradiated by a smile that like a ray of light illuminated the crystal tears, and whispered,

'I shall be happy when you return.'

Then they parted, and Albion, during his voyage over the wide ocean, often thought for comfort on her last words.

It is a common superstition that the words uttered by a friend on separating are prophetic, and these certainly portended nothing but peace.

IV

In due course of time they arrived at the Glass Town, and were welcomed with enthusiastic cordiality.

After the duke had visited his kingdom, he returned to the chief metropolis, and established his residence there at Salamanca Palace.

The Marquis of Tagus, from the noble beauty of his person, attracted considerable attention wherever he went, and in a short period he had won and attached many faithful friends of the highest rank and abilities.

From his love of elegant literature and the fine arts in general, painters and poets were soon among his warmest admirers. He himself possessed a most sublime genius, but as yet its full extent was unknown to him.

One day, as he was meditating alone on the world of waters that rolled between him and the fair Marina, he determined to put his feelings on paper in a tangible shape that he might hereafter show them to her when anticipation had given place to fruition. He took his pen, and in about a quarter of an hour had completed a brief poem of exquisite beauty. The attempt pleased him and soothed the anguish that lingered in his heart. It likewise gave him an insight into the astonishing faculties of his own mind; and a longing for immortality, an ambition of glory, seized him.

[Albion's subsequent work, a] tragedy, wreathed the laurels of fame round his brow, and his after-productions, each of which seemed to excel the other, added new wreaths to those which already beautified his temples.

I cannot follow him in the splendour of his literary career, nor even mention so much as the titles of his various works. Suffice it to say he became one of the greatest poets of the age; and one of the chief motives that influenced him in his exertions for renown was to render himself worthy to possess such a treasure as Marina. She, in whatever he was employed, was never out of his thoughts, and none had he as yet beheld among all the ladies of the Glass Town

– though rich, titled, and handsome strove by innumerable arts to gain his favour – whom he could even compare with her.

V

One evening Albion was invited to the house of Earl Cruachan, where was a large party assembled. Among the guests was one lady apparently about twenty-five or twenty-six years of age. In figure she was very tall, and both it and her face were of a perfectly Roman cast. Her features were regularly and finely formed, her full and brilliant eyes jetty black, as were the luxuriant tresses of her richly-curled hair. Her dark glowing complexion was set off by a robe of crimson velvet trimmed with ermine, and a nodding plume of black ostrich feathers added to the imposing dignity of her appearance.[12]

Albion, notwithstanding her unusual comeliness, hardly noticed her till Earl Cruachan rose and introduced her to him as the Lady Zelzia Ellrington. She was the most learned and noted woman in Glass Town, and he was pleased with this opportunity of seeing her.

For some time she entertained him with a discourse of the most lively eloquence, and indeed Madame de Staël[13] herself could not have gone beyond Lady Zelzia in the conversational talent. On this occasion she exerted herself to the utmost, as she was in the presence of so distinguished a man, and one whom she seemed ambitious to please.

At length one of the guests asked her to favour the company with a song and tune on the grand piano. At first she refused, but, on Albion seconding the request, rose, and taking from the drawing room table a small volume of poems, opened it at one by the Marquis of Tagus. She then set it to a fine air and sang as follows, while she skilfully accompanied her voice upon the instrument:

> I think of thee when the moonbeams play
>   On the placid water's face;
> For thus thy blue eyes' lustrous ray
>   Shone with resembling grace . . .[14]
>
> Oh! for the day when once again
>   Mine eyes will gaze on thee,

> But an ocean vast, a sounding main,
>   An ever howling sea,
>   Roll on between
>   With their billows green,
>   High tost tempestuously.

This song had been composed by Albion soon after his arrival at the Glass Town. The person addressed was Marina. The full rich tones of Lady Zelzia's voice did ample justice to the subject, and he expressed his sense of the honour she had done him in appropriate terms.

When she had finished, the company departed, for it was then rather late.

VI

As Albion pursued his way homewards alone, he began insensibly to meditate on the majestic charms of Lady Zelzia Ellrington, and to compare them with the gentler ones of Marina Angus. At first he could hardly tell which to give the preference to, for though he still almost idolised Marina, yet an absence of four years had considerably deadened his remembrance of her person.

While he was thus employed, he heard a soft but mournful voice whisper,

'Albion!' He turned hastily round, and saw the form of the identical Marina at a little distance, distinctly visible by the moonlight.

'Marina! My dearest Marina!' he exclaimed, springing towards her, while joy unutterable filled his heart. 'How did you come here? Have the angels in heaven brought you?'

So saying he stretched out his hand, but she eluded his grasp, and slowly gliding away, said: 'Do not forget me; I shall be happy when you return.'[15]

Then the apparition vanished. It seemed to have appeared merely to assert her superiority over her rival, and indeed the moment Albion beheld her beauty he felt that it was peerless.

But now wonder and perplexity took possession of his mind. He could not account for this vision except by the common solution of

supernatural agency, and that ancient creed his enlightened understanding had hitherto rejected until it was forced upon him by this
extraordinary incident.[16]

One thing there was, however, the interpretation of which he
thought he could not mistake, and that was the repetition of her
last words: 'I shall be happy when you return.' It showed that she
was still alive, and that which he had seen could not be her wraith.
However, he made a memorandum of the day and hour, namely,
the 18th of June 1815, twelve o'clock at night.

From this time the natural melancholy turn of his disposition
increased, for the dread of her death before he should return was
constantly before him; the ardency of his adoration, and desire to
see her again, redoubled.

At length, not being able any longer to bear his misery, he
revealed it to his father; and the duke, touched with his grief and
the fidelity of his attachment, gave him full permission to visit
England and bring back Marina with him to Africa.

VII

I need not trouble the reader with a minute detail of the
circumstances of Albion's voyage, but shall pass on to what
happened after he arrived in England.

It was a fair evening in September 1815 when he reached
Strathelleraye. Without waiting to enter the halls of his fathers, he
proceeded immediately to Oakwood House. As he approached it,
he almost sickened, when, for an instant, the thought that she
might be no more passed across his mind. But summoning hope to
his aid, and resting on her golden anchor, he passed up the lawn
and gained the glass doors of the drawing room.

As he drew near a sweet symphony of harp music swelled on his
ear. His heart bounded within him at the sound. He knew that no
fingers but hers could create those melodious tones, with which
now blended the harmony of a sweet and sad, but well-known
voice. He lifted the vine branch that shaded the door and beheld
Marina, more beautiful, he thought, than ever, seated at her harp,
sweeping with her slender fingers the quivering chords.

Without being observed by her, as she had her face turned from him, he entered; sitting down, he leaned his head on his hand, and, closing his eyes, listened with feelings of overwhelming transport to the following words:

> Long my anxious ear hath listened
>   For the step that ne'er returned;
> And my tearful eye hath glistened,
>   And my heart hath daily burned,
>   But now I rest.[17]

> All my days were days of weeping;
>   Thoughts of grim despair were stirred;
> Time on leaden feet seemed creeping;
>   Long heart-sickness, hope deferred
>   Cankered my heart.

Here the music and singing suddenly ceased. Albion raised his head. All was darkness except where the silver moonbeams showed a desolate and ruined apartment, instead of the elegant parlour that a few minutes before had gladdened his sight.

No trace of Marina was visible, no harp or other instrument of harmony; and the cold lunar light streamed through a void space instead of the glass door. He sprang up, and called aloud,

'Marina! Marina!' But only an echo as of empty rooms answered. Almost distracted, he rushed into the open air. A child was standing alone at the garden gate, who advanced towards him and said,

'I will lead you to Marina Angus. She has removed from that house to another.'

Albion followed the child till they came to a long row of tall dark trees leading to a churchyard, which they entered, and the child vanished, leaving Albion beside a white marble tombstone on which was chiselled:

MARINA ANGUS
She died
18th of June 1815
at
12 o'clock
midnight.[18]

When Albion had read this, he felt a pang of horrible anguish wring his heart and convulse his whole frame. With a loud groan he fell across the tomb and lay there senseless a long time, till at length he was waked from the deathlike trance to behold the spirit of Marina, which stood beside him for a moment, and then, murmuring

'Albion, I am happy, for I am at peace,' disappeared!

For a few days he lingered round her tomb, and then quitted Strathelleraye, where he was never again heard of.

The reason of Marina's death I shall briefly relate. Four years after Albion's departure, tidings came to the village that he was dead. The news broke Marina's faithful heart. The day after, she was no more.

October, 1830

The Rivals[19]

Scene – *a thick forest, under the trees of which* LADY ZENOBIA ELLRINGTON *is reposing, dressed in her usual attire of a crimson velvet robe and black plumes. She speaks:*

'Tis eve: how that rich sunlight streameth through[20]
The inwoven arches of this sylvan roof!
How those long, lustrous lines of light illume,
With trembling radiance, all the agèd boles
Of elms majestic as the lofty columns
That proudly rear their tall forms to the dome
Of old cathedral or imperial palace!
Yea, they are grander than the mightiest shafts
That e'er by hand of man were fashioned forth
Their holy, solemn temples to uphold.
And sweeter far than the harmonious peals
Of choral thunder, that in music roll
Through vaulted isles, are the low forest sounds
Murmuring around: of wind and stirrèd leaf,
And warbled song of nightingale or lark

Whose swelling cadences and dying falls
And whelming gushes of rich melody
Attune to meditation, all serene,
The weary spirit; and draw forth still thoughts
Of happy scenes half veilèd by the mists
Of bygone times. Yea, that calm influence
Hath soothed the billowy troubles of my heart
Till scarce one sad thought rises, though I sit
Beneath these trees, utterly desolate.
But no, not utterly, for still one friend
I fain would hope remains to brighten yet
My mournful journey through this vale of tears;
And, while he shines, all other, lesser lights
May wane and fade unnoticed from the sky.
But more than friend, e'en he can never be.
                    [*Heaves a deep sigh.*]
That thought is sorrowful, but yet I'll hope.
What is my rival? Nought but a weak girl,
Ungifted with the state and majesty
That mark superior minds. Her eyes gleam not
Like windows to a soul of loftiness;
She hath not raven locks that lightly wave
Over a brow whose calm placidity
Might emulate the white and polished marble.
                    [*A white dove flutters by.*]
Ha! what art thou, fair creature? It hath vanished
Down that long vista of low-drooping trees.
How gracefully its pinions waved! Methinks
It was the spirit of this solitude.
List! I hear footsteps; and the rustling leaves
Proclaim the approach of some corporeal being.

[*A young girl advances up the vista, dressed in green, with a garland
of flowers wreathed in the curls of her hazel hair. She comes towards*
LADY ZENOBIA, *and says:*

Lady, methinks I erst have seen thy face.
Art thou not that Zenobia, she whose name
Renown hath borne e'en to this far retreat?

LADY ELLRINGTON

Aye, maiden, thou hast rightly guessed. But how
Did'st recognise me?

GIRL

In Verreopolis
I saw thee walking mid those gardens fair
That like a rich, embroidered belt surround
That mighty city; and one bade me look
At her whose genius had illumined bright
Her age, and country, with undying splendour.
The majesty of thy imperial form,
The fire and sweetness of thy radiant eye,
Alike conspired to impress thine image
Upon my memory, and thus it is
That now I know thee as thou sittest there
Queen-like, beneath the over-shadowing boughs
Of that huge oak tree, monarch of this wood.

LADY ELLRINGTON [*smiling graciously*]

Who art thou, maiden?

GIRL

Marian is my name.

LADY ELLRINGTON [*starting up: aside*]

Ha! my rival! [*Sternly*] What dost thou here alone?

MARIAN [*aside*]

How her tongue changed! [*Aloud*] My favourite cushat dove,
Whose plumes are whiter than new-fallen snow,
Hath wandered, heedless, from my vigilant care.
I saw it gleaming through these dusky trees,
Fair as a star, while soft it glided by,
So have I come to find and lure it back.

LADY ELLRINGTON

Are all thy affections centred in a bird?

For thus thou speakest, as though nought were worthy
Of thought or care saving a silly dove!

MARIAN

Nay, lady, I've a father, and mayhap
Others whom gratitude or tenderer ties,
If such there be, bind my heart closely to.

LADY ELLRINGTON

But birds and flowers and such trifles vain
Seem most to attract thy love, if I may form
A judgement from thy locks elaborate curled
And wreathed around with woven garlandry,
And from thy whining speech, all redolent
With tone of most affected sentiment.
    [*She seizes* MARIAN, *and exclaims with a violent gesture*]
Wretch, I could kill thee!

MARIAN

                    Why, what have I done?
How have I wronged thee? Surely thou'rt distraught!

LADY ELLRINGTON

How hast thou wronged me? Where didst weave the net
Whose cunning meshes have entangled round
The mightiest heart that e'er in mortal breast
Did beat responsive unto human feeling?

MARIAN

The net? What net? I wove no net; she's frantic!

LADY ELLRINGTON

Dull, simple creature! Can'st not understand?

MARIAN

Truly, I cannot. 'Tis to me a problem,
An unsolved riddle, an enigma dark.

LADY ELLRINGTON
I'll tell thee, then. But, hark! What voice is that?

VOICE [*from the forest*]
Marian, where art thou? I have found a rose
Fair as thyself. Come hither, and I'll place it
With the blue violets on thine ivory brow.

MARIAN
He calls me; I must go; restrain me not.

LADY ELLRINGTON
Nay, I will hold thee firmly as grim death.
Thou need'st not struggle, for my grasp is strong.
Thou shalt not go: Lord Arthur shall come here,
And I will gain the rose despite of thee!
Now for mine hour of triumph. Here he comes.

[LORD ARTHUR *advances from among the trees, exclaims on
seeing* LADY ELLRINGTON.]

LORD ARTHUR
Zenobia! How cam'st thou here? What ails thee?
Thy cheek is flushed as with a fever glow;
Thine eyes flash strangest radiance; and thy frame
Trembles like to the wind-stirred aspen tree!

LADY ELLRINGTON
Give me the rose, Lord Arthur, for methinks
I merit it more than my girlish rival;
I pray thee now grant my request, and place
That rose upon my forehead, not on hers.
Then I will serve thee all my after-days
As thy poor handmaid, as thy humblest slave,
Happy to kiss the dust beneath thy tread,
To kneel submissive in thy lordly presence.
Oh! turn thine eyes from her and look on me
As I lie here imploring at thy feet,
Supremely blest if but a single glance

Could tell me that thou art not wholly deaf
To my petition, earnestly preferred.

LORD ARTHUR

Lady, thou'st surely mad! Depart, and hush
These importunate cries. They are not worthy
Of the great name which thou hast fairly earned.

LADY ELLRINGTON

Give me that rose, or I to thee will cleave
Till death these vigorous sinews has unstrung.
Hear me this once and give it me Lord Arthur.

LORD ARTHUR [*after a few minutes' deliberation*]

Here, take the flower, and keep it for my sake.
     [MARIAN *utters a suppressed scream, and sinks to the ground.*]

LADY ELLRINGTON [*assisting her to rise*]

Now I have triumphed! But I'll not exult;
Yet know, henceforth, I'm thy superior.
Farewell, my lord; I thank thee for thy preference!
     [*Plunges into the wood and disappears.*]

LORD ARTHUR

Fear nothing, Marian, for a fading flower
Is not symbolical of constancy.
But take this sign; [*gives her his diamond ring*] enduring
     adamant
Betokens well affection that will live
Long as life animates my faithful heart.
Now let us go; for see, the deepening shades
Of twilight darken our lone forest path;
And, lo! thy dove comes gliding through the mirk,
Fair wanderer, back to its loved mistress' care!
Luna will light us on our journey home:
For see, her lamp shines radiant in the sky,
And her bright beams will pierce the thickest boughs.
          [*Exeunt, curtain falls.*]
                              December, 1830

The Bridal

I

In the autumn of the year 1831, being weary of study, and the melancholy solitude of the vast streets and mighty commercial marts of our great Babel, and being fatigued with the ever-resounding thunder of the sea, with the din of a thousand self-moving engines, with the dissonant cries of all nations, kindreds, and tongues: in one word, being tired of Verdopolis and all its magnificence, I determined on a trip into the country.

Accordingly, the day after this resolution was formed, I rose with the sun, collected a few essential articles of dress, packed them neatly in a light knapsack, arranged my apartment, partook of a wholesome repast, and then, after locking the door and delivering the key to my landlady, I set out with a light heart and joyous step.

After three days of continued travel, I arrived on the banks of a wide and profound river, winding through a vast valley embosomed in hills whose robe of rich and flowery verdure was broken only by the long shadow of groves, and here and there by clustering herds and flocks lying, white as snow, in the green hollows between the mountains. It was the evening of a calm summer day when I reached this enchanting spot. The only sounds now audible were the songs of shepherds, swelling and dying at intervals, and the murmur of gliding waves.

I neither knew nor cared where I was. My bodily faculties of eye and ear were absorbed in the contemplation of this delightful scene, and, wandering unheedingly along, I left the guidance of the river and entered a wood, invited by the warbling of a hundred forest minstrels. Soon I perceived the narrow, tangled wood-path to widen, and gradually it assumed the appearance of a green, shady alley.

At length I entered a glade in the wood, in the midst of which was a small but exquisitely beautiful marble edifice of pure and dazzling whiteness. On the broad steps of the portico two figures were reclining, at sight of whom I instantly stepped behind a low, wide-spreading fig tree, where I could hear and see all that passed without fear of detection. One was a youth of lofty stature and remarkably graceful demeanour, attired in a rich purple vest and mantle, with closely fitting white pantaloons of woven silk, displaying to advantage the magnificent proportions of his form. A richly adorned belt was girt tightly round his waist from which depended a scimitar whose golden hilt, and scabbard of the finest Damascus steel, glittered with gems of inestimable value. His steel-barred cap, crested with tall, snowy plumes, lay beside him, its absence revealing more clearly the rich curls of dark, glossy hair clustering round a countenance distinguished by the noble beauty of its features, but still more by the radiant fire of genius and intellect visible in the intense brightness of his large, dark, and lustrous eyes.

The other form was that of a very young and slender girl, whose complexion was delicately, almost transparently, fair.[21] Her cheeks were tinted with a rich, soft crimson, her features moulded in the utmost perfection of loveliness; while the clear light of her brilliant hazel eyes, and the soft waving of her auburn ringlets, gave additional charms to what seemed already infinitely too beautiful for this earth. Her dress was a white robe of the finest texture the Indian loom can produce. The only ornaments she wore were a long chain which encircled her neck twice and hung lower than her waist, composed of alternate beads of the finest emeralds and gold; and a slight gold ring on the third finger of her left hand, which, together with a small crescent of pearls glistening on her forehead (which is always worn by the noble matrons of Verdopolis), betokened that she had entered the path of wedded life. With a sweet vivacity in her look and manner, the young bride was addressing her lord thus, when I first came in sight of the peerless pair:

'No, no, my lord; if I sing the song, you shall choose it. Now, once more, what shall I sing? The moon is risen, and, if your decision is not prompt, I will not sing at all!' To this he answered,

'Well, if I am threatened with the entire loss of the pleasure if I defer my choice, I will have that sweet song which I overheard you singing the evening before I left Scotland.'

With a smiling blush she took a little ivory lyre, and, in a voice of the most touching melody, sang the following stanzas:

A dark veil is hung
O'er the bright sky of gladness,
And, where birds sweetly sung,
There's a murmur of sadness;
The wind sings with a warning tone
Through many a shadowy tree;
I hear, in every passing moan,
The voice of destiny.[22]

When the lady had concluded her song, I stepped from my place of concealment, and was instantly perceived by the noble youth (whom, of course, every reader will have recognized as the Marquis of Douro).

He gave me a courteous welcome, and invited me to proceed with him to his country palace, as it was now wearing late. I willingly accepted the invitation, and, in a short time, we arrived there.

II

It is a truly noble structure, built in the purest style of Grecian architecture, situated in the midst of a vast park: embosomed in richly wooded hills, perfumed with orange and citron groves, and watered by a branch of the Gambia, almost equal in size to the parent stream.

The magnificence of the interior is equal to that of the outside. There is an air of regal state and splendour, throughout all the lofty domed apartments, which strikes the spectator with awe for the lord of so imposing a residence. The marquis has a particular pride in the knowledge that he is the owner of one of the most splendid, select, and extensive libraries now in the possession of any individual. His picture and statue galleries likewise contain many of the finest works, both of the ancient and modern masters, particularly the latter, of whom the marquis is a most generous and munificent patron. In his cabinet of curiosities I observed a beautiful casket of wrought gold. I likewise noticed a brace of pistols, most exquisitely wrought and highly furnished.

[The marquis's list of treasures, most of which reflect on

his own glory, includes 100 gold and silver medals (literary and scientific honours); a gold vase (for composition of the best Greek epigram); a silver bow and quiver (for excellence in archery); a gold bit, bridle, and spurs (for horsemanship); several dried wreaths of myrtle and laurel.]

But what interested me more than all these trophies of victory and specimens of art and nature – costly, beautiful, and almost invaluable as they were – was a little figure of Apollo, about six inches in height, curiously carved in white agate, holding a lyre in his hand, and placed on a pedestal of the same valuable material, on which was the following inscription:

In our day we beheld the god of Archery, Eloquence, and Verse, shrined in an infinitely fairer form than that worn by the ancient Apollo, and giving far more glorious proofs of his divinity than the day-god ever vouchsafed to the inhabitants of the old pagan world. Zenobia Ellrington implores Arthur Augustus Wellesley to accept this small memorial, and consider it as a token that, though forsaken and despised by him whose good opinion and friendship she valued more than life, she yet bears no malice.

There was a secret contained in this inscription which I could not fathom. I had never before heard of any misunderstanding between his lordship and Lady Zenobia, nor did public appearances warrant a suspicion of its existence. Long after, however, the following circumstances came to my knowledge. The channel through which they reached me cannot be doubted, but I am not at liberty to mention names.

III

One evening about dusk, as the Marquis Douro was returning from a shooting excursion into the country, he heard suddenly a rustling noise in a deep ditch on the roadside. He was preparing his fowling piece for a shot when the form of Lady Ellrington started up before him. Her head was bare, her tall person was enveloped in the tattered remnants of a dark velvet mantle. Her dishevelled hair hung in wild elflocks over her face, neck, and shoulders, almost concealing her features, which were emaciated and pale as death. He stepped back a few paces, startled at the sudden and ghastly apparition. She threw herself on her knees before him, exclaiming in wild, maniacal accents,

'My lord, tell me truly, sincerely, ingenuously, where you have been. I heard that you had left Verdopolis, and I followed you on foot five hundred miles. Then my strength failed me, and I lay down in this place, as I thought, to die. But it was doomed I should see you once more before I became an inhabitant of the grave. Answer me, my lord: Have you seen that wretch Marian Hume? Have you spoken to her? Viper! Viper! Oh, that I could sheathe this weapon in her heart!'

Here she stopped for want of breath, and, drawing a long, sharp, glittering knife from under her cloak, brandished it wildly in the air. The marquis looked at her steadily, and, without attempting to disarm her, answered with great composure,

'You have asked me a strange question, Lady Zenobia; but, before I attempt to answer it, you had better come with me to our encampment. I will order a tent to be prepared for you where you may pass the night in safety, and, tomorrow, when you are a little recruited by rest and refreshment, we will discuss this matter soberly.'[23]

Her rage was now exhausted by its own vehemence, and she replied with more calmness than she had hitherto evinced,

'My lord, believe me, I am deputed by heaven to warn you of a great danger into which you are about to fall. If you persist in your intention of uniting yourself to Marian Hume you will become a murderer and a suicide. I cannot now explain myself more clearly; but ponder carefully on my words until I see you again.'

Then, bowing her forehead to the earth in an attitude of adoration, she kissed his feet, muttering at the same time some unintelligible words. At that moment a loud rushing, like the sound of a whirlwind, became audible, and Lady Zenobia was swept away by some invisible power before the marquis could extend his arm to arrest her progress, or frame an answer to her mysterious address. He paced slowly forward, lost in deep reflection on what he had heard and seen. The moon had risen over the black, barren mountains ere he reached the camp. He gazed for awhile on her pure, undimmed lustre, comparing it to the loveliness of one far away, and then, entering his tent, wrapped himself in his hunter's cloak, and lay down to unquiet sleep.

Months rolled away, and the mystery remained unsolved. Lady Zenobia Ellrington appeared as usual in that dazzling circle of which she was ever a distinguished ornament. There was no trace of wandering fire in her eyes which might lead a careful observer to imagine that her mind was unsteady. Her voice was more subdued and her looks pale, and it was remarked by some that she avoided all (even the most commonplace) communication with the marquis.

In the meantime the Duke of Wellington had consented to his son's union with the beautiful, virtuous, and accomplished, but untitled, Marian Hume. Vast and splendid preparations were in the making for the approaching bridal, when just at this critical juncture news arrived of the Great Rebellion headed by Alexander Rogue. The intelligence fell with the suddenness and violence of a thunderbolt. Unequivocal symptoms of dissatisfaction began to appear at the same time among the lower orders in Verdopolis. The workmen at the principal mills and furnaces struck for an advance in wages, and, the masters refusing to comply with their exorbitant demands, they all turned out simultaneously. Shortly after, Colonel Grenville, one of the great mill-owners, was shot.[24] His assassins, being quickly discovered and delivered up to justice, were interrogated by torture, but they remained inflexible, not a single satisfactory answer being elicited from them.

The police were now doubled. Bands of soldiers were stationed in the more suspicious parts of the city, and orders were issued that no citizen should walk abroad unarmed. In this state of affairs Parliament was summoned to consult on the best measures to be taken. On the first night of its sitting the house was crowded to excess. All the members attended, and above a thousand ladies of the first rank appeared in the gallery. A settled expression of gloom and anxiety was visible in every countenance. They sat for some time gazing at each other in the silence of seeming despair.

At length the Marquis of Douro rose and ascended the tribunal.

It was on this memorable night he pronounced that celebrated oration which will be delivered to farthest posterity as a finished specimen of the sublimest eloquence. The souls of all who heard him were thrilled with conflicting emotions. Some of the ladies in the gallery fainted and were carried out. My limits will not permit me to transcribe the whole of this speech, and to attempt an abridgement would be profanation. I will, however, present the reader with the conclusion. It was as follows:

> I'll call on you, my countrymen, to rouse yourselves to action. There is a latent flame of rebellion smouldering in our city, which blood alone can quench: the hot blood of ourselves and our enemies freely poured forth! We daily see in our streets men whose brows were once open as the day, but which are now wrinkled with dark dissatisfaction, and the light of whose eyes, formerly free as sunshine, is now dimmed by restless suspicion. Our upright merchants are ever threatened with fears of assassination from those dependants who, in time past, loved, honoured, and reverenced them as fathers. Our peaceful citizens cannot pass their thresholds in safety unless laden with weapons of war, the continual dread of death haunting their footsteps wherever they turn. And who has produced this awful change? What agency of hell has effected, what master spirit of crime, what prince of sin, what Beëlzebub of black iniquity, has been at work in the kingdom? I will answer that fearful question: Alexander Rogue! Arm for the battle, then, fellow-countrymen; be not faint-hearted, but trust in the justice of your cause as your banner of protection, and let your war shout in the onslaught ever be: "God defend the right!"[25]

When the marquis had concluded this harangue, he left the house amidst long and loud thunders of applause, and proceeded to a shady grove on the river banks. Here he walked for some time inhaling the fresh night wind, which acquired additional coolness as it swept over the broad rapid river; he was just beginning to recover from the strong excitement into which his enthusiasm had thrown him, when he felt his arm suddenly grasped from behind, and turning round, beheld Lady Zenobia Ellrington standing beside him, with the same wild, unnatural expression of countenance which had before convulsed her features.

'My lord,' she muttered, in a low, energetic tone, 'your eloquence, your noble genius has again driven me to desperation. I am no longer mistress of myself, and if you do not consent to be mine, and mine alone, I will kill myself where I stand.'

'Lady Ellrington,' said the marquis coldly, withdrawing his hand from her grasp, 'this conduct is unworthy of your character. I must beg that you will cease to use the language of a madwoman, for I do assure you, my lady, these deep stratagems will have no effect upon me.'

She now threw herself at his feet, exclaiming in a voice almost stifled with ungovernable emotion:

'Oh! do not kill me with such cold, cruel disdain. Only consent to follow me, and you will be convinced that you ought not to be united to one so utterly unworthy of you as Marian Hume.'

The marquis, moved by her tears and entreaties, at length consented to accompany her. She led him a considerable distance from the city to a subterraneous grotto, where was a fire burning on a brazen altar. She threw a certain powder into the flame, and immediately they were transported through the air to an apartment at the summit of a lofty tower.[26] At one end of this room was a vast mirror, and at the other a drawn curtain, behind which a most brilliant light was visible.

'You are now,' said Lady Ellrington, 'in the sacred presence of one whose counsel, I am sure, you, my lord, will never slight.'

At this moment the curtain was removed, and the astonished marquis beheld Crashie,[27] the divine and infallible, seated on his golden throne, and surrounded by those mysterious rays of light which ever emanate from him.

'My son,' said he, with an august smile, and in a voice of awful harmony, 'fate and inexorable destiny have decreed that in the hour you are united to the maiden of your choice, the angel Azazel[28] shall smite you both, and convey your disembodied souls over the swift-flowing and impassable river of death. Hearken to the counsels of wisdom, and do not, in the madness of self will, destroy yourself and Marian Hume by refusing the offered hand of one who, from the moment of your birth, was doomed by the prophetic stars of heaven to be your partner and support through the dark, unexplored wilderness of future life.'

He ceased. The combat betwixt true love and duty raged for a few seconds in the marquis's heart, and sent his lifeblood in a tumult of agony and despair burning to his cheek and brow. At length duty prevailed, and, with a strong effort, he said in a firm, unfaltering voice:

'Son of Wisdom! I will war no longer against the high decree of heaven, and here I swear by the eternal—'

The rash oath was checked in the moment of its utterance by some friendly spirit who whispered in his ear:

'There is magic. Beware.'

At the same instant Crashie's venerable form faded away, and in its stead appeared the evil genius, Danhasch,[29] in all the naked hideousness of his real deformity. The demon soon vanished with a wild howl of rage, and the marquis found himself again in the grove with Lady Ellrington.

She implored him on her knees to forgive an attempt which love alone had dictated, but he turned from her with a smile of bitter contempt and disdain, and hastened to his father's palace.

About a week after this event the nuptials of Arthur Augustus, Marquis of Douro, and Marian Hume were solemnized with unprecedented pomp and splendour. Lady Ellrington, when she thus saw that all her hopes were lost in despair, fell into deep melancholy, and while in this state she amused herself with carving the little image before mentioned. After a long time she slowly recovered, and the marquis, convinced that her extravagances had arisen from a disordered brain, consented to honour her with his friendship once more.

I continued upwards of two months at the Marquis of Douro's country place, and then returned to Verdopolis, equally delighted with my noble host and his fair, amiable bride.

August, 1832

Zenobia and Rogue
(from *The Foundling*)

[Arthur and Marian being married, Zenobia seeks solace, or revenge, by uniting herself to Arthur's rival, Alexander Rogue. A scene depicting their version of wedded bliss follows.]

I trust my reader will excuse me if I now change the scene to Ellrington Hall. About a week after the fête at Lord Selby's, Lady Zenobia was sitting alone in her boudoir, when a servant entered and informed her that Lord Ellrington would be with her in less than an hour.

'Very well,' said she, 'I am prepared to receive him at any time.' The servant bowed and left the room.

She sat for some time with her head resting on her hand, and her eyes fixed on a Greek copy of Æschylus' tragedies which lay before her. This was the first interview she had had with Rogue since their quarrel at the ball, and she now dreaded the consequences of his resentment which she knew would not be softened by delay, but, on the contrary, increased in violence, when he should have an opportunity of giving it vent. At first her countenance betrayed no symptom of emotion, but after a little while large round drops appeared trembling in her dark eyes, and falling thence to the learned page on which they rested. Presently she started from the table and, hurriedly pacing the apartment, exclaimed in a low tremulous voice,

'What means this weakness? Why do I thus dread one whom I ought to despise? Oh, that I should have resigned myself into the hands of such a man, in a moment of pique at love neglected, contemned, spurned; in an hour of false, fleeting admiration of abused and degraded talents, I yielded up my liberty and received the galling yoke of worse than Egyptian bondage. Arthur! Arthur! Why did I ever see you? Why did I ever hear your voice? If love for another did not occupy my whole heart, absorb my whole existence, perhaps I might endure the cruelty of this man with less utter, less unendurable misery. Perhaps I might, by unwearied patience, by constant and tender submission, win some portion of his regard, some slight share of his affection. But now it is impossible. I cannot love him. I cannot even appear to love him, and therefore I must hereafter drag out the remnant of my wretched life in sorrow and woe, in hopeless and ceaseless mourning.'

Here she stopped, threw herself on to a sofa, and for a long time wept aloud and bitterly.

Steps were now heard in the corridor.

[Zenobia is interrupted by her foppish brothers, in flight from Rogue, who has threatened to behead them 'on a log of wood like so many chickens'.]

Lady Zenobia could scarcely refrain from smiling at this piteous relation. Sensible, however, that no time was to be lost in providing for her brothers' safety, she ordered them immediately to make their escape by means of a private door, which she pointed out, and to hasten to Waterloo Palace, and there implore the Duke of Wellington to protect them till the storm should have blown over.

They were no sooner gone than Rogue arrived in earnest. He entered the room with a firm step, but Zenobia shuddered to see the savage light of intoxication glancing in his, at all times, fiery eye. Having seated himself, he drew out a pair of pistols, placed them on the table, pulled his wife rudely towards him, and addressed her thus:

'Well, termagant, I suppose you thought I'd forgotten your insolent behaviour to me about a week ago, but I assure you if that was your opinion you're very much mistaken. Kneel at my feet this instant, and humbly and submissively ask pardon for all past offences, or—'

'Never,' said she, while a smile of scorn curled her lips, 'never will I so far degrade myself. Do not hope, do not imagine that I will.'

'I neither hope nor imagine anything about the matter, but I'm certain of it; at least, if you refuse, an ounce of cold lead shall find its way to your heart. Do you think I will have you dancing and manoeuvring before my very face with that conceited, impertinent, white-livered puppy?'

'Dare not, at your peril, to speak another insulting word of the Marquis of Douro.'

'Fool,' said Rogue, in a voice of thunder, while flames seemed actually darting from his eyes. 'Fool and madwoman, is this the language calculated to screen either you or him from the terrible effects of my wrath? You may grovel now in the dust. You may kneel and implore my forgiveness till your bold tongue rots and refuses to move. I will not grant it now were every angel celestial and infernal to command me.'

'Base villain, I scorn your forgiveness. I trample your offers of mercy under foot. And think not to harm the marquis: he is far above your power. That blood-stained, that crime-blackened hand, could not harm one hair of his noble head. Yet know, wretch, that though I honour him thus highly, though I look upon him as more than man – as an angel, a demigod – yet rather than break my faith even with you I would this instant fall a corpse at your feet.'

'Liar,' said Rogue. 'These words shall be your sentence and I will execute quickly, but you shall not die the easy death of having your brains blown out. No! I'll thrust this sharp blade slowly through you, that you may feel and enjoy the torture.'

Here he drew a long glittering sword from its scabbard, twisted his hand in her thick black hair, and was just in the act of striking her as she lay unresisting and motionless, when a strong and sudden grasp arrested his arm from behind. Half choked with fury he turned round. The hideous visage of Montmorency[30] met his fire-flashing eyes, rendered ten times more frightful by the loathsome grin which wrinkled his misshapen features. Shuddering with passion and disgust, he demanded what had emboldened him thus to intrude on his privacy.

'Nothing, my beloved friend,' replied he, 'but firstly the desire of doing you good, and secondly of doing myself no harm. I was walking in the corridor when I heard your dear, well-known voice raised a little above the customary pitch. Anxious to know what could thus have excited my friend, and desirous to share his gratification if the cause were pleasure, and to alleviate his sufferings if pain, I crept on tiptoe to the door. There, by looking through the keyhole, I beheld as pretty a tragedy as one could wish to set eyes on, but when I saw that matters were approaching a crisis, I remembered that the gallows often follows murder, and were we to lose you just now our cause would not soon recover from the shock; my fine dreams of ambition would be in some measure blighted; and, moreover, the unfailing spring, the well of the waters of life eternal, whereat I am wont to quench the thirsting of my soul after righteousness, would at once and forever be dried up. Prompted by these considerations, I magnanimously denied myself the delight of witnessing your play to the end. I stepped forward like a hero, bearded the lion in his wrath, and effected the deliverance of this fair damsel in distress.'

'Well,' replied Rogue sneeringly, 'since the brother of my heart has interposed, I will permit that woman to escape the punishment due to her crimes this once.'

The truth was that Rogue who, though scarcely a man, is not yet altogether a monster, was somewhat moved at seeing the deadly paleness that overspread his wife's face, and the attitude of passive helplessness in which she lay stretched before him; besides, it must be urged, in palliation of his violence, that the provocation he had received was such as no man either could or ought to have endured in silence. He, however, disdained to shew his emotion. Pushing her aside with his foot he exclaimed,

'Get up, heap of baseness, and begone instantly from my presence.' She did not attempt to move. He looked at her more closely and found that the fear of death had so far overcome her as to occasion a fainting fit. With a loud and deep oath he rung the bell,[31] and commanded the servant who answered his summons to 'carry that woman away'.

June, 1833

PART III
Mary

❋

A Peep into a Picture Book

[Charles, in search of postprandial entertainment, leafs through a set of volumes entitled 'The Aristocracy of Africa'.]

It is a fine, warm, sultry day, just after dinner. I am at Thornton Hotel. The general is enjoying his customary nap; and while the serene evening sunshine reposes on his bland features and unruffled brow, an atmosphere of calm seems to pervade the apartment.

What shall I do to amuse myself? I dare not stir lest he should awake; and any disturbance of his slumbers at this moment might be productive of serious consequences to me: no circumstance would more effectually sour my landlord's ordinarily bland temperament. Hark! there is a slight, light snore, most musical, most melancholy; he is firmly locked in the chains of the drowsy god. I will try. At the opposite end of the room three large volumes that look like picture books lie on a sideboard; their green watered-silk quarto covers and gilt backs are tempting, and I will make an effort to gain possession of them.

With zephyr-step and bosomed breath I glide onward to the sideboard; I seize my prize; catlike I creep back and being once more safely established in my chair I open the volumes to see if the profit be equivalent to the pains.

[The first two portraits are those of Rogue, now known as Alexander Percy, Earl of Northangerland, and of his wife, Zenobia.]

A mighty phantom has answered my spell: an awful shape clouds the magic mirror! Reader, before me I behold the earthly tabernacle of Northangerland's unsounded soul! There he stands: what a vessel to be moulded from the coarse clay of mortality! What a plant to spring from the rank soil of human existence! And the vessel is without flaw: polished, fresh, and bright from the last process of the maker. The flower has sprung up to mature beauty, but not a leaf is curled, not a blossom faded. This portrait was taken ere the lights and shadows of twenty-five summers had fallen across the wondrous labyrinth of Percy's path through life. Percy! Percy! Never was humanity fashioned in a fairer mould. The eye follows, delighted, all those classic lines of face and form; not one unseemly curvature or angle to disturb the general effect of so much refined regularity; all appears carved in ivory. The grossness of flesh and blood will not suit its statuesque exactness and speckless polish. A feeling of fascination comes over me while I gaze on that Phidian[1] nose, defined with such beautiful precision; that chin and mouth chiselled to such elaborate perfection; that high, pale forehead, not bald as now, but yet not shadowed with curls, for the clustering hair is parted back, gathered in abundant wreaths on the temples, and leaving the brow free for all the gloom and glory of a mind that has no parallel to play over the expanse of living marble which its absence reveals. The expression in this picture is somewhat pensive, composed, free from sarcasm except the fixed sneer of the lip and the strange deadly glitter of the eye whose glance – a mixture of the keenest scorn and deepest thought – curdles the spectator's blood to ice. In my opinion this head embodies the most vivid ideas we can conceive of Lucifer, the rebellious archangel: there is such a total absence of human feeling and sympathy; such a cold frozen pride; such a fathomless power of intellect; such passionless yet perfect beauty – not breathing and burning and full of lightning, blood, and fiery thought and feeling like that of some others whom our readers will recollect – but severely studied, faultlessly refined, as cold and hard and polished and perfect as the most priceless brilliant.[2] Northangerland has a black drop in his veins that flows through every vessel, taints every limb, stagnates round his heart, and there, in the very citadel of life, turns the glorious blood of the Percys to the bitterest, rankest gall. Let us leave him in that shape, bright with beauty, dark with crime. Farewell, Percy!

I turn the leaves and behold – his countess! What eyes! What raven hair! What an imposing contour of form and countenance! She is perfectly grand in her velvet robes, dark plume, and crown-like turban. The lady of Ellrington House, the wife of Northangerland, the prima donna of the Angrian Court, the most learned woman of her age, the modern Cleopatra, the Verdopolitan de Staël: in a word, Zenobia Percy! Who would think that that grand form of feminine majesty could launch out into the unbridled excesses of passion in which her ladyship not unfrequently indulges? There is fire in her eyes, and command on her brow; and some touch of a pride that would spurn restraint in the curl of her rich lip. But all is so tempered with womanly dignity that it would seem as if neither fire nor pride nor imperiousness could awaken the towering fits of ungoverned and frantic rage that often deform her beauty.[3]

[Though Zenobia is here solemnly pictured with a 'large clasped volume', Charles confesses that he has on more than one occasion been the physical victim of her terrific rage. He moves on to a portrait of the grave but kindly Duke of Fidena, in the course of which we learn that Arthur's wife Marian, rejected for a new love, has died of a broken heart.]

I have watched him for hours while he sat on a sofa with his lovely wife beside him, and the youthful Marchioness of Douro sitting at his feet; and heard the benignant simplicity with which he poured out the stores of his varied and extensive erudition, answering so kindly and familiarly each question of the fair listeners, mingling an air of conjugal tenderness in his manner to his wife, and an earnest melancholy gentleness in that to Marian such as always characterized his treatment of her. Poor thing! She looked on him as her only friend: her brother, her adviser, her unerring oracle. With the warm devotedness that marked her disposition, she followed his advice as if it had been the precept of inspired revelation. Fidena could not err; he could neither think nor act wrongly; he was perfect. Those who thought him too proud were very much mistaken. *She* never found him so. Nobody had milder and softer manners; nobody spoke more pleasingly. Thus she would talk and then blush with anger if any one contradicted her too exclusively favourable opinion. Fidena, I believe, regarded Marian as a delicate flower planted in a stormy situation, as a lovely, fragile being that needed his careful protection; and that protection he would have extended to her at the hazard of life itself. To the last he tried to support her. Many lone days he spent in watching and cheering her during her final lingering sickness. But all the kindness, all the tenderness in the world were insufficient to raise that blighted lily, so long as the sunshine of those eyes which had been her idolatry was withered; and so long as the music of that voice she had loved so fondly and truly sounded too far off to be heard. Fidena was in the house when she died. On quitting the bedside, as he hung over his adopted sister for the last time, a single large tear dropped on the little worn hand he held in his, and he muttered half aloud,

'Would to God I had possessed this treasure; it should not thus have been thrown away.'

Marian's portrait comes next to Fidena. Every one knows what it is like: the small delicate features, dark blue eyes full of wild and tender enthusiasm, beautiful nutty curls, and frail-looking form, are familiar to all; so I need not pause on a more elaborate detail.

[The convenience with which Marian is here despatched suggests that Charlotte had lost interest in her first, sentimental heroine – she even gets the colour of her eyes wrong. Arthur now reappears, sporting a new title – the Duke of Zamorna – and a new wife: Mary Henrietta, daughter, from his first marriage, of Alexander Percy.]

Fire! Light! What have we here? Zamorna's self, blazing in the frontispiece like the sun on his own standard. All his usual insufferableness or irresistibleness, or whatever the ladies choose to call it, surrounding him like an atmosphere, he stands as if a thunderbolt could neither blast the light of his eyes nor dash the effrontery of his brow. Keen, glorious being! Tempered and bright and sharp and rapid as the scimitar at his side, when whirled by the delicate yet vigorous hand that now grasps the bridle of a horse, to all appearance as viciously beautiful as himself. O, Zamorna! what eyes those are glancing under the deep shadow of that raven crest! They bode no good. Man nor woman could ever gather more than a troubled, fitful happiness from their kindest light. Satan gave them their glory to deepen the midnight gloom that always follows where their lustre has fallen most lovingly. This, indeed, is something different from Percy. All here is passion and fire unquenchable. Impetuous sin, stormy pride, diving and soaring enthusiasm, war and poetry, are kindling their fires in all his veins, and his wild blood boils from his heart and back again like a torrent of new-sprung lava. Young duke? Young demon! I have looked at you till words seemed to issue from your lips in those fine electric tones, as clear and profound as the silver chords of a harp, which steal affections like a charm. I think I see him bending his head to speak to some lady while he whispers words that touch the heart like a melody that's sweetly played in tune. A low wind rises, sighs slowly onward. Suddenly his plumes rustle; their haughty shadow sweeps over his forehead; the eye, the full, dark, refulgent eye, lightens most gloriously; his curls are all stirred; smiles dawn on his lips. Suddenly he lifts his head, flings back the feathers and clusters of bright hair. And, while he stands erect and godlike, his *regards* (as the French say) bent on the lady, whoever it be – who by this time is, of course, seriously debating whether he be man or angel – a momentary play of indescribable expression round the mouth, and a faint elevation of the eyebrows, tell how the stream of thought runs at that moment; the mind which so noble a form enshrines! Detestable wretch! I hate him!

But just opposite, separated only by a transparent sheet of silver paper, there is something different: his wife, his own matchless Henrietta! She looks at him with her serene eyes as if the dew of placid thought could be shed on his heart by the influence of those large, clear stars. It reminds me of moonlight descending on troubled waters. I wish the parallel held good all the way, and that she was as far beyond the reach of sorrows arising from her husband's insatiable ambition and fiery impetuosity as Diana is above the lash of the restless deep. But it is not so: her destiny is linked with his. And however strangely the great river of Zamorna's fate may flow; however awful the rapids over which it may rush; however cold and barren the banks of its channel and however wild; however darkly beached and stormily billowed the ocean into which it may finally plunge: Mary's must follow. Fair creature! I

could weep to think of it. For her sake, I hope a bright futurity lies
before her lord. Pity that the shadow of grief should ever fall where
the light of such beauty shines. Every one knows how like the
duchess is to her father;[4] his very image cast in a softer – it could
not be a more refined – mould. They are precisely similar, even to
the very delicacy of their hands. As Byron[5] says, her features have
all the statuesque repose, the calm classic grace, that dwell on the
earl's. She, however, has one advantage over him: the stealing,
pensive brilliancy of her hazel eyes, and the peaceful sweetness of
her mouth, impart a harmony to the whole which the satanic sneer
fixed on the corresponding features of Northangerland's face totally
destroys.

May–June, 1834

From *My Angria and the Angrians*

[A dashing Zamorna, in disguise, dazzles a bevy of
aristocratic young ladies, and then confronts his wife, now
caught in the midst of the escalating conflict between her
husband and her father.]

At this moment a gentleman of tall and powerful figure dashed
through the multitude and at one bound cleared the paling erected
before the hustings, mounted them very unceremoniously, and
stretching out his arms as he stood erect in the front, said, in a
clear trumpetlike voice that rose over and almost quelled the din,

'Men of Angria, before one among you strides a step homeward,
let all join in our grand national anthem.' [The anthem being
sung], he jumped from his station, and keeping still within the
paling, came slowly walking along towards the ladies' seats. Of
course, they all looked at him, and I thought many a bright eye
lingered on his form and followed it anxiously as he passed. He
regarded them too with a careless and condescending smile which
brightened into flashing pride as his glance turned on the now
departing multitude. He paused just opposite to where I sat[6] and
thus I was enabled to take a full and leisurely view of him.

He seemed to be in the full bloom of youth; his figure was

toweringly, overbearingly lofty, moulded in statuelike perfection, and invested with something which I cannot describe; something superb, impetuous, resistless; something, in short, no single word can altogether express. His hair was intensely black, curled luxuriantly, but the forehead underneath, instead of having the swarthy tinge proper to such Italian locks, looked white and smooth as ivory. His eyebrows were black and broad, but his long eyelashes and large clear eyes were deep sepia brown. The wreaths on his temples were brought so low as to meet the profusely curled raven whiskers and mustachios, which hid his mouth and chin, and shadowed his fair-complexioned cheeks. I thought these symbols of manhood much too strong and abundant for his evident juvenility. When he smiled, lips and teeth appeared such as any lady might have envied, coral-red and pearl-white. The upper lip was very short – Grecian – and had a haughty curl which I knew well.[7] At the first glance I discerned him to be a military man.

'That's a proper man,' said Maria Percy when she had carefully surveyed him. 'One of the few I should condescend to look twice at. Pray, does any one here know him? Ask my sister-in-law Cecilia there, and Lady Richton – they are whispering intelligently.'

'Did Maria mention my name?' asked the mild, arch Cecilia Percy, bending forward.

'Yes, girl, I wish to know if you are acquainted with that black-headed Titan?'

'No!' she replied dryly. 'Are you, Matilda?' (to Lady Richton).

'No,' was the brief response.

'On my honour I'll ask his name,' continued Maria.

'Surely you will not,' interposed Edith coldly, 'he cannot be any one of much consequence.'

'I will though, and that too in a manner which shall not make him proud of the notice.'

'Do, do,' said Lady Sydney, 'you always go to the root of the matter at once, Maria.' In all the pride of her rank and beauty the princess bent over the stage.

'Come hither, sir,' said she imperiously. He turned his head, but not his person.

'Well, pretty one, what do you want?' was the astounding

familiar address to one of the proudest and fairest women of Africa. It only spirited Maria to go forward.

'What do I want, sir? Nothing more than your name, that I may report you to the proper authorities for having intruded within the paling.'

'Good,' said the stranger, 'you desire me to bear testimony against myself? Not so, sparkler.'[8]

'I will have you arrested on the spot, if you do not obey me. My servants are at hand,' continued the roused and angry princess.

'Wilt thou?' said the stranger in a lowered and changed tone. Maria started, blushed over neck, brow and temples, and sunk back in her seat as quiet as a lamb. He laughingly advanced towards her.

'Come, madam,' said he, 'I had no intention to quarrel with one who is so perfectly unknown to me as yourself. My name is Major Albert Howard; I was not aware that any restriction existed regarding this paling, so you must forgive my intrusion.'

'I do,' said Maria, bowing and smiling very graciously. Major Albert smiled too, but his haughty head refused to bend, and in silence he moved slowly away.

'How could I be so obtuse,' murmured Maria when he was gone. Cecilia's fair face again leaned over her shoulder.

'*Him* for a wager, sister,' she said archly.

'Or else his wraith,' returned the princess.

*

Major Howard crossed the silent square. He did not ascend the vestibule, but stole very softly round a wing of the edifice and stopped at a private door before which a sentinel was pacing. 'Stand!' said the man as that tall shadow-like form approached. 'Arise,' was the brief reply. Instantly the musket rung reversed on the pavement, and its bearer drew back with an air of profound reverence. He touched the call bell which returned a faint silver sound. The door instantly unclosed and he entered. I lingered a moment behind. Through the open door I saw his valet disencumbering him of the roquelaure.[9]

'Will your lordship have a change of dress now or not?' he asked.

'No, it signifies little. Where is your lady?'

'In the purple saloon, I believe, my lord. She gave Mr Robert
S'death[10] an audience there half an hour since.'

'S'death! Hum, scoundrel! what can his business have been?'

With these words he walked away; I followed, of course.
Creeping up the little marble staircase which terminated a small
but elegant hall, I presently entered a long, lamplit, sounding,
lonely corridor. I think few but the major would have ventured to
wake such an echo as did his brass-shod boots in abodes so regally,
so grandly silent. He turned off soon into the interior chamber,
and after him I wandered through a suite of rooms, bewilderingly
magnificent, and all the more impressive from the light which
revealed them: soft, solemn moonshine pensively stealing through
the Grecian windows, and tinting with pearl and silver whatsoever
its lustre touched.

He paused at the folding doors of one apartment, opened them
gently, and without again entirely closing them, went in. They
were just sufficiently ajar to allow me a full view of the penetralia.
Here warm lights were glowing over the rich deep sombre hangings,
dazzling carpets, and Tyrian couches. Queen Mary Henrietta
appeared in the midst alone, partially reclined on the piled cushions
of a purple silk ottoman, beautiful, delicate as a dream, all fair and
soft and tranquil and imperial.

Aye! I now felt I was in a king's palace: the host of loveliness
which dazzled me so at Zamorna faded away.[11] They were people
of this world, who went in flocks, and laughed and talked and
jested socially. But this was a clear, large star of beauty, appropriated and dwelling apart in its own cloudless quarter of the sky; a
priceless pearl which a strong man had found, and which he kept
and guarded jealously.

Yet royal as was Queen Mary's solitude, it appeared likewise
melancholy. I did not envy her. She seemed cut off by greatness
from commerce with her kind. Still, the haughty expression of her
brow and of her beaming moonlight eyes told it was no matter of
regret to her. Happy, however, she was not, but pensive, mournful,
and disconsolate, and as she impatiently turned her cheek on the
cushion which supported it, and veiled her forehead with her hand,
the tears of some secret sorrow trickled through these slender
fingers.

An ebony table stood at her side on which lay an unfolded paper, and there her eye seemed to linger with intense anxiety. Major Albert fixed on her a long and steadfast gaze. Ere he withdrew it she looked up and saw him. The convulsed start with which she sprang from her couch bespoke an overwrought mind. For a moment she stood bewildered. The disguise had scattered her ideas. One word, however – her own name 'Mary' whispered in a low tone, and accompanied by a gentle smile – sufficed to complete the recognition. She did not run forward, but said softly and sadly,

'Ah Zamorna, did you think *I* could be blinded by a mask like that? Where have you been my lord? And how long is it since you went? I scarcely know how time passes.'[12]

The duke curled his lips, walked to the fire, and was silent. Just then he actually, for once in his life, felt displeased with himself. The duchess spoke again.

'Do tell me where you have been, Adrian,[13] I only want to know that.'

'What ails you, Henrietta?' said he quickly.

'I am very sorrowful, as I have been for a long while now.'

Zamorna's hand went to the gold chain across his bosom and he looked as gloomy as night.

'Am I to have the old story?' he said, glancing at her and then letting his eye fall. She did not reply and he went on,

'S'death has been with you, has he not?'

'He has, my lord.'

'And what was the fiend's errand?'

'He came from my father, sire.'

'That I did not doubt. He is ever the messenger of Satan. And what said he of thy father, dove?'

'That his health and spirits droop more in a foreign country than they did at home. He likewise brought this letter, which I would offer your majesty, only I fear –'

'Fear nothing, child. It cannot contain sentiments more infernal than those I give him credit for, so let us see the precious document.'

'I trust, sire, you will think more favourably of my father when you have seen his heart there disclosed,' said Henrietta as she gave the paper to her husband. He sat down. The shaded lustre dependent from the saloon ceiling gave him light. With compressed lips and settled aspect he perused Northangerland's famous letter to the Angrians.[14] Not a sound interrupted the silence which reigned around while the duke was thus employed, except the rustling sheets as he turned them over.

Mary watched him intently. With an unconscious movement she stole by degrees nearer to him till she stood at his side. Then weary of standing she kneeled on one knee, and resting against his sofa, looked up into her lord's face with so fond, so tender, so appealing an expression, that nothing I have seen either in sculpture or painting could equal the feeling of pathos it conveyed.

He concluded and laid the paper down. His cheek had become brightly flushed towards the end and his eyes were assuming an excited and flashing glow.

'Sire, may I speak?' asked the queen, clasping her hands with earnestness.

He heard her voice, but I think not her words. His spirit was far off in another region, and, regarding her surpassing loveliness with a faint abstracted smile, he gathered his energies in profound thought.

Mary took the smile for consent, and drawing still closer, she addressed him thus:

'I know, sire, you will now, with your kingly candour, confess that Lord Northangerland means you no harm. He calls Zamorna his noble king, and warmly declares his admiration of him. O, Adrian, if you knew how much I love my father you would appreciate the sufferings I have lately endured. I saw your aspect darken whenever he passed before you. I knew you hated him and I never spoke a word. I bade him farewell – it might be for the last time. I watched the vessel that bore him from Africa lessen and vanish, and I still kept silence. I heard on all sides hints thrown out that the queen had no influence, or that she was coldly apathetic. So my brother Edward taunted me to my face, and I endured this also. Hardest of all sire, I feared – was it without reason? – that your dislike of Percy began to mingle with your feelings towards his wretched daughter. I wept alone, and though my heart nearly broke with the unnatural effort, I laid my finger on my lips still. I had a reason for this conduct which I scarcely dared whisper to myself. It was the appalling dread that your majesty's aversion might be well founded – that Percy might in truth be Zamorna's bitter foe; and whether right or wrong, just or impious, I stood prepared to sacrifice my father's very life, truly as I loved him, to the interests of him I could not help adoring with blind, infatuated, consuming zeal. My own life, my own happiness, I will not speak of; they seemed as dust in the balance. But sire, when two hours since I received that letter, when I had read it, the delusion at once passed away. I knew then that Northangerland was true to you, and I blessed him with my whole soul for it. My father has been wronged sire, vilely and wickedly wronged. He has human feelings, but a superhuman intellect. Errors may have resulted from this incongruity, and these he says he will not defend, and after that noble confession who shall dare to accuse him? My king, my husband, my very deity, smile at me once more, and tell me that Percy shall again be your right hand. O, sire! he is worth all the jackals that throng round you now. He is a true and royal lion, worthy to consort with yourself, while his detractors are inferior to the dust your foot has prest. Am I to lie down on a sleepless pillow tonight Zamorna? Am I to eat the bread and drink the waters of bitterness, or, blessed with the forgiving light of your countenance, am I to sleep in peace and awake in safety?'

Her enthusiasm as she knelt, almost crouched, in her earnest pleading at his feet, her sweet and swelling tones, her whole aspect, quickly recalled Zamorna's absent thoughts, and he heard the latter part of her prayer with deep attention. The monarch's hand shook through the influence of some strong internal emotion as he passed it over his broad white brow and then let it slowly fall on his queen's head, bowed before him like a storm-beaten lily.

She burst into happy tears the moment she felt his fingers laid caressingly on her golden curls.

'Be calm, love; be calm, my dear Mary,' said he in that still, dewlike voice of his. 'I would indeed receive your father back with open arms, for his gentle daughter's sake, if sincerity had prompted one fourth part of the sentiments his letter contains. But no, Mary; I see nothing like the light of truth. One hollow wheel turns with a still hollower; and all the mass of machinery weaves together a veil of deceit that might blind Machiavel's eyes, but I have cast it from me and I'll walk my own path steadfastly, turning neither to the right hand nor the left.' Mary sighed deeply.

'Am I never to see my father again then?' said she.

'I trust you will, love, in this very palace. I even prophesy that before a month passes he will be Premier of Angria again. It is my determination to throw no obstacles in his way. His genius, so grandly developed in that letter, I want: and if possible I will have it. But by God's help, I will beware of his insidious wickedness.'

'He loves you, sire,' again interposed Henrietta. The duke smiled. He gently raised his wife, and having placed her on his own sofa, began himself to pace the room with folded arms and thoughtful forehead. His quickened step soon shewed that the current of his meditations was running high and strong.

He paused. Mary looked at him. There he stood with the red firelight flashing over him, one foot advanced, his head proudly raised, his kindled eyes fixed on the opposite wall and filled with a most inspired glory: that tinge of insanity, which certainly mingles with his blood, was looking through their fierce dilated zones, as if it glared out at visions which itself had poured through the air.

'We walk together,' he exclaimed aloud. 'Our hands shall be twined, our purposes must be one. He has no heart, and I'll rend mine from my bosom before its quick, hot pulsations shall interfere with what I see, with what I feel, with what I anticipate by day and night. Why else were we born in one century? His sun should have set before mine rose, if their blended shining was not destined to set earth on fire. By the great genii! It spreads! What? Farther, farther; a deeper, longer, gorier vista. I'll follow: you dare not beckon where I dare not go. Hah! it is stopped, filled up. Blackness, blackness, where am I? The day went down suddenly! All is utterly dark. Spirit! Percy! I have seen the end of my battles. How time hastens – twenty years did you say? Gathered in the span, as at this distance, it seems of one hour. Life slides from under me and there is the gulf of eternity. Eternity! Deep, bodiless, formless, what sails there? Why is there no sound? Such a stony silence, such a desolate vacancy. There should have been stars in the space. Who said I might remember? A vain hope; thought slips already. Earth, existence, I have been great in both, but I remember no more my greatness.'

He ceased, his eyes had become fixed, his face looked ashen and lifeless, but with one hand on his breast and the other resting on a stand of lamps he still stood rigidly upright.

While he spoke, my attention had been too much absorbed to notice what passed at the other end of the saloon. But now I heard a voice saying, 'You have seen him so before, Mary?' I looked around. A gentleman in black stood beside the duchess, and his powdered hair and sternly statuesque physiognomy at once announced the Duke of Wellington. He wore a travelling dress, and had evidently only just arrived at the palace. Mr Maxwell [the steward] accompanied him. Henrietta seemed calm and collected, only she trembled all over.

'I have seen the duke so twice before,' said she, 'both times then I was alone, and I never spoke a word of it to any living creature. Was your grace aware of these paroxysms?'

'Aye! aye, Mary, and stranger ones than these, or at least more dangerous. Is Alford in the house?'

'Yes, but I beg your grace will not send for him. Zamorna is not senseless now. He would be infuriated by the slightest movement towards the bell or door. I committed that mistake once, and I shall never forget the tone and look with which he commanded me to desist.'

'Humph,' replied my father. 'Like a possessed corpse.'

'Send for no one, I tell you,' said Mary quickly. 'I will venture to approach him myself, if you dare not, Maxwell. I say no man on earth knows what those have to suffer, who, idolizing Zamorna as I do, see him in his dark moments. I verily believe he has revelations which other people have not, or else his imagination is burning as a hot coal. But look! He moves, I'll go to him.' She was about to approach, but the Duke of Wellington placed his strong sinewy arms round her and held her firmly back.

'Be still, my love,' said he, 'I would not trust him at this moment.'

Zamorna slowly paced the saloon and then he drew towards that group. I was glad just then I did not form a part of it. He stopped within half a yard of them, and fixed upon them such an aspect, such eyes: it was evident he saw neither his father, his wife, nor Maxwell. The organs of vision were still and glazed; they looked through and beyond all solid objects, with motionless intensity – motionless except an occasional fluttering of the eyelid and long lashes.

They watched the transient visions imagination had portrayed, then they turned slowly upwards. His face whitened more and more. Something like foam became apparent on his lip, and he knitted his brow convulsively.[15]

The Duke of Wellington turned to Maxwell.

'Carry my daughter from the room,' he said. 'Never mind how she struggles, and return yourself instantly.'

The steward having obeyed these orders, my father in turn closed and locked the three doors of the apartment, not omitting the folding door, and so my post of observation being destroyed, I saw no more.

> [Northangerland does return to Angria, and with him a
> semblance of calm, here happily interrupted by the birth of
> royal twins.]

Well the Duchess of Zamorna has done it at last, and in right, good, dashing Angrian style. Her subjects are delighted: they absolutely worship her. It comes so properly up to their ideas – somewhat out of the common line – the thing accomplished, and a trifle to spare. Angria will have nothing trite. There must be flash and bustle and rising-sun-ism about all her affairs, especially where the king is concerned. Well they have it.

On the 5th of October 1834, about twelve o'clock high noon, I was sitting in the front drawing room of Julia Place. All at once, without any sound of previous warning, the window before which I sat was shaken by a strong iron thrill of sound, at first too stunning to admit of comprehension. After a moment's intermission it burst or rung out again, and then I knew it to be the united peal of all the bells in the cathedral and the churches. Twelve times was that mighty crash repeated. Then the bonds of sound seemed loosened, the chain of union apparently burst with the violence of the concussion, and they rung abroad through the sunny and cloudless sky, filling its echoes with so sweet, so exulting, so inspiring a strain, that instinctively I shouted 'Hurrah!' and rushed from the house into the street.

It was full of people. How they had gathered so quickly I know not. All were talking as fast and loud, and elbowing their way as vigorously and unceremoniously, as if each man was charged with a matter of life and death. Bets I heard were going fast, and all seemed to hang on the alternative 'son or daughter, daughter or son', for such was the keynote that ruled the chaos of sound around me.

'What is the matter?' asked I of a stout, able-bodied Angrian who happened to stand near.

'Matter?' he replied. 'Why man, our bonny queen – God bless her – has been doing her duty to her husband, her king and her country. Unto us a child is born. Whether it be son or daughter we can't tell yet, but two soldiers of the horseguards have just ridden full gallop down Parliament Street in the direction of the batteries, with orders about the artillery. Ten salutes will be fired if it's a boy you know, and only five if it be a girl. *If*, do I say? There's no if about the matter: it must be a boy.' And with this characteristic asseveration he turned on his heel.

The batteries on the east bank of the river are distinctly visible from the end of Julia Place. In that direction all eyes were anxiously turned. Ere long a flash of fire, a cloud of smoke, a long loud deepening roar belched from the bristling line of cannons and rolled over the water – gave the first welcome to the royal stranger. Another, a third, a fourth, a fifth came and went. All the city rested in expectation. When the red balls of the sixth discharge at length fell and rebounded on the river's breast, Julia Place spoke in a shout to Parliament Street, Parliament Street roared Huzza to Adrian Road, Adrian Road called to Palace Square: Adrianopolis, in short, rose in a living earthquake of exultation. Ten was numbered by the east battery, the appointed number. An interval of six or seven minutes ensued, and to the astonishment of all, the west battery caught up the dying echo. Crash after crash rattled round the city till ten more salutes were numbered.

At this moment a gentleman on horseback dashed through the throng, his face full of glee, and his eyes sparkling with pleasure.

'Bravo Angrians!' exclaimed he, waving his hat round his head.

'Fling up your caps and your wigs, men. Here I am fresh from the palace. Such news I never heard the like for good. Twins! my lads, twins! and both thriving, handsome, healthy boys. There's for you.'

The crowds were actually convulsed with enthusiasm at this intelligence. I left them, darkening the sun with their headgear, leaping, roaring, and hurrahing like mad. During that day I visited the palace, but could find no rest for the sole of my foot.

[Charles, snooping as usual, manages to pick up from the steward a hint that all is not well between Zamorna and Northangerland, and later to get a peep at the little princes.]

'What does the duke think about the matter?' asked I. 'Is he glad?'

'Why, Lord Charles,' returned Maxwell, 'my master, you know, is rather difficult to fathom sometimes. All last night and this day has he been shut up in his study, and nobody but the earl his father-in-law, Lady Helen Percy,[16] and Doctor Alford have been admitted to speak with him until about half an hour after his children were born, when he sent for me, to give some written orders. I found him walking very restlessly up and down the room, Lord Northangerland sitting near the mantlepiece, as sadly thoughtful as if death instead of life had been added to the house. Zamorna smiled at me as I entered, and very condescendingly put his hand into mine. It trembled and felt cold. I offered my humble congratulations with heartfelt sincerity.

' "Thank you, William," he said quickly. "I hope the country will be as pleased as yourself. Quite in the Angrian style – two instead of one. Well, I am glad the matter is over at any rate."

'He talked to me about five minutes longer, rather hurriedly, and his eyes shone as he spoke, with that fitful kind of light they always have when his feelings are much excited. His right hand never left the eye-glass chain and scarlet breast ribbon a minute. On the whole I believe he is well-pleased.'

My influence with two of the duchess's ladies procured me a sight of the young princes. I entered their nursery on tiptoe. It is all hung with white and silver damask, and their cradle is veiled with white satin curtains, silver-fringed and tasselled.

I saw the little fairies through a thin web of point lace suspended above them. They are just like the Duke of Zamorna's other children – delicate and beautiful as if made out of modelled wax, with tiny ringlets of pale brown hair on their small snowy foreheads, and their father's eyes gleaming large, full, and dark underneath. It is strange that hereditary feature should (like Northangerland's nose) be transmitted with such exactness – Ernest, Julius, and the present pair of whelps all precisely alike in that particular. I understand they will be christened with much pomp and splendour next week. Mr Maxwell, an unerring authority, gave me their intended names and titles.

The eldest, that is, the heir apparent[17] of Angria and Wellington'sland by right of four or five minutes' seniority, will be called Victor Frederic Percy Wellesley, Marquis of Arno. The name of the youngest is Julius Warner di Enara Wellesley, Earl of Saldanha.

[A splendid christening is described, followed by the presentation, which is marred only by the ominous absence of the twins' grandfather.]

Amongst the gentlemen I looked in vain for Lord Northangerland. He was not there. Shaver afterwards told me that during the whole of that day he remained shut up in the regal gloom of Northangerland House, a prey to profound melancholy.

But as the gates of the great entrance rolled back, a side door also unclosed. Two tall, dark-haired ladies glided out and, passing among the pillars of the vestibule, paused between the two huge central columns. Each, as she stood still, stretched to the full view of the multitude a small beautiful image clad in sweeping white robes, with great, brown sparkling eyes, whose light shone from under the shade of ostrich plumes drooping over them in snowy pendency. The unusual size of these orbs communicated a strange, rather wild expression to their faces, whose features were otherwise delicately sweet.

The Angrians welcomed their infant princes with a shout loud as from numbers without number numberless. The bands struck up and the banners waved exultingly. And now somewhat darkened the door of the palace a crested figure, in stature taller than the sons of men. It had risen on a sudden and, with a quick impetuous gesture, it descended the flight of steps and advanced to the lawn-like space kept clear in front.

'Well, Angrians, that's what heaven has sent you!' exclaimed Zamorna, pointing to his children. 'They are yours as well as mine. I dedicate them from their birth. Being born for Angria's good, they must live for her glory, and die if need be for her existence. I rejoice in their creation for your sakes. I love them as much for their connection with the land whose sun is now shining on them, as I do for the blood that runs in their veins and the flesh which covers their bones, though that blood and flesh be my own or dearer than my own. If I could, Angrians, I would permit every individual man here present to bless my children with his embrace and benediction.'

He turned and approached the nurses. I think his little scions had scarcely seen him so near before, for as the lofty shade drew nigh, they clung, without screaming, but with a scared and astonished look, to their female guardians. He smiled, and bending his head and proud mourning plumes over one of them, Victor Frederic I think, kissed it, and saying something in a very soft voice, gently took it to his bosom. The small creature yet gave no note of disapprobation; its tiny cheek even dimpled with an answering smile . . .

Sorry I am, reader, to announce that I can give no further description of the presentation. Just as Zamorna was delivering up his child, I unfortunately, in stretching out of a window of the palace where I had established myself, and whence I had hitherto viewed the affair, lost my balance and fell down a perpendicular eight of twenty feet. I was taken up for dead, and till next morning I continued in a state of utter insensibility. Excuse this hiatus.

October, 1834

Zamorna denounces Northangerland before Parliament: *from the* Verdopolitan Intelligencer

[Relations between Zamorna and Northangerland continue to disintegrate; the rebellion which will drive the duke from office and into exile is imminent. Here he publicly challenges his foe, still hoping for a last-minute reconciliation.]

'My lord Northangerland. It is well known that you and I have run up a long score against each other. Let me see: the accounts have been accumulating for the space of five months – all the world is waiting to see the settlement. It shall be gratified tonight. I do not represent myself as a dove in the midst of serpents, as a lamb compassed by wolves. No, I too am a serpent, and it was the infliction of my own venomous fang, the utterance of my own threatening hiss, which called all my brother dragons about me. I too am a wolf, and it was my own ravening and insatiable ferocity which made the whole horde of wolves single me out. That was as it should be. I do not complain; I deserved it, Percy! That is not what rouses in my heart a feeling of mixed passions which has no name in language. That blended sensation of bitter disappointment, of keen rage, of unquenchable thirst for revenge can never be awakened by any act of my open enemy. It is reserved for the moment which reveals a cold, corrupt, radically black-hearted traitor in the man whom I thought my right-hand councillor.

' "My lord," your look now says, "I have not hated you, Zamorna." I know that insinuating meekness of mouth and eye. O! Percy, cast off that mask: it curdles my blood to see it. What I hate most in all your conduct, what I abhor more than the league with my foes, is the tone of pretended candour and partiality you have chosen to assume towards me. Am I not aware, my lord, that the man never breathed whom you could regard with the feeling of friendship? Do I not know that you are unable to tolerate your fellow-creatures, that your soul is too cold and vitiated for sympathy with them? Have I yet to learn that the conformation of your strange nervous system obliges you to hate that man worst whom, by a stretch of dissimulation, you have pretended to admire; and that consequently I, of all living men, am the most utterly abominable to you? Happily this has been taught me by sharp experience. Do you think me a fool?

> [Zamorna proceeds with an itemized list of Percy's treacherous deeds: providing money to buy arms for Angria's enemies; persecuting with 'rabid hostility' Zamorna's 'best and greatest ministers'; allowing publication of 'vile and detestable falsehoods' in his newspaper.]

'Time passes rapidly, and I must draw to a close. Percy, I have made up a catalogue of your crimes. You have hated my friends and you have loved my enemies. Can we then any longer act together? Impossible. Yet it grieves me to part, knowing how wide, how deep, how impassable a chasm will intervene between us the moment the last link of the binding chain dissolves. Oh my lord! I once thought differently of you. When we combated together last year I would have stabbed the man to the heart who should have told me you were so black, so hollow a traitor as I now find you to be. But it recks not mourning over the past. Where the tree has fallen, so it must lie. Yet I once dreamt (it was but a dream) that we might together have done something which historians should pause over in wonder before they recorded it, that we might have raised a nation fit to be described by the grand symbol of the cedar which Ezekiel applied to Assyria.

[Zamorna then quotes, almost verbatim, Ezekiel 31, 3–8.][18]

'With your aid had I hoped to do this; and without your aid do I still hope to do it. The sands are out in the glass: the moments of grace are departed. We must resolve now. Shall I extend the olive or draw the sword? Decide now. I tremble not, Northangerland. My cause is better than yours, for treachery is not on my side. I have not caressed with the hand what I abhorred in the spirit; my lips have not spoken what my actions belied. No: and therefore, feeling myself to be wronged, my revenge now we part shall be as bitter as I can make it. I'll strike from under you the only prop left to support your exhausted and world-weary heart.[19] Now may the God of Battles, the God whose existence you deny, and whose law I daily transgress, may that mighty and merciful being defend with his right arm the justest cause. We are both darkly spotted in his holy sight. But in the dust I confess my sin; in the ashes I acknowledge my iniquity; in hope I implore forgiveness; in faith I lean on him as on the rock of my defence; in sincerity I worship at his altars, and what can I more? My lord, I demand the seals of office in your possession. You have ceased to be Premier of Angria.' The duke was silent a moment. He then drew quite close to Lord Northangerland, and taking the earl's hand in both his, recommenced speaking in a very low but emphatic tone. The blood mounted to his cheeks; his eyes glittered fiercely.

'Take this warning. I will do as I have said; if eternal death were the immediate consequence, my resolution would remain unshaken. Think, Percy. Think. Much hangs on the next five minutes. All shall go if we part. Not one drop of the blood, not one remnant of the race shall remain: you may never after wash out the deed I am about to commit in my blood. Speak. Shall it be so? Pronounce your own sentence, and that of all you love in the world.'

March, 1835

Zamorna's Exile

[The poem, originally seventy-two stanzas,[20] is a long soliloquy delivered by Zamorna as he is carried into exile, after his defeat at the hands of Northangerland's forces.]

I

1. And, when you left me, what thoughts had I then?
   Percy, I would not tell you to your face;
   But, out of sight and thought of living men,
   Wandering away on the lone ocean's face,
   I may say what I think and how and when
   The mood comes on me; I will give it space,
   Confessing, like a dying man to heaven
   Anxious alone to have his sins forgiven.

2. Not caring what the world he leaves may say,
   Heedless of its forgotten hate and scorn,
   But giving full and free and fearless way
   To secrets that the fear of death has torn
   From his concealing bosom, where they lay
   Scorching the soul in which their sparks were born –
   I give my dreams to the wild wind and sea.

3. You are a fiend; I've told you that before;
   I've told it half in earnest, half in jest;
   I've sworn it when the very furnace-roar
   Of hell was rising fiercely in my breast;
   And calmly I confirm the oath once more,
   Adding however, as becomes me best,
   That I'm no better, and we two united
   Each other's happiness have fiendlike blighted.

4. How oft we wrung each other's callous hearts,
   Conscious none else could so effectively
   Waken the pain, or venom the keen darts
   We shot so thickly, so unsparingly
   Into those sensitive and tender parts
   That, veiled from all besides, ourselves could see
   Like eating cankers, pains that heaven had dealt
   On devotees to crime, sworn slaves of guilt.

5. And still our mutual doom accomplishing,
   Blind as the damned, our antitypes; if one
   Had in his treasures some all-priceless thing,
   Some jewel that he deeply doated on
   Dearer to him than life, the fool would fling
   That rich gem to his friend; he could not shun
   The influence of his star, though well he knew
   His friend that treasure to the winds would strew.

6. Percy, your daughter was a lovely being;
   Truly, you must have loved her: her sweet eyes
   Showed in their varied lustre – changing, fleeing –

Such warm and intense passion; that which lies
In your own breast and, save to the All-seeing,
Not fully known to any, could not rise
To stronger inspiration than their ray,
Revealed when I had waked her nature's wildest play.

7. Well, sir, when Mary on some pleasant even
   Has sat beside you – perhaps at Percy Hall –
   And, in the richest, purest light of heaven
   You've seen the curls around her temples fall;
   And when the coming gloom of dark has given
   A tone of such sad loveliness to all,
   Could you look on her, sire, think that she
   Must sometime be a prey to such as me?

8. I well remember, on our marriage day,
   An hour or two after the bridal rite,
   We'd somehow chanced to find our way
   Into a huge and empty hall, whose light,
   Streaming through painted windows, shed its ray
   On nothing save ourselves, the floor of stone,
   And the pure fountain falling there alone.

9. I gazed on her Ionian[21] face, so fair
   In all its lines, so classically straight
   Her marble forehead, with the haloing hair
   Sunnily clustered round it, whereon sate
   A shade that soon might deepen into care,
   Even such care as had gloomed there of late;
   Though then 'twas but the sadness said to lie
   On the fair brow of those who early die.

10. I asked her if she loved me, and she said
    That she would die for me, with *such* a glance!
    Talk of the fiery, arrowy lustre bred
    By the hot southern suns of Spain and France –
    I say again, as I before have said,
    Our western tenderness does so enhance

    The ardour of our women's souls and spirits,
    That naught on earth such fire divine inherits.

11. She said she'd die for me – and now she's keeping
    Her word far off at Alnwick[22] o'er the sea;
    The very wind around this vessel sweeping
    Will steal unto her pillow whisperingly
    And murmur o'er her form, which shall be sleeping
    Ere long beneath some quiet, pall-like tree:
    I would she were within my reach just now,
    Not long that shade should haunt her Grecian brow.

12. She'd feel the stream of life run strong again
    If I could only take her to my breast;
    She'd feel a balm poured on her aching pain;
    Her day-long weariness would know a rest;
    But then, there's the profound, wide, thundering main,
    Tossing between us its triumphant crest
    Of snow-white foam; and then I've pledged my faith
    To break her father's heart by Mary's death!

13. A holy resolution, and it will
    Be visited upon me thirty-fold,
    For human nature feels a shuddering chill
    To hear of life for bloody vengeance sold:
    An animal passion when unmoved, and still
    And vulture-like it fixes its stern hold
    Deep in the very vitals of its slave,
    Making his bosom but a hungry grave.

14. And so, my lord, if you have ruined me,
    And ruined all the hopes I ever cherished,
    I've paid you back, and that abundantly:
    You'll feel it when that flower of yours has perished;
    And dark and desolate that hour shall be,
    When the place where my dazzling lily flourished
    Shall know no more its past magnificence,
    Death having gathered it and borne it hence.

II

1. Of late our ship along the coast of France
   Was gliding in the gentle gales which blow
   Off from the storied walls of old Provence;
   We saw Marseilles frown on the waves below:
   It's pleasant when the sunny billows dance
   All gladsomely around the vessel's prow,
   And when a town and shore before you lie,
   The home of thousands 'neath their native sky.

2. I stood upon the deck; the vessel's rails
   I was convulsive grasping, for around
   The life and gaiety of proud Marseilles
   Were poured upon the harbour; not a sound
   Rung o'er the deep but glad as chiming bells
   It spoke of life, and made my bosom bound
   With a wild wish for freedom, worse than vain –
   My breast but struck the stronger 'gainst a chain.

3. At that dark moment, something spoke my name –
   My title, rather, which ought now to die –
   'Twas from a female that the soft sound came:
   She said in French, 'Zamorna, will you buy?'
   I turned – it was like the kindling of a flame
   To utter that word 'neath an alien sky:
   I saw a girl beside me, dusk and tall,
   Her face all shaded by her tresses' fall.

4. The curls as bright and black as jet descended
   From under the Provençal hat she wore;
   A basket, full of grapes and vine leaves blended
   With roses, all in Gallic taste, she bore;
   And as on her my silent gaze I bended
   She offered me her rich corbeille[23] once more,
   Murmuring, in the soft tone of sympathy,
   'You shall not buy them: you shall have them free!'

5. I took a rosebud, dropping in its stead
   A coin of my own ruined kingdom, graced
   With the wreathed impress of my own wise head,
   And then – you know my ways – however placed,
   Were it upon the scaffold, flaming red
   With noble blood and forms all death defaced,
   Or were it underneath the gallows-tree,
   I'd kiss the lovely lips that pitied me.

6. Well, when I lifted up the fruit-girl's head
   To give her that salute, the black curls parted,
   And the revealed and flashing eyeballs shed
   A ray upon me not unknown; I started
   And, half indignantly, I would have said,
   'This must not be,' but then so broken-hearted,
   So full of dying hope was that dark eye,
   I could not put its mute petition by.[24]

7. And so I turned again towards the town
   And looked down on its vast and busy quay;
   And meekly obstinate the girl sat down
   Beside me on the deck and murmuringly
   She said, 'Zamorna, I have borne your frown
   Often before, and now I dare not be
   Delicate in my duties; those must dwell
   In gloom habitual who would serve you well.

8. 'I stayed in Angria, sire, until the hour
   Was past when I could serve my master there;
   Until they had dug up the cherished flower
   He gave unto my sleepless, deathless care;
   Until they'd broken his own domestic bower,
   Shivered his shrine, and scattered in the air
   The relics he loved well; and, this task done,
   I rose and followed where my lord was gone.

9. 'I will be with you, sire; you'll want me soon
   In that lone, dreary island where you go;

You'll sicken of the melancholy tune
The waves will play around you in their flow;
And, wandering on its shore with shipwrecks strewn,
You'll feel its solitude – full well I know –
Go to your heart: and then a wretch like me
Might serve you still in that extremity.'

10. She spoke; I made no answer, we were now
Leaving the harbour of Marseilles behind;
S'death had weighed anchor, and the Rover's prow
Was flashing through the wave before the wind:
The gleaming walls and towers began to grow
Dim in the distance; scarce the eye might find
More than the misty outlines of their forms
Shadowy as rocks obscured by coming storms.

11. Our captain came, and swore that she should stay:
He'd have no boats sent off to land, not he;
She might have known the ship was under weigh,
She saw it moving through the severed sea;
And, by his soul, and by the light of day,
He'd never stir a step to pleasure me;
And Mina smiled to see her end was gained:
Fortune had favoured her, and she remained.

12. Now, for my Mary's sake, I have not given
One smile or gleam of love to that poor slave;
And I have seen her woman's feelings riven
With pangs that made her look down on the wave
As if it were her home, her hope of heaven,
Because a semblance of repose it gave:
She sees I do not want her; none can tell
What torments from that chill conviction swell.

13. I cannot spurn her, though my wife is dying
Cheerless and desolate in solitude;
This moment, like a faithful dog, she's lying
Crouched at my feet, for with a sad, subdued,

Untiring constancy she's ever trying
To gain one word, or even one look, imbued
With some slight touch of kindness; 'There, then take
A brief caress, for all thy labour's sake.'

14. I did but press her little hand, and press
The taper fingers as a brother might;
And she looked upward in her meek distress,
While such a glad, adoring ray of light
Shot from her large black eyes, as if to bless
A god for mercies given, and full and bright
The gathered tear ran over; then again
They bent their radiance on the solemn main.

[Mina brings to Zamorna the tragic intelligence that his
eldest son, Ernest, who had been left behind in Mina's care,
has been savagely murdered by his foes.]

III

1. How did I feel when Mina ceased her speaking,
I, stronger than an Indian in my love
For that which now beyond the power of waking
Sleeps in its gory grave? There's heaven above,
And earth around me, and beneath me, shaking
With cries of the tormented, hell may move:
But neither from hell nor earth nor righteous heaven
Can rest or comfort to my heart be given.

2. Thou whom I nurtured in my bosom, child;
Thou whom I doated on and fondly cherished;
Thou to die thus, when I was far exiled!
In gloom, in grief, in agony he perished,
Sundered from me by that storm dread and wild
Which was sent over Angria: all that flourished
Fairest upon her plains died in the blast,
Leaving her lorn and barren as it passed.

3. You would not save him, Percy, nor will I
   Save yours from desolation: with wild pleasure
   I'll now call down the doom from the most high,
   His curse upon my head in fullest measure;
   I'll fit me for a passage to the sky
   By heaving overboard my choicest treasure:
   Yea, I'll leave all, take up my cross and follow;
   All flesh is grass, all joys are vain and hollow.

4. King, Dog, and Fiend, you cannot tell me now
   The thing I would not do to make another
   Feel the same horror that bedews my brow
   With bloody sweat: hot, harried crime may smother
   The choking, suffocating thoughts that grow
   Like fungi round my wrecked heart and wither
   Its vital greenness, deeply, deeply eating
   Into my life-pulse hotly, madly beating.

5. Mina, come hither; weep no more; I love you
   As a hawk loves a lark; I've cast away
   Patrician ladies throned as high above you
   As that large star serene above the ray
   The glow-worm flings; let not this world's scorn move you
   And waste not in my passion's fiery ray:
   I know that you can bear a fierce caress;
   My arm grows strong, nerved by my heart's distress.

6. You'll never fear nor tremble to draw nigh
   When I am scarce myself, with torment stinging;
   Into the principle of life you'd die
   To save my bosom from a moment's wringing;
   Faithful, devoted martyr! Through her eye,
   Her soul, a ray of fevered joy is clinging
   Because I said she might the victim be
   Of a chained vulture, caged amid the sea.

7. Beautiful creature! Once so innocent,
   With such a seriousness and strength of mind
   Beaming upon her youthful brow, and blent
   With what seemed like religion; so refined,
   So firm in principle, her soul ne'er bent
   Nor wavered midst the soft voluptuous wind:
   A western blast around the wild rose blew
   But shook not from it one pure drop of dew.

8. I'll go and sit beside her and recline
   My forehead on her shoulder; there, all's calm;
   Her faithful heart was blest as it felt mine
   Beating against it; now, denied the balm
   Blown o'er the summer sea by gales divine,
   Singing as sweet as some old mournful psalm,
   I'll bow resigned, a man of many woes;
   The sea shall soothe me, saddening as it flows.

9. Tormented! O, tormented! Mina, love,
   Thy neck is wet with tears; they would come forth;
   I cannot one brief hour of respite prove
   The sweetest sights and sounds that bless this earth;
   Only the fiend to busier madness move
   That eats my life away: what is their worth?
   Nothing! O Mina love, I cannot rest,
   I could not if Heaven's glories round me pressed.

10. And it is misery, when all's so bright
    In earth and sea and sky, as they were wooing
    My mind to sympathy; and in their light,
    Their evening light, I feel around me growing
    Some thing no words can tell: an inward night,
    Downward unceasingly, and darkly flowing
    In clouds – yes, pity me, and wildly strain
    Thy master to thy breast: 'tis all in vain!

11. Wave thy soft ringlets round me, press my brow
    With that cool supple hand, and point again
    Unto that western sky: I see its glow,
    I feel it rosily upon the main
    Pouring its flush; I hear the cooing flow
    Of the hushed waters lulling their deep strain,
    Answering the winds as those enkindled seas
    Respond to the bright burning sunset's blaze.

12. I seem to have lived for nothing: wandering
    Through all my early youth, 'mong fields of flowers,
    Tracking the green paths where the fairest spring,
    Culling the richest bloom of dells and bowers;
    When, all at once, the unredeeming wing
    Of some cold blast, swept by with sleety showers,
    Scattered the roses and buds and leaves away,
    Save one or two left shrivelled by decay.

13. That simile's absurd: all words are weak:
    Tongue cannot utter what the victim feels
    Who lies outstretched upon that burning lake
    Whose flaming eddy now beneath me reels –
    All that breathes happiness seems to forsake
    His blighted thoughts: a demon hand unseals
    That little well so treasured in man's breast
    Whose drop of hope so sweetens all the rest.

14. And out it flows and slips unseen away,
    Trickling to nothingness, and leaving gall,
    Rank gall behind: such bitter, briny spray
    As might be brought up by a sulphurous squall
    From the Dead Lake, the Sodomitish Sea:
    But, halt! I've said enough; and yonder wave
    Shall give my words an unrevealing grave.

July, 1836

The Return of Zamorna

I

The last days of autumn were now dimly closing. A little of the softness of summer still lingered in the air, but the leaf-strewn walks and embrowned groves of Alnwick prophesied how nigh were the snows of winter. Mary had risen wan and pallid from the bed that a month since it seemed she never would leave again. Too feeble to bear the chill of October and the scent of decaying woods and flowers, she never walked but in the lengthened and sounding corridors of the hall, and there she would pace about hour after hour, resting herself at intervals in the seats at the latticed windows, silent, abstracted, in an unbroken reverie, from sunrise to midnight.

Wasted and blanched as she looked, her attendants wondered often how she could bear to walk so long, but her uncomplaining melancholy awed them too much for expostulation. They never dared advise her to seek more repose, and there, all day long, the light rustle of her dress might be heard as she traversed the measured walk with noiseless and languid tread, more like a flitting shade than a living woman.

What thoughts absorbed her spirit through these dreary hours? She seldom, I am told, was seen to weep, though now and then a tear that had been gathering long on her eyelid would fall like a single pearl on the pavement.

Occasionally on Sunday evening, when the sun just before its setting was diffusing a placid glow over the park, she would go to Lady Helen's drawing room; and leaning from the open casement, would listen to the bells of Alnwick Minster ringing two miles off for evening service. I can well imagine what associations the holy chime, the consecrated day and hour, would bring.

Miss Clifton [her maid] told me that she continued to wear, round her neck, a little miniature of the duke which she had worn constantly since their marriage, but that she never opened the case that contained it. There was a marble medallion of his head too in one of her rooms, but on no occasion did she seem to be aware whose likeness it was. She had lost the substance and she was too ardent, too wildly devoted in her adoration of what had been riven from her grasp to care anything for the cold, lifeless shadow.

But oh! by day, by night, when she woke, when she lay down, how would her thoughts ever wander: aimless, guideless, she unknowing where, conscious only that they were stretching still seaward.

How would they brood over the visions of a broad ocean without either isle or shore or ship, with the moon of the most serene night mirrored in its depths, and over all the phantasm flung the pervading feeling that in those waves her hope, her happiness, her god, her heaven were merged.[25]

Meantime she scarce seemed to grow worse from day to day, yet she lived almost without food. What she took in the course of the whole four and twenty hours would scarce have sufficed a healthy appetite for a single repast.

But now November was passing away, and the rough and tempestuous days of December were drawing rapidly on. She could no longer walk in the corridor, whose damp atmosphere, if she breathed it a moment, brought on a faint and threatening cough. She sat, therefore, in a large apartment, exquisitely fitted up with all the luxuries and all the decorations of refined art Lady Helen could devise as likely for a moment to divert her attention. The walls were painted with sweet Italian scenes: groups of figures amidst the gleaming statues and blushing roses of some stately garden; a lake with a sweep of sunny shore in the distance; and the sky of a southern clime canopying all.

Amidst these splendours Mary would sit from morning to night in one place, almost in one position. To have seen her thus would have been a striking spectacle, as richly dressed as when she sat throned in Adrianopolis, the centre of the most dazzling court in the world. Morning after morning her ladies robed her as they had been accustomed to do.

'Many a time,' said one of them to me, 'I have thought, whilst placing the rings on her little thin nerveless fingers, and clasping the chains of pearl about her wasted neck all over as white and clear as marble – I have thought it would not be long before we should have to dress her corpse in its shroud and to lay her out, young as she was and divinely beautiful, stiff and icy in her coffin.'

It would have been well for her if this dream of life could have lasted unbroken, for if far indeed removed from all affinity with happiness, it was at least a relief from the pangs of extreme misery; but every now and then it might be told by the sudden restlessness which would seize her, by the fever that would concentrate in her chest, by the clasping of her little consumptive hands, and by the agonized and delirious expression of her eye, that she had been wakened to a wilder and clearer recollection of her sorrows.

> [Mary delivers a long, heartrending speech to her grand-
> mother, recalling the old, happy days and her love for her
> father and for Zamorna.]

It was after such a wild awakening of woes as this that the unfortunate queen had retired one dreary night to her chamber, and had thrown herself, sick with despair, on her splendid bed. All her attendants had by her own desire left her. She would not be undressed and there she lay, arrayed in rich satin, with a clear chain of brilliants quivering round her neck, the shadowy ray of a single lamp shining on her white face and lighting the tears on her eyelashes and on her soft pure cheeks.

Perhaps human suffering of similar kind has never surpassed what she felt then: that intense yearning after what she knew was unattainable; that dying away of hope; that conviction that happiness would never return more; that fearful ebb of spirits which seems to bring death so near and to invest it with a form so terrible.

It was a tempestuous night. A hollow and continuous wind howled in the dark air, and rain came, driven in fitful showers against the windows. In such circumstances a superstitious horror began to creep over Mary's mind, which her shattered nerves were but ill able to resist.

She looked round the gloomy and spacious room and she thought, 'How shall I pass the night that lies before me?' Her mind conjured up ghastly ideas of beings from another world, of strange unthought-of visitants with aspects divested of human sympathy congealed to stone and full of such meaning as nothing mortal could witness and live.

She longed for a moment's relief, she prayed for it with hands clasped, shuddering lest some voice of unearthly tone should answer her prayer.

As she finished the ejaculation, whilst the cold sweat was starting from her forehead, her eye, drooping from its raised glance to God, fell on a small cabinet opposite her bed. A white square of paper like a folded letter arrested her meandering glance.

[The letter turns out to be from Zamorna, who assures her that he is near by and well, and plans to reclaim her after he has settled the score with his foes.]

I should like to have you in my arms for a moment [the letter continues], but I suppose that is not to be as yet. If you are strong enough, come down to the park gates tomorrow at nine o'clock in the morning, and you will perhaps see me; but don't expect to speak to me. I am not lurking about like a felon, but following my calling in an independent way. I defy the devil himself either to catch or retain me just now. There's a lock of my hair enclosed. You've romance enough about you to like the gift. I'm not your husband at present and I don't intend to be for a little while, but I shall keep thinking of you whenever I've a minute's leisure, and if your guardians don't take care they'll find themselves outwitted by and by.

This letter sounds rather hard and rough but I've had something to go through lately. I don't intend to die in a hurry.

Good-bye.

A.W.

Reader, how shall I describe the sensations these words – this letter – flashed upon Mary Percy? Five minutes ago and she had been flung on the bed, bloodless and faint, with the aspect, with the feelings of one dying in bitter grief. Strange terrors conjured by despair out of the night had been pressing darkly round her, and now a few words had changed almost her identity.

She seemed to comprehend at once that she had been living in a world of hideous phantasms, which till now she had mistaken for realities. The undefined horror which had overspread all associations connected with Alnwick, every room in the house, and every walk in the garden, cleared off. A bright, a rational hope softly prevailed over despair.

She knew Zamorna was not yet hers nor she Zamorna's, but he was alive, he was in Africa, he remembered her. There lay his letter, there lay a lock of his own hair, severed but lately from his own head. And as she hung over the soft curl of dark chestnut, glanced again at the well-known autograph, and felt rushing back to her excited mind recollections of the seductive smiles and tones and aspect that she, of all the flowers of Africa, had been singled out to enjoy alone, small scruple did the western lady feel at the thought of yielding herself to the prescribed and desperate wanderer's guidance.

The idea that she was not his wife did indeed once cross her brain, and therewith came a reminiscence of certain reckless and slippery traits in his character. But as she passed the chamber with these thoughts sending the blood in crimson to her cheeks, it might be told by one lofty moment with which she raised her head, and by the resolved enthusiasm sparkling in her eyes, that no doubt, no misgiving, no check of prudence could restrain her imperious will for a moment. All her strong feelings were concentrated in one desire. The gathered flood was pausing on the brow of the fall: there were reeds waving beside it; there were flowers and willows; but which wand, which blossom, can arrest the impending dash?

II

[The next morning finds Mary, long before nine, waiting by the river for a sight of her beloved.]

Oh! how long seemed the two weary hours of her morning vigil. At first, upheld by excitement, she did not feel the charnel chill of the air; but her spirits, so broken by lengthened suffering, could not long endure suspense. She looked along the path by the riverside. She looked up the clear blue stream itself. All was still and speckless. The leafless shrubs alone trembled gently at intervals.

'Was it but a sweet dream?' she asked herself, and she had scarce spoken when her morbid imagination almost made the supposition a certainty. Her cough, irritated by the cold, came on with violence. By nature she was not formed to bear disappointment. Her strength both of body and mind sunk away at once; and wishing, almost expecting, to die on the spot, she sat down on the mossy stone and yielded to a burst of drear lamenting.

She had sat thus a long, long time, her head sunk on her knees, overwhelmed with the weight of woe that, a moment lightened, had fallen back with tenfold heaviness; when suddenly there proceeded from the river a sound like the intermittent dash of oars. It drew nearer and nearer. There was a pause, and a hoarse voice called out.

'What the devil! Are you going to run the barge ashore?'

'Stand back,' was the reply, 'I know what I'm about.' The words were few but they made Miss Percy start. She bounded up like a deer, across the path, down the slope, through the narrow copse of hazels. Amongst the sedges and luxuriant aquatic plants, she stood ancle-deep in the pure wave. But the voice again arrested her.

'Lady!' it exclaimed, hailing her across the broad stream. 'Stop! the river's deep. If it were not so I'd tell you, my sweet lass, to venture further and wade to me.'

'Be still, you wild dog. That's a real lady,' said the voice that had spoken first.

There was a rush through the waves, and from behind the shade of a little islet plumed with majestic willows, and close to the shore, swept a barge, heavily laden. A group of watermen were lying on the packages at one end. At the other stood erect a very tall figure leaning on an oar.

'Look,' he said, lifting his clear sonorous tones again over the murmur of the Derwent, 'look, I'll send her like a race horse under that thicket!'

With an athletic and flashing stroke, he dissevered the wave and brought his barge with a swoop close up to the bank, just beneath where Mary stood. She saw herself within five or six yards of a young man of unusually erect and lofty figure, dressed in a checked shirt and loose canvas trousers, without shoes or stockings; his symmetrical bony and almost fleshless feet as white as marble, bare on the wet planks of the barge; his neck bare too, his high features and thin cheeks, bloodless and sallow, savagely shadowed by dark and profuse whiskers. His hair of the darkest chestnut had evidently not been acquainted with shears for months. It floated in long, wild curls on the wind, and encumbered his neck like the luxuriant mane of a desert steed. His lips bore a laughing and reckless expression, but his eyes had a character of ferocity which made one glad to elude their sudden quick glance.

As the barge neared and was borne slowly away by the current of the Derwent, the favouring wind filling its large sail, Mary saw him turn and fix on her so eager, so hawklike a glance – while the classic lips curled with such a fond and sunny smile – that, dizzy with the tumultuous feelings, the wild pulsations, the burning and impatient wishes that smile and glance excited, she closed her eyes in momentary blindness.

When she looked again the boat had become a speck. He was gone almost before she had had time for recognition. His image had passed over the surface of her mind, and scarce an instant had been allowed to seize and fix it, but it was he. She knew it, she had felt it, and now she would return home and live on the bright vision of that morning till another, less fleeting, should be vouchsafed to her.

He looked very worn and pale, but there were the same superb lines.

'Would I could follow him; I must, I must go to Ellrington Hall.[26] The thought gives me new life. There will be hope of another glimpse and I can watch my tremendous father. I'll set off this very day. Alnwick is a ghastly dungeon. I can live in it no longer. O God! Look upon Zamorna: guard his life, give him victory, crush his foes, and above all in life, or death, let him not forget me!'

[In the next scene Mina Laury, who has tended the grieving duke throughout his exile, reappears and announces to Zamorna's faithful ally, Warner, that he is alive and has returned to Angria. Word spreads, and reaches an elated band of the duke's old followers, who all rush off to join him.]

III

[Mary has arrived in Verdopolis; the newspapers are filled with accounts of Zamorna's success. Northangerland's defeat seems imminent; he is besieged by three of his mistresses who fear the duke's wrath if they are captured.]

'Oh! Alexander, my Alexander! You will save me from every insult, you will save me from danger. Don't let me be guillotined – don't, don't. Look at my neck – you would not like it to be gashed with the sharp axe; and they are coming – they will take me – they will behead me. Look, he smiles! Are you glad? Well it is all your own doing. You have brought them. You would not listen to me, and slay whilst you had the power. I wanted you to kill, and you only banished. Fool, it serves you right – he is come back. I wish he may take you and shoot you.'

'Thank you, my love,' said the earl, 'I need some good wishes and I'm likely to get them. Meantime, what has occasioned this burst of fondness? Any special news this morning?'

Louisa paused a moment to gather strength for her overwhelming reply, and during that momentary space the door was dashed to the wall. Two other females rushed into the room: one a tall, imperial Verdopolitan in robes of the revolutionary crimson, sweeping and ample; the other a dark vivacious foreigner in spotless white. In a whirl of dishevelled locks and floating array they flung themselves round the knees of Northangerland.

Louisa was in his arms and for an instant thus he stood, zoned with beauty, the whole three weeping wildly at his feet, and at intervals ejaculating detached words of horror and consternation.

'By heaven!' exclaimed the earl, with a reckless and peculiar laugh, 'I shall be murdered now, however. Verily this is too much of a good thing. But,' he continued more sternly, 'I must know the meaning of this. What has happened?'

Louisa and Madame Lalande (the dark lady in white) answered only by cries of 'Save us, save us, we are lost.' They seemed wholly taken up with their own distress.

'Oh!' shrieked Louisa, 'what shall I do if I am captured? Think of Enara, of the bloody Hartford, of the savage grinding Warner. I shall be broken on the wheel, or burnt alive, and I cannot endure pain. I never could. When I pricked my finger I would scream.'

'Et moi aussi!' chimed in Lalande. 'And those barbarous Angrians hate the French. I am worse off, Percy, than this bagatelle.[27] Take most care of me.'

At these words, Lady Greville, the fair and regal Verdopolitan, sprung from her kneeling posture. Her countenance, when she lifted it up, though expressing by the bold outline somewhat too free a system of thought and action, showed a far nobler soul than the dark, small, selfish physiognomies of her rivals.

[Lady Greville, pushing aside her hysterical rivals, acquaints Northangerland with Zamorna's latest advances, and with the more dangerous fact that the tide of feeling has now turned away from him and back to the duke.]

'Lalande, what shall I do, empress?'

'Leave Verdopolis, my lord. Fly with me, to Orléannois, to my own Château de Bois. There rest till the storm blows over.'

'Très bien, ma belle! That is your dictum. Now, Vernon, what do you say?'

'I say that I am horrified, that I already feel my joints stretched by the rack, and see myself bound and led captive by an escort of Tiger-cavalry. Oh, St Cloud! I wish I were there. Let us go on board a packet immediately. There is the St Antoine about to leave yonder dock. Come, come, I will go as I am. Cover me with your cloak, Alexander. Never mind Caroline; she is a child, and is safe.[28] Fiends will not harm her; and as for Miss Percy, she has but to play the frightened dove and fly from the hawks of war into her lover's bosom. She'll find her account now, in loving the rebellious, red-handed détenu!'[29]

Miss Percy, who had been standing near a window, gazing with frenzied feelings upon the scene, came forward when her name was mentioned.

'Oh, father,' she said, 'You are on the very verge of ruin, and these creatures will thrust you into it. You are wrecked, and you cannot swim, for they cling to you.

'Wretches!' she continued, kindling into passion as she spoke. 'They do not care for you; they are absorbed in their own pitiful terrors. And your other followers, your crew of slaves who have licked your feet, and eaten and wasted your bread, instead of gathering about you, they are drawing off. They will leave you. Deserted, solitary as you are, even I, your daughter, cannot give my whole heart to you. There was a time – I almost wish it would return – when I loved nothing, looked up to nothing, worshipped nothing but my father: Oh, do not leave Verdopolis; rouse the people. You must not be deserted.'

'I shall not,' returned the earl, rising. 'These fellows dare not all at once. A train of their carriages are at the door even now, and I hear them in the anteroom, clamorous for audience. Ladies, leave me. You Lalande, and you Louisa, go to St Cloud and Orléannois. You, Georgiana, I will see again his evening.'

As the three, obedient at once to the voice of decided command, glided from the room, Northangerland turned to his daughter.

'Mary,' said he, 'all this is very much my own work, and I am not more unhappy at this crisis than in hours of dead calm, so shed no tears for the matter; and as for these Angrians, do as you will. I'll not restrain you, only if you should feel particularly interested in any of them, remember you've no ring on that third finger of yours. This I say specially – Good-bye! – you'll cut me to the heart if you forget that last information.' With these words he left the room.

IV

[The forces of Northangerland and Zamorna clash; victory for the latter seems inevitable, so committed are they to their leader and their cause.]

A thinned and wasted band they were now: but so resolved, so devoted, so unanimous, so inspired by the strength and spirit of him that led them, they were resistless; or, if crushed and overpowered by numbers, it was with the last drop of blood in the last man's heart alone that they would yield.

But the record of all this and of much more, I leave to those who are much better able to describe it than I am,[30] and again I sink back to the details of private life.

Distracted as Verdopolis was, Northangerland never once asked his daughter to leave it; and she, spellbound amidst the hurricane, remained lingering about the unquiet halls and tumultuous saloons of Ellrington House, watching the nearing of the crisis, the gradual deepening of the plot, exulting and trembling by turns. And as in every paper she saw, from every tongue she heard the name of Zamorna, reflecting silently to herself on the change which had taken place in a fortnight's time.

Yes, fourteen days ago she was alone at Alnwick, buried amongst its solitary groves, existing faintly in a strange dream, the stir of war asleep around her. She thought of the nights she had lain alone, in a large antique room, on a wide stately bed. She remembered how the silence of the night, the pallid glimmer of the lamps used to strike her mind. She recalled the dreamy lethargy which seemed to steal over her instead of sleep, when past joys seemed to swim away to doubt, to oblivion, and she would dread that all the recollections she dwelt on so fondly were but a void delusion. Then she used to fear to breathe the name of Zamorna, lest it should be an imaginary sound never whispered before in mortal ear; and doubts of the reality of life, of the earth, of the changeful sky and the profound sea, would come like dim clouds over her faculties and quench them for a moment in vacancy.

All this was over now. The triumphant, the plumed, the crowned Zamorna was within twelve miles of her. Africa, half in terror, and half in ecstasy, was ringing with his name. Yes, he was rising again like a revived sun over the piles of calumny, of scorn, of dishonour, heaped, as a trophy of his foe's success, over his buried name.

And now it was within the verge of possibility that she might once more be taken to his arms, and forget her days of weariness, her nights of woe, on the heavenly rest his breast afforded.

On these things she sat musing late one stormy night. She had gone up into her chamber with the intention of retiring to rest, but the fit of thought came over her. She had sunk into a chair near her dressing table, and with her head on her hand was all absorbed in recollection and anticipation.

A door in this apartment opened on to a narrow staircase leading by a private outlet to the garden, and often before her marriage had she stolen down this to meet Lord Douro in the dim, sequestered walks, beside some moonlit fountain or gleaming form of marble.

The strange enchantment that called her to him recurred to her mind at this hour: the mystic and eager glance with which he would welcome her; his figure as she caught the first glimpse of him through the trees, standing by the falling fountain, watching intently for her appearance, silent with composed and intent aspect; then his laugh when she sprang into his arms, his embrace, his murmured and impassioned epithet of fondness –

'Surely,' she said as these thoughts rushed vividly upon her, 'he will not forget me in the tumult of victory. He will ask me to be his wife again. At any rate he will wish to see me.'

The words had scarce passed her lips when she heard a suppressed, creaking sound as if the door from the garden was carefully opened. A cold blast of wind blew in, and raised the carpet near the inner door. She distinctly heard it closed and the bolt drawn. She heard a cough at the bottom of the staircase. She started to her feet. She felt beside herself. A wild idea rushed upon her with immense power. She put it back.

'My father's house at such a time – through Verdopolis – a crown, honour, life, staked upon his freedom – I was mad to imagine it for a moment.' The idea died away. All was again silent. She sat down. The sounds she had heard were so uncertain, they might have been all fancy. But hush! A voice spoke in the little passage.

'Wait there, Eugene.[31] Watch, listen. I shall be with you in an hour.' It needed no more. The tone was like music: native, idolized, glorious music.

She sprang to the door. She dashed it open. Down the staircase she swept, into the little dark hall. She encountered a tall figure, scarce visible in the gloom. Furs and ample drapery enveloped it. It caught her yielding form on its airy descent, surrounded, shadowed her with the folds of sable, clasped her to a warm, throbbing bosom, and impressed on her lips one long, fervent, ardent kiss.

December 1836–January 1837

PART IV

Mina

Mina Laury [1]

The Cross of Rivaulx! Is that a name familiar to my readers? I
rather think not. Listen then: it is a green, delightful, and quiet
place half way between Angria and the foot of the Sydenham Hills;
under the frown of Hawkscliffe, on the edge of its royal forest. [2]
You see a fair house, whose sash windows are set in ivy grown
thick and kept in trim order; over the front door there is a little
modern porch of trellis work, all the summer covered with a
succession of verdant leaves and pink rose-globes, buds and full-
blown blossoms. Within this, in fine weather, the door is constantly
open and reveals a noble passage, almost a hall, terminating in a
staircase of low white steps, traced up the middle by a brilliant
carpet. You look in vain for anything like a wall or gate to shut it in:
the only landmark consists in an old obelisk with moss and wild flowers at its base and an half obliterated crucifix sculptured on its side.

Well, this is no very presuming place, but on a June evening not
seldom have I seen a figure, whom every eye in Angria might
recognise, stride out of the domestic gloom of that little hall and
stand in pleasant leisure under the porch whose flowers and leaves
were disturbed by the contact of his curls. Though in a sequestered
spot, the Cross of Rivaulx is not one of Zamorna's secret houses;
he'll let anybody come there that chooses.

The day is breathless, quite still and warm. The sun, far declined
for afternoon, is just melting into evening, and sheds a deep amber
light. A cheerful air surrounds the mansion whose windows are up,
its door as usual hospitably apart, and the broad passage reverber-
ates with a lively conversational hum from the rooms which open
into it. The day is of that perfectly mild, sunny kind that by an
irresistible influence draws people out into the balmy air: see, there

are two gentlemen lounging easily in the porch, sipping coffee from the cups they have brought from the drawing room; a third has stretched himself on the soft moss in the shadow of the obelisk. But for these figures, the landscape could be one of exquisite repose.

Two, [in military dress], are officers from the headquarters of Zamorna's grand army; the other, reclining on the grass, a slight figure in black, wears a civil dress. That is Mr Warner, the home secretary. Another person was standing by him whom I should not have omitted to describe. It was a fine girl, dressed in rich black satin, with ornaments like those of a bandit's wife in which a whole fortune seemed to have been expended; but no wonder, for they had doubtless been the gift of a king. In her ears hung two long clear drops, red as fire, and suffused with a purple tint that showed them to be the true oriental ruby. Bright delicate links of gold circled her neck again and again, and a cross of gems lay on her breast, the centre stone of which was a locket enclosing a ringlet of dark brown hair – with that little soft curl she would not have parted for a kingdom.

Warner's eyes were fixed with interest on Miss Laury as she stood over him, a model of beautiful vigour and glowing health; there was a kind of military erectness in her form, so elegantly built, and in the manner in which her neck, sprung from her exquisite bust, was placed with graceful uprightness on her falling shoulders. Her waist too, falling in behind, and her fine slender foot, supporting her in a regulated position, plainly indicated familiarity from her childhood with the sergeant's drill. All the afternoon she had been entertaining her exalted guests – the two in the porch were no other than Lord Hartford and Enara – and conversing with them, frankly and cheerfully. These were the only friends she had in the world. Female acquaintance she never sought, nor if she had sought, would she have found them. And so sagacious, clever, and earnest was she in all she said and did, that the haughty aristocrats did not hesitate to communicate with her often on matters of first-rate importance.

Mr Warner was now talking to her about herself.

'My dear madam,' he was saying in his usual imperious and still dulcet tone, 'it is unreasonable that you should remain thus exposed to danger. I am your friend – yes, madam, your *true* friend. Why do you not hear me and attend to my representations of the case? Angria is an unsafe place for you. You ought to leave it.' The lady shook her head.

'Never. Till my master compels me, his land is my land.'

'But – but, Miss Laury, you know that our army have no warrant from the Almighty. This invasion may be successful at least for a time; and then what becomes of you? When the duke's nation is wrestling with destruction, his glory sunk in deep waters, and himself striving desperately to recover it, can he waste a thought or a moment on one woman?'

Mina smiled.

'I am resolved,' said she. 'My master himself shall not force me to leave him. You know I am hardened, Warner; shame and reproach have no effect on me. I do not care for being called a camp follower. In peace and pleasure all the ladies of Africa would be at the duke's beck; in war and suffering he shall not lack one poor peasant girl. Why, sir, I've nothing else to exist for. I've no other interest in life. Just to stand by his grace, watch him and anticipate his wishes, or when I cannot do that, to execute them like lightning when they are signified; to wait on him when he is sick or wounded, to hear his groans and bear his heart-rending animal patience in enduring pain; to breathe if I can my own inexhaustible health and energy into him, and oh, if it were practicable, to take his fever and agony; to guard his interests, to take on my shoulders power from him that galls me with its weight; to fill a gap in his mighty train of service which nobody else would dare to step into: to do all that, sir, is to fulfil the destiny I was born to. I know I am of no repute amongst society at large because I have devoted myself so wholly to one man. And I know that he even seldom troubles himself to think of what I do, has never and can never appreciate the unusual feelings of subservience, the total self-sacrifice I offer at his shrine. But then he gives me my reward, and that an abundant one.

'Mr Warner, when I was at Fort Adrian and had all the yoke of governing the garrison and military household, I used to rejoice in my responsibility, and to feel firmer, the heavier the weight assigned me to support. When my master came over, as he often did to take one of his general surveys, or on a hunting expedition with some of his state officers, I had such delight in ordering the banquets and entertainments, and in seeing the fires kindled up and the chandeliers lighted in those dark halls, knowing for whom the feast was made ready. It gave me a feeling of ecstasy to hear my young master's voice, to see him moving about secure and powerful in his own stronghold, to know what true hearts he had about him. Besides, sir, his greeting to me, and the condescending touch of his hand, were enough to make a queen proud, let alone a sergeant's daughter.

'Then, for instance, the last summer evening that he came here, the sun and flowers and quietness brightened his noble features with such happiness, I could tell his heart was at rest; for as he lay in the shade where you are now, I heard him hum the airs he long, long ago played on his guitar. I was rewarded then to feel that the house I kept was pleasant enough to make him forget Angria and recur to home. You must excuse me, Mr Warner, but the west, the sweet west, is both his home and mine.' Mina paused and looked solemnly at the sun, now softened in its shine and hanging exceedingly low. In a moment her eyes fell again on Warner. They seemed to have absorbed radiance from what they had gazed on: light like an arrow point glanced in them as she said,

'This is my time to follow Zamorna. I'll not be robbed of those hours of blissful danger when I may be continually with him. I am not afraid of danger; I have strong nerves; I will die or be with him.'

'What has fired your eyes so suddenly, Miss Laury?' asked Lord Hartford, now advancing with Enara from their canopy of roses.

'The duke, the duke,' muttered Enara. 'You won't leave him, I'll be sworn.'

'I can't, general,' said Mina.

'No,' answered the Italian, 'and nobody shall force you. You shall have your own way, madam, whether it be right or wrong. I hate to contradict such as you in their will.'

'Thank you, general, you are always so kind to me.' Mina hurriedly put her little hand into the gloved grasp of Enara.

'Kind, madam?' said he, pressing it warmly, 'I'm so kind that I would hang the man unshriven who should use your name with other than the respect due to a queen.' The dark, hard-browed Hartford smiled at his enthusiasm.

'Is that homage paid to Miss Laury's goodness or to her beauty?' asked he.

'To neither, my lord,' answered Enara briefly, 'but to her worth, her sterling worth.'

'Hartford, you are not going to despise me? Was that a sneer?' murmured Mina aside.

'No. No, Miss Laury,' replied the noble general seriously. 'I know what you are; I am aware of your value. Do you doubt Edward Hartford's honourable friendship? It is yours on terms such as it was never given to a beautiful woman before.'

Before Miss Laury could answer, a voice from within the mansion spoke her name.

'It is my lord!' she exclaimed, and sped like a roe over the sward, through the porch, along the passage, to a summer parlour, whose walls were painted fine pale red, its mouldings burnished gilding, and its window curtains artistical draperies of dark blue silk, covered with gold waves and flowers.

Here Zamorna sat alone; he had been writing. One or two letters, folded, sealed, and inscribed with western directions lay on the table beside him. He had not uncovered since entering the house three hours since, and either the weight of his dragoon helmet, or the gloom of its impending plumes, or else some inward feeling, had clouded his face with a strange darkness.

Mina closed the door and softly drew near; without speaking or asking leave, she began to busy herself in unclasping the heavy helmet. The duke smiled faintly as her little fingers played about his chin and luxuriant whiskers; and then, the load of brass and sable plumage being removed, as they arranged the compressed masses of glossy brown ringlets, and touched with soft cool contact his feverish brow. Absorbed in this grateful task she hardly felt that his majesty's arm had encircled her waist; yet she did feel it, too, and would have thought herself presumptuous to shrink from his endearment. She took it as a slave ought to take the caress of a sultan, and obeying the gentle effort of his hand, slowly sunk on to the sofa by her master's side.

'My little physician,' said he, meeting her adoring but anxious upward gaze with the full light of his countenance, 'you look at me as if you thought I was not well – feel my pulse.' She folded the proffered hand, white, supple, and soft with youth and delicate nurture, in both her own; whether Zamorna's pulse beat rapidly or not, his handmaid's did as she felt the slender grasping fingers of the monarch laid quietly in hers.

He did not wait for the report, but took his hand away again, and laying it on her raven curls said, 'So, Mina, you won't leave me, though I never did you any good in the world. Warner says you are resolved to continue in the scene of war.'

'To continue by your side, my lord duke.'

'But what shall I do with you, Mina? Where shall I put you? My little girl, what will the army say when they hear of your presence? You have read history; recollect that it was Darius³ who carried his concubines to the field, not Alexander. The world will say Zamorna has provided himself with a pretty mistress. He attends to his own pleasures and cares not how his men suffer.'

Poor Mina writhed at these words as if the iron had entered into her soul. A vivid burning blush crimsoned her cheek, and tears of shame and bitter self-reproach gushed at once into her bright black eyes. Zamorna was touched acutely.

'Nay, my little girl,' said he, redoubling his haughty caresses and speaking in his most soothing tone, 'never weep about it. It grieves me to hurt your feelings, but you desire an impossibility and I must use strong language to convince you that I cannot grant it –'

'Oh! don't refuse me again,' sobbed Miss Laury. 'I'll bear all infamy and contempt to be allowed to follow you, my lord. My lord, I've served you for many years most faithfully and I seldom ask a favour of you. Don't reject almost the first request of the kind I ever made.' The duke shook his head, and the meeting of his exquisite lips, too placid for the term compression, told he was not to be moved.

'If you should receive a wound, if you should fall sick,' continued Mina, 'what can surgeons and physicians do for you? They cannot watch you and wait on you and worship you like me; you do not seem well now, the bloom is so faded on your complexion and the flesh is wasted round your eyes. My lord, smile and do not look so calmly resolved. Let me go!'

Zamorna withdrew his arm from her waist. 'I must be displeased before you cease to importune me,' said he. 'Mina, look at that letter, read the direction,' pointing to one he had been writing. She obeyed: it was addressed to Her Royal Highness Mary Henrietta, Duchess of Zamorna, Queen of Angria.

'Must I pay no attention to the feelings of that lady?' pursued the duke, whom the duties of war and the conflict of some internal emotions seemed to render rather peculiarly stern. 'Her public claims must be respected whether I love her or not.' Miss Laury shrunk into herself. Not another word did she venture to breathe. An unconscious wish of wild intensity filled her that she were dead and buried, insensible to the shame that overwhelmed her. She saw Zamorna's finger with the ring on it still pointing to that awful name, a name that raised no impulses of hatred, but only bitter humiliation and self-abasement. She stole from her master's side, feeling that she had no more right to sit there than a fawn has to share the den of a royal lion; and murmuring that she was very sorry for her folly, was about to glide in dismay and despair from the room. But the duke, rising up, arrested her, and bending his lofty stature over as she crouched before him, folded her again in his arms. His countenance relaxed not a moment from its sternness, nor did the gloom leave his magnificent but worn features, as he said,

'I will make no apologies for what I have said because I know, Mina, that, as I hold you now, you feel fully recompensed for my transient severity. Before I depart, I will speak to you one word of comfort, which you may remember when I am far away, and perhaps dead. My dear girl! I know and appreciate all you have done, all you have resigned, and all you have endured for my sake. I repay you for it with one coin, with what alone will be to you of greater worth than worlds without it. I give you such true and fond love as a master may give to the fairest and loveliest vassal that ever was bound to him in feudal allegiance. You may never feel the touch of Zamorna's lips again. There, Mina.' And fervently, almost fiercely, he pressed them to her forehead. 'Go to your chamber. Tomorrow you must leave for the west.'

'Obedient till death,' was Miss Laury's answer, as she closed the door and disappeared.

[Meanwhile . . . though Zamorna has apparently directed a letter to his wife in this past scene, he persists in his decision to repudiate her and get revenge on her father, Northangerland, by breaking her heart. Weeks pass without a word from Zamorna, and Mary begins to pine away.]

The duchess dropped her head on her hand.

'Is the sun shining hot this evening?' said she. 'I feel very languid and inert.' Alas, it was not the mild sun of April glistening even now on the lingering rain drops of the morning which caused that sickly languor. 'I wish the mail would come in,' continued the duchess. 'How long is it since I've had a letter now, Amelia?'

'Three weeks, my lady.'

'If none comes this evening, what shall I do, Amelia? I shall never get on till tomorrow. Oh, I do dread those long, weary, sleepless nights I've had lately, tossing through many hours on a wide, lonely bed, with the lamps decaying round me. Now I think I could sleep if I only had a kind letter for a talisman to press to my heart all night long. Amelia, I'd give anything to get from the east this evening a square of white paper directed in that light, rapid hand. Would he but write two lines to me signed with his name.'

'My lady,' said Miss Clifton, as she placed a little silver vessel of tea and a plate of biscuit before her mistress, 'you will hear from the east this evening, and that before many minutes elapse. Mr Warner is in Verdopolis and will wait upon you immediately.' It was pleasant to see how a sudden beam of joy shot into the settled sadness of Queen Mary's face.

'I am thankful to heaven for it,' exclaimed she. 'Even if he brings bad news it will be a relief from suspense; and if good news, this heart sickness will be removed for a moment.'

As she spoke, a foot was heard in the antechamber, there was a light tap at the door. Mr Warner entered closely muffled, as it was absolutely necessary that he should avoid remark, for the sacrifice of his liberty would have been the result of recognition. With something of chivalric devotedness in his manner he sunk on one knee before the duchess, and respectfully touched with his lips the hand she offered him. A gleam of eager anxiety darted into his eyes as he rose, looked at her, and saw the pining and joyless shadow which had settled on her divine features, her blanched delicacy of complexion.

'Your grace is wasting away,' said he abruptly, the first greeting being past. 'You are going into a decline; you have imagined things to be worse than they really are; you have frightened yourself with fantastic surmises.'

[Despite his desire to console her, Warner does not bring the longed-for letter. In desperation, Mary resolves to return with him to the front.]

'I cannot try one effort to soften him, separated by one hundred and twenty miles. He would think of me more as a woman, I am sure, and less as a bodiless link between himself and my terrible father if I were near at hand. Warner, this irritation throughout all my nerves is unbearable. I am not accustomed to disappointment and delay in what I wish. When do you return to Angria?'

'Tomorrow, my lady, before daylight, if possible.'

'And you travel incognito, of course?'

'I do.'

'Make room in your carriage then for me. I must go with you. Not a word, I implore you, Mr Warner, of expostulation. I should have died before morning if I had not hit upon this expedient.' Mr Warner heard her in silence and saw it was utterly vain to oppose her, but in his heart he hated the adventure. He saw its rashness and peril; besides he had calculated the result of the duke's determination over and over again. He had weighed advantages against disadvantages, profit against loss, the separation from the father against the happiness of the daughter, and in his serene and ambitious eye, the latter scale seemed far to kick the beam. He bowed to the duchess, said she should be obeyed, and left the room.

[Upon their arrival at the front Warner immediately meets with Zamorna.]

'I knew you were come, Howard,' said he, 'for I heard your voice below a quarter of an hour since. Well, have you procured the documents?'

'Yes, and I have delivered them to your grace's private secretary.'

'They were at Wellesley house, of course?'

'Yes, in the duchess's own keeping. She said you wished them to be preserved with care.

'Her grace,' continued Warner after a brief pause, 'asked very anxiously after you.'

The stern field-marshal look came over the duke, as he lay giantlike on his couch, and the momentary mildness melted away.

'I need not ask you how Mary Wellesley looks,' said he in his deep undertone, 'because I know better than you can tell me. I say, Howard, did she not ask you for a letter?'

'She did; she almost entreated me for one.'

'And you had not one to give her,' answered his sovereign, while with a low bitter laugh he turned on his couch and was silent.

Warner paced the room with a troubled step. 'My lord, are you doing right?' exclaimed he, pausing suddenly. 'The matter lies between God and your conscience. I know that the kingdom must be saved at any hazard of individual peace or even life; I advocate expediency, my lord, in the government of a state; I allow of equivocal measures to procure a just end; I sanction the shedding of blood and the cutting up of domestic happiness by the roots to stab a traitor to the heart. But nevertheless I am a man, sire, and after what I have seen during the last day or two, I ask your majesty with solemn earnestness: is there no way by which the heart of Northangerland may be reached except through the breast of my queen?'

> [Zamorna remains obdurate, and Warner finally quits
> him, with the intelligence that there is 'a lady' in the next
> room who wishes an audience with him.]

About ten minutes after Warner's departure, the lady in question entered the room by an inner door. Zamorna was now risen from his couch and stood in full stature before the fire. He turned to her at first carelessly, but his keen eye was quickly lit up with interest when he saw the elegant figure, whose slight, youthful proportions and graceful carriage, agreeing with her dress, produced an effect of such ladylike harmony. While dropping a profound obeisance, she contrived so to arrange her large veil as to hide her face. As she did this, her hand trembled; then she paused and leaned against a bookcase near the door.

Zamorna now saw that she shook from head to foot. Speaking in his tone of most soothing melody, he told her to draw near, and placed a chair for her close by the hearth. She made an effort to obey but it was evident she would have dropped if she had quitted her support. His grace smiled, a little surprised at her extreme agitation.

'I hope, madam,' said he, 'my presence is not the cause of your alarm,' and advancing, he kindly gave her his hand and led her to a seat. As she grew a little calmer he addressed her again in tones of the softest encouragement.

'I think Mr Warner said you are the wife of an officer in my army. What is his name?'

'Archer,' replied the lady, dropping one silver word for the first time.

'And have you any request to make concerning your husband? Speak out freely, madam; if it be reasonable, I will grant it.' She made some answer, but in a tone too low to be audible.

'Be so kind as to remove your veil, madam,' said the duke. 'It prevents me from hearing what you say distinctly.' She hesitated a moment, then as if she had formed some sudden resolution, she loosened the satin knot that confined her bonnet, and taking off both it and her veil, let them drop on the carpet. His majesty now caught a glimpse of a beautiful blushing face, but in a moment clusters of curls fell over it, and it was likewise concealed by two delicate little white hands with many rings sparkling on the taper fingers.

The sovereign of the east was nonplussed; he had an acute eye for most of these matters, but he did not quite understand the growing, trembling embarrassment of his lovely suppliant. He repeated the question he had before put to the lady respecting the nature of her petition.

'Sire,' said she at length, 'I want your majesty's gracious permission to see my dear, dear husband once more in this world before he leaves me forever.' She looked up, parted from her fair forehead her auburn curls, and raised her wild brown eyes, tearful and earnest and imploring, to a face that grew crimson under their glance.

The king's heart beat and throbbed till its motion could be seen in the heaving of a splendid chest. He seemed fixed in his attitude, standing before the lady, slightly bent over her, an inexpressible sparkle commencing and spreading to a flash in his eyes, the current of his lifeblood rising to his cheek, and his forehead dark with solemn, awful, desperate thought.

Mary clasped her hands and waited. She did not know whether love or indignation would prevail. She saw that both feelings were at work. Her suspense was at an end: the thundercloud broke asunder in a burst of electric passion! He turned from his duchess and flung open the door. A voice rung along the halls of Angria House summoning Warner – a voice having the spirit of a trumpet, the depth of a drum in its tone –

[Warner is duly rebuked in true imperial style, and dismissed.]

Warner, whose angelic philosophy had been little shaken by this appalling hurricane, would have stopped to give his grace a brief homily on the wickedness of indulging in violent passions; but a glance of entreaty from the duchess prevailed on him to withdraw in silence.

It was with a sensation of pleasurable terror that Mary found herself again alone with the duke. He had not yet spoken one harsh word to her. It was awful to be Zamorna's sole companion in this hour of his ire but how much better than to be one hundred and twenty miles away from him. She was soon near enough. The duke, gazing at her pale and sweet loveliness till he felt there was nothing in the world he loved half so well – conscious that her delicate attenuation was for his sake, appreciating too the idolatry that had brought her through such perils to see him at all hazards – threw himself impetuously beside her and soon made her tremble as much with the ardour of his caresses as she had done with the dread of his wrath.

'I'll seize the few hours of happiness you have thrown in my way, Mary,' said he, as she clung to him and called him her adored glorious Adrian, 'but these kisses and tears of thine, and this intoxicating beauty, shall not change my resolution. I *will* rend you, my lovely rose, entirely from me; I'll plant you in your father's garden again: I must do it, he compels me.'

'I don't care,' said the duchess, swallowing the delicious draught of the moment, and turning from the dark future to the glorious present shrined in Zamorna. 'But if you do divorce me, Zamorna, will you never, never take me back to you? Must I die inevitably before I am twenty?' The duke looked at her in silence; he could not cut off hope.

'The event has not taken place yet, Mary, and there lingers a possibility that it may be averted. But, love, should I take the crown off that sweet brow, the crown I placed over those silken curls on the day of our coronation, do not live hopeless. You may on some moonlight night hear Adrian's whistle under your window when you least expect it. Then step out on to the parapet; I'll lift you in my arms from thence to the terrace. From that time for ever, Mary, though Angria shall have no queen, a Percy shall have no daughter.'

'Adrian,' said the duchess, 'how different you are, how very different when I get close to you. At a distance you appear quite unapproachable. I wish, I wish my father was as near to you now as I am – or at least almost as near; because I am your creeping plant, I twine about you like ivy, and he is a tree to grow side by side with you. If he were in this room I should be satisfied.'

What answer Zamorna made I know not, but he brought down the curtain.

*

[An interval ensues; Zamorna is ultimately victorious and the rebellion put down; he is reconciled with Northanger-land, against the vigorous objections of his advisors, and Mary is saved from the death which could surely have followed a permanent separation from her 'Adrian'. However, we next see Zamorna trying to extricate himself once again from his tenacious 'creeping plant'. He has bid good-bye to his family and is about to set off for Angria.]

The barouche stood at the door, the groom and the valet were waiting, and the duke, with a clouded countenance, was proceeding to join them, when his wife came forwards.

'You have forgotten me, Adrian –' she said in a very quiet tone, but her eye meantime flashed expressively. He started, for in truth he had forgotten her.

'Good-bye then, Mary,' he said, giving her a hurried kiss and embrace. She detained his hand.

'Pray, how long am I to stay here?' she asked. 'Why do you leave me at all? Why am I not to go with you?'

'It is such weather,' he answered. 'When this storm passes over I will send for you –'

'When will that be?' pursued the duchess, following in his steps as he strode into the hall.

'Soon – soon my love – perhaps in a day or two – there now – don't be unreasonable – of course you cannot go today –'

'I can and I will,' answered the duchess quickly. 'I have had enough of Alnwick, you shall not leave me behind you.'

'Go into the room, Mary. The door is open and the wind blows on you far too keenly. Don't you see how it drifts the snow in –'

'I will not go into the room. I'll step into the carriage as I am. If you refuse to wait till I can prepare, perhaps you will be humane enough to let me have a share of your cloak –' She shivered as she spoke. Her hair and her dress floated in the cold blast that blew in through the open entrance, strewing the hall with snow and dead leaves.

'You might wait till it is milder. I don't think it will do your grace any good to be out today –'

'But I must go, Mary – the Christmas recess is over and business presses.'

'Then do take me; I am sure I can bear it.'

'Out of the question. You may well clasp those small, silly hands – so thin I can almost see through them; and you may well shake your curls over your face – to hide its paleness from me, I suppose. What is the matter? Crying? Good! What the devil am I to do with her? Go to your father, Mary. He has spoilt you.'

'Adrian, I cannot live at Alnwick without you,' said the duchess earnestly, 'It recalls too forcibly the very bitterest days of my life. I'll not be separated from you again except by violence –'

The task of persuasion was no very easy one, for his own false play, his alienations, and his unnumbered treacheries had filled her mind with hideous phantoms of jealousy, had weakened her nerves and made them a prey to a hundred vague apprehensions: fears that never wholly left her except when she was actually in his arms or at least in his immediate presence.

'I tell you, Mary,' he said, regarding her with a smile half expressive of fondness – half of vexation – 'I tell you I will send for you in two or three days –. Probably I shall be a week in Angria, not more –'

'A week! and your grace considers that but a short time? To me it will be most wearisome –'

'The horses will be frozen if they stand much longer,' returned the duke, not heeding her last remark. 'Come, wipe your eyes and be a little philosopher for once. There, let me have one smile before I go. A week will be over directly – this is not like setting out for a campaign.'

'Don't forget to send for me in two days,' pleaded the duchess as Zamorna released her from his arms.

'No, no, I'll send for you tomorrow – if the weather is settled enough. And,' half mimicking her voice, 'don't be jealous of me, Mary – unless you're afraid of the superior charms of Enara and Warner. Good-bye –' He was gone. She hurried to the window; he passed it. In three minutes the barouche swept with muffled sound round the lawn, shot down the carriage road, and was quickly lost in the thickening whirl of the snow storm.

[Mina, in the meantime, waits patiently for Zamorna at Rivaulx. As it happens, Lord Hartford is desperately in love with Mina; outraged by Zamorna's careless treatment of her, he decides to visit her and propose. He makes several attempts to broach the subject, but Mina pointedly avoids taking his meaning. Finally, however, his ardour becomes unmistakeable.]

Miss Laury agitatedly rose; she approached Hartford.

'My lord, you have been very kind to me, and I feel very grateful for that kindness. Perhaps sometime I may be able to repay it – we know not how the chances of fortune may turn; the weak have aided the strong. I will watch vigilantly for the slightest opportunity to serve you, but do not talk in this way. I scarcely know whither your words tend.' Lord Hartford paused a moment before he replied. Gazing at her with bended brows and folded arms, he said,

'Miss Laury, what do you think of me?'

'That you are one of the noblest hearts in the world,' she replied unhesitatingly. She was standing just before Hartford, looking up at him, her hair falling back from her brow, shading with exquisite curls her temples and her slender neck. Her small sweet features, with that high seriousness deepening their beauty, were lit up by eyes so large, so dark, so swimming, so full of pleading benignity: an expression of alarmed regard, as if she at once feared for, and pitied, the sinful abstraction of a great mind.

Hartford could not stand it. He could have borne female anger or terror, but the look of enthusiastic gratitude, softened by compassion, nearly unmanned him. He turned his head for a moment aside, but then passion prevailed. Her beauty when he looked again struck through him a maddening sensation, whetted to acuter power by a feeling like despair.

'You shall love me!' he exclaimed desperately. 'Do I not love you? Would I not die for you? Must I in return receive only the cold regard of friendship? I am no platonist, Miss Laury – I am not your friend. I am, hear me, madam, your declared lover. Nay, you shall not leave me, by heaven! I am stronger than you are –' She had stepped a pace or two back, appalled by his vehemence. He thought she meant to withdraw; determined not to be so balked, he clasped her at once in both his arms and kissed her furiously rather than fondly. Miss Laury did not struggle.

'Hartford,' said she, steadying her voice, though it faltered in spite of her effort, 'this must be our parting scene. I will never see you again if you do not restrain yourself.' Hartford saw that she turned pale and he felt her tremble violently. His arms relaxed their hold. He allowed her to leave him. She sat down on a chair opposite and hurriedly wiped her brow, which was damp and marble-pale.

'Now, Miss Laury,' said his lordship, 'no man in the world loves you as I do. Will you accept my title and my coronet? I fling them at your feet.'

'My lord, do you know whose I am?' she replied in a hollow, very suppressed tone. 'Do you know with what a sound those proposals fall on my ear, how impious and blasphemous they seem to be? Do you at all conceive how utterly impossible it is that I should ever love you? I thought you a true-hearted faithful man; I find that you are a traitor.'

'And do you despise me?' asked Hartford.

'No, my lord, I do not.' She paused and looked down. The colour rose rapidly into her pale face; she sobbed, not in tears, but in the overmastering approach of an impulse born of a warm heart. Again she looked up. Her eyes had changed, their aspect burning with a wild bright inspiration.

'Hartford,' said she, 'had I met you long since, before I left home and dishonoured my father, I would have loved you. O, my lord, you know not how truly. I would have married you and made it the glory of my life to cheer and brighten your hearth. But I cannot do so now – never.

'I saw my present master when he had scarcely attained manhood. Do you think, Hartford, I will tell you what feelings I had for him? No tongue could express them: they were so fervid, so glowing in their colour, that they effaced everything else. I lost the power of properly appreciating the value of the world's opinion, of discerning the difference between right and wrong. I have never in my life contradicted Zamorna, never delayed obedience to his commands. I could not! He was sometimes more to me than a human being, he superseded all things: all affections, all interests, all fears or hopes or principles. Unconnected with him, my mind would be a blank – cold, dead, susceptible only of a sense of despair. How I should sicken if I were torn from him and thrown to you! Do not ask it – I would die first. No woman that ever loved my master could consent to leave him. There is nothing like him elsewhere. Hartford, if I were to be your wife, if Zamorna only looked at me, I should creep back like a slave to my former service. I should disgrace you as I have long since disgraced all my kindred. Think of that, my lord, and never say you love me again –'

[Hartford, stung to recklessness, finally insults Mina by a sarcastic reference to her as Zamorna's 'gentle mistress' whom he visits when he is tired by 'the turmoil of business and the teasing of matrimony'. They part abruptly, in bitterness.

More desperate than ever, Hartford challenges Zamorna to a duel; furious that 'a coarse Angrian squire' should seek to 'possess anything that had ever been mine', the duke inflicts a near-fatal wound on his rival.

Having dismissed Hartford, and unaware of the ensuing duel, Mina returns to her daily tasks, and to waiting for the duke. Mary, less patient than Mina, can wait no longer, and sets out for Zamorna's country house. An accident with her carriage lands her instead at Mina's Cross of Rivaulx, which is on the grounds of the duke's estate.]

Miss Laury was sitting after breakfast in a small library. Her desk lay before her, and two large ruled quartos filled with items and figures which she seemed to be comparing. Behind her chair stood a tall, well-made, soldierly, young man with light hair. His dress was plain and gentlemanly; the epaulette on one shoulder alone indicated an official capacity. He watched with a fixed look of attention the movements of the small fingers, which ascended in rapid calculation the long columns of accounts. It was strange to see the absorption of mind expressed in Miss Laury's face; the gravity of her smooth, white brow, shaded with drooping curls; the scarcely perceptible and unsmiling movement of her lips – though those lips in their rosy sweetness seemed formed only for smiles. An hour or more lapsed in the employment, the room meantime continuing in profound silence broken only by an occasional observation addressed by Miss Laury to the gentleman behind her concerning the legitimacy of some items, or the absence of some stray farthing, wanted to complete the necessary of the sum total. In the balancing of the books she displayed a most businesslike sharpness and strictness. The slightest fault was detected and remarked on in few words, but with a quick searching glance. However, the accountant had evidently been accustomed to her surveillance, for on the whole his books were a specimen of mathematical correctness.

'Very well,' said Miss Laury, as she closed the volumes. 'Your accounts do you credit, Mr O'Neill. You may tell his grace that all is quite right. Your memoranda tally with my own exactly.' Mr O'Neill bowed.

'Thank you, madam.' Taking up his books, he seemed about to leave the room. Before he did so, however, he turned and said,

'The duke wished me to inform you, madam, that he would probably be here about four or five o'clock in the afternoon.'

'Today?' asked Miss Laury in an accent of surprise.

'Yes, madam.' She paused a moment, then said quickly,

'Very well, sir.' Mr O'Neill now took his leave with another bow of low and respectful obeisance. Miss Laury returned it with a slight abstracted bow; her thoughts were all caught up and hurried away by that last communication. For a long time after the door had closed, she sat with her head on her hand, lost in a tumultuous flush of ideas – anticipations awakened by that simple sentence, 'The duke will be here today.'

The striking of the timepiece roused her. She remembered that twenty tasks waited her direction. Always active, always employed, it was not her custom to while away hours in dreaming. She rose, closed her desk, and left the quiet library for busier scenes.

Four o'clock came and Miss Laury's foot was heard on the staircase, descending from her chamber. She crossed the large, light passage, an apparition of feminine elegance and beauty. She had dressed herself splendidly: the robe of black satin became at once her slender form, which it enveloped in full and shining folds, and her bright, blooming complexion, which it set off by the contrast of colour. Glittering through her curls there was a band of fine diamonds, and drops of the same pure gem trembled from her small, delicate ears. These ornaments, so regal in their nature, had been the gift of royalty, and were worn now chiefly for the associations of soft and happy moments which their gleam might be supposed to convey.

She entered her drawing room and stood by the window. From thence appeared one glimpse of the highroad, visible through the thickening shades of Rivaulx; even that was now almost concealed by the frozen mist in which the approach of twilight was wrapt. All was very quiet, both in the house and in the wood. A carriage drew near, she heard the sound. She saw it shoot through the fog. But it was not Zamorna.

She had not gazed a minute before her experienced eye discerned that there was something wrong with the horses – the harness had got entangled, or they were frightened. The coachman had lost command over them, they were plunging violently. She rung the bell; a servant entered; she ordered immediate assistance to be despatched to that carriage on the road. Two grooms presently hurried down the drive to execute her commands, but before they could reach the spot, one of the horses, in its gambols, had slipped on the icy road and fallen. The others grew more unmanageable, and presently the carriage lay overturned on the roadside. One of Miss Laury's messengers came back. She threw up the window.

'Anybody hurt?'

'I hope not much, madam.'

'Who is in the carriage?'

'Only one lady, and she seems to have fainted. She looked very white when I opened the door. What is to be done, madam?' Miss Laury, with Irish frankness, answered directly,

'Bring the lady in directly, and make the servants comfortable.'

'Yes, madam.'

Miss Laury shut her window; it was very cold. Not many minutes elapsed before the lady, in the arms of her own servant, was slowly brought up the lawn and ushered into the drawing-room.

'Lay her on the sofa,' said Miss Laury. The lady's travelling cloak was carefully removed, and a thin figure became apparent in a dark silk dress: the cushions of down scarcely sunk under the pressure, it was so light.

Her swoon was now passing off. The genial warmth of the fire, which shone full on her, revived her. Opening her eyes, she looked up at Miss Laury's face, who was bending close over her, wetting her lips with some cordial. Recognising a stranger, she shyly turned her glance aside. She looked keenly round the room, and seeing the perfect elegance of its arrangement, the cheerful and tranquil glow of a hearthlight, she appeared to grow more composed.

'To whom am I indebted for this kindness? Where am I?'

'In a hospitable country, madam. The Angrians never turn their backs on strangers.'

'I know I am in Angria,' she said quietly, 'but where? What is the name of this house, and who are you?'

Miss Laury coloured slightly. It seemed as if there were some undefinable reluctance to give her real name; she knew she was widely celebrated – too widely; most likely the lady would turn from her in contempt if she heard it. Miss Laury felt she could not bear that.

'I am only the housekeeper,' she said. 'This is a shooting lodge belonging to a great Angrian proprietor –'

'Who?' asked the lady, who was not to be put off by indirect answers. Again Miss Laury hesitated; for her life she could not have said 'His Grace the Duke of Zamorna.' She replied hastily,

'A gentleman of western extraction, a distant branch of the great Pakenhams – so at least the family records say, but they have been long naturalised in the east –'

'I never heard of them,' replied the lady. 'Pakenham? That is not an Angrian name!'

'Perhaps, madam, you are not particularly acquainted with this part of the country –'[4]

'I know Hawkscliffe,' said the lady, 'and your house is on the very borders, within the royal liberties,[5] is it not?'

'Yes, madam. It stood there before the great duke bought up the forest manor, and his majesty allowed my master to retain this lodge and the privilege of sporting in the chase.'

'Well, and you are Mr Pakenham's housekeeper?'

'Yes, madam.' The lady surveyed Miss Laury with another furtive side-glance of her large, majestic eyes. Those eyes lingered upon the diamond earrings, the bandeau of brilliants that flashed from between the clusters of raven curls; then passed over the sweet face, the exquisite figure of the young housekeeper; and finally were reverted to the wall with an expression that spoke volumes. Miss Laury could have torn the dazzling pendants from her ears; she was bitterly stung.

'Everybody knows me,' she said to herself. ' "Mistress" I suppose is branded on my brow –'

[Realizing that Mina is lying, Mary asks for a room to withdraw to and concocts her own story: she is 'Mrs Irving', whose husband is a minister from the north. Mary retires; Mina, below, awaits Zamorna's arrival.]

Five o'clock now struck. It was nearly dark. A servant with a taper was lighting up the chandeliers in the large dining room where a table, spread for dinner, received the kindling lamplight upon a starry service of silver. It was likewise flashed back from a splendid sideboard, all arranged in readiness to receive the great, the expected, guest.

Tolerably punctual in keeping an appointment – when he meant to keep it at all – Zamorna entered the house as the fairylike voice of a musical clock in the passage struck out its symphony to the pendulum. The opening of the front door, a bitter rush of the night wind; then the sudden close and the step advancing were the signals of his arrival.

Miss Laury was in the dining room looking round and giving the last touch to all things. She just met her master as he entered. His cold lip pressed to her forehead, and his colder hand clasping hers, brought the sensation which it was her custom of weeks and months to wait for, and to consider, when attained, as the single recompense of all delay and all toil, all suffering.

'I am frozen, Mina,' said he. 'I came on horseback for the last four miles and the night is like Canada.' Chafing his icy hand to animation between her own warm and supple palms, she answered by the speechless but expressive look of joy, satisfaction, and idolatry which filled and overflowed her eyes.

'What can I do for you, my lord?' were her first words, as he stood by the fire raising his hands cheerily over the blaze. He laughed.

'Put your arms around my neck, Mina, and kiss my cheek as warm and blooming as your own.'

If Mina Laury had been Mina Wellesley, she would have done so; and it gave her a pang to resist the impulse that urged her to take him at his word. But she put it by and only diffidently drew near the arm chair into which he had now thrown himself, and began to smooth and separate the curls on his temples. She noticed, as the first smile of salutation subsided, a gloom succeeded on her master's brow, which, however he spoke or laughed afterwards, remained a settled characteristic of his countenance.[6]

'What visitors are in the house?' he asked. 'I saw the groom rubbing down four black horses before the stables as I came in.'

'A carriage was overturned at the lodge gates about an hour since; as the lady who was in it was taken out insensible, I ordered her to be brought up here and her servants accommodated for the night.'

'And do you know who the lady is?' continued his grace. 'The horses are good – first rate.'

'She says her name is Mrs Irving, and that she is the wife of a Presbyterian minister in the north, but –'

'You hardly believe her?' interrupted the duke.

'No,' returned Miss Laury. 'I must say I took her for a lady of rank. She has something highly aristocratic about her manners and aspect, and she appeared to know a good deal about Angria.'

'What is she like?' asked Zamorna. 'Young or old, handsome or ugly?'

'She is young, slender, not so tall as I, and I should say rather elegant than handsome; very pale and cold in her demeanour. She has a small mouth and chin and a very fair neck –'

'Perhaps you did not say to whom the house belonged, Mina?'

'I said,' replied Mina smiling, 'the owner of the house was a great Angrian proprietor, a lineal descendant of the western Pakenhams, and that I was his housekeeper.'

'Very good; she would not believe you. You look like an Angrian country gentleman's dolly. Give me your hand, my girl. Are you not as old as I am?'

'Yes, my lord duke. I was born on the same day, an hour after your grace.'

'So I have heard, but it must be a mistake. You don't look twenty, and I am twenty-five, my beautiful western. What eyes! Look at me, Mina – straight and don't blush –' Mina tried to look, but she could not do it without blushing. She coloured to the temples.

'Pshaw!' said his grace, putting her away. 'Pretending to be modest. My acquaintance of ten years cannot meet my eye unshrinkingly. Have you lost that ring I once gave you, Mina?'

'What ring, my lord? You have given me many.'

'That which I said had the essence of your whole heart and mind engraven in the stone as a motto.'

'Fidelity?' asked Miss Laury, and she held out her hand with a graven emerald on her forefinger.

'Right,' was the reply. 'Is it your motto still?' And with one of his haughty, jealous glances he seemed trying to read her conscience. Miss Laury at once saw that late transactions were not a secret confined between herself and Lord Hartford. She saw his grace was unhinged and strongly inclined to be savage; she stood and watched him with a sad, fearful gaze.

'Well,' she said, turning away after a long pause, 'If your grace is angry with me, I've very little to care about in this world –' The entrance of servants with the dinner prevented Zamorna's answer . . .

It was not till after the cloth was withdrawn and the servants had retired that the duke, whilst he sipped his single glass of champagne, recommenced the conversation he had before so unpleasantly entered upon.

'Come here, my girl,' he said, drawing a seat close to his side. Mina never delayed nor hesitated, through bashfulness or any other feeling, to comply with his orders.

'Now,' he continued, leaning his head towards hers, and placing his hand on her shoulder, 'are you happy, Mina? Do you want anything?'

'Nothing, my lord.' She spoke truly. All that was capable of yielding her happiness on this side of eternity was at that moment within her reach. The room was full of calm. The lamps hung as if they were listening; the fire sent up no flickering flame, but diffused a broad, still, glowing light over all the spacious saloon. Zamorna touched her. His form and features filled her eye, his voice her ear, his presence her whole heart. She was soothed to perfect happiness.

'My Fidelity,' pursued that musical voice, 'if thou hast any favour to ask, now is the time. I'm all concession – as sweet as honey, as yielding as a lady's glove. Come, Esther, what is thy petition and thy request?[7] Even to the half of my kingdom it shall be granted.'

'Nothing,' again murmured Miss Laury. 'Oh, my lord, nothing. What can I want?'

'Nothing?' he repeated. 'What, no reward for ten years' faith and love and devotion? No reward for the companionship in six months' exile? No recompense to the little hand that has so often smoothed my pillow in sickness, to the sweet lips that have many a time in cool and dewy health been pressed to a brow of fever? None to the dark Milesian[8] eyes that once grew dim with watching through endless nights by my couch of delirium? Need I speak of the sweetness and fortitude that cheered sufferings known only to thee and me, Mina, of the devotion that gave me bread when thou wert dying of hunger, and that scarcely more than a year since? For all this and much more must there be no reward?'

'I have had it,' said Miss Laury, 'I have it now –'

'But,' continued the duke, 'what if I have devised something worthy of your acceptance? Look up now and listen to me.' She did look up, but she speedily looked down again. Her master's eye was insupportable; it burnt absolutely with infernal fire.

'What is he going to say?' murmured Miss Laury to herself. She trembled.

'I say, love,' pursued the individual, drawing her a little closer to him, 'I will give you as a reward a husband – don't start now – and that husband shall be a nobleman, and that nobleman is called Lord Hartford! Now, madam, stand up and let me look at you.' He opened his arms and Miss Laury sprang erect like a loosened bow.

'Your grace is anticipated!' she said. 'That offer has been made me before. Lord Hartford did it himself three days ago.'

'And what did you say, madam? Speak the truth now. Subterfuge won't avail you –'

'What did I say? Zamorna, I don't know – it little signifies. You have rewarded me, my lord duke, but I cannot bear this. I feel sick.' With a deep short sob, she turned white, and fell, close by the duke, her head against his foot.

This was the first time in her life that Miss Laury had fainted, but strong health availed nothing against the deadly struggle which convulsed every feeling of her nature when she heard her master's announcement. She believed him to be perfectly sincere; she thought he was tired of her and she could not stand it.

I suppose Zamorna's first feeling when she fell was horror; and his next, I am tolerably certain, was intense gratification. People say I am not in earnest when I abuse him, or else I would here insert half a page of deserved vituperation: deserved and heartfelt. As it is, I will merely relate his conduct, without note or comment. He took a wax taper from the table and held it over Miss Laury. Hers could be no dissimulation: she went white as marble and still as stone. In truth, then, she did intensely love him with a devotion that left no room in her thoughts for one shadow of an alien image. Do not think, reader, that Zamorna meant to be so generous as to bestow Miss Laury on Lord Hartford. No; trust him; he was but testing in his usual way the attachment which a thousand proofs daily given ought long ago to have convinced him was undying.

While he yet gazed, she began to recover. Her eyelids stirred; then slowly dawned from beneath the large black orbs that scarcely met his before they filled to overflowing with sorrow. Not a gleam of anger, not a whisper of reproach; her lips and eyes spoke together no other language than the simple words,

'I cannot leave you.' She rose feebly, and with effort. The duke stretched out his hand to assist her. He held to her lips the scarcely tasted wine glass. 'Mina,' he said, 'are you collected enough to hear me?'

'Yes, my lord.'

'Then listen. I would much sooner give half – aye, the whole of my estates to Lord Hartford than yourself. What I said just now was only to try you.' Miss Laury raised her eyes, sighed like awaking from some hideous dream, but she could not speak.

'Would I,' continued the duke, 'would I resign the possession of my first love to any hands but my own? I would far rather see her in her coffin. I would lay you there as still, as white, and much more lifeless than you were stretched just now at my feet, before I would for threat, for entreaty, for purchase, give to another a glance of your eye, a smile from your lip. I know you adore me now, for you could not feign that agitation; and therefore I will tell you what a proof I gave yesterday of my regard for you. Hartford mentioned your name in my presence, and I revenged the profanation by a shot which sent him to his bed little better than a corpse.'

Miss Laury shuddered, but so dark and profound are the mysteries of human nature, ever allying vice with virtue, that I fear this bloody proof of her master's love brought to her heart more rapture than horror. She said not a word, for now Zamorna's arms were again folded round her; again he was soothing her to tranquillity, by endearments and caresses that far away removed all thought of the world, all past pangs of shame, all cold doubts, all weariness, all heartsickness resulting from hope long-deferred. He had told her that she was his first love, and now she felt tempted to believe that she was likewise his only love. Strong-minded beyond her sex, active, energetic, and accomplished in all other points of view, here she was as weak as a child. She lost her identity. Her very way of life was swallowed up in that of another.

[The tête-à-tête is interrupted by Zamorna's valet, who calls him from the room to deliver the embarrassing intelligence that 'Mrs Irving', now wandering about the halls, bears a disconcerting resemblance to his wife, the duchess.]

'I was walking carelessly through the passage about ten minutes since, when I heard a step on the stairs – a light step, as if of a very small foot. I turned, and there was a lady coming down. My lord, she was a lady!'

'Well, sir, did you know her?'

'I think, if my eyes were not bewitched, I did. I stood in the shade screened by a pillar and she passed very near without observing me. I saw her distinctly, and may I be damned this very moment if it was not –'

'Who, sir?'

'The duchess!!' There was a pause, which was closed by a remarkably prolonged whistle from the duke. He put both his hands into his pockets and took a leisurely turn through the room. 'You're sure?' he said. 'I know you dare not tell me a lie in such matters. Aye, it's true enough, I'll be sworn. Mrs Irving, wife of a minister in the north. A satirical hit at my royal self, by God. Pale, fair neck, little mouth and chin. Very good! I wish that same little mouth and chin were about a hundred miles off. What can have brought her? Anxiety about her invaluable husband? Could not bear any longer without him? Obliged to set off to see what he was doing? If she had entered the room unexpectedly about five minutes since – God! I should have had no resource but to tie her hand and foot. It would have killed her. What the devil shall I do? Must not be angry, she can't do with that sort of thing just now. Talk softly, reprove her gently, swear black and white to my having no connection with Mr Pakenham's housekeeper –' Closing his soliloquy, the duke turned again to his valet.

'What room did her grace go into?'

'The drawing room, my lord. She's there now.'

'Well, say nothing about it, on pain of sudden death. Do you hear sir?' He laid his hand on his heart and Zamorna left the room to commence operations.

Softly unclosing the drawing room door, he perceived a lady by the hearth. Her back was towards him, but there could be no mistake. The whole turn of form, the style of dress, the curled auburn head: all were attributes of but one person, of his own unique, haughty, jealous little duchess. He closed the door as noiselessly as he had opened it, and stole forwards.

The duchess felt a hand press her shoulder, and she looked up. The force of attraction had its usual result, and she clung to what she saw.

'Adrian! Adrian!' was all her lips could utter.

'Mary! Mary!' replied the duke, allowing her to hang about him. 'Pretty doings! What brought you here? Are you running away, eloping in my absence?'

'Adrian, why did you leave me? You said you would come back in a week, and it's eight days since you left me. Do come home –'

'So, you actually have set off in search of a husband,' said Zamorna, laughing heartily, 'and been overturned and obliged to take shelter in Pakenham's shooting box!'

'Why are you here, Adrian?' enquired the duchess, who was far too much in earnest to join in his laugh. 'Who is Pakenham and who is that person who calls herself his housekeeper? Why do you let anybody live so near Hawkscliffe without ever telling me?'

'I forgot to tell you,' said his grace. 'I've other things to think about when those bright hazel eyes are looking up at me. As for Pakenham, to tell you the truth – he's a sort of left-hand cousin of your own, being natural son to the old admiral, my uncle, in the south; his housekeeper is his sister. Voilà tout. Kiss me now.' The duchess did kiss him, but it was with a heavy sigh. The cloud of jealous anxiety hung on her brow undissipated.

'Adrian, my heart aches still. Why have you been staying so long in Angria? O, you don't care for me! You have never thought how miserably I have been longing for your return. Adrian –' she stopped and cried.

'Mary, recollect yourself,' said his grace. 'I cannot be always at your feet. You were not so weak when we were first married. You let me leave you often then without any jealous remonstrance.'

'I did not know you so well at that time,' said Mary, 'and if my mind is weakened, all its strength has gone away in tears and terrors for you. I am neither so handsome nor so cheerful as I once was. But you ought to forgive my decay because you have caused it.'

'Mary, never again reproach yourself with loss of beauty till I give the hint first. Believe me now, in that and every other respect, you are just what I wish you to be. You cannot fade any more than marble can – at least not to my eyes. As for your devotion and tenderness, though I chide its excess sometimes because it wastes and bleaches you almost to a shadow, yet it forms the very firmest chain that binds me to you. Now cheer up. Tonight you shall go to Hawkscliffe; it is only five miles off. I cannot accompany you because I have some important business to transact with Pakenham which must not be deferred. Tomorrow I will be at the castle before dawn. The carriage shall be ready, I will put you in, myself beside you. Off we go, straight to Verdopolis, and there for the next three months I will tire you of my company, morning, noon, and night. Now, what can I promise more? If you choose to be jealous, why, I can't help it. I must then take to soda water and despair, or have myself petrified and carved into an Apollo for your dressing room. Lord! I get no credit with my virtue –' By dint of lies and laughter the individual at last succeeded in getting all things settled to his mind. The duchess went to Hawkscliffe that night. Keeping his promise, for once, he accompanied her to Verdopolis the next morning –

Lord Hartford still lies between life and death. His passion is neither weakened by pain, piqued by rejection, nor cooled by absence. On the iron nerves of the man are graven an impression which nothing can efface.

For a long space of time, good-bye reader. I have done my best to please you, and though I know that through feebleness, dullness, and iteration my work terminates rather in failure than triumph, yet you are bound to forgive, for I have done my best –

January, 1838

PART V

Elizabeth

❋

Henry Hastings

PROLOGUE

A young man of captivating exterior, elegant address, and most gentlemanlike deportment is desirous of getting his bread easy, and of living in the greatest possible enjoyment of comfort and splendour, at the least possible expense of labour and drudgery. To this end he begs to inform the public that it would suit him uncommon well to have a fortune left him, or to get a wife whose least merit should not be her pecuniary endowment.

The advertiser is not particular as to age, nor does he lay any stress on those fleeting charms of a merely personal nature – which, according to the opinion of the best-informed medical men of all ages, a few days' sickness or the most trivial accident may suffice to remove.

On the contrary, an imperfect symmetry of form – a limb laterally, horizontally, or obliquely bent aside from the line of rigid rectitude; or even the absence of a feature, as an eye too few, or a row of teeth minus – will be no material objection to this enlightened and sincere individual, provided only satisfactory testimonials be given of the possession of that one great and paramount virtue, that eminent and irresistible charm: C-A-S-H! address C.T.[1] – care of Mr Graeme Ellrington, No. 12 Chapel Street, Verdopolis. *P.S.* None need apply whose property – personal, landed, and funded – amounts to less than 20,000£ sterling. The advertiser considers himself a cheap bargain at double this sum.

Such was the advertisement that lately appeared in the columns of a metropolitan paper, being the last resource of an unoffending and meritorious individual who, penniless and placeless, found himself driven upon the two horns of a hideous dilemma, and (all attempts to raise the wind by less desperate methods having failed) compelled either to write or to wed.

For the last six months I have been living on, as it were, turtle-soup and foie gras; I have been rowing and revelling and rioting to my heart's content. But now, alas, my pockets are empty and my pleasures are gone; I must either write a book or marry a wife, to refill the one and to recall the other.

Which shall I do? Hymen with a waving torch invites me – but no, I am beloved by too many to give up my liberty to one. Fascinating as a pheasant, I will still be free as an eagle. Wail not then, O dark-eyed daughters of the west! Lament not, ye ruddy virgins of the east! Sit not in sackcloth, soft maids of the sunny south; nor weep upon the hill tops, proud damsels of the north; nor yet send the voice of mourning from afar, O ye mermaids of the island realm! Charles Townsend will not marry. He is yet too young, too frisky, too untamed, to submit to the sober bonds of matrimony. Charles Townsend will still be the handsome bachelor, the cynosure of neighbouring eyes, the tempting apple of discord to the African fair. Charles Townsend, therefore, gets pen, ink and paper and sits down to write a book – though his charming noddle is about as empty of ideas as his pocket is of pence. 'Regardez comme nous allons commencer –'

CHAPTER I

I have clean forgotten what day of the month it was, or even what month in the year – whether the last week in September or the first week in October – that I, comfortably seated in an Angrian stagecoach, found myself comfortably rolling up from Adriano-polis.

However, it was autumn; the woods were turning brown. It was the season of partridge shooting, for the popping of guns was continually to be heard over the landscape and, as we whirled past Meadowbank, the seat of John Kirkwall Esq. M.P., I recollect catching a glimpse from the coach window of three or four young gentlemen in green shooting jackets, followed by a yelling train of pointers and a brassy-browed gamekeeper. A gentleman opposite to me observed,

'That is Mr Frank Kirkwall.' At the same time he smiled significantly, as good as to add, 'a scoundrelly young blade'. 'And I believe,' he continued, 'the other with the gun is no other than Lord Vincent James Warner, the youngest brother of the premier.'

'Indeed!' exclaimed a voice at my side. At the same moment a person I had not before observed leaned forward and almost rudely pushed past me to get a look from the window. The person was a lady and therefore I could not well resent her want of ceremony; so I waited patiently till she chose to sit down again, and then I said with a jocular smile,

'You seem interested, ma'am, in the lieutenant.'

'Why,' she answered, 'I don't often see celebrated men.'

'I am not aware that that young chap is particularly celebrated,' was my reply.

'Yes, but his brother, you know,' responded the lady with clearness of expression '– and I believe the lieutenant himself is an officer of the illustrious 19th.'[2]

'Illustrious ma'am! A parcel of blackguards!' exclaimed the gentleman who had spoken before.

'Yes, they are,' said the lady, who seemed not strongly inclined to dispute any opinion uttered by another. 'They are certainly very wild and reckless according to all accounts. But then, after all, they have performed gallant exploits. Evesham would never have been won but for them.'

'Fit for nothing but storming towns,' answered the gentleman. 'And that's dirty work, after all – bloody work, ma'am.'

'Yes, it is,' again assented she. 'But if we have war, there must be bloodshed; and then the 19th have other things to do than that, and they have never failed – at least the newspapers say so.'

'They always prime so well before they explode. I've understood, ma'am, that that honourable regiment mostly drinks up de trop in time of action.' I expected the lady would turn enthusiastic and indignant at this, but she only smiled.

'Indeed, sir! Well then, they do their duty much better than most men do sober.'

'I can tell you, ma'am, on the best authority, that at Westwood, half an hour before General Thornton put himself at their head to make the final charge, every officer and almost every private of the nineteenth were as drunk as they could sit in their saddles.'

'Very plucky!' said the lady, still not at all roused. 'Yet that charge was most noble and successful. Was it not said that Lord Arundel thanked them on the field of battle for their gallantry?'

'Don't know,' said the gentleman coldly, 'and if he did, madam, his lordship is very little better than they are.'

'No, certainly,' said she. 'I should think his courage to be much of the same order.'

Until the commencement of the little dialogue above recorded, I had not been sufficiently attracted by my fellow-passenger to give her more than the slightest cursory glance imaginable. But I now scrutinised her a little more closely. I remembered indeed that early that morning as, after travelling all night, our vehicle was traversing a wild tract of country, its speed had suddenly been checked by a cry of 'Coach! Coach!' On looking out, I perceived that we had neared a little inn just where a branch path, winding down from among the loneliest hills, formed a junction with the great high road. By the grey light was just discernible a female figure in a shawl, bonnet, and veil, waiting at the inn door, and a woman-servant standing guard over certain paraphernalia of boxes and packages. The luggage was hoisted onto the top of the coach and the lady was helped inside, where, being but little and thin, she was easily stowed away between myself and a stout woman in a plurality of cloaks. I just saw her shake hands with her attendant. She said something which sounded like 'Good-bye, Mary'; then, as the coach dashed off, she sat well back behind my shoulder, and comfortably hid in her veil and shawl, gave herself up to most unsocial and unfascinating taciturnity.

One can't feel interest in a person that will neither speak nor look. After the lapse of nearly four mortal hours' silence, I had completely forgotten her existence, and should never have remembered it again if that sudden push of hers towards the window had not reminded me of it. The few sentences she subsequently uttered prevented her from sinking again into immediate oblivion, and though no one could have deducted a character from them, yet they were sufficiently marked to make me feel a little curiosity as to what and who she might be.

I had already made two or three attempts to get a view of her face, but in vain. Her bonnet and veil effectually shaded it from observation. Besides, I thought she intentionally turned from me, and though she had talked freely enough to the crusty middle-aged manufacturer opposite, I had not yet been able to draw a syllable of conversation from her. By her voice I concluded she must be a young person, though her dress was of that general simple nature that almost any age might have adopted it: a dark silk gown and heavy chenille shawl, a straw bonnet plainly trimmed, completed a costume unpretending but not unladylike.

Thinking at last that the best way to get a look at her was to begin to talk, I turned rather suddenly towards her for the purpose of commencing a conversation. Meantime, while I had been thinking of her, she, I found, had also been thinking of me; and as she sat shrinking behind me, she had taken the opportunity of my seeming abstraction to scrutinise my physiognomy most closely. Consequently, when I made the unexpected movement of turning my head, I saw her veil thrown back and her eyes fixed full on me with a gaze of keen, sharp observation.

I protest I felt almost flattered by the discovery. However, I soon recovered my wonted self-possession sufficiently to take revenge by an answering stare of, I flatter myself, at least equal intensity. The lady exhibited some command of countenance; she only coloured a little, and then, looking towards the window, remarked it was a beautiful country we were entering upon. It was, for we were now in the province of Zamorna, and the green and fertile glades of March were unfolding on either side of the noble road. Had the lady been very old and very ugly I would have said no more to her; had she been young and extremely handsome I would have commenced a series of petits soins and soft speeches.

Young indeed she was, but not handsome. She had a fair, rather wan complexion, dark hair smoothly combed in two plain folds from her forehead, features capable of much varied expression, and a quick wandering eye of singular and by no means commonplace significance.[3]

'You are a native, madam, I presume, of Angria?'

'Yes,' said she.

'A fine, thriving nation yours. No doubt you're very patriotic?'

'O, of course,' was her answer, and she smiled.

'Now I shouldn't wonder if you take a great deal of interest in politics,' continued I.

'People who live in retired places often do,' she returned.

'You are not from any particular district then, ma'am?'

'No; a solitary hilly country on the borders of Northangerland.' And as she spoke, I remembered the place where she had been taken up, just at the corner of a bypath winding away amongst untrodden hills.

'You must find a pleasant change in visiting this busy, stirring region,' said I. 'Were you ever in Zamorna before?'

'Yes, it is a splendid province – the most populous and wealthy of all the seven.'

'I dare say, now, you think it is worthy of giving a title to your gallant young monarch, eh, madam? You Angrian ladies are all very loyal I know.'[4]

'Yes,' she said, 'I suppose the women of Angria have that character. But I understand it is not peculiar to them. Most African ladies admire his grace, don't they?'

'They make a great profession of doing so, ma'am, and of course you are not an exception.'

'O, no!' she said with extreme coolness. 'I never had the happiness of seeing him, however.'

'Perhaps that is the reason you speak so indifferently about him. I am quite astonished; all his fair subjects with whom I have conversed on the topic before speak in raptures.'

She smiled again. 'I make a point of never speaking in raptures, especially in a stagecoach.'

'Except about the gallant 19th,' I interposed significantly. Then, with my most insinuating air, 'Perhaps some hero of that heroic corps is honoured with your especial interest?'

'All of them are, sir; I like them the better because they are so abused.'

'Humph,' said I, taking a pinch of snuff, 'I see how it is, madam. You don't scruple to admire in general terms any body of men, but you decline coming to individuals.'

'Just so,' said she gaily. 'I'm not free to condescend on particulars.'

'Do you travel far on this road, ma'am?'

'No, I get out at the Spinning Jenny in Zamorna – the inn where the coach stops.'

'Then you are going to visit some friends in that city?'

'I expect to be met there.'[5]

This was an answer so indirect that it was as good as a rebuff. It was evident this young woman did not intend to make anybody the confidant either of her opinions or plans.

'She may keep her secrets to herself then,' thought I, a little huffed at her reserve, and folding my arms, I resumed my former silence, and so did she hers.

It was about noon when we got into Zamorna. The bustle of a market day was throughout all the streets of the thriving commercial city. As the coach stopped at the Spinning Jenny, I saw my fellow-traveller give an anxious glance from the window as if in search of those she expected to meet her. I thought I would keep an eye upon her movements, for my curiosity was a little piqued concerning her.

The door being opened, I was just stepped out into the inn yard, and was offering my hand to assist her in alighting, when a man in livery pushed up and forestalled me in that office. Touching his hat to the lady, he enquired what luggage she had. She gave him her orders and in five minutes I saw her enter a handsome travelling carriage. The trunks and portmanteaus being stowed away in the same conveyance, and a touch being given to the horses, the whole concern rolled lightly off, and in a twinkling had vanished like a dream.

'Surely she can't be anybody of consequence,' thought I. 'She has little of the bearing or mien of an aristocrat. That quiet aspect and plain demure dress scarcely harmonize with so splendid an equipment.'[6]

[Two scenes follow. The first includes a portrait by Charles of the opening of Parliament, which is relevant because it contains a sarcastic description of Sir William Percy; Townsend describes him as vain, lazy, foppish.

The second scene consists of a conversation between Charles and Lord Macara Lofty (opium addict, leader of the Republican Party) about Sir William; again he is portrayed as a foppish womanizer. Charles agrees to visit with Macara the next day.

Sir William is important since he is later attracted to Elizabeth, and becomes the object of her love. His diary will form part of the subsequent narrative.]

CHAPTER 2

Lord Macara's apartments are in a street of splendid lodging houses mostly let to M.P.s towards the West End. The evening of the next day being very wet, and the wind besides being high, I called a hackney coach, and at the appointed hour was set down under the imposing portico of his hotel. His valet let me in and I was shewn through a well-lighted hall and up a handsome flight of stairs to a drawing room of small size but tasteful arrangement, cheerfully shining in the light of a good fire and of four tall wax candles burning on the table. I perceived at once that Macara had been thoughtful enough to provide female superintendence. Her lady-ship was there, seated in a low chair by the hearth, and playing with the silken ears of a little spaniel. A lady, if there be but one in an apartment, always rivets the attention first, and I did not look for other visitors until I had satisfactorily scanned Louisa's easy figure.

'Down, Pepin, down,' she was saying as she tantalised the pigmy with a bit of biscuit. Then again, changing her tone, 'Poor thing, come,' and she laid her slim hand lightly on its head and soothed it till the reclining creature sprang into her lap. There it was caressed for a while, still with the same aristocratic hand whose touch seemed lighter than foam, shaking her head meantime in affected rebuke so as to produce a pretty waving motion in her big curls and cause them to stray readily upon her cheeks and neck. This charming pantomime having been acted a due length of time, she saw fit to start and acknowledge my approach.

'Dear Mr Townsend, how you frighten me with stealing into the room! Pray, how long have you been standing at the door watching me and Pepin?'

'Perhaps five minutes, madam. It's rude I know, but you must excuse me. The picture was such a pretty one.'

'Now,' said she, turning to a person in another part of the room whom I had not noticed before, 'we'll have no flattery tonight, will we, sir?'

'Not from me at least, ma'am,' answered a voice from a dark corner.

'You never flatter, I know,' she continued.

'I've not done lately,' was the reply. 'My tongue is out of practice.'

'Perhaps you disdain all soft nonsense,' said she.

'I'm a novice – a novice –' answered the Unseen hastily. 'I don't understand it.'

'Come and learn, then,' interposed I. 'At Louisa's feet who would be a novice in Love's worship long?'

'Curse it, I'm cold!' ejaculated the gentleman, and rising hastily from the sofa where he had been lounging, he strode forward on to the hearth.

The gentleman, as he spread his hands over the fire, regarded me from top to toe with a rapid sharp glance that implied in its sidelong scrutiny anything rather than an open comfortable shade of mind. I pretended not to look at him, but yet from one corner of my eye I took a sufficiently scrutinising survey of his person and demeanour. He was a man of a muscular and powerful frame, though not tall; of a worn and haggard aspect, though not old or even middle-aged. His hair had no gloss upon it, though it was jet-black and thick. Little care had been bestowed upon its arrangement; it crossed his forehead in disordered flakes, and yet his dress was good and fashionable. Judging by the man's face, he must have been blessed with a devilish temper. I never saw such a mad, suspicious irritability as glinted in his little black eyes. His complexion, of a dark sallowness, aided the effect of a scowl which seemed habitual to his hard, beetling brow.

Leaning on the mantle piece, he looked at Louisa. What a contrast was there between him and her!

'I've not seen his lordship, madam; where is he?'

'O, he'll be down soon. But the viscount's health is really so very indifferent now; during the last week he has never left his bed till it was time to go to the House.'

'Hum!' said the gentleman; then, after a pause of some minutes during which he looked ferociously into the fire, he added, 'Dash it – I feel a want!' The marchioness was now playing with her dog; her attention being wholly taken up with its gambols, the dark stranger turned to me, and putting his thumb to his nose-end, said with a felicitous politeness,

'Do you?'

'Can't say,' was my response.

' 'Cause,' he continued, 'If your case is a similar one to my own, I know the whereabouts and we'll apply a remedy.' I thanked him for his civility but said I was well enough, and for the present at least would dispense with his medicine.

'You don't take?' returned he. 'However, please yourself. Every man to his mind, as the man said; but I must corn or it's no go.'

He walked towards a door and opened it. There was a room within; I watched him walk up to the far end where was a lamp hanging over a sideboard. Decanters and glasses stood there. He filled a glass and drank it. Another – again – again – again – even to the mysterious number of seven times. He returned wiping his lips with a handkerchief.

Just then the door opened and a figure in slippers and dressing gown came bending into the apartment.

'Glad to see you, my lord,' said the stranger, advancing very brusquely. 'I've come according to invitation, you see. I hope your lordship's well.'

'Indifferent, Mr Wilson, indifferent.[7] I've made an effort to rise on your account. Louisa, will you lend me your arm to a seat – I don't feel strong this morning.'

'Certainly, my dear viscount,' said the marchioness, and rising, she supported her friend to an easy chair set by the hearth. He leant back on the cushions and thanked her with a placid patient smile. To look at him now a stranger might have thought him a saint. He was as white as a sheet – every feature expressed extreme exhaustion – but his eye glittered with temporary excitement.

'What have you been doing with yourself since last night?' asked I with surprise.

'O, I took cold,' he answered. 'Cold always weakens me so. But I shall be better soon, Townsend. You and Mr Wilson don't know each other, I believe. Let me introduce you – Townsend, Mr Wilson – Wilson, Mr Townsend.'

Wilson bowed to me with an assured impudent air, and then he sat down immediately in front of the fire, folded his arms on his broad chest, and favoured me with one or two of his pleasant, ingenuous glances.

'My lord,' he said, addressing Macara, 'I hadn't expected to meet company here.'

'O, Mr Townsend is a friend,' returned Lord Macara. 'I hope you and he will soon be on the best terms.'

'Have you ever been in the army, sir?' asked Mr Wilson turning to me. It was evident the man was too mad or too muddy to have any perception of my real identity. So I answered calmly, No, though I had a large circle of military friends.

[‘Wilson’ proceeds to deny with vehemence that he is from Angria, though Townsend has remarked on his Angrian twang.]

'It's the Scotch accent!' exclaimed he. 'I'll stand to it – it's the Scotch accent – I was born in Rosstown and brought up in Rosstown – and I'll break any man's bones who shall dare –'

'Mr Wilson, take some coffee,' interposed the voice of Louisa and that lady stood before him in a bending attitude with the cup in her hand and the smile of persuasion on her lips, almost as lavish of her fascinations to the commercial traveller[8] as she could have been to her high and aristocratic lover, the fastidious Earl of Northangerland.

Wilson looked at her, and taking the cup she offered him said, 'Were it poison I'd drink it.'

'I hope it will act as a sedative,' said she, smiling gently.

'No, madam, as a fiery stimulant. This draught, given by you, makes me a soldier again.' He swallowed the coffee. 'Now,' he continued, flashing at her with a glance of fierce sentiment, 'I've done what you bid me. I wish it were a harder task.'

'I can impose one you will think harder,' returned she. 'Restrain that haughty temper of yours. Be quiet for at least five minutes. See, I seal your lips.' She sportively touched his mouth with her finger, and laughing, returned to her seat.

'There,' said Lord Macara, 'you cannot break a prohibition so delivered . . .'

On that [tableau] I will dwell no more – it is enough to say that I saw Wilson put into Macara's carriage that night blind-drunk. Where it took him I do not know, for the night was so cold and tempestuous I could not be at the pains to follow him. The viscount I left sitting in his easy chair very still, with a leering, vacant simper fixed on his lips. Louisa had driven home to Azalea Bower some hours before, after lavishing the softest attentions on the intoxicated Wilson. I thought I could discern that Macara had employed her to act the basilisk, and lure, by her dangerous charms, the reckless ruffian into his power. During the conversation of the evening, when wine removed restraint, I heard hints of political machinations. Wilson spoke of his associates, of his pals, a short time before he fell under the table. He drank in a brimming bumper damnation to the soldan and his satellites. He insisted that I should pledge him, to which I made no objection, I knew nothing who the soldan might be. I did not even know, though perhaps I might guess – but n'importe.[9]

CHAPTER 3

[Charles has just finished tea, a few days later, and is drowsing by the fire; his romantic reverie is rudely interrupted.]

'Hillo!' I shouted, starting up. 'Let the fire alone will ye, or I'll shiver your skull with the poker!' Somebody laughed, and as I opened my eyes and woke up, I perceived that the flame was ascending the chimney more brilliantly than before, and that fresh fuel had been added within the last few minutes. A dusk form was bending over the hearth in the very act of replacing the poker against the support.

'Who are you?' I demanded.

'Look!' was the concise answer. I did look and not small was my astonishment to discern an individual attired in the dress, and bearing all the insignia of, a policeman. There was no mistaking the dark blue uniform faced with red, the white gloves, the staff and sword stick.

'Who sent you and what do you want?' I again interrogated.

'Only your company for a short distance,' returned the man. 'No need to alarm yourself, Mr Townsend, it's only a trifle. The nobs want a word or two of you. Meantime, if you'll use your eyes you'll see I'm a friend. If it were not for previous acquaintances, I should not have made bold to come upon you so sudden-like –'

[The policeman turns out to be Charles's old friend Ingham, who hustles him into a hackney and takes him down to the station for questioning about his evening with 'Wilson'. The inquiry is conducted by Sir William Percy and Mr Moore, Jane's father.][10]

'Well now, to come to the point. Where were you last Thursday?'

'In Verdopolis.'

'Where were you on the evening of that day?'

'I'm cursed if I can recollect.'

'Perhaps in that case I may be able to refresh your memory. You know Clarges Street?'

'Yes.'

'Is it not chiefly occupied by lodging houses?'

'Very likely.'

'Can you recall the names of any individuals to whom these lodgings are let?'

'Perhaps I might by tomorrow night at this time –'

'You were there last Thursday evening.'

'Was I?'

'Lord Macara Lofty occupies apartments in that street, Mr Townsend, and you were there as a guest of his lordship's last Thursday evening. Now you are required on your oath to say what visitors you met on that occasion.

'Hum!' thought I. 'Here's some enquiry.' I paused, I rapidly ran over in my own mind the state of the business, I calculated whether I had any interest in concealing names and screening the noble viscount. I weighed the affair and adjusted the balance as evenly as I could; and as, after due consideration, I could not discern that one atom of advantage would accrue to me by telling a lie, I resolved to speak the truth.

'I was at Clarges Street last Thursday,' said I, 'and I saw Lord Lofty and the honourable Miss Vernon. I took tea with them –'

'You were alone then in their company?' 'No, there was a sort of lap dog, a poodle or spaniel of the name of Pepin –' Sir William interposed a word.

'You and the poodle then were invited to meet each other I presume, Mr Townsend, and the noble viscount had not troubled himself to ask a third person?'

'Yes, a very respectable bag man –'

'Of the name of Wilson?'

'Just so –'

'Will you describe the person of this gentleman? Was he tall?'

'He was, in comparison of the poodle –'

'Mr Townsend, this won't do. I must demand proper answers to my questions. I request you again to give me a description of Mr Wilson.'

'I will then,' said I, 'and it shall be done con amore. He was a middle-sized man with a deep open chest, a very dark skin, strong black hair and whiskers; a dissipated, profligate look, a kind of branded brow hanging over his eyes with a scowl; a remarkably bass voice for a man under thirty – which I should judge him to be – though strong drink and bad courses had ploughed lines in his face which might better have suited three score. He called himself a Scotchman, but had none of the Scotch physiognomical characteristics –'

'Did he talk much?'

'No.'

'Had you any wine in the course of the evening?'

'Just a drop.'

'Did Mr Wilson profess teetotalism?'

'Hardly.'

'Was he quite sober when he left the house?'

'I daresay he would be by next day at noon.'

'Was he carried out or did he walk?'

'Something between the two. He walked to the top of the stairs, fell to the bottom, and was carried to Lord Macara's carriage.'

'Who went home with him?'

'No one except the coachman.'

'Did you see the carriage drive off?'

'Yes; for that matter, I saw two carriages. At the moment I was labouring under the complaint called second sight.'

'In what direction did it drive? Up Clarges Street or down?'

[The interrogation continues; at its conclusion, Moore and Sir William are convinced of Wilson's real identity, and Townsend is permitted to leave. He concludes by marvelling over the cooperation between his two interrogators, usually at extreme odds politically: Moore is Hartford's 'tool'; Hartford (Henry's commanding officer) and Sir William are bitter enemies.]

CHAPTER 4

Where the Olympian crept along, slow, deep, and quiet, after escaping from the rushing mill dams of Zamorna, a thin ice was beginning to crisp upon its surface. A frost was setting in that evening which already had hardened the road down Hartford Dale to such iron-firmness that when any solitary carriage passed up at that late hour, the sound of its wheels tinkled among the dusk woods as if they had rolled over metal. Ascending above the dimness of the valley, a full moon filled the cloudless and breathless winter twilight with a sort of peace the largest star could but have faintly typified. Yet here was no summer softness: it was cold, icy, a night of marble; fast beneath its influence did bagmen urge their gigs, and rejoicingly did mailcoach guards wind their horns, when the lights of Zamorna flashed in the distance and the vision of a tankard of hot ale and rum flashed upon their inward eye.

A man in a cloak came over the Bridge of Zamorna and, turning down the dale, held a straight course along the causeway of that noble road. He walked on foot with his cloak gathered about him, his head and chest erected, and his hat so set on his brow that the brim rested very near on the bridge of his nose. Hartford Woods,

unfolding on each hand, shewed in a fissure between their dark
sweep of shade the sky filled with the glorious rising moon – which
moon looked intently upon the traveller with that melancholy
aspect it has always worn since the flood. The man stinted his
stride a moment, when on his right hand he passed the great gates
of Hartford Hall, and beheld far within, towering amid the stretch
of grounds, the wide front and wings of that lordly seat.

While you gaze, reader, on those long windows shining in
moonlight, on those stately and turret-like chimneys and that
gleaming roof, the traveller has hurried on. Where is he? Not on
the road; has he vanished? Follow me and we shall see. He crossed
a stile in that hedge – the field beyond was steep, green, and wide.
He skirted it quickly and then, with a faster stride than ever, he
threaded the broad far-stretching ings[11] of the Olympian. Distant
now from the main road, he pursued a lone track through the
silence of lanes and fields. Not a creature crossed his path. Flocks
and herds were folded; the farms here are vast and the farmhouses
far asunder. This was Lord Hartford's land, let in long leases half
a century ago.

Well, he was now four miles away from Zamorna, and the bells
of a church were heard far away chiming nine at night; he stopped
till they had ceased ringing, perhaps to listen, perhaps to draw
breath. At last he came to a field with a very noble row of
magnificent old trees down the sides, and close along their trunks
a broad gravelled footpath which their boughs overhung like
arches. Following this road, he came soon to the house called
Massinger Hall: an ancient spacious dwelling, situated all alone in
those wide fields, very solitary and impressive, with a sombre
rookery frowning behind it. The pillars of the garden gate were
crowned with stone balls, as also were the gables of the house, and
in the garden, on the lawn, there was a stone pillar and a time-
stained dial plate. Massinger Hall was as silent as the grave; all the
front was black, except where the moonlight shone on the masses
of ivy clustered around every casement. Yet it was not ruined; a
calm, stately order pervaded the scene. It was only antique, lonely,
and gray.

The man in the cloak roamed backwards and forwards before
the front of the hall, pausing sometimes as if to listen, and when

no sound was audible and no light streamed from the many closed and frost-wrought casements, wandering on again with the same measured stride. At length from within the house a sound was heard of the deep bark of some large dog – not near at hand, but in a remote room away at the back. Fearful, evidently, of discovery, the traveller started at the noise. In a moment he had turned the corner of the house and stood sheltered under the more retired gable. Here at last his eye met some sign of habitation. The gable had but one large window, almost like that of a church – long and low, opening upon the turf of the lawn – and from this window glowed a reflection of warm light upon all the garden shrubs about it. Everyone knows how distinctly the interior of a lamp-lit room can be seen at night when there is no shutter or blind to screen the window, and as the stranger knelt on the ground behind a large laurel whose branches were partly shot over the lattice, he could see into the very penetralia of the grim house as distinctly as if he had been actually within its walls.

About the window there hung the festoons and drapery of a heavy moreen[12] curtain, deep crimson in colour. These, looped up, showed a long room, glittering on all sides with the reflection of firelight from the darkest panels of oak. The room was carpeted and in the middle was a massive table having the raven gloss of ebony. There were no candles, no lamps burning, but a glowing hearth. This might have been a cheerful room when filled with company, but tonight it wore, like the rest of Massinger Hall, an air of proud gloom almost too impressive to the imagination.

A figure came towards the window and then paced back again and was almost lost in the shadow of the opposite end. Again it appeared, drawing near slowly. As slowly, it withdrew to the dusk of distance. To and fro it paced with the same measured step, down the whole length of the large old parlour, and there was nothing else visible: a single person walking about there in that remote mansion, embosomed amid boundless fields.

This person was a woman – rather, a girl of about nineteen. She looked like one who lived alone, for her dress shewed none of the studied arrangement and decorative taste by which women – young women especially – endeavour to please those with whom they associate. She looked also like one who lived too much alone, for the expression of her face, as she roamed to and fro, was fixed and dreamy. Whether at this moment her thoughts were sad or bright, I cannot tell; but they were evidently very interesting, for she had forgot heaven above and earth beneath and all things that are thereon, in the charm that they wrapped about her. No doubt it was to excite in her mind these feverish dreams that she had left the curtains of the great window undrawn, so that whenever she looked towards it, there was the moon gliding out into a broad space of blue sky from behind the still, tall spire of a poplar, and under her beams, spreading to the horizon, there were wide solitary pastures, with the noblest timber of the province along their swells.

At last she is waking,[13] and it's time, for a clock somewhere in the house struck ten five minutes ago. She shakes off her trance with a short sigh, walks to the fire, stirs it, and then thinks she'll let down the window curtains.

Being not very tall, she stept on to a chair for this purpose.[14] But she quickly jumped down again, for as she was stretching her hand to loose the crimson rope, a man rose from behind the laurel branches and stood straight up with his foot on the very sill of the window. The young woman gave back and looked towards the door. Considerable dismay and amazement were at first depicted in her face, but before she had time to run away, the apparition had passed the thin barrier of the glass door and stood in her very presence.

Most considerately, he closed the lattice behind him, and also let down the curtains, a feat his stature enabled him to perform much more conveniently than the lady could have done. Then he took off his hat and, while he ran his fingers through his thick hair, said in an ordinary masculine voice,

'Now, Elizabeth, I suppose you know me?'

But this greeting, easy as it was, seemed for a while to produce no answering token of recognition. The young woman looked again and again in complete astonishment. At last, some conviction seemed fastening on her mind. It excited strong feeling; she lost the very little colour which had tinged her complexion before; and at last she said in a peculiar voice, a voice flesh and blood human beings never use but when the strongest and strangest sensations are roused,

'Henry! Can it be you?' Smiling as well as he could, in a kind of way that shewed he was not used to that sort of thing, the man in the cloak offered his hand. It was clasped in two that together were not as large as that one, and wrung and pressed with wild and agitated eagerness. The girl would not speak till she had cleared her voice, so as to be able to utter her words without making hysterical demonstrations. Then she said her visitor was cold, and drew him towards the fire.

'I shall do, Elizabeth – I shall do,' said the man, 'only you get a trifle calmer – come, come, I don't know that I've exactly deserved much of a welcome.'

'No, but I must give it you when I can't help it,' she answered sharply. 'Sit down – I never thought you were alive – according to the newspapers you were in France. Why have you left it for a country where you can't be safe? Do you think the police have a glimpse of suspicion which route you have taken? How cold you are, Henry – it is two years tonight since I saw you; sit down.' There was a large antique armchair on each side of the hearth, and he threw himself into one with the abandonment of a weary man.

'I've not had two hours' sleep for the last three nights,' said he. 'How their damned police have dogged me since they got fairly on the scent –'

'What! officers are in pursuit of you now!' exclaimed the girl in a tone of dread.

'Yes, yes; but I think I've shown them a trick in coming here. They'd think Angria would be the last cover the Fox would take. Give me a draught of wine, Elizabeth, I'm almost done.'

She went out of the room hurriedly, looking round at his harrassed, pallid face as she closed the door. In her absence, he dropped his head upon the arm of the chair and gave expression to his sufferings in a single groan, the language of a strong man's distress. When her step was heard returning, he started up, cleared his countenance, and sat erect. She brought wine, which he took from her hand and swallowed eagerly.

'Now,' said he, 'all's right again. Come, you look sadly scared, Elizabeth – but with regard to you I'm just the same Harry Hastings that I always was. I daresay by this time you've learnt to think of me as a kind of ogre –' He looked at her with that kind of mistrust

born of conscious degradation, but his suspicions were allayed by
the expressive glance with which she answered him. It said more
convincingly than words: 'your faults and yourself are separate
existences in my mind, Henry'.

Now reader, how were those two connected? They were not
lovers; they were not man and wife; they must have been – a
marked resemblance in their features attested it – brother and
sister. Neither were handsome. The man had wasted his vigour
and his youth in vice; there was more to repel than charm in the
dark fiery eye sunk far below the brow, an aspect marked with the
various lines of suffering, passion, and profligacy. Yet there were
the remnants of a strong and steady young frame, a bold martial
bearing in proud, confident, and ready action, which in better days
had won him smiles from eyes he adored like a fanatic. But you
remember, reader, what I said of Wilson. I need not paint his
portrait anew, for this was Wilson: just the same dark reprobate in
the lonely oak parlour of Massinger Hall, as he had been in Lord
Lofty's elegant drawing room at Verdopolis.

His sister was almost as fair as he was dark, but she had little
colour. Her features could lay no claim to regularity, though they
might to expression; yet she had handsome brown eyes, and a
ladylike and elegant turn of figure. Had she dressed herself stylishly
and curled her hair, no one would have called her plain. But in a
brown silk frock – a simple collar, and hair parted on her forehead
in smooth braids – she was just an insignificant, unattractive young
woman, wholly without the bloom, majesty, or fullness of beauty.
She looked like a person of quick perceptions and dexterous
address; when the first tumult of emotion consequent on the
adventure of the night had subsided, she spoke to her brother with
an assumed tone of cheerfulness, as if desirous to avert from his
vigilant jealousy those pangs of anguish which his changed appearance, his dreadful and death-struck prospects, must have forced
into her heart. He had gone away a young soldier full of hope:
what career of life must that have been which had brought him
back a Cain-like wanderer with a price upon his blood?[15]

'I am not as bad as you think me,' said Henry Hastings suddenly.
'I'm a man that has been atrociously wronged. I'll tell you,
Elizabeth, a black tale about Adams and that gutter-blood, that

Fiend of Hell, Lord Hartford. They envied me – but I suppose you're on their side, so it's no use talking –'

'You think I care more about Hartford and Adams than I do about you, do you, Henry? And I know so little of you as to suppose you would shoot a man dead without a galling and infamous provocation?'[16]

'Aye – but besides that, I'm a deserter, and no doubt at Pendleton[17] everybody is very patriotic and it's ultra heterodox to hate an Angrian renegade one whit less than the devil. My father, for instance, would he see me, d'ye think?'

'No.'

The answer was short and decisive, but Hastings would not have tolerated evasion. The truth was a bitter pill, but he swallowed it in silence.

'Well, I don't care!' he exclaimed after a pause. 'I'm a man yet, and a better man than most of those that hate me, too. Don't think I've been spending the last two years in puling and whining, either, Elizabeth. I've lived like a prince at Paris, a good life, and feasted so well on pleasure that a little pain comes in conveniently to prevent a surfeit. Then this pursuit will soon blow over. I'll keep close with you at Massinger till the hounds are baffled, and then I'll slip down to Doverham, take ship, and emigrate to one of the Islands. I'll make myself rich there, and when I've built a good house and got an estate full of slaves, I'll stand for a borough. Then I'll come back. After seven years' absence they can't touch me. I'll speak in Parliament. I'll flatter the people. I'll set hell burning through the land. I'll impeach half the peerage for their brutal corruptions and tyrannies. If Northangerland be dead, I'll apothosize his memory.[18] Let my bloody-handed foes remember that.'

Instead of softening the renegade's excited ferocity, and reasoning against his malignant vindictiveness, Miss Hastings caught his spirit and answered in a quick excited voice.[19]

'You have been basely persecuted. You have been driven to desperation – I know it and I always did know it. I said so on the day that Mr Warner came to Pendleton and told my father you were broken by a court martial for desertion. My father took out his will and, while Mr Warner looked on, drew a long line through your name and said he disowned you forever. Our landlord said he had done right, but I told him he had done wrong and unnaturally. My father was then scarcely himself, and he is always quick and passionate as his son. He knocked me down, in Mr Warner's presence. I got up and said the words over again. Mr Warner said I was an undutiful daughter, and was adding by my obstinacy to my father's misery. I cared nothing for his reproof, and I left Pendleton a few weeks after. I've been earning my bread since by my own effort.'

'So I heard,' returned Hastings, 'and that is the reason you are at Massinger, I suppose.'

'Yes, the house belongs to the Moores. Old Mr Moore died lately, and his son, the barrister, is going to reside here. I am keeping it for him while he and his daughter are in Verdopolis. Miss Moore pretends to have a great regard for me and says she can't live without me, because I flatter her vanity and don't rival her beauty. And I teach her to speak French and Italian, which of course is a convenience.'[20]

'Well, Elizabeth, can you keep me here in safety for a day or two?'

'I'll do my best. There are only two or three old servants in the house. But, Henry, you are sick with weariness. You must have something to eat and go to bed directly. I'll order a room to be prepared for you –'

While Elizabeth Hastings leaves the parlour to find her way through dark passages to the distant kitchen, we also will turn for a time from the contemplation of her and her brother. My candle is nearly burnt out and I must close the chapter.

CHAPTER 5

SIR WILLIAM PERCY'S DIARY

[The first entry in Sir William's diary recounts a romantic dream about a French woman with whom he has been involved; the passage, which confirms earlier descriptions of him as a womanizer, reveals the pleasure he finds in the fantasy of being irresistible, and his own intention never to marry. The hunt for Hastings is his next theme.]

Just given audience to Ingham, my police Inspector. He tells me that he has quite ascertained that Wilson has left his haunts about town. My lads have smoked every hole where he could hide with such strong fumes of brimstone that he's been forced into flight – an important object gained. It's easier to chase the Fox over an open campaign than in the broken ground and pits and holes of a rabbit warren like Verdopolis – aye, or Paris either. Drove to York Place to communicate the intelligence to Moore. The oily-tongued, smooth-faced toadie of a blackguard cut-throat was sly enough to see the advantage at once. He rubbed his hands and said, chuckling, 'We have him now, Sir William. Only a little patience, a little time, and we'll all be in at the death –' But what tack has Hastings taken? My lads must disperse far and wide.

I've ordered some to Edwardston to watch the east road, and some to Alnwick to guard the west, and some to Freetown to bestride the north. If he does escape me, he's a devil and not a man; yet he has skill in baffling pursuit. Again and again, when the hounds were on his very haunches, he has doubled and slipped. I wonder what charm the miserable ruffian can find in life to make him stick to it so? In Paris, I more than once so hemmed him in and harrassed him, so crushed him to the wall, that he must have been at the verge of absolute starvation. The man would have cut his throat long since if he had been left alone. But while others seek his life to take it, his obstinate nature will lead him to defend the worthless possession to the last.

Today, while thinking about him, I recollected a little incident which I may hereafter turn to account in discovering his lair. Some months since I chanced to go to the opera one night. While I was sitting in my box and thinking myself in my full dress uniform an uncommonly killing sight, I observed a sort of sensation commencing round me, and heard, amidst many whispers and a rising hum of admiration, the words often repeated, 'It is the beautiful Angrian!' Translate me – if I didn't at first think they were alluding to myself!

The words 'Spare my blushes' were at my tongue's end, and I was beginning to consider whether it would or would not be necessary to acknowledge so much polite attention by a grateful bow, when I perceived that the heads and eyes of the ninnies were not turned towards me, but in a clean opposite direction, to a box where a tall young woman was sitting in the middle of a crowd of most respectable-looking masculine individuals, who one and all wanted nothing but a tail to make the prettiest counterfeit monkeys imaginable. The young woman shone in blond and satin – with plumes enough on her head to waft an ostrich from Arabia. The liberal display of neck and arms showed plainly enough that she knew both were as white and round and statuesque as if Phidias had got up from the dead to chisel them out of the purest marble he could find from the quarries of Paros,[21] and the pearls circling them round showed that she had taste enough to be aware how effective was the contrast between the dazzling living flesh and the cold gleaming gem. She'd a nose like Alexander the Great's, and large blue imperial eyes, bright with the sort of ecstasy that a woman, flattered with conviction of her own divinity, must feel glowing at her heart. Nature had given her a profusion of hair, and art had trained it into long silky ringlets bright as gold.

She was a superb animal, there's not a doubt of it. I hardly know a face or form in Africa that would not have looked dim by her side; a dim, dusk foil she had indeed to her diamond lustre, a little shade just at her elbow,[22] hustled backwards and forwards by the men, pagans that were crowding to the shrine of this idol.

While I was looking at her, Townsend came into my box.

'D'ye see how triumphant Jane Moore is looking tonight?' said he.

'Yes,' I answered, 'she's poisoning half the female peerage with envy. But who in heaven's name has she got at her side, Townsend? Who can the little blighted mortal be? Somebody she's hired at so much a night to keep near her for the purpose of shewing her off?' Townsend took a sight with his opera glasses.

'D'ye mean that pale, undersized young woman dressed as plainly as a Quakeress in grey, with her hair done à la Victoria Delph? Small credit to her taste for that same. I think a few curls wouldn't have been amiss, to relieve her singular features a trifle. And yet I don't know; there's something studied about her dress. Everything suits: white scarf, plain silver ribbon in her hair –' I interrupted.

'D'ye know who she is, Townsend? Is she some heiress that

has sufficient attractions of purse to dispense with those of person?'

'Hardly, I think; for if you observe, she has not a single man in her train. If she'd had brass now, half that raff of young Angrian scamps that are pressing their attentions upon Miss Moore would have turned their thoughts to the holder of the money bags. It strikes me now, as that girl looks towards us, I've seen her face before. I have. I'm sure it was in a stagecoach on the Angrian road. I travelled with her some distance and I remember, from what she said, I thought her a sharp, shrewd customer enough.'

'Did you hear her name?'

'No.' Here the conversation dropped, for I could take no particular interest in a person of that sort.

But a day or two after, I went to dine at Thornton's. It was a blowout for the Angrians on the occasion of their omni-gathering at the commencement of the Verdopolitan season, and I was a trifle late, as is my way occasionally. When I entered the drawing room they were already marshalling themselves for dinner. Jane Moore was the first person I saw, and three gentlemen were offering her their arms at once. While I was watching their manoeuvres, all the other ladies had found conductors. Lo, I was last in the long train of plumes and robes, and to my horror and consternation, nothing left for me to patronise but the same little dusk apparition I had seen at the opera: the plain, pinched protégée of Miss Moore's.

'Well,' thought I, 'she may go by herself before I offer her my arm,' and pretending not to see her, I carelessly followed the rest and took my place, with all the ease and coolness of my natural habits, at the very bottom of the table.

She came stealing after; there was a single chair below mine, and into this, being the only seat vacant, she was obliged to induct herself. However, I'd a pleasant pretty girl on the other side of me, an Augusta Lonsdale, and one of the stately Ladies Seymour opposite to me. So, having formed the determination not to notice my left-hand neighbour by word or look, I made myself very comfortable.

Your Angrians have always a deal of laughing and conversation over their meals, and the party were exceedingly merry. Looking up the table, I saw a great many handsome women, and much glittering of jewellery and sparkling of bright eyes. Invitations to take wine were also passing from lip to lip, and bows were interchanged across the table with infinite suavity. Ladies were leaning their heads to hear the flatteries of the men at their sides, and for my part, I was cajoling Miss Augusta Lonsdale with the finest possible compliments on the bloom of her complexion and the softness of her smile.

When all this flow of enjoyment was at its height, I chanced to look round for the purpose of taking some vegetables a footman was handing, and my eye unfortunately fell on the little individual I had resolved not to see. She was eating nothing, listening to nothing; not a soul had addressed a word to her, and her face was turned towards a large painting of a battle which, in that room by lamplight, had a peculiar aspect of gloom and horror.

I can't pretend to say what thoughts were in her mind, but something she beheld in the rolling clouds of smoke, in the tossed manes and wild eyes of charging horses, in the bloody forms of men trampled beneath their hoofs, had filled her eyes with tears. More likely, however, she felt herself solitary and neglected. There is no bitterness the human heart knows like that of being alone and despised, while around it hundreds are lorded and idolized.

I think I should have spoken to her, but something suggested to me, 'Everybody has their own burdens to bear. Let her drink the chalice fate commands to her lips.' Besides, there was something that suited my turn of mind in the idea of a neglected human being turning from the hollow world, glittering with such congenial and selfish splendour before her, to the contemplation of that grim vision of war, and finding in the clouds of battle dust and smoke, there melting into air, something that touched her spirit on the quick.

I would not break the charm by trying to remove the sorrow. When a tear trickled from her eyelash to her cheek, she hastily lifted her handkerchief to wipe it away, and then, roused to recollection, called into her face an indifferent expression, and turning from the picture, looked like a person without an idea, alien from those she was with. I took good care to seem engaged in deep discourse with Augusta Lonsdale, that she might not suspect what scrutiny she had been the subject of a moment before.

After dinner, when the ladies had retired to the drawing room, I was, as I always am, one of the first to follow them. I hate sotting over the decanters: it's a vulgar beastly habit. The whole of that evening I watched the protégée very closely, but she evinced no other habit that took my fancy. She got a little more notice: several ladies talked to her, and she entered into conversation with a good deal of fluency and address. She assented, and gave up her opinion, and listened with becoming interest to whatever others had to say. She asked Miss Moore to sing just when Miss Moore wanted to be asked. She ran over the list of her finest songs where Jane's grand show-off voice is most efficiently displayed. And when the lady had fairly commenced, she retired from the piano and left room for her admirers to crowd about her.

In two hours, she had grown quite a favourite with the female part of the company; the men she never looked at, nor seemed once desirous of attracting their attention. Yet the creature, on a close examination, was by no means ugly. Her eyes were very fine and seemed as if they could express anything. She'd a fair, smooth skin, and a hand as fine as a fairy's; her feet and ancles were like those of a crack dancer in an opera-ballet corps, but her features were masked with an expression foreign to them. Her movements were restrained and guarded; she wanted openness, originality, frankness.

Before the evening was over, I contrived to learn her name and family: it was Elizabeth Hastings, the sister of that devil Henry.

I have never seen her since – till today I had forgotten her. But it struck me all at once that if I could find her out I might, by proper management, get some useful intelligence respecting her brother. I'll call on Miss Moore and ask her a few careless questions about her protégée, taking care to throw in deprecating remarks and a general air of contempt and indifference. A careful gleaner finds corn of good grain where a fool passes by and sees only stubble.

CHAPTER 6

[Sir William, continued]

Feb. 10th[23] Dedicated the whole of this morning to an easy lounge in Miss Moore's boudoir. How much wisdom there is in taking things quietly: I carry on my machinations amidst the velvet and down of a lady's chamber. Jane Moore certainly knows how to fascinate. She is what the world calls exquisitely sweet-tempered. A sweet temper in a beautiful face is a divine thing to gaze on, and she has a kind of simplicity about her which disclaims affectation. She does not know human nature; she does not penetrate into the minds of those about her; she does not fix her heart fervently on some point which it would be destructive to take it from; she has none of that strong refinement of the senses which makes some temperaments thrill with undefined emotion at changes or chances in the skies or the earth, in a softness in the clouds, a trembling of moonlight in water, an old and vast tree, the tone of the passing wind at might, or any other little accident of nature which contains in it more botheration than sense.[24]

Well, and what of that? Genius and enthusiasm may go and be hanged. I did not care a damn for all the genius and enthusiasm on earth when Jane rose from her nest by the fire, and stood up in her graceful height of stature with her hand held out to welcome me; and,

'Good morning, Sir William,' those fresh lips said with such a frank smile, I liked my name better for being uttered by her voice. 'Sit down, close to the fire, you must be very cold.' So I did sit down, and in two minutes she and I were engaged in the most friendly bit of chat imaginable.

Jane asked me if I was getting warm, and rang for some more coal for my special benefit. Then she enquired when I thought of going down into Angria, for she hoped whenever I chanced to be about Zamorna I would be sure to pay them a visit, provided only they were at home.

'You've never been to our new house,' said she. 'You know we've left Kirkham Lodge since my grandfather died.'

'Indeed,' said I, 'but you live in the neighbourhood still, I suppose?'

'O, yes, it's the family place near Massinger – an old queer sort of house – but papa intends to pull it down and build a proper seat. I'm rather sorry, because the people at Zamorna will be sure to say it is pride.'

'O, you shouldn't mind envy,' I returned, and then by way of changing the conversation I made a remark on the beauty of an ornamental vase on the mantelpiece, the sides of which were exquisitely painted with a landscape of Grecian ruins and olives, and a dim mountain background.

'Is it not beautiful!' she said, taking it down. 'It was done by the sister of poor Captain Hastings. By the bye, colonel, it is very cruel of you to hunt young Hastings as they say you do – he was such a clever, high-spirited fellow.'

'Aye, he shewed high spirit in that bloody murder of Adams,' I returned.

'Adams was not half as nice a man as he,' returned Jane. 'He was very arrogant. I daresay he insulted poor Hastings shamefully. I once met him and I told papa, when I came home, I thought he was a very proud disagreeable man.'[25]

'Then you think his subaltern did right to shoot him through the brain?'

'No, not right. But it is a pity Hastings should die for it. I wish you knew his sister, colonel, you would be very sorry for her.'

'His sister – who is she? Not that very plain girl I saw with you one night at the opera?'

'You wouldn't call her plain if you knew her, colonel,' said Jane with the most amiable earnestness of manner. 'She is so good and so clever. She knows everything very nearly and she's quite different to other people. I can't tell how –'

'Well,' said I, 'she's not a person, my dear Miss Moore, to attract my attention much. Is she really a friend of yours?'

'I won't tell you, colonel, because you speak so sneeringly of her.' I laughed.

'And so I suppose this paragon bothers you a great deal about her murdering brother? Tells you tales of his heroism and genius and sorrows?'

'No,' said Jane, 'there's one very odd thing I've often wondered at. She never mentions him. And somehow I never dare to talk on the subject; for she has her peculiarities and, if she happened to take offence, she'd leave me directly.'

'Leave you! What! does she live with you?'

'She's my governess, in a sense,' said Miss Moore. 'I learn French and Italian of her. She went to school at Paris, and she speaks French very well.'

'Where do the Hastings come from?' I enquired.

'From Pendleton, up in Angria; quite a rough, wild country – very different to Zamorna. There's no good society there at all, and the land is very little cleared. I once rode over to the neighbourhood on horseback when I was on a visit to Sir Markham Howards, and I was quite astonished at the moors and mountains. You've no idea: hardly any green fields, and no trees, and such stony bad roads.

'I called at old Mr Hastings' house. They don't live like us there – he's considered a gentleman and his family is one of the oldest in that part of the country. He was sitting in his kitchen – what they call the house. It was wonderfully clean, the floor scoured as fair nearly as this marble, and a great fire in the chimney such as we have in our halls. Still, it looked strange; Mr Hastings was roughly dressed and had his hat on. He spoke quite with an Angrian accent, far broader than General Thornton's, but I liked him very much, he was so hospitable. He called me a bonny lass and said I was as welcome to Colne-Moss Tarn as the day.'

'Was Captain Hastings at home then?' I enquired.

'No, it was soon after he had entered the army, when everybody was talking in his praise, and his songs were sung at public dinners and meetings. But Elizabeth Hastings was at home, and she did look such an elegant ladylike being, in that homely place. But though she's quite fastidious in her refinement, I really believe she likes those dreary moors and that old manor house far better than Zamorna or even Verdopolis. Isn't it odd?'

'Very,' said I. Jane continued.

'I often wonder what it was that made her leave Pendleton and go out into the world as she has done. Papa thinks it is for something her father has said or done against Henry, for old Mr Hastings is an exceedingly obstinate, passionate man; indeed, all the family are passionate.[26] Elizabeth has never been home for two years, and now she's living by herself at our old place, Massinger Hall. Such a lonely situation and such gloomy old rooms – I wonder she can bear it –'

This last sentence of Miss Moore's comprised the information I wished to obtain, so it was not necessary I should prolong my visit much further. After a few minutes further, I took a final gaze on her kind, handsome face, shook hands, made my parting bow and exit. Man, when I got home, I found Ingham waiting for me with an important piece of intelligence. He had succeeded in ascertaining that the dog Wilson had certainly gone in an easterly direction. Angria is the word then. I'll set off tomorrow; and as to this Massinger Hall, I mean to see the interior of it before two more suns set.

CHAPTER 7

[This portion of Sir William's diary concludes, and Town-send's narrative resumes long enough to describe first Henry's character, and then the 'insult' for which, apparently, he murdered Adams.]

The stillest time of a winter's day is often the afternoon, especially when the desolation of snow and tempest without seem to give additional value to the comfort of a warm hearth and sheltering roof within. Near the close of a wild day, just before twilight's shadows began to fold over the world, Captain Hastings and his sister were sitting by the hearth of the oak parlour at Massinger Hall. Hastings watched the dreary snow storm careering past that large Gothic casement, and after a long silence he said,

'There will be deep drifts on Boulshill[27] –' The man was in a gloomy mood and so was his sister, for neither of them was the brightest, mildest, or gentlest of human beings. One had the horror of a violent death always before him, and the other had the consciousness that the murderer, an outlaw, a deserter, and a traitor, were all united in the person of her only brother.

'And you think no intercession on your behalf would be listened to at court?' said Elizabeth Hastings, recurring to a conversation they had engaged in some minutes previously.

'I think they are all unhanged villains at court,' replied Henry in a deep rough voice –

Before proceeding with my narration, I would pause a minute for the character of Captain Hastings. The 19th regiment, of which the renegade had once been an officer, had lost from its bold, bad ranks a man well-calculated to sustain the peculiar species of celebrity which that corps have so widely earned. He was, at the outset of his career, just what a candidate for distinction there ought to have been. Before vice fired her canker in him, he was a strong, active, athletic man, with all the health of his native hills glowing in his dark cheeks; with a daring ferocity of courage always awake in his eyes; with an arrogance of demeanour that bore down weaker minds, and which, added to an intellect strong in the wings as an eagle, drew round him wherever he went a train of besotted followers.

But the man was mutinous and selfish and accursedly malignant. His mind was of that peculiarly agreeable conformation, that if anyone conferred a benefit upon him, he instantly jumped to the conclusion that they expected some act of mean submission in return; and the consequence was, he always bit the hand that caressed him. Then his former patrons looked coldly at him, shrugged their shoulders, and drew off in disgust, while Hastings followed their retreat with a howl of hate and a shout of defiance. Thus he ruined his public prospects: those already in high places swore, till the bottom of hell was moved by their oaths, that they'd go bodily to Beelzebub before Hastings should rise an inch. No doubt these aristocratic vows will be fulfilled all in good time – but meanwhile the captain, like a wise man, thought he'd be beforehand with them. Ambition would not carry him fast enough to Pandemonium,[28] so he harnessed the flying steeds of pleasure to aid it.

His passions were naturally strong, and his imagination was warm to fever. The two together made wild work, especially when Drunken Delirium lashed them up to a gallop that the Steeds of the Apocalypse thundering to Armageddon[29] would have emulated in vain. He was talked of everywhere for his excesses. People heard of them with dismay; the very heroes of the 19th held up their saintly hands and eyes at some of his exploits and exclaimed, 'Dang it! that beats everything!'

One day, during the campaign of the Cirhala, Hastings was on duty somewhere, when a man in an officer's cloak rode by on horseback. He reined up and said,

'Hastings, is that you?'

'Yes,' said the captain, not looking up from the butt end of his rifle on which he was leaning, for he knew the voice and the figure too, and it galled him that anything should come near him whose approach it would be necessary to recognise by an act of homage. However the horseman was alone, so, as there were no witnesses of the humiliation, Hastings at last condescended to lift his military cap from his brow.

'You're going to the dogs I understand, Hastings,' continued the other. 'What the devil do you think your constitution's made of, man –?'

'Devilment, if I may judge from what I feel,' answered the suffering profligate with the air of a rated[30] bulldog.

'D'ye mean to stop?' continued the interrogator.

'I've no present intention of that sort.'

'Well, perhaps you're in the right,' continued the horseman, coolly managing his restless charger, which fretted impatiently beneath the restraint of the rein. 'Perhaps you're in the right, lad. It would be hardly worth your while to stop now, you're a lost worn-out broken up scoundrel.' The captain bowed.

'Thank you, my lord – that's God's truth however.'

'I once had a pleasure in looking at you,' added his adviser. 'I thought you a fine, promising fellow that was fit for anything. You're now just a poor devil – nothing more.'

'And that's God's truth too,' was the answer. The horseman stooped a moment from his saddle, laid his hand on Hastings' shoulder, and with a remarkably solemn air ejaculated,

'Damn you, sir!' The horse was then touched with the spur and it sprang off as if St Nicholas had ridden it.

It was evening when this interview took place and the next morning Hastings shot Colonel Adams.

[The narrative now returns to Sir William's diary.]

CHAPTER 8

Feb. 18th – Stancliffe's is a real nice, comfortable inn. I always feel
as content as a king when I'm seated in that upper room of theirs
that looks out on the court house. I'd a wretchedly cold journey
from Verdopolis down to Zamorna; very wet and dreary day, got
in just about noon; felt very philanthropic and benevolent when I
was shewn into the aforesaid upper room with a good fire, and as
pretty a little luncheon as eye could wish to see set out on the table.
Having appeased the sacred rage of hunger, I began to consider
whether I should order fresh horses to my barouche and drive
forward to Massinger. But a single glance towards the window
settled that matter: such driving, pelting rain; such a bitter
disconsolate wind; such sunless gloom in the sky; streets brown
and shining with wet, clattering with pattens,[31] and canopied by
umbrellas.

'No, it's no go,' I said to myself. 'I'll give anybody leave to cut
off my ears that shall catch me romancing in search of old halls
today.' So I just laid me down easy on the sofa that stood convenient
to the fireside, and with the aid of the last number of 'Rookwood's
Northern Magazine' and a glass of pleasant Madeira placed on a
little stand within the reach of my arm, I proposed spending an
afternoon at once rational and agreeable. Well, for two hours all
went uncommon well. The fire burnt calm and bright, the room
was still, the elements without gibbered more infernal moans than
ever; and I, hanging over the pages of a deliciously besotted tale,
was just subsiding into a heavenly slumber when, knock – knock
– knock; some fiend of Tartarus tapped at the door.

> [A messenger from Lord Hartford brings a note requesting
> Sir William's 'immediate attendance'; he is ready to close in
> for the kill.]

Having achieved the perusal of this dispatch, I found myself
giving utterance to a whistle and at the same instant the spirit
moved me to ring the bell and order a horse. In about a quarter of
an hour after I had been dreaming on a couch under the dozy
influence of a stupid tale, I found myself perched up in a saddle,

dashing over the bridge of Zamorna like a laundrymaid heading a charge of cavalry.

When I got to Hartford Hall I found a carriage drawn up at the entrance, and four of my own police ready-mounted in the disguise of postillions. One of them was Ingham. He doffed his cap.

'Scent's as strong as stink, sir,' says he. Encouraged by this agreeable hint, I alighted and hastened into the house to obtain more precise information. Passing through the hall I perceived the door of the dining room was open so I walked in. The Great Creole[32] had just concluded his dinner and was in the act of helping himself to a glass of wine when I entered. His gloves and his hat lay on a sidetable, and a servant stood with his cloak over his arm waiting to assist him on with it.

'Well, Percy,' he began with his growling bass voice as soon as ever his eye caught me. 'I hope the rascal is about to be disposed of at last. Fielding, is my cloak ready?'

'Yes, my lord.'

'Will you take wine, Sir William? Fielding, the carriage is at the door I suppose?'

'Yes, my lord.'

'You have nothing to detain you I presume, Sir William; time is precious.[33] Fielding, have the police had the whisky I ordered?'

'Yes, my lord.'

'I got upon the train only this morning, Sir William. I laid my plans instantly. Fielding, did you load my pistols?'

'Yes, my lord.'

'A desperate scoundrel like that ought to be guarded against. By God, if he resists, if he proves troublesome, a small thing will make me blow his brains out. Fielding, my cloak. Help me on with it.'

'Yes, my lord.'

'By God, I wish he may only give me sufficient pretext. I'll provide for him handsomely. Ha! ha! Provided he'll save me the trouble of a trial, I'll put him out of pain a little quicker. Sir William, you're ready?'

'Yes, my lord.'

The baron swallowed another bumper of his claret, then drew on his gloves and pulled his hat over his broad black eyebrows – so as half to shade the orbs flickering underneath – with an unaccustomed smile kindled partly by wine and partly by the instinct of bloodhound exultation. Out he strode into the hall, and I followed.

Before getting into the carriage, I just stepped up to my two innocents and inquired how they were off for soap, alias firearms, for I knew the stag would gore when brought to bay. The dear babes shewed me each a couple of chickens nestling in his bosom. I was satisfied and took my seat calmly by the side of my noble friend. How my heart warmed towards him in the close proximity of our relative positions, especially when I looked at his visnomy,[34] and saw him dissevering his lips with a devilish grin and setting his clenched teeth against the wild sheets of rain that, as we whirled down his park, came driving in our faces.

Evening was now setting in, and all the woods of the dale were bending under the gloom of heavy clouds and rushing to the impetus of the tremendous wind. As we swept out at the town gates, which swung back at our approach with a heavy clang, lights glanced from the porter's lodge; they were gone in a moment and on we thundered through rain and tempest and mist, Hartford cursing his coachman every five minutes and ordering him to make the horses get over the ground faster. I shall not soon forget that ride. My sensations were those of strange, bloodthirsty excitement; woods and hills rolled by in dusky twilight, spangled with lights from the scattered houses of the valley, while rain drove slanting wildly over everything, and the swollen and roaring Olympian seemed running a mad race with ourselves.

The first intimation we had of a near approach to the hall was the rushing of trees above us, and the vision of vast, dusky trunks lining the road with a long colonnade of timber. Hartford now countermanded his former orders to Johnson and desired him to drive softly, a mandate easily obeyed, for the path was carpeted with a thick bed of withered leaves never cleared since last autumn; over these the wheels passed with a dead, muffled sound, scarcely heard at all through the confusion of wind and rain and groaning branches.

The carriage suddenly stopped, and when I looked up, there was the dim outline of a gate with balls upon the pillars; beyond, rising above trees, I saw a stack of chimneys and a gable end.

'Here we are!' said Hartford, and he jumped out as eager and impatient for his prey as the most unreclaimed tiger of the jungle.

'Have you got the manacles?' I asked quietly, bending over to Ingham.

'Yes, sir, and a strait waistcoat.'

There were four policemen. One of them was to be stationed behind, one in front of the house, to bar all egress; the two others were destined for the business of the interior. I now led my men to their posts; all the garden paths were dark and wet. The house was silent, all the windows closed, and not a beam of light streaming from their panes.

My lads having received their orders, I stole round to join Lord Hartford. He was waiting for me on the front door steps; I could just discern his dusk, cloaked figure standing there like a goblin.

'Is all right?' said he.

'All's right,' I answered. He turned to the door, lifted the knocker, and to the sound of his summons a long, desolate echo answered from within. In the interval that followed, how utterly I forgot that drenching rain. Wild wind and utter darkness enveloped me round. A door opened, and a very light but very rapid step was heard to run quickly up the passage; then another step and a hollow treading sound as of one ascending oaken stairs; then a pause, a silence of some minutes. Hartford began again with his growling solo of oaths.

'Hustling the lumber into concealment, I suppose,' said he. He gave another, louder rap, and in two minutes more the withdrawing of a bolt and the rattling of a chain was heard. The heavy front door turned, grating on its hinges, and a woman-servant stood before us with a light. The look with which she scanned us said plainly enough: 'Who can be making such a noise at this time of night?'

'Is Miss Hastings at home?' I asked.

'Yes, sir.'

'Can we see her?'

'Walk forward, sir.' And still with a perplexed air, the woman led the way through a long passage, and opening a door in the side, asked us to step in. She left her light on the table, and closing the door, went away.

It was an apartment with the chill of a vault on its atmosphere, furnished in drawing-room style – but without fire in its bright steel grate, without light in its icy chandelier, whose drops streamed from the ceiling like a cold, crystal stalactite. The mirror between the windows looked as if it had never reflected a human face for ages; the couch, the chairs, the grand piano, all stood like fixtures never to be moved.

The turning of the door handle caused me also to turn, and having so done, I saw a young female enter the room, curtsy to myself and Lord Hartford, and then stand with her fingers nervously twined in a watch chain round her neck, her eyes fixed on us with a look of searching, yet apprehensive inquiry.

'We shall want a few minutes' conversation with you, Miss Hastings,' said Hartford, shutting the door and handing a chair, while the stern arrogance of the dissipated old rake instantly softened to gentle condescension at the sight of a petticoat.

'I believe I am speaking to Lord Hartford,' said she, summoning a kind of high-bred, composed tact into her manner, though the ladylike trembling of her thin white hands let me into the secret as to the reality of that composure.

'Yes, madam, and I wish to treat you as considerately as I can. Now come, be under no alarm – sit down –'

'Now for my vinaigrette,' [brought by Sir William, in anticipation of Elizabeth's collapse] thought I, for already the nervous being had lost her front of calmness and was beginning to look sick. She took the chair Hartford brought her.

'I am only surprised at your lordship's visit. I am not alarmed. There is nothing to alarm me.' And a respectful air of reserve was assumed.

'I can trust to your sense,' said his lordship politely. 'You will receive the communication I have to make with proper fortitude, I am sure. It grieves me that you happen to be the sister of a man proscribed by the law, but justice must have its course, madam, and it is now my painful duty to tell you that I am here tonight for the purpose of arresting Captain Henry Hastings on a charge of murder, desertion, and treason.'

'Will she swoon now?' thought I, but humph – no, up she got like a doe starting erect at the sound of horns.

'But Henry Hastings is not here,' said she, and she stood within a pace or two of Hartford looking up into his face as if she were going to challenge him. His lordship, still drawing it mild, shook his head.

'It won't do, Miss Hastings, it won't do,' said he. 'Very natural that you should wish to screen your brother, but my information is decisive, my plans are laid. There are four policemen about the house. Your doors are guarded. So now compose yourself. Stay here with Sir William Percy. I am going to execute my warrant, and in two minutes the thing will be done.' Sparks of fire danced in Miss Hastings' eyes.

'Dare your lordship intend to search the house?' said she.

'Yes, madam, every cranny of it from the hall to a rat hole.'

'And every cranny of it from the hall to a rat hole is free for your lordship's inspection,' she rejoined. Hartford moved towards the door.

'I shall certainly attend your lordship,' she pursued, and turning sharply to the table, she took up the candle and walked after him, thus leaving me very unceremoniously in the dark. I heard Hartford stop in the passage.

'Miss Hastings, you must not follow me.' There was a pause. 'I must lead you back to the drawing room.'

'No, my lord –'

'I must –'

'Don't,' in an intreating tone, 'I'll show you every room.' But Hartford insisted. She was obliged to retreat. Still she did not yield; she only backed as the baron advanced, a little overawed by his towering stature and threatening look. She made a stand at the drawing room door.

'Will you compel me to use coercive measures?' said his lordship. He laid a hand on her shoulder. One touch was enough. She shrunk away from it into the room. Hartford shut the door and she was left standing, her eyes fixed on the vacant panels. Mechanically she replaced the candle on the table; and then she wrung her hands and turned a distressed, wild glance on me.

It was now my turn to address her, and my knowledge of her character shewed me in what way to proceed. Here, I saw, was little strength of mind, though there was a semblance of courage:

the result merely of very overwrought and ardent feeling. Here was a being made up of intense emotions, in her ordinary course of life always smothered under the diffidence of prudence and a skilful address: but now, when her affections were about to suffer almost a death-stab, when incidents of strange excitement were transpiring around her, on the point of bursting forth like lava, still she struggled to keep wrapt about her the veil of reserve and propriety.

She sat down at a distance from me and turned her face from the light to evade the look with which I followed all her movements. I walked towards her chair.

'Miss Hastings, you look very much agitated. If it would be a relief to you, you shall accompany the officers on their search. I have authority to give you permission. I am sorry for you, my poor girl.' She turned more and more away from me as I spoke. She leant her eyes and forehead on her hand and when I uttered those last words, there was a short irrepressible sob. Every part of her frame quivered, and she gave way to despair. She got over it as soon as she could, and thanked me for my compassion.

'I may go?' she said. I gave her leave, and, as quick as thought, she was gone.

'But I must follow,' thought I, and it required my fastest stride to overtake her. The lower rooms had been clearly examined. We heard the policeman's tramp in the lobby overhead. She was speeding up the old staircase as if her feet had been winged. Hartford confronted her at the top of the stairs. He frowned prohibition and stretched out his arm to impede passage, but she darted under the bar, sprang before Ingham, who was just in the act of opening a chamber door; darted in before him, exclaiming,

'Henry, the window!' and clapping the door to, tried with all her strength to hold it and to bolt it till the murderer should have time to escape.

'The vixen!' thought I. 'The witch! That's the consequence of minding female tears.' I sprang to Ingham's assistance. In her agony she had had strength to hold it against him for a fraction of time. I put my foot and hand to the door; the inefficient arm within failed. She was flung to the ground by the force of the rebound. I and my myrmidons rushed in.

The room was dark, but there, by the window, was the black outline of a man, madly tearing at the stanchions and bolt by which the old lattice was secured. It was a nightmare.

'Seize him!' thundered Hartford. 'Man your pistols! Shoot him dead if he resists –' There was a flash through the dark chamber – a crack – somebody's pistol had exploded. Another, louder crash – the whole framework of the lattice was dashed in, bars, glass, and all. The cold, howling storm swept through the hollow. Hastings was gone.

I gave a glance to see if I could follow, but there was an unfathomed depth of darkness down below. I thought of legs jammed into the body like a telescope. To the outside I shouted. I cleared the stairs at two bounds, made for the front door, and followed by I know not what hurly-burly of tramping feet, rushed onto the front. The contest was already begun.

I saw a huddled struggle of two figures in deadly grips. There sprung a flash of fire between them and the ringing crack of a pistol split the air again. The mass of wrestling mortality dissolved, the arms of one were loosened from the body of the other, and a heavy weight fell on the grass. Off sprang one survivor, bounding like a panther – but he was surrounded, he was hemmed in; the three remaining policemen cut across the lawn, interrupted his flight. He was too stunned to struggle more, and while two held him down on his knees, the third fixed his hands in a pair of bracelets more easily put on than taken off.

Just as this ceremony was completed, the moon for the first time that night came rolling out of a cloud. She was in her wane, but the decayed orb gave light enough to shew me the features I longed to see. He was in the act of rising up, his head was bare, his face lifted a little. A gloom – cold, wan, and wild – revealed the aspect, the expression of the man I had followed for eighteen months and hunted down in blood at last – of that daring, desperate miscreant, Henry Hastings the Angrian!

CHAPTER 9

[A section of the narrative has apparently been lost. In the
next scene, narrated again by Townsend, Elizabeth asks the
Duchess of Zamorna to seek a pardon for Henry, who, since
his arrest, has further complicated matters by making an
attempt on Zamorna's life. Being in the position of supplicant
is a cause of some distress to the proud Elizabeth.]

When she stepped into the imperial breakfast room, the tears were
so hot and blinding in her eyes, she could scarcely discern into
what a region of delicate splendour her foot had intruded. She saw,
however, a table before her, and at the table there was a lady
seated. When she had cleared the troublesome mist from her
vision, she perceived that the lady was engaged with some loose
sheets that looked like music, conversing, as she turned them over,
with a person who stood behind her chair. That person was Sir
William Percy, and when Miss Hastings entered, as his royal sister
did not appear to notice her approach, he observed coolly,

'The young woman is in waiting. Will your grace speak to her?'

Her grace raised her head: not quickly as your low persons do
when they are told an individual is expecting their attention, but
with a calm, deliberate movement, as if it was a thing of course
that somebody should be waiting the honour of her notice. Her
grace's eyes were very large and very full. She turned them on Miss
Hastings, let them linger a moment over her figure, and then
withdrew them again.

'A sister of Captain Hastings, you say,' she remarked, addressing
her brother.[35]

'Yes,' was the answer. Her grace turned the leaves of a fresh
sheet of music, put it quietly from her, and once more regarded the
petitioner. Miss Hastings stood that gaze, her temper so refractory
at the time she could almost have curled her lip in token of defying
it. Yet, as she stood opposite the fair princess, she felt by degrees
the effect of that beautiful eye changing her mood, awakening a
new feeling; and her heart confessed, as it had a thousand times
done before, the dazzling omnipotence of beauty, the degradation
of personal insignificance.

'Come forward,' said the duchess. Miss Hastings barely moved a step. Still she would hardly endure the tone of dictation.

'Explain to me what you wish in your present circumstances and I will consider if I can serve you.'

'I presume,' returned Miss Hastings, looking down and speaking in a low, quick voice, not at all supplicatory, 'I presume your royal highness is aware of the situation of Captain Hastings. My present circumstances are to be inferred from that situation –' And so she abruptly stopped.

'I do not quite comprehend you,' returned the duchess, 'I understand you came as a petitioner –'

'I do,' was the answer. 'But perhaps I have done wrong. Perhaps your royal highness would rather not be troubled with my request. I know what seems of importance to private individuals is often trivial to the great.'

'I assure you I regard your brother's case with no unconcerned eye. Perhaps I may have already done all that I can to obtain a remission of his sentence.'

'In that case, I thank your grace; but if your grace has done what you can, it follows that your grace can do no more. So it would be presumption in me to trouble your grace further.'

The duchess seemed rather puzzled. She looked at the little stubborn sight before her with a perplexed air and did not condescend to continue the conversation till Miss Hastings should choose to explain.

That individual, in the meantime, liable always to quick and strong revulsions of feeling, began to recollect that she was not going the right way to work if she intended to make an impression in favour of her brother.

'What a fool I am,' she thought to herself, 'to have spent the best part of my life in learning how to propitiate the vices and vanity of these aristocrats; and now, when my skill might do some good, I am on the point of throwing it all away for the sake of a pique of offended pride. Come, let me act like myself, or that Beautiful Woman will order her lackey to shew me to the door directly.'

So she came a little nearer to the chair where the Queen of Angria was seated, and looking up, she said with the emphatic earnestness of tone and manner peculiar to her,

'Do hear the few words I have to say.'

'I said before I would hear them,' was the haughty reply – a reply intended to show Miss Hastings that great people are not to be wantonly trifled with.

'Then,' continued the petitioner, 'I have nothing to urge in extenuation of my brother. His crimes have been proved against him. I have only to ask your grace to remember what he was before he fell; how warm his heart was towards Angria; how bold his actions were in her cause. It is not necessary that I should tell your royal highness of the energy that marks Captain Hastings' mind, of the powerful and vigorous talent that distinguished him above most of his contemporaries. The country rung with his name once, and that is proof sufficient.'

'I know he was a brave and able man,' interposed the duchess, 'but that did not prevent him from being a very dangerous man.'

'Am I permitted to reply to your royal highness?' asked Miss Hastings. The duchess signified her permission by a slight inclination of the head.

'Then,' said Miss Hastings, 'I will suggest to your grace that his courage and his talents are the best guarantee against dishonourable meanness, against treachery. If my brother's sovereign will condescend to pardon him, he will, by that gracious action, win back a most efficient subject to his standard.'

'An efficient subject!' repeated the duchess. 'A man free from treachery! You are aware, young woman, that the king's life has been endangered by the treasonable attempt of the very man whose cause you are pleading. You know that Captain Hastings went near to become a regicide –'

'But the attempt failed,' pleaded she, 'and it was in distraction and despair that Hastings hazarded it –'

'Enough!' said the duchess, 'I have heard you now, and I think you can say nothing more to me which can throw fresh light on the subject. I will give you my answer. Captain Hastings' fate will be regarded by me with regret, but I consider it inevitable. You seem shocked. I know it is natural you should feel, but I cannot see the use of buoying up your expectations with false hopes. To speak candidly, I have already used all the influence I possess in Hastings' behalf. Reasons were given me why my request should meet with a denial, reasons I could not answer; and therefore I was silent. If I recur to the subject again, it will be with reluctance, because I know that the word passed will not be revoked. However, I promise to try. You need not thank me. You may go.' And, she turned her head quite away from Miss Hastings. The hauteur of her exquisite features expressed that, if more was said, she did not mean to listen to it.

Her humble subject looked at her a moment. It was difficult to say what language was spoken by her dark glowing eyes: indignation, disappointment, and shame seemed to be the prevailing feelings. She felt that somehow she did not take with the Duchess of Zamorna, that she had hit on a wrong tack, had made a false impression at first; that she had injured her brother's cause, rather than benefited it. Above all she felt that she had failed thus signally before the eyes and in the presence of Sir William Percy. She left the room quite heartsick.

[After Elizabeth's departure, Sir William remains in conversation with his sister. The unpleasantness of his character is further confirmed as he reveals to the duchess, out of sheer spite, another recent amour of her philandering husband – this time with the Angrian beauty, Jane Moore.]

CHAPTER 10

To Lord Hartford,
Colonel of the 19th regiment of infantry,
Judge of the court martial at Zamorna.

My Lord,
I have received his majesty's commands to lay before you the following decision, sanctioned by his majesty in council, concerning the prisoner Hastings, now in your lordship's custody in the county jail of Zamorna. It is desired that your lordship shall proceed forthwith to lay before him the following articles, on agreeing to which the prisoner is to be set at liberty with the reservations hereafter stated:

Firstly, he is to make a full confession as to how far he was connected with the other individuals included with himself in the sentence of outlawry;

Secondly, he is to state all he knows of the plans and intentions of those individuals;

Thirdly, he is to give information where he last saw those individuals; also where he now supposes them to be; also how far they were concerned with the late massacre in the east and the disembarkation of French arms at Wilson's Creek; also whether these persons are connected with any foreign political incendiaries; also, and this your lordship will consider an important question, whether the courts of the southern states have maintained any secret correspondence with the Angrian renegades; whether they have given them any encouragement directly or indirectly.

Should Hastings consent to give such answers to these questions as his majesty and the government shall deem satisfactory, his sentence of death will be commuted to degradation from his rank as an officer in the Angrian army, expulsion from the 19th regiment, and compulsory service as a private soldier.

Should Hastings decline answering all or any of these questions, after being allowed half an hour for deliberation, your lordship will cause his sentence to be executed without reserve. His majesty particularly requests that your lordship will not delay complying with his commands on these points, as he thinks it is high time the affair were brought to a conclusion.

> I have the honour to remain
> your lordship's obedient humble servant,
> H. F. Etrei,
> Secretary at War,
> Verdopolis, March 18th, 1839

It was March, the 19th day of the month, and Tuesday by the week.[36] The day was fine, the sky bright blue with a hot sun, and far on the horizon those silver-piled towering clouds that foretell the rapid showers of spring. There had been rain an hour ago, but the fresh breeze had dried it up, and only here and there a glittering pool of wet remained on the bleached street pavement. One could tell that in the country the grass was growing green, that the trees were knotty with buds and the gardens golden with crocuses. Zamorna, however, and the citizens of Zamorna, thought little of these rural delights. Tuesday was market day; the piece hall[37] and the commercial buildings were as throng as they could stand. The Stuartville Arms, the Wool-Pack, and the Rising Sun were all astir with the preparations for their separate market dinners, and the waiters were almost run off their feet with answering the countless calls for bottoms of brandy, glasses of gin and water, and bottles of north-country ale.

No doubt there is some affair of importance transacting at the court house opposite, for the doors are besieged with a gentlemanly crowd of black and green and brown velvet-collared frock coats, and black and drab beaver hats. Moreover, every now and then, the doors open and an individual comes out, turns hastily down the steps across the way to Stancliffe's; there, calls impatiently for wine; having swallowed what is brought him, runs with equal haste back again, a lane being simultaneously opened for him by the crowd through which he passes, with absorbed important gravity, looking neither to the left hand nor the right. The door is jealously closed as he enters, allowing you but one glimpse of a man with a constable's staff standing inside.

On the morning in question, I was myself one of the crowd about the court house doors, and I believe I stood four mortal hours at the bottom of a flight of broad steps, looking up at the solid and lofty columns supporting the portico above.[38] Ever since nine o'clock the court martial had been assembled within. It was known throughout all Zamorna that Henry Hastings, the renegade, was at this moment undergoing a rigid examination, on the result of which hung the issues of life and death. Yes: just now the stern Hartford occupied his seat as judge; the crafty Percy sat by, watching every transaction, ferreting out every mystery, urging relentlessly the question that would fain be eluded. All round are ranged the martial jury, while the few gentlemen privileged to be spectators sit on benches near; and then the prisoner Hastings. Imagine him: at this instant the mental torture is proceeding. A broad gleam of sunshine rests on the outside walls of the court house. The pillared front and noble roof rise against the unclouded sky. But if Judas Hastings is selling his soul to about a score of devils sitting upon him in judgement, what thought has he to spare for the cheerful daylight?

[Townsend and some fellow-observers discuss at length the odds as to whether or not Hastings will turn traitor to save his life. Finally the court house doors open and the occupants begin to emerge.]

Then, 'There's Hastings!' And when I looked up there was a man emerging from the shade of the portico, dressed in black, with his single-breasted coat buttoned close over his broad chest, and his hat drawn down on his brow. I can hardly say that I saw his face; and yet one glimpse I caught, as he raised his head for a moment and threw a hurried glance over the crowd. The expression of that glance was one to be soon caught and long retained. It denoted the jealous suspicion of a bad man who expects others to hate, and the iron hardihood of a vindictive man who resolves to hate others in return. His teeth were set, his countenance was one dark scowl. He seemed like one whose mind was troubling him with the gall of self-abhorrence. A policeman got into the hackney coach. Then Hastings entered it and a second policeman followed him. The vehicle drove away. Not a sound followed his departure, neither cheer nor hoot.

'He's Judas, I'll lay my life on it,' said I.

Two hours had not elapsed before the result of the day's proceedings was known all over Zamorna. Hastings had accepted conditions: had delivered a mass of evidence against his quondam friends, whose purport, as yet a secret, would erelong be indicated by the future proceedings of government; had yielded his captain's commission; had taken the striped jacket and scarlet belt of a private; and, in recompense, had received the boon of life. Life without honour, without freedom, without the remnant of a character. So opens the new career of Henry Hastings, the young hero, the soldier poet of Angria! 'How are the mighty fallen!'[39]

CHAPTER II

Sir William Percy, like his father, is very tenacious of a favourite idea, any little pet whim of his fancy, and the less likely it is to be productive of good, either to the individual who conceived it, or to others, the more carefully it is treasured and the more intently it is pursued. Northangerland has all his life been a child chasing the rainbow, and into what wild abysses has the pursuit often plunged him! How often has it seduced him from his serious aims!

Sir William, being of a cooler and less imaginative temperament than his father, has never yielded to delirium like this – compared to Northangerland he is a man of marble – but still marble under a strange spell, capable of warming to life like the sculpture of Pygmalion. He is a being of changeful moods. Now the loveliest face will call from him nothing but a sneer on female vanity; and again, an expression flitting over ordinary features, a transient ray in an eye neither large nor brilliant, will fix his attention and throw him into romantic musing, merely because it chanced to harmonize with some preconceived whim of his own capricious mind. Yet having once caught an idea of this kind, having once received the seeds of this sort of partiality – inclination, fondness – call it what you will, his heart offered a tenacious soil likely to hold fast, to nurture long, to cultivate secretly, but surely, the unfolding germ of what might in time grow to a rooted passion.

Sir William, busied with the debates of cabinet councils, living in an atmosphere of turmoil, still kept in view that little private matter of his own: that freak of taste; that small, soothing amusement; his fancy for Miss Hastings. She had dropped out of his sight, he hardly knew where. After that audience with his royal sister, he had never troubled himself to enquire after her. The last view he had of her face was as it looked, flushed with painful feeling, when she retired from the presence-chamber.

The warm-hearted young man chuckled with internal pleasure at the recollection of the cold, indifferent mien he had assumed as he stood behind the royal chair. He knew at the time she would apply to him no more, that she would thenceforth shun his very shadow, fearful lest her remotest approach should be deemed an unwelcome intrusion. He knew she would leave Verdopolis that very hour if possible, and he allowed her to do so without a parting word from him.

Still, Miss Hastings lingered in his recollection; still, he smiled at the thought of her ardour; still, it pleased him to picture again the quick glances of her eye when he spoke to her, glances in which he could read so plainly what she imagined buried out of sight in her inmost heart. Still, whenever he saw a light form, a small foot, an intelligent thin face, it brought a vague feeling of something agreeable, something he liked to dwell on. Miss Hastings therefore was not by any means to be given up. No, he would see her again sometime. Events might slip on. One thing he was certain of: he need be under no fear of the impression passing away.

So, when he came again to Zamorna, having ascertained that she was still there, he began to employ his little odds and ends of leisure time in quiet speculations as to how, when, and where he should reopen a communication with her. It would not do at all to conduct the thing in an abrupt straightforward way. He must not seem to seek her. He must come upon her sometime as if by accident. Then too, this business of her brother's must be allowed to get out of her head. He would wait a few days, till the excitement of his trial had subsided, and the renegade was fairly removed from Zamorna and on his march to the quarters and companions assigned him beyond the limits of civilization. Miss Hastings would then be very fairly alone in the world, quite disembarrassed from friends and relations, not perplexed with a multitude of calls on her attention. In such a state of things an easy chance meeting with a friend would, Sir William calculated, be no unimpressive event. He'd keep his eye then on her movements and, with care, he did not doubt he should be able to mould events so as exactly to suit his purpose.

Well, a week or two passed on; Hastings' trial, like all nine days' wonders, had sunk into oblivion. Hastings himself was gone: to the sound of fife, drum, and bugle the Lost Desperado had departed, leaving behind him the recollection of what he had been, a man; the reality of what he was, a monster. It was very odd, but his sister did not think a pin the worse of him for all his dishonour. It is private meanness, not public infamy, that degrades a man in the opinion of his relatives.[40] Miss Hastings heard him cursed by every mouth, saw him denounced in every newspaper. Still, he was the same brother to her he had always been. Still, she beheld his actions through a medium peculiar to herself. She saw him go away with a triumphant hope (of which she had the full benefit, for no one else shared it) that his future actions would nobly blot out the calumnies of his enemies. Yet, after all, she knew he was an unredeemed villain. Human nature is full of inconsistencies; natural affection is a thing never rooted out where it has once really existed.

These passages of excitement being over, Miss Hastings very well satisfied that her brother had walked out of jail with the breath of life in his body, and having the aforesaid satisfactory impression on her mind that he was the finest man on the top of this world, began to look about her and consider how she was to make out life. Most persons would have thought themselves in a very handsome fix, majestically alone in the midst of trading Zamorna. However, she set to work with the activity of an emmet,[41] summoned her address and lady-manners to her aid, called on the wealthy manufacturers of the city and the aristocracy of the seats round, pleased them with her tact, her quickness, with the specimens of her accomplishments; and in a fortnight's time had raised a class of pupils, sufficient not only to secure her from want, but to supply her with the means of comfort and elegance.[42] She was now settled to her mind, she was dependent on nobody, responsible to nobody.

She spent her mornings in her drawing room surrounded by her class, not wearily toiling to impart the dry rudiments of knowledge to yawning, obstinate children, a thing she hated and for which her sharp, irritable temper rendered her wholly unfit,[43] but instructing those who had already mastered the elements of education; reading, commenting, explaining, leaving it to them to listen; if they failed, comfortably conscious that the blame would rest on her pupils, not herself. The little dignified governess soon gained considerable influence over her scholars, daughters many of them of the wealthiest families in the city. She had always the art of awing young ladies' minds with an idea of her superior talent, and then of winning their confidence by her kind, sympathizing affability.

She quickly gained a large circle of friends, had constant invitations to the most stylish houses of Zamorna, acquired a most

impeccable character for ability, accomplishment, obliging disposition, and most correct and elegant manners. Of course her class
enlarged, and she was as prosperous as any little woman of five feet
high and not twenty years old need wish to be. She looked well,
she dressed well: plainer, if possible, than ever, but still with such
fastidious care and taste. She moved about as brisk as a bee. Of
course, then, she was happy.

No. She'd plenty of money, scores of friends, good health,
people making much of her everywhere. But still the exclusive,
proud being thought she had not met with a single individual equal
to herself in mind, and therefore not one whom she could love.
Besides, it was respect, not affection, that her pompous friends felt
for her, and she was one who scorned respect. She never wished to
attract it for a moment, and still it always came to her. She was
always burning for warmer, closer attachment. She couldn't live
without it, but the feeling never woke, and never was reciprocated.
O, for Henry, for Pendleton, for one glimpse of the Warner Hills.

Sometimes when she was alone in the evenings, walking through
her handsome drawing room by twilight, she would think of home,
and long for home, till she cried passionately at the conviction that
she should see it no more. So wild was her longing that when she
looked out on the dusky sky, between the curtains of her bay
window, fancy seemed to trace on the horizon the blue outline of
the moors, just as seen from the parlour at Colne-moss. The evening
star hung over the brow of Boulshill, the farm fields stretched away
between. And when reality returned – houses, lamps, and streets
– she was frenzied. Again, a noise in the house seemed to her like
the sound made by her father's chair when he drew it nearer to the
kitchen hearth; something would recall the whine or the bark of
Hector and Juno, Henry's pointers. Again, the step of Henry
himself would seem to tread in the passage, and she would
distinctly hear his gun deposited in the house-corner. All was a
dream. Henry was changed, she was changed, those times were
departed for ever. She had been her brother's and her father's
favourite; she had lost one and forsaken the other. At these
moments, her heart would yearn towards the lonely old man in
Angria till it almost broke. But pride is a thing not easily subdued.
She would not return to him.[44]

Very often too – as the twilight deepened and the fire, settling to clear red, diffused a calm glow over the papered walls – her thoughts took another turn. The enthusiast dreamed about Sir William Percy. She expected to hear no more of him. She blushed when she recollected how, for a moment, she had even dared to conceive the presumptuous idea that he cared for her. But still, she lingered over his remembered voice and look and language with an intensity of romantic feeling that very few people in this world can form the remotest conception of. All he had said was treasured in her mind; she could distinctly tell over every word, she could picture vividly as life his face, his quick hawk's eye, his habitual attitudes. It was an era in her existence to see his name, or an anecdote respecting him, mentioned in the newspapers. She would preserve such paragraphs to read over and over again when she was alone. There was one which mentioned that he was numbered amongst the list of officers designed for the expected campaign in the east, and thereupon her excitable imagination kindled with anticipation of his perils and glories and wanderings. She realized him in a hundred situations: on the verge of battle, in the long weary march, in the halt by wild river banks. She seemed to watch his slumber under the desert moon – with large-leaved jungle plants spreading their rank shade above him. Doubtless she thought the young hussar would then dream of someone that he loved – some beautiful face would seem to bend over his rough pillow, such as had charmed him in the saloons of the capital.

> And with that thought came an impulse
>   Which broke the dreamy spell,
> For no longer on the picture
>   Could her eye endure to dwell.
> She vowed to leave her visions
>   And seek life's arousing stir,
> For she knew Sir William's slumber
>   Would not bring a thought of her.[45]

Such were Miss Hastings's musings, such were almost the words that arranged themselves like a song in her mind: words neither spoken nor sung. She dared not so far confess her frenzy to herself. Only once she paused in her walk through the drawing room by the open piano, laid her fingers on the keys, and wakening a note or two of plaintive melody, murmured the last lines.

Instantly snatching her hand away, and closing the instrument with a clash, she made some emphatic remark about unimitigated folly, then lighted her bed-candle and, it being now eleven at night, hastened upstairs to her chambers as fast as if a nightmare had been behind her.[46]

CHAPTER 12

One mild, still afternoon, Miss Hastings had gone out to walk. She was already removed from the stir of Zamorna, and slowly pacing along the causeway of Girnington Road. The high wall and trees enclosing a gentleman's place ran along the road side; the distant track stretched out into a quiet and open country. Now and then a carriage or a horseman rolled or galloped past, but the general characteristic of the scene and day was tranquillity. Miss Hastings, folded in her shawl and with her veil down, moved leisurely on, in as comfortable a frame of mind as she could desire; inclined to silence and with no one to disturb her by talking; disposed for reverie; at liberty to indulge her dreams unbroken. The carriages that passed at intervals kept her in a state of vague expectation. She always raised her eyes when they drew near, as if with the undefined hope of seeing somebody, she hardly knew whom – a face from distant Pendleton, perhaps.

Following a course she had often taken before, she soon turned into a by-lane with a worn white causeway running under a green hedge and, on either hand, fields. The stillness now grew more perfect as she wandered on. The mail road disappeared behind her, the sense of perfect solitude deepened. That calm afternoon sun seemed to smile with a softer lustre. Away in a distant field a bird was heard singing with a fitful note, now clear and cheerful, now dropping to pensive silence.

She came to an old gate; the posts were of stone, mouldering and grey. The wooden paling was broken, clusters of springing leaves grew beside it. This gate opened into a large and secluded meadow, or rather into a succession of meadows, for the track worn in the grass led on through stiles and gates from pasture to pasture to an unknown extent. Here Miss Hastings had been accustomed to ramble for many an hour, indulging her morbid propensity for castle-building, as happy as she was capable of being except when now and then scared by hearing the remote and angry low of a great Girnington bull which haunted these parts.[47]

On reaching the gate she instinctively stopped to open it. It was open, and she passed through. She stopped with a start. By the gate post lay a gentlemanly-looking hat and a pair of gloves, with a spaniel coiled up beside them, as if keeping guard. The creature sprung forward at the approach of a stranger and gave a short bark, not very furious. Its instinct seemed to tell it that the intruder was not of a dangerous order. A very low whistle sounded from some quarter, quite close at hand; yet no human being was visible from whom it could proceed. The spaniel obeyed the signal, whined, and lay down again. Miss Hastings passed on. She had hardly set her foot in the field when she heard the emphatic ejaculation, 'Bless my stars!' distinctly pronounced immediately behind her.

Of course she turned. There was a hedge of hazels on her right hand under which all sorts of leaves and foliage grew green and soft. Stretched full-length on this bed of verdure, with the declining sun resting upon him, she saw a masculine figure, without a hat and with an open book in his hand, which it is to be supposed he had been perusing, though his eyes were now raised from the literary page and fixed on Miss Hastings. It being broad daylight and the individual being denuded as to the head – features, forehead, hair, whiskers, blue eyes, etcetera, etcetera were all distinctly visible – of course my readers know him: Sir William Percy and no mistake, though what he could possibly be doing here ruralizing in a remote nook I candidly confess myself not sufficiently sagacious to divine.

Miss Hastings being, as my readers are aware, possessed with certain romantic notions about him, got something of a start at this unexpected meeting. For about five minutes she'd little to say, and indeed was deeply occupied in collecting her wits and contriving an apology for what she shuddered to think Sir William would consider an unwelcome intrusion. Meantime the baronet gathered himself up, took his hat, and came towards her with a look and smile that implied anything rather than annoyance at her presence.

'Well, you've not a single word to say to me. How shocked you look, and pale as a sheet. I hope I've not frightened you.'

'No, no –' with agitation in the tone, 'but it is an unusual thing to meet anybody in these fields –' and she feared she had perhaps disturbed Sir William – she was sorry – she ought to have taken the spaniel's hint and retreated in time.

'Retreated? What from? Were you afraid of Carlo? I thought he saluted you very gently. Upon my word I believe the beast had sense enough to know that the newcomer was not one his master would be displeased to see. Had it been a great male scarecrow in jacket and continuations,[48] he'd have flown at his throat.' The tone of Sir William's voice brought back again like a charm the feeling of confidence Miss Hastings had experienced before in conversing with him. It brought back, too, a throbbing of the heart and pulse, a kindling of the veins which soon flushed her pale face with suffusing colour.

'I was not afraid of Carlo,' said Miss Hastings.

'What, then, were you afraid of; surely not me?' She looked up at him. Her natural voice and manner, so long disused, returned to her.

'Yes,' she said quickly, 'you and nothing else. It is so long since I had seen you, I thought you would have forgotten me and would think I had no business to cross your way again. I expected you would be very cold and proud.'

'Nay, I'll be as warm as you please. As to pride, I calculate you are not exactly the sort of person to excite that feeling in my mind.'

'I suppose, then, I should have said contempt: you are proud, no doubt, to your equals or superiors. However, you have spoken to me very civilly, for which I am obliged, as it makes me unhappy to be scorned.'

'May I ask if you're quite by yourself here?' inquired Sir William. 'Or have you companions near at hand?'

'I'm alone. I always walk alone.'

'Humph. I'm alone likewise; and as it's highly improper that a young woman such as you should be wandering by herself in such a lot of solitary fields, I shall take the liberty of offering my protection whilst you finish your walk, and then seeing you safe home.'

Miss Hastings made excuses. She could not think of giving Sir William so much trouble. She was accustomed to manage for herself. There was nothing in the world to be apprehended. The baronet answered by drawing her arm through his.

'I shall act authoritatively,' said he. 'I know what's for the best.' Seeing she could not so escape, she pleaded the lateness of the hour; it would be best to turn back immediately.

'No.' Sir William had a mind to take her half a mile further. She wouldn't be able to get back to Zamorna before dark and as he was with her she needn't fear. On they went then, Miss Hastings hurriedly considering whether she was doing anything really wrong and deciding that she was not, that it would be sin and nonsense to throw away the moment of bliss Chance had offered her. Besides, she had nobody in the world to find fault with her, nobody to whom she was responsible, neither father nor brother.[49] She was her own mistress, and she was sure it would be cant and prudery to apprehend harm.

Having thus set aside scruples, and wholly yielded herself to the wild delight fluttering at her heart, she bounded on with so light and quick a step Sir William was put to his mettle to keep pace with her.

'Softly, softly,' said he at last. 'I like to take my time in a ramble like this. One can't walk fast and talk comfortably at the same time.'

'The afternoon is so exceedingly pleasant,' returned Miss Hastings, 'and the grass is so soft and green in these fields, my spirits feel cheerier than usual. But to please you, I'll draw in.'

'Now,' continued the baronet. 'Will you tell me what you're doing in Zamorna and how you're getting on?'

'I'm teaching, and I have two classes of twelve pupils each. My terms are high – first-rate – so I'm in no danger of want.'

'But have you money enough? Are you comfortable?'

'Yes, I am as rich as a Jew. I mean to begin to save for the first time in my life, and when I've got two thousand pounds, I'll give up work and live like a fine lady.'

'You're an excellent little manager for yourself. I thought now, if I left you a month or two unlooked after, just plodding on as you could, you'd get into straits or difficulty and be glad of a friend's hand to help you out; but somehow you contrive provokingly well.'

'Yes, I don't want to be under obligations.'

'Come, let me have no proud speeches of that sort. Remember, Fortune is ever changing, and the best of us are not exempt from reverses. I may have to triumph over you yet.'

'But if I wanted a sixpence, you would be the last person I should ask for it,' said Miss Hastings, looking up at him with an arch expression very natural to her eyes, but which seldom indeed was allowed to shine there.

'Should I, young lady? Take care; make no rash resolutions. If you were compelled to ask, you would be glad to go to the person who would give most willingly. And you would not find many hands so open as mine would be. I tell you plainly it would give me pleasure to humble you. I have not yet forgotten your refusal to accept that silly little cross.'⁵⁰

'Nay,' said Miss Hastings, 'I knew so little of you at that time I felt it would be quite a shame to take presents from you.'

'But you know me better now, and I have the cross here. Will you take it?' He produced the green box from his waistcoat pocket, took out the jewel, and offered it.

'I won't,' was the answer.

'Humph!' said Sir William. 'I'll be revenged sometime. Such nonsense!' He looked angry, an unusual thing with him.

'I don't mean to offend you,' pleaded Miss Hastings, 'but it would hurt me to accept anything of value from you. I would take a little book, or an autograph of your name or a straw or a pebble. But not a diamond –' The attachment implied by those words was so very flattering, and at the same time expressed with such utterly unconscious simplicity, that Sir William could not suppress a smile. His forehead cleared.

'You know how to turn a compliment after all, Miss Hastings,' said he. 'I'm obliged to you. I was beginning to think myself a very unskilful general, for, turn which way I would, and try what tactics I chose, the Fortress would never give me a moment's advantage. I could not win a single outwork. However, if there's a friend in the Citadel, if the heart speaks for me, all's right.' Miss Hastings felt her face grow rather uncomfortably hot. She was confused for a few minutes and could not reply to Sir William's odd metaphorical speech. The baronet squinted towards her one of his piercing sideglances and, perceiving she was a trifle startled, he whistled a stave to give her time to compose herself, affected to be engaged with his spaniel; then, when another squint had assured him that the flush was subsiding on her cheek, he drew her arm a little closer, and recommenced the conversation on a fresh theme.

'Lonely, quiet, meadows these,' said he. 'And all this country has something very sequestered about it. I know it well, every lane and gate and stile.'

'You've been here before, then?' returned Miss Hastings. 'I've often heard that you were a rambler.'

'I've been here by day and by night; I've seen these hedges bright as they are now in sunshine, and throwing a dark shade by moonlight. If there were such things as fairies, I should have met them often, for these are just their haunts: foxglove leaves and bells, moss like green velvet, mushrooms springing at the roots of oak trees, thorns a hundred years old grown over with ivy – all precisely in the fairy-tale style.'

'And what did you do here?' enquired Miss Hastings. 'What made you wander alone, early and late? Was it because you liked to see twilight gathering in such lanes as these, and the moon rising over such a green swell of pasture as that, or because you were unhappy?'

'I'll answer you with another question,' returned Sir William. 'Why do *you* like to ramble by yourself? It is because you can think, and so could I. It never was my habit to impart my thoughts much, especially those that gave me the most pleasure, so I wanted no companion. I used to dream, indeed, of some nameless being, whom I invested with the species of mind and face and figure that I imagined I could love. I used to wish for some existence with finer feelings and a warmer heart than what I saw round me. I had a kind of idea that I could be a very impassioned lover – if I met with a woman who was young and elegant and had a mind above the grade of an animal.'

'You must have met with many such,' said Miss Hastings, not shrinking from the conversation, for its confidential tone charmed her like a spell.

'I've met with many pretty women; with some clever ones; I've even seen one or two that I thought myself in love with for a time. But a few days, or at most weeks, tired me of them. I grew ennuyé with their insipid charms and turned again to my ideal Bride. Once indeed I plunged over head and ears into a mad passion with a real object – but that's over.'

'Who was she?'

'One of the most beautiful and celebrated women of her day. Unfortunately she was appropriated. I could have died to win that woman's smile; to take her hand and touch her lips I could have suffered torture. And to obtain her love, to have the power of clasping her in my arms and telling her all I felt, to have my ardour returned, to hear in her musical earnest voice the expression of responsive attachment, I could, if the devil had asked me, have sold my redemption and consented to take the stamp of the hoof on both my hands.'[51]

'Does she live in Angria?'

'Yes. Now ask me no more questions for I'll not answer them. Come, give me your hand and I'll help you over this stile. There! We're out of the fields now. Were you ever so far as this before?'

'Never,' said Miss Hastings, looking round. The objects she saw were not familiar to her. They had entered upon another road, rough, rutty, and grown over. Not a house or a human being was to be seen; but immediately before them stood a church, with a low tower and a little churchyard, scattered over with a few headstones and many turf mounds. About four miles off stretched a line of hills, darkly ridged with heath, now all empurpled with a lovely sunset. Miss Hastings' eye kindled as she caught them.

'What moors are those?' she asked quickly.

'Ingleside and the Scars,' replied Sir William.

'And what is that church?'

'Scar Chapel.'

'It looks old. How long do you think it is since it was built?'

'It is one of the earliest date in Angria. What caps me is why the devil any church at all was set down in a spot like this where there is no population.'

'Shall we go into the churchyard?'

'Yes, if you like. You'd better rest there for a few minutes, for you look tired.'

In the centre of the enclosure stood an ancient yew, gnarled, sable, and huge. The only raised tomb in the place rested under the shadow of this grim old sentinel.

'You can sit down here,' said Sir William, pointing to the monument with his cane. Miss Hastings approached, but before she took her seat on the slab, something in its appearance caught her attention. It was of marble, not stone; plain and unornamented, but gleaming with dazzling whiteness from the surrounding turf. At first sight it seemed to bear no inscription, but looking nearer, one word was visible: 'RESURGAM'. Nothing else, no name, date or age.

'What is this?' asked Miss Hastings. 'Who is buried here?'

'You may well ask,' returned Sir William, 'but who d'ye think can answer you? I've stood by this grave many a time when that church clock was striking twelve at midnight, sometimes in rain and darkness, sometimes in clear quivering starlight; looked at that single word and pondered over the mystery it seemed to involve, till I could have wished the dead corpse underneath would rise and answer my unavailing questions.'

'And have you never learnt the history of this tomb?'

'Why, partly –'

'Tell me what you know then,' said Miss Hastings, raising her eyes to Sir William's with a look that told him how magical was the effect, how profound was the interest, of all this sweet confidential interchange of feeling. It was more bewitching even than the open language of love. She had no need to blush and tremble. She had only to listen when he spoke to feel that he trusted her, that he deemed her worthy to be the depository of those half-romantic thoughts he had never perhaps breathed into human ear before. These sensations might all be delusive, but they were sweet and, for the time, Doubt and Apprehension dared not intrude their warnings.

'Come, sit down,' said the baronet, 'and you shall hear all I can tell you. I see you like anything with the savour of romance in it.'

'I do,' replied Miss Hastings. 'And so do you, Sir William – only you're rather ashamed to confess it.'

He smiled and went on: 'Well, the first clue I got to this business was by a rather remarkable chance . . .'

[Sir William, hunting one day, comes upon a stranger weeping over the tomb. As he strides away, William perceives him to be the Duke of Zamorna. Beneath the stone lies another of his conquests, Rosamund, formerly his ward, who has died of a broken heart, or by suicide. Whichever, the stone stands as a monument to the dangers of excessive passion; as Sir William puts it, Rosamund 'loved his majesty not wisely, but too well'.]

'Now, Elizabeth, what do you say to such a business as that?'

'It seems the Duke of Zamorna never forsook her, and that he remembered her after she was dead,' remarked Miss Hastings.

'Oh! and that's sufficient consolation! As the Duke of Zamorna is a very fine, proud god incarnate, I suppose. God damn!'

'The Duke of Zamorna is a sort of scoundrel from all that ever I heard of him; but then, most men of rank are, from what I can understand.'

'Were you ever blessed with a sight of his majesty?' inquired Sir William.

'Never.'

'But you've seen his portraits, which are one and all very like. Do you admire them?'

'He's handsome, no doubt.' .

'O, of course, killingly, infernally handsome: such eyes and nose, such curls and whiskers! And then his stature! Magnificent! And his chest two feet across – I never knew a woman yet who did not calculate the value of a man by the proportions of his inches.'

Miss Hastings said nothing, she only looked down and smiled.

'I'm exceedingly nettled and dissatisfied,' remarked Sir William.

'Why?' inquired Miss Hastings, still smiling.[52]

Sir William, in his turn, gave no answer; he only whistled a stave or two. After a moment's silence he looked all round him with a keen, careful eye. He then turned to his companion.

'Do you see,' said he, 'that the sun is set and that it is getting dark?'

'Indeed it is,' replied Miss Hastings, and she started instantly to her feet. 'We must go home, Sir William. I had forgotten – how could I let time slip so?'

'Hush,' said the young baronet, 'and sit down again for a few minutes. I will say what I have to say.' Miss Hastings obeyed him.

'Do you see,' he continued, 'that everything is still round us, that the twilight is deepening, that there is no light but what that rising half moon gives?'

'Yes.'

'Do you know that there is not a house within two miles and that you are four miles from Zamorna?'

'Yes.'

'You are aware then that in this shade and solitude you and I are alone?'

'I am.'

'Would you have trusted yourself in such a situation with any one you did not care for?'

'No.'

'You care for me then?'

'I do.'

'How much?' There was a pause – a long pause. Sir William did not urge the question impatiently. He only sat keenly and quietly watching Miss Hastings and waiting for an answer. At last she said in a very low voice,

'Tell me first, Sir William Percy, how much you care for me.'

'More than, at this moment, I do for any other woman in the world.'

'Then,' was the heartfelt rejoinder, 'I adore you. And that's a confession death should not make me cancel.'

'Now, Elizabeth,' continued Sir William, 'listen to the last question I have to put, and don't be afraid of me. I'll act like a gentleman whatever your answer may be. You said just now that all men of rank were scoundrels. I'm a man of rank. Will you be my mistress?'

'No.'

'You said you adored me.'

'I do, intensely. But I'll never be your mistress. I could not, without incurring the miseries of self-hatred.'

'That is to say,' replied the baronet, 'you are afraid of the scorn of the world.'

'I am. The scorn of the world is a horrible thing, and more especially, I should dread to lose the good opinion of three persons: of my father, of Henry, and of Mr Warner. I would rather die than be despised by them. I feel a secret triumph now in the consciousness that though I have been left entirely to my own guidance, I have never committed an action, or narrated a word, that would bring my character for a moment under the breath of suspicion! My father and Mr Warner call me obstinate and resentful; but they are both proud of the address I have shewn in making my way through life, and keeping always in the strictest limits of rectitude. Henry, though a wild wanderer himself, would blow his brains out if he heard of his sister adding to the pile of disgrace he had heaped so thickly on the name of Hastings.'

'You would risk nothing for me then?' returned Sir William. 'You would find no compensation for the loss of the world's favour in my perfect love and trusting confidence? It is no pleasure to you to talk to me, to sit by my side as you do now, to allow your hand to rest in mine?' The tears came into Miss Hastings' eyes.

'I dare not answer you,' she said, 'because I know I should say something frantic. I could no more help loving you than that moon can help shining. If I might live with you as your servant I should be happy. But as your mistress! Is is quite impossible.'[53]

'Elizabeth,' said Sir William, looking at her and placing his hand on her shoulder, 'Elizabeth, your eyes betray you. They speak the language of a very ardent, very imaginative temperament. They confess not only that you love me, but that you cannot live without me. Yield to your nature, and let me claim you this moment as my own.'

Miss Hastings was silent, but she was not going to yield. Only the hard conflict of passionate love with feelings that shrank horror-struck from the remotest shadow of infamy compelled her, for a moment, to silent agony. Sir William thought his point was nearly gained.

'One word,' said he, 'will be sufficient; one smile or whisper. You tremble. Rest on my shoulder. Turn your face to the moonlight and give me a single look.'

That moonlight shewed her eyes swimming in tears. The baronet, mistaking these tears for the signs of resolution fast dissolving, attempted to kiss them away. She slipt from his hold like an apparition.

'If I stay another moment God knows what I shall say or do,' said she. 'Good-bye, Sir William. I implore you not to follow me. The night is light. I am afraid of nothing but myself. I shall be in Zamorna in an hour. Good-bye, I suppose, forever!'

'Elizabeth!' exclaimed Sir William. She lingered for a moment. She could not go. A cloud just then crossed the moon; in two minutes it had passed away. Sir William looked towards the place where Miss Hastings had been standing. She was gone.

The churchyard gate swung to. He muttered a furious curse, but did not stir to follow. There he remained, where she had left him, for hours, as fixed as the old yew whose black arms brooded over his head. He must have passed a quiet night: church and graves and tree, all mute as death, Lady Rosamund's tomb alone proclaiming in the moonlight, 'I shall rise'.

[The final scenes turn from Elizabeth to Zamorna. First Northangerland's wife, Zenobia, calls on Zamorna to complain of her husband's infidelities. Then Zamorna visits his own wife, Mary, in her chamber; she has been pining since hearing from Sir William of Zamorna's tête-à-tête with Jane Moore. Zamorna's terrible power over Mary is immediately clear. With a facile lie he brings her around; they kiss, and retire. While these episodes detract from the unity of plot, they underscore, bitterly, the story's themes: men are scoundrels, ready to exploit their women in whatever way suits them; women's devotion in general makes them easy prey; the power of sexual passion is particularly treacherous, leading in the instance of Zenobia and Mary to regular humiliation, withstood only in Elizabeth's case because of her peculiar, fierce sense of personal integrity.]

1839

Farewell to Angria

I have now written a great many books, and for a long time have
dwelt on the same characters and scenes and subjects. I have
shown my landscapes in every variety of shade and light which
morning, noon, and evening, the rising, the meridian, and the
setting sun, can bestow upon them. Sometimes I have filled the
air with the whitened tempest of winter: snow has embossed the
dark arms of the beech and oak, and filled with drifts the parks
of the lowlands or the mountain pass of wilder districts. Again,
the same mansion with its woods, the same moor with its glens,
has been softly coloured with the tints of moonlight in summer,
and in the warmest June night, the trees have clustered their full-
plumed heads over glades flushed with flowers. So it is with
persons. My readers have been habituated to one set of features,
which they have seen now in profile, now in full face, now in
outline, and again in finished painting – varied but by the change
of feeling or temper or age; lit with love, flushed with passion,
shaded with grief, kindled with ecstasy; in meditation and mirth,
in sorrow and scorn and rapture; with the round outline of
childhood, the beauty and fulness of youth, the strength of
manhood, and the furrows of thoughtful decline; but we must
change, for the eye is tired of the picture so oft recurring, and
now so familiar.

Yet do not urge me too fast, reader: it is no easy theme to
dismiss from my imagination the images which have filled it so
long; they were my friends and my intimate acquaintances, and
I could with little labour describe to you the faces, the voices, the
actions, of those who peopled my thoughts by day, and not
seldom stole strangely even into my dreams by night. When I
depart from these I feel almost as if I stood on the threshold of a
home and were bidding farewell to its inmates. When I strive to
conjure up new inmates I feel as if I had got into a distant country
where every face was unknown, and the character of all the
population an enigma which it would take much study to comprehend and much talent to expound. Still, I long to quit for
awhile that burning clime where we have sojourned too long – its

skies flame, the glow of sunset is always upon it. The mind would cease from excitement and turn now to a cooler region where the dawn breaks grey and sober, and the coming day for a time at least is subdued by clouds.

1839

Notes

*

Jane Austen

VOLUME THE FIRST

1. (p. 39) *Martha Lloyd*: With her sister Mary, close friends and neighbours of the young Jane and Cassandra Austen; Martha was later to become the second wife of Francis Austen.
2. (p. 40) *The Valley of Tempé* comes from Mlle de Scudéry's seventeenth-century romantic novel, *The History of the Princess Elismonda*.
3. (p. 43) See *OED*, *brace*, a pair; *leash*, a brace and a half, three.
4. (p. 45) See *OED*, *fesse*, a pale blue colour; *fess* is also a Hampshire dialect word for 'conceited', 'proud' (*English Dialect Dictionary*).
5. (p. 46) *Francis Austen*: Jane's fifth brother (1774–1865); he attended the Royal Naval College at Portsmouth, and fought at sea in the Napoleonic War, becoming an admiral in Nelson's navy.
6. (p. 49) Richardson's *Sir Charles Grandison* (1753–4) was one of Jane Austen's favourite novels.
7. (p. 52) This sentence is erased in the MS.
8. (p. 54) The insufferable Charles Adams's views on female excellence seem to look forward to those expressed by Mr Darcy in *Pride and Prejudice* (Chapter 8).
9. (p. 54) Brian Wilks remarks on the frequency of man-traps and spring-guns on the great estates of the time (*Jane Austen*, p. 12); normally these were to discourage poachers, but Charles Adams doubtless hopes to preserve himself from his many admirers.
10. (p. 64) *Jane Cooper*: Jane's cousin; she was at school in 1783 at Southampton with the two Austen girls, and very probably saved their lives by promptly reporting their dangerous illness to the Austens.
11. (p. 70) *Charles Austen*: Jane's youngest brother (1779–1852); like his brother Francis, he became a naval officer. Though at sea for extended periods, both brothers maintained a close bond with their family.
12. (p. 72) The rattle John Thorpe, in *Northanger Abbey*, boasts that his

horse makes ten miles an hour in harness; although this is no doubt an
exaggeration, nineteen miles in eighteen hours (5 a.m.–11 p.m.) is
surely a very feeble pace. As the distance between Bath and London is
107½ miles, Mr Clifford still has a fair trip ahead of him.

13. (p. 72) Mr Clifford's already feeble pace seems to have slowed even
more, as the total distance between Devizes and Basingstoke is roughly
forty miles; Overton, Dean, Clarkengreen, and Worting are all villages
near Steventon.

14. (p. 73) *Cassandra Austen*: Jane's elder sister (1773–1845), her closest
friend and confidante throughout her lifetime.

15. (p. 75) *Mrs Austen*: Jane's mother, Cassandra Leigh Austen
(1739–1827), daughter of the Rev. Thomas Leigh of All Souls, Oxford,
niece of Theophilus Leigh, Master of Balliol College, Oxford.

16. (p. 78) *James Austen*: Jane's eldest brother (1765–1819), succeeded his
father as rector of Steventon; while at Oxford he edited a periodical
and tried his hand at verse.

17. (p. 78) *The School for Jealousy and The Travelled Man*: The absence of
any reference to these plays in histories of the drama, and indeed the
way in which Jane jokingly mentions them, suggest that they may have
been written by James himself, the most literary of her brothers.

18. (p. 80) These sentences are erased in the MS.

19. (p. 83) *Rev. George Austen*: Jane's father (1731–1805), son of a surgeon,
William Austen; he won an open scholarship at St John's, Oxford, took
orders in 1760, and was presented upon his marriage with the livings
of Steventon and Deane by his wealthy relatives, Thomas Knight and
Francis Austen.

20. (p. 84) *and dress*: erased in the MS.

21. (p. 85) *Edward Austen*: (1768–1852), Jane's third brother, who was
adopted by the family of Thomas Knight, and made their heir;
nonetheless he remained close to his original family, and Chawton
Cottage, where Mrs Austen and her two daughters lived after leaving
Bath, was on his estate.

22. (p. 85) *The Three Sisters* includes a number of elements that are to be
developed in later novels. Mr Watts, as the 'eligible' but odious
bachelor, looks forward to Mr Collins; Mrs Stanhope, as the mother
determined to marry off her daughters no matter how unsavoury the
suitor, to Mrs Bennet. The pattern of two sensible, sensitive girls
(Sophy and Georgiana) *v.* one vain one (Mary) looks forward to the
later opposition of Jane and Elizabeth to Lydia. The handsome Mr
Brudenell, who betrays his capacity for caddishness by egging Mary
on, may be a prototype of *Mansfield Park*'s Henry Crawford. Mary's
distaste for her fiancé brings to mind Maria Bertram's feelings for Mr

Rushworth; the intolerance of both girls is exacerbated by the introduction of a handsome stranger.

23. (p. 86) This phrase is erased in the MS.

24. (p. 90) This phrase is erased in the MS.

25. (p. 91) The following phrase is erased in the MS.: 'Pearls as large as those of the Princess Badroulbadour in the fourth volume of the Arabian Nights, and rubies, emeralds, topazes, sapphires, amethysts, turkeystones, agate, beads, bugles and garnets . . .'. Austen seems to have decided that the stylistic excess of this passage would undercut the cumulative effect of real folly that has been built up through Mary's previous speeches.

26. (p. 92) *Which is the Man*: a sentimental comedy by Hannah Cowley (1743–1809), given its first performance at Covent Garden in February 1782.

27. (p. 94) This phrase is erased in the MS. The details of his connection would at once explain Mr Brudenell's familiar position at the Duttons', and permit him to be fair game for all the young women, Duttons and Stanhopes alike.

28. (p. 97) Although this fragment, dedicated to Jane's niece on 2 June 1793, is cancelled in the MS, I have included it as a rare attempt at preaching. The following Ode, dated the next day, suggests that she was quick to abandon her pious stance.

VOLUME THE SECOND

1. (p. 99) Southam notes in his edition of *Volume the Second* that Austen herself has amended the traditionally accepted 'Freindship' to read 'Friendship': a change that 'may not be welcome to those of Jane Austen's devotees who value her spelling for its charm' (Volume II, p. vii). Eliza de Feuillide (1761–1813) was Jane's cousin, who often visited the Austens at Steventon. Her first marriage was to a French count who was guillotined during the Terror; she was later to marry Henry Austen.

2. (p. 99) *a regular detail . . . of your life*: the retelling of 'the life', a standard feature of the romantic novel, was earlier parodied by Charlotte Lennox in *The Female Quixote* (1752).

3. (p. 102) *We . . . convinced* replaces the following paragraph: 'I cannot pretend to assert that any one knocks, tho' for my own part, I own I rather imagine it is a knock at the Door that somebody does. Yet as we have no ocular Demonstration . . .'

4. (p. 103) *how it happened* was that Edward has been travelling west instead of south, and is over 100 miles off course.

5. (p. 107) *We fainted* . . .: Southam notes that this may be an allusion to a stage direction from Sheridan's *The Critic* (1779): 'They fainted alternately in each other's arms.'

6. (p. 108) A phrase follows, 'When we were somewhat recovered from the overpowering effusions of our . . .', which is cancelled in the MS; this is actually the sentence with which Letter 10 opens; perhaps Jane, when recopying her text, accidentally skipped from 8 to 10, catching her mistake after the first sentence.

7. (p. 114) Laura and Sophia's response to poor Graham seems to look forward to that of Marianne Dashwood to Edward Ferrars.

8. (p. 116) *although . . . Hall*: this phrase replaces two earlier cancelled versions in the MS: 'as it was a most agreable Drive' and 'from its wonderful Celebrity'. *Gretna Green*, a Scottish village near the English border, was the frequent setting for clandestine unions. As *the* place to run off to, it will also be the choice of Lydia Bennet (*Pride and Prejudice*, chapter 47).

9. (p. 118) *He was like them* . . . : the sentimental poet William Shenstone (1714–63), in his *Essays on Men and Manners*, remarked that 'all trees have a character analogous to that of men'.

10. (p. 119) Thomas Wolsey (*c.* 1475–1530), powerful cardinal-archbishop under Henry VIII, who, despite his papal aspirations, ended in disgrace, accused of treason.

11. (p. 120) It is suggested by Southam that Laura's ravings may be an imitation of Tilburnia in Sheridan's *The Critic* (III, i), or perhaps a parody of Lear (*King Lear*, IV, vi).

12. (p. 120) Southam points out that Cassandra was soon to turn seventeen – in January 1791.

13. (p. 122) Southam compares Laura's speech to one of Joseph Surface in *The School for Scandal* (IV, iii), a play in which Jane had taken part.

14. (p. 123) See *OED, basket*: the overhanging back compartment on the outside of a stagecoach.

15. (p. 124) The reference is to William Gilpin's *Observations, relative chiefly to Picturesque Beauty . . . particularly the Highlands of Scotland, 1789.*

16. (p. 125) *Edinburgh to Sterling*: Jane refers back to this when writing to Cassandra in August 1814 (Letter 99): 'my own coach between Edinburgh and Sterling'.

17. (p. 125) As late as *Sanditon* (1817), the hypochondriacal Arthur Parker is to reveal his 'Earthy Dross' by his appetite for buttered toast, though he draws the line at green tea (chapter 10).

18. (p. 126) *for want of people . . . we could perform*: Southam observes that 'this would remind Jane Austen's family audience of their own theatricals . . . They too sometimes had difficulty in raising a cast'.

19. (p. 128) This collection of five letters, of which only two are here included, was dedicated to Jane's cousin, Jane Cooper; the letters show her to be experimenting with a range of voices.

20. (p. 130) *in her way*: on her way; in other words, picking Maria up is no real favour at all.

21. (p. 131) Lady Greville seems to be an early version of Lady Catherine de Bourgh, with a bit of Mrs Norris thrown in.

22. (p. 132) See *OED, break*: to become bankrupt.

23. (p. 132) See *OED, bench: the King's Bench*: the seat of justice, in which originally the sovereign presided.

24. (p. 132) Austen has tinkered a fair bit with this passage, in which Maria, as she 'talks back' to Lady Greville, looks forward to Elizabeth Bennet and her spunky resistance to Lady Catherine: 'but your Ladyship knows best' is cancelled after 'I fancy not'; 'Just as your Ladyship chooses' is cancelled before 'I never saw him there', which was first 'it is the same to me'; 'Laughing' is replaced by 'being thought too saucy'. She seems to be working at letting Maria be spirited without quite being rude.

25. (p. 133) Lady Greville's refusal to descend from her carriage is a peculiar form of insult later to be practised on Mrs Collins by Lady Catherine.

26. (p. 133) The image of Maria walking to a dinner party perhaps foreshadows that of Elizabeth Bennet as she walks three miles cross-country to visit her ill sister at Netherfield.

27. (p. 134) This letter is from a section entitled simply *Scraps*, dedicated to Jane's niece Fanny, daughter of Edward Austen; it is included because the female philosopher, Julia Millar, seems to be an early version of Mary Bennet. Amongst the selections from Volume the Second that I have not included are *The History of England* ('by a partial, prejudiced, and ignorant Historian . . . There will be very few Dates in this History'), and *Lesley Castle*, which is dedicated to Jane's fourth brother Henry (1771–1850); he was in the Oxford militia, became a banker, and ended as a clergyman; he served as intermediary between Austen and her publisher.

374   *Jane Austen*

VOLUME THE THIRD

1. (p. 136) The fragment seems originally to have been called *Kitty*, which has been erased in the first paragraph, and replaced by Catharine, but has been allowed to stand elsewhere in the MS.

2. (p. 137) This phrase is erased in the MS.

3. (p. 138) Jane's early distaste for the 'option' of becoming a governess looks forward to that expressed so unequivocally by Jane Fairfax in *Emma* (see, for example, chapter 35).

4. (p. 138) As Chapman points out in his edition of Volume the Third, Cecilia Wynne's fate is similar to that experienced by Jane's own Aunt Philadelphia Austen, 'who was shipped to Madras in 1752 and became Mrs Hancock within seven months'.

5. (p. 139) Mr Dudley looks forward to a number of clergymen, notably Mr Collins and Mr Elton, ill-suited to their profession; and his daughter, to a long line of fortune-hunters.

6. (p. 139) Kitty's aunt was first named 'Peterson', but the MS has been emended here and elsewhere to read 'Percival'. The *OED* cites *Mrs* as the title 'prefixed to the name of an unmarried lady' to 1791.

7. (p. 140) The contrast between Catharine and a 'typical' heroine looks forward to the opening paragraphs of *Northanger Abbey*, and the introduction of Catherine Morland in similar terms.

8. (p. 141) Cf. Mrs Elton's determination to imitate her friends (Selina, Clara, and the two Milmans) and neglect her music now that she is 'a married woman' (*Emma*, chapter 32).

9. (p. 141) The portrait of Camilla is markedly similar to that of *Northanger Abbey*'s Isabella Thorpe.

10. (p. 141) This phrase is erased in the MS.

11. (p. 141) Charlotte Smith (1749–1806), a romantic, Gothic novelist comparable to Ann Radcliffe; *Emmeline, The Orphan of the Castle* (1788) was her first novel; *Ethelinde* appeared in 1790, just two years before the dedication of *Catharine*.

12. (p. 142) *Grasmere*: a village and lake in the heart of the Lake District.

13. (p. 142) The device of using literary ignorance as a means of reflecting general moral shallowness reappears in chapters 6 and 7 of *Northanger Abbey*, in which we are treated to the Thorpes' 'views' of *The Mysteries of Udolpho*, *Sir Charles Grandison* and *Camilla*.

14. (p. 142) Matlock is *in* Derbyshire, Scarborough is on the sea in Yorkshire (into which Camilla believes they are not going); Chapman remarks that her geography 'may remind us of Mrs Bennet's idea of Newcastle . . . or of Mrs Musgrove's ignorance of the Bahamas'.

15. (p. 143) *I believe . . . else*: this phrase is erased in the MS. Mrs Percival looks forward in some ways to Miss Bates (though in her hypochondria she is closer to Mr Woodhouse); but Austen seems here to have decided against giving Kitty Emma's sharpness of tongue.

16. (p. 143) Jane's fierce antipathy for Elizabeth I, which seems largely to be based on her imprisonment and execution of Mary, is expounded at length in her *History of England*, where Elizabeth is 'the destroyer of all comfort, the deceitful Betrayer of trust reposed in her, and the murderess of her cousin'.

17. (p. 145) See *OED*, *to find in*: to supply with.

18. (p. 146) The superficiality of *Northanger Abbey*'s Mrs Allen and Isabella is similarly underscored by their fixation upon dress (e.g. chapters 9 and 15).

19. (p. 148) Camilla may mean 'difficult to please', 'particular', or 'critical'; it is difficult to be sure as *OED* supplies seventeen separate definitions for *nice*: Henry Tilney is to tease Catherine Morland for her imprecise use of the same word ('do you not think Udolpho the nicest book in the world?' *Northanger Abbey*, chapter 14).

20. (p. 148) *If so . . . having it*. This sentence is erased in the MS, again apparently to moderate the sharpness of Kitty's tongue.

21. (p. 148) This phrase is erased in the MS.

22. (p. 151) *of . . . disposition*: in the MS this phrase replaces 'of their being disposed to like one another', which is erased.

23. (p. 152) This phrase is erased in the MS.

24. (p. 152) Mrs Stanley, as the defective mother whose bad judgement is all too clearly manifested in the form of Camilla, looks forward to the likes of Mrs Dashwood and Mrs Bennet.

25. (p. 152) The Regency walking dress has replaced a mere bonnet in the MS.

26. (p. 153) Originally, the MS read 'gone but half an hour . . . in another hour and a half she might be there'. The changes make Kitty both more serious as a letter writer, and less vain, in that she requires little time to dress.

27. (p. 154) This phrase is erased in the MS.

28. (p. 154) *for . . . powder*: this phrase is erased in the MS. Presumably the purpose of this and the preceding deletion is to de-emphasize Kitty's vanity, the better to contrast with Stanley's.

29. (p. 155) As the loquacious, comical confidante-maid, Anne is a hangover from the Gothic tradition (e.g. *Udolpho's* Annette) who disappears in Austen's mature works.

30. (p. 155) See *OED*, *hack*: a horse let out for hire.

31. (p. 156) See *OED*, *courtesy*: 'customary expression of respect; . . . the

action of inclining, bowing'. I have kept the MS form as the modern substitute seems less expressive.

32. (p. 157) With his wit, charm, good looks, and vanity, young Stanley seems most to look forward to that later breath of fresh air, Frank Churchill.

33. (p. 157) *I took her for you*: yet, in his introductory speech, Stanley claimed Kitty to be 'too well known to me by description to need any information of [her name]'.

34. (p. 163) *William Pitt* (1759–1806), English statesman and Prime Minister at the time of *Catharine*'s composition.

35. (p. 166) *It* replaces the following phrase in the MS: 'Why in fact, it is nothing more than being young and handsome – and that . . .'

36. (p. 167) See *OED*, *impudent*: shameless, indelicate.

37. (p. 167) *Her intimacies . . . amiss to her*: this phrase is erased in the MS. Perhaps in retrospect this effective charge of promiscuity seemed excessive, even from Mrs Percival.

38. (p. 169) See *OED*, *calculated*: fitted, suited (to 1722).

39. (p. 169) Jane's own judgement of Richard III, according to her *History of England*, seems to be rather *un*decided: 'It has indeed been confidently asserted that he killed his two nephews and his wife, but it has also been declared that he did *not* . . . Whether innocent or guilty, he did not reign long in peace . . .' Chapman raises the possibility that Jane had read Horace Walpole's *Historic Double* on the character of Richard III.

40. (p. 170) The *Sermons*, by the Scottish divine, Hugh Blair (1718–1800), were in five volumes, the first of which appeared in 1777; *Cœlebs in Search of a Wife*, by Hannah More (1745–1833), a fictional piece exposing the corruption of the Regency, appeared in 1809. These two titles were added, obviously much later, replacing Secker's *Lectures on the Catechism of the Church of England* (1769). Chapman points out that Blair's *Sermons* were admired by Mary Crawford; generally, the works of both More and Blair were enormously popular.

41. (p. 174) *To think every body is in love with me*: a standard pitfall for romantic heroines (e.g. Arabella in Charlotte Lennox's *The Female Quixote*). All too soon, however, Kitty is seen to be forgetting her lesson. Swayed by Camilla's words, Kitty's judgement starts to falter, and we find her (by p. 176) beginning to think, and speak, with an extravagance alarmingly reminiscent of *Love and Friendship*'s Laura.

42. (p. 176) Chapman notes that, from here on, 'a slight change in hand, and a more obvious change in the colour of the ink', suggest that remainder of the MS was written after the rest. For the first time 'Mrs Percival' stands, and is not an interlinear correction for 'Mrs Peterson'.

Charlotte Brontë

PART I: ORIGINS OF ANGRIA

1. (p. 181) This excerpt was reprinted by Mrs Gaskell in her *Life*. 'Maria' was the eldest Brontë girl, the model for Helen Burns in *Jane Eyre*, who died (as did Elizabeth, the second daughter) in 1825 of a fever contracted at Cowan Bridge School. 'Tabby' was Tabitha Akroyd, the devoted family servant, who stayed with them until she was in her eighties, and used to delight the children with her fairy stories. 'Aunt' is the sister of Mrs Brontë, who came to the parsonage to keep house after her death; according to Gaskell, the aunt's fear of taking cold eventually led her to pass 'nearly all her time, and [take] most of her meals, in her bed-room'.

   In his edition of Gaskell's *Life*, Alan Shelstone notes that 'Christopher North' was the pseudonym for *Blackwood*'s founder, John Wilson, and that the peculiarity of some of the company's names is explained by the pseudonymous nature of many of the contributions.

2. (p. 182) Branwell, in his *History of the Young Men* (December 1830) reports that Emily's and Anne's soldiers were named Parry and Ross, after their heroes, the explorers.

3. (p. 183) Wise and Symington note that Maimoune, daughter of a genie king, is a figure from the *Arabian Nights*.

4. (p. 183) The leader of the group, though not mentioned here, is the Duke of York.

5. (p. 184) See *OED*, *oxeye* 6: 'Those Dreadful Storms on the Coasts of Guinea, which the Seamen call the Ox-Eye, from their Beginning; because at first it seems no bigger than an Ox's-Eye' (C. Purshall, 1705).

6. (p. 186) See *OED*, *genius* 2: a demon or spiritual being in general. Now chiefly in the plural, *genii*, (the singular being replaced by 'genie'), as a rendering of Arab *jinn*, the collective name of a class of spirits . . . supposed to interfere powerfully in human affairs.

7. (p. 188) *Arabian Nights* was not the only source of magical material for Charlotte. Gérin notes a striking parallel from James Ridley's *Tales of the Genii* (1764): 'as soon as they arrived at the Palace [the Genius] led her little charges into a spacious Saloon, where on 28 Thrones of Gold sat the good race of the Genii; and beneath, on carpets covering the whole saloon, were numberless of the lower class of Genii, each with 2 or more of the Faithful under their charge'.

8. (p. 188) Cf. Charlotte's own words on first seeing her soldier in *The History of the Year*: as Fannie Ratchford reports in *The Brontës' Web of Childhood*, the children themselves became the chief genii, aptly named Tallii, Brannii, Emmii and Annii.

9. (p. 191) The exchange between Murray, O'Donell, and the duke is of interest for a number of reasons: first, it demonstrates the easy and absolute power of the duke, which will be passed on to his son Arthur, Duke of Zamorna; second, the sneering Murray looks forward, possibly, both to the duke's sour second son, Charles, and to the later character of Henry Hastings; third, the reference to civil war foreshadows the later destructive conflict between Zamorna and Percy.

10. (p. 191) Fifteen thousand men, but no mention of any women! We are not enlightened as to how this substantial demographic increase has come about.

11. (p. 192) The date of 1827 is confusing, as is the previous one of 1816, which has been altered in the manuscript, the '6' first reading '4' and then '5'. The chronology of the first part of the story, presented with great care, suggests that Arthur would have returned to England in mid-October 1794; we are then specifically told that roughly twenty years pass before he comes back as duke to Africa. Thus we would expect the first date, and also, probably, the second, to read 1814, as it hardly seems likely that the African group would wait over a decade after the departure of the Duke of York to select a new leader.

12. (p. 193) Snug the room may be; otherwise this scene seems clearly to foreshadow Jane Eyre's imprisonment in the Red Room (chapter 2) and her perception, real or otherwise, of Mr Reed's ghost.

PART II: MARIAN V. ZENOBIA

1. (p. 195) Charlotte here spells the Marquis's title *Duro*, but later it is consistently *Douro*, perhaps after a river in Spain, near the border of Portugal. The Douro runs through the province of Zamora, possibly the source for Arthur's later title, Duke of Zamorna. Though he ages roughly ten years in the decade 1829–39, Charlotte feels free to take some liberties with chronology; the next piece, written in 1830, finds Arthur only nineteen years old.

2. (p. 196) The names of Albion and Marina are pseudonyms for Arthur Wellesley and Marian Hume (Arthur's first wife); Cornelius is, presumably, Charles (Arthur's brother) and Zelzia reappears as Zenobia, who later marries Arthur's rival, Percy. The narrator of this story, the ill-tempered Charles, is to become Charlotte's narrator in many of

her subsequent tales. He prefaces this story with a confession that it is told 'out of malignity for the injuries that have lately been offered me . . . the conclusion [in which Marian dies] is wholly destitute of any foundation in truth, and I did it out of revenge.' (It is perhaps worth noting that resurrection was a common event in the Brontës' early works.) Charlotte adds her own note at the end of the preface: 'I wrote this in four hours. – C.B.'

3. (p. 197) See *OED*, *nae sheepshank* (Sc.); a person or thing of no small importance.

4. (p. 198) See *OED*, *hoodie*: the hooded or royston crow.

5. (p. 198) *Albion*: ancient Celtic or pre-Celtic name of Great Britain; thus an appropriate pseudonym for Arthur.

6. (p. 198) *Apollo Belvedere*: see *OED belvedere*, '[a. It. *belvedere* "a faire sight . . ."] *1834* . . . Apollo Belvedere, a celebrated statue of Apollo, placed . . . in the Belvidere of the Vatican, whence it derives its present name.'

7. (p. 200) Marian/Marina is fifteen when she and Arthur/Albion first fall in love. Albion, as we have been told, is nineteen.

8. (p. 201) Glass Town is the city constructed in the 'Twelve Adventurers'; its name later became Verreopolis, and finally Verdopolis.

9. (p. 201) Gérin (*Charlotte Brontë*, p. 43) notes that the work of the artist John Martin included 'vast perspectives of the lost cities of the ancient world', such as Nineveh and Babylon. Between 1826 and 1837, Martin's engravings were printed regularly in the *Annuals*, and Mr Brontë himself owned four of them. Thus they were accessible to the little Brontës, 'upon whom Martin's imagery was to have a decisive influence'; cf. also the description of the undersea temple in 'An Adventure in Ireland'.

10. (p. 201) *Ninus*: King of Assyria, of which Nineveh was the capital; *Belus*: an Asiatic king, founder of Babylon.

11. (p. 201) *Astarte*: an early relative of Aphrodite, and the dead beloved of the hero in Byron's *Manfred*. (See also *Paradise Lost*, I, 439.) *Semele*: mother of Dionysius.

12. (p. 203) The glamorous Zelzia/Zenobia looks forward to Jane Eyre's rival, Blanche Ingram (chapter 17), who is 'tall as a poplar, moulded like a Diana', with 'noble bust . . . dark eyes and black ringlets . . . Her face was like her mother's [who had Roman features].' Mrs Ingram, too, wears 'a crimson velvet robe'. While Zelzia's ostrich feather adds to the 'imposing dignity of her appearance', Jane's later, sharper tongue remarks that Mrs Ingram's turban 'invested her (I suppose she thought) with a truly imperial dignity'. Gérin notes that the Brontës' knowledge of the latest fashions in London dress came

from their perusal of the *Annuals*, which printed 'portraits of the
hostesses in the news' (*Charlotte Brontë*, p. 49).

13. (p. 203) Madame de Staël, the French novelist (1766–1817), widely
admired and sought after in her own day; 'from her earliest years a
romp, a coquette, and passionately desirous of prominence and
attention' (*Encyclopedia Brittanica*, 1911).

14. (p. 203) Zelzia's song continues as follows:

> I think of thee when the snowy swan
>   Glides calmly down the stream;
> Its plumes the breezes scarcely fan,
>   Awed by their radiant gleam.
>
> For thus I've seen the loud winds hush
>   To pass thy beauty by,
> With soft caress and playful rush
>   'Mid thy bright tresses fly.
>
> And I have seen the wild birds sail
>   In rings thy head above,
> While thou hast stood like lily pale
>   Unknowing of their love.

15. (p. 204) This scene, most dramatically, looks forward to the time when
Jane Eyre, nearly worn down by St John Rivers' persistent proposals
(chapter 35), hears Mr Rochester's voice calling her, and resolves to
return to Thornfield. It is also, perhaps, reminiscent of the confronta-
tion between Byron's Manfred and the spirit of his beloved Astarte,
who calls his name, foretells his death, and then slips away.

16. (p. 205) Cf. Jane's response: 'Down superstition! . . . This is not thy
deception, nor thy witchcraft: it is the work of nature.'

17. (p. 206) Marina's song continues as follows:

> Nature's self seemed clothed in mourning;
>   Even the star-like woodland flower,
> With its leaflets fair, adorning
>   The pathway to the forest-bower,
>   Drooped its head.
>
> From the cavern of the mountain,
>   From the groves that crown the hill,
> From the stream, and from the fountain,
>   Sounds prophetic murmured still,
>   Betokening grief.

> Boding winds came fitful, sighing,
>   Through the tall and leafy trees;
> Birds of omen, wildly crying,
>   Sent their calls upon the breeze
>   Wailing round me.
>
> At each sound I paled and trembled,
>   At each step I raised my head,
> Hearkening if it his resembled,
>   Or if news that he was dead
>   Were come from far.

18. (p. 206) Jane Eyre, later comparing notes with Mr Rochester, discovers that she heard his voice at the same moment ('last Monday night, somewhere near midnight') that he had called her name (chapter 37).

19. (p. 207) *The Rivals* is one piece in a two-volume collection entitled *Visits in Verreopolis*. In a preface, Charlotte's narrator, Charles Wellesley, notes that 'I have nothing to say, except that Verreopolis means the Glass Town, being compounded of a Greek and French word to that effect; and that I fear the reader will find this the dullest and dryest book I have ever written. With this fair warning I bid him good-bye.'

20. (p. 207) This verse form – five-beat lines, unrhymed couplets – is the predominant one used by Byron in his dramatic poem, *Manfred*.

21. (p. 214) Marian Hume, with her fragile beauty and her blend of childish and womanly qualities, seems pretty clearly to be an early version of the little countess, Paulina Mary Home of *Villette*, of whom, for example, Charlotte is later to write: 'a tinge of summer crimson heightened her complexion; her curls fell full and long on her lily neck; her white dress suited the heat of June' (chapter 30). Marian also shares her auburn curls with Byron's Haidée (see *Don Juan*, II).

22. (p. 215) Wise and Symington note that Marian's song is an earlier composition, first appearing in an 1831 manuscript. The last three verses are as follows:

> Then, O Lord of the Waters! the great and all-seeing!
> Preserve in thy mercy his safety and being;
>   May he trust in thy might
>   When the dark storm is howling,
>   And the blackness of night
>   Over heaven is scowling;
> But may the sea flow glidingly
>   With gentle summer waves;
> And silent may all tempests lie
>   Chained in Æolian caves!

Yet, though ere he returnest long years will have vanished,
Sweet hope from my bosom shall never be banished:
    I will think of the time
  When his step, lightly bounding,
    Shall be heard on the rock
  Where the cataract is sounding;
When the banner of his father's host
    Shall be unfurled on high,
To welcome back the pride and boast
    Of England's chivalry!

Yet tears will flow forth while of hope I am singing;
Still Despair her dark shadow is over me flinging;
    But, when he's far away,
  I will pluck the wild flower
    On bank and on brae
  At the still, moonlight hour;
And I will twine for him a wreath
    Low in the fairy's dell;
Methought I heard the night wind breathe
    That solemn word: 'Farewell!'

23. (p. 217) Charlotte adds the following explanatory note: 'It is the custom in Verdopolis, where perhaps forty or fifty noblemen, with their attendants, go to shoot or hunt wild beasts and birds in the desolate and uninhabited Mountains of the Moon, to form a sort of camp for their mutual protection and defence. These camps sometimes contain upwards of a hundred individuals.'

24. (p. 218) The theme of labour unrest and assassination of an unpopular employer, which looks back to the Luddite movement (1811–13), is later developed in *Shirley*, with the storming of Robert Moore's mill, and the attempt on his life.

25. (p. 219) The Brontës being ardent followers of all Parliamentary proceedings, it is not surprising that oratorical brilliance should figure prominently amongst Arthur's broad range of skills.

26. (p. 220) This handy magical powder seems to be an import from *Arabian Nights*. The abrupt transition, from Parliament to fairyland, is a perfect illustration of Gérin's observation: '[Charlotte] did not turn away from the real world in distaste; she hugged it to her heart, and integrated it into her dreams, investing the England of the early nineteenth century with all the magic of an Arabian Nights' entertainment' (*Charlotte Brontë*, p. 30).

27. (p. 220) Crashie is a potent deity in the Brontë pantheon.

28. (p. 220) For Azazel, see *Paradise Lost*, I, 534: 'a Cherube tall:/Who forthwith from the glittering Staff unfurld/Th' Imperial Ensign'.

29. (p. 221) *Danhasch*: an evil genie from the *Arabian Nights*.

30. (p. 224) *Montmorency*: one of Rogue's co-conspirators.

31. (p. 225) For the form see *OED*, ring v², pa.t.: 'On the batter'd shield Rung the loud lance' (1797, Southey, *Joan of Arc*, VI).

PART III: MARY

1. (p. 227) *Phidian*: in the style of Phidias, a famed Athenian sculptor (born *c*. 490 BC). It is tempting to propose the young Percy, with his cold, Grecian beauty, as an early model for St John Rivers.

2. (p. 227) The contrast between Percy's ice and Zamorna's fire evidently looks forward to that between Rivers and Rochester in *Jane Eyre*. Charlotte's language as she makes the contrast is oddly like her later criticism of Jane Austen: 'what throbs fast and full, though hidden, what the blood rushes through, what is the unseen seat of life and the sentient target of death – this Miss Austen ignores' (from a letter to W. S. Williams, 12 April 1850).

3. (p. 228) Zenobia's witch-like propensities, her jealousy and ungovernable passion, perhaps look forward to Bertha Rochester.

4. (p. 231) Given the fatal attraction that Arthur/Zamorna feels for Rogue/Northangerland, it is hardly suprising that he should find himself drawn to the daughter as well. This passage prepares for a later development in the Angrian saga: to punish Northangerland for his treachery, Zamorna decides to repudiate Mary, and by killing the daughter, to destroy her father.

5. (p. 231) Byron's judgement is, obviously, the last word.

6. (p. 231) Charles is, as usual, the narrator of the piece.

7. (p. 232) Charles has little difficulty penetrating his brother's disguise.

8. (p. 233) See *OED*, *sparkler*: one who sparkles; especially a vivacious, witty, or pretty young woman (1713).

9. (p. 233) See *OED*, *roquelaure*: named after the Duke of Roquelaure; a cloak reaching to the knee worn by men in the eighteenth and early nineteenth centuries (1716).

10. (p. 234) *S'death*: one of Percy's allies.

11. (p. 234) The 'host of loveliness' refers to the aristocratic bevy observed by Charles at Zamorna, an Angrian province. King of Angria has now been added to the list of Arthur's titles.

12. (p. 235) The first part of their conversation apparently refers to Zamorna's habitual philandering.

13. (p. 235) Adrian is Mary's special name for her husband.

14. (p. 236) The letter, composed by Branwell, is printed by Wise and Symington in vol. I, pp. 457–61.

15. (p. 239) Gérin notes that Branwell's 'heated imagination often led to seizures that had the likeness of fits' (*Charlotte Brontë*, p. 89).

16. (p. 242) *Lady Helen*: Northangerland's mother, Mary's grandmother.

17. (p. 243) Ernest and Julius are Zamorna's, but not Mary's, sons.

18. (p. 246) The fact that Charlotte omits verses 5 and 6, and reverses 7 and 8, suggests that she was quoting from memory. If so, her accuracy is formidable.

19. (p. 246) Here Zamorna refers to his plan to destroy Mary by repudiating her.

20. (p. 247) The eight-line stanza form is the same as that used by Byron in *Don Juan*.

21. (p. 249) *Ionian*: a branch of the Greek people mentioned by Homer, renowned for their music and architecture, as well as their conquests.

22. (p. 250) Alnwick is a family home to which Mary has been 'exiled' after being repudiated by Zamorna.

23. (p. 251) See *OED*, *corbeille*: 'an elegant fruit or flower basket' (1800).

24. (p. 252) The mysterious fruit-girl turns out to be Zamorna's devoted mistress, Mina Laury, who has followed him into exile. Though she does not play a major role in the early Angrian saga, her connection with Zamorna evidently began years ago, when they were both fifteen.

25. (p. 259) Mary has been told, and believes, that Zamorna was drowned in a storm at sea.

26. (p. 264) Ellrington Hall is Northangerland's Verdopolitan residence.

27. (p. 266) *bagatelle*: trifle.

28. (p. 266) Caroline is the illegitimate daughter of Northangerland and Louisa – who does not here allow her feelings of maternal tenderness to stand in the way of her instincts for survival.

29. (p. 266) *détenu*: prisoner.

30. (p. 268) It was generally left to Branwell to take charge of military matters. In September 1836, while Charlotte was at Roe Head, Branwell wrote that he had decided to have Mary die; 'the news affected Charlotte like a family loss' (*Charlotte Brontë*, p. 107). But during the 1836–7 Christmas break, when The Return of Zamorna was composed, Mary was evidently allowed to be resurrected.

31. (p. 269) Eugene is the duke's valet.

PART IV: MINA

1. (p. 271) This story is a conflation of two episodes, written over a two-year period. The first part, from the *History of Angria*, written in April 1836, takes place chronologically before *Zamorna's Exile* and *Return* – the duke is still intent on his scheme to repudiate his wife – and concludes on p. 283. The later half reveals Zamorna to have fallen considerably in Charlotte's estimation, if not in that of his other worshippers.

2. (p. 271) Hawkscliffe is Zamorna's country estate.

3. (p. 276) Darius III (*c.* 380–330 BC), 'outgeneralled and outfought' by the invading Alexander, 'his defeat being aggravated by his personal cowardice' (*Oxford Classical Dictionary*).

4. (p. 291) Mina does not, of course, realize that she is talking to the Queen of Angria; Mary clearly begins to suspect that Mina is *someone's* mistress, but *whose* she does not divine.

5. (p. 291) See *OED, liberty*, the district over which a person's privilege extends.

6. (p. 293) Zamorna, we remember, is fresh from his duel with Hartford.

7. (p. 295) Cf. *The Book of Esther*, vii, 2: 'And the King said again unto Esther on the second day at the banquet of wine, What is thy petition, queen Esther? and it shall be granted thee: and what is thy request? and it shall be performed, even to the half of the kingdom.' Unlike Esther, however, Mina has no petition.

8. (p. 295) See *OED, Milesian*, 'of or pertaining to King Milesius or his people; Irish'; (from *Milesius* [Miledh], a fabulous Spanish king whose sons are reputed to have conquered and reorganized the ancient kingdom of Ireland about 1300 BC).

PART V: ELIZABETH

1. (p. 301) Charles is still Charlotte's narrator, but his last name has become Townsend. Evidently he has ceased to be Zamorna's brother.

2. (p. 303) Townsend's fellow traveller is Elizabeth Hastings, whose interest in, and defence of, the 'illustrious 19th' will later be explained by the fact that her beloved brother, Henry, has been an officer in that regiment.

3. (p. 305) The parallels between Elizabeth's personal appearance and that of Jane Eyre and Charlotte herself are striking.

4. (p. 306) Charles refers, of course, to the Duke of Zamorna, heart-throb of all the ladies – except for the independent Miss Hastings.

5. (p. 307) Elizabeth's spunk, and her gift for repartee, again look forward to Jane Eyre.

6. (p. 307) The 'splendid equipment' is that of the society beauty, Jane Moore. Elizabeth (who reappears in chapter 4), is employed as Jane's companion.

7. (p. 310) 'Wilson' is the pseudonym of the fugitive, Henry Hastings, brother of Elizabeth. 'Louisa' is the mistress of Northangerland, previously encountered in the *Return of Zamorna*.

8. (p. 311) Wilson claims to be a Scotch trader, but Townsend has recognized him as 'some scoundrelly broken officer . . . who dared not own his country and had blotted out his family name'.

9. (p. 312) The 'soldan' is Zamorna, upon whose life Hastings will later make an attempt – at the instigation of Macara and his crew.

10. (p. 313) The two men thus relentlessly tracking Elizabeth's brother are her present employer and the man who will seek to become her lover.

11. (p. 316) See *OED*, *ing*; meadow-land.

12. (p. 317) See *OED*, *moreen*; a coarse, woollen fabric.

13. (p. 318) Cf. the tense shifts, for dramatic effect, in *Jane Eyre* (e.g. chapters 22 and 23).

14. (p. 318) The portrait of Elizabeth – her plain dress, her affinity with the moon, her small stature – is again reminiscent of Jane Eyre.

15. (p. 320) In an 1834 letter, Charlotte warns her pious friend Ellen Nussey against Byron's *Cain*, but calls it a 'magnificent poem'. Emily's sympathy for the Cain-figure is evident in the character of Heathcliff.

16. (p. 321) Henry is sought for the murder of Adams.

17. (p. 321) *Pendleton*: the Hastings' birthplace. Pendle Hill is a landmark near Haworth. Gérin points out, in *Five Novelettes*, that Angria is becoming more like Yorkshire and less like Africa.

18. (p. 321) Northangerland, Zamorna's foe, was Branwell's special hero as well as Henry's.

19. (p. 321) Cf. the attempts of Louisa, the establishment beauty, to soothe Hastings.

20. (p. 322) Elizabeth's employment as Jane Moore's companion, and her evident sour feelings about it, coincide with Charlotte's first experience as a governess in the spring of 1839.

21. (p. 324) *Paros*: the second largest of the Cyclades, a centre of Aegean trade, and famous for its marble.

22. (p. 324) The 'little shade' is, of course, Elizabeth Hastings. The contrast between the two women here looks forward to that between Blanche Ingram and Jane Eyre, or Ginevra Fanshawe and Lucy Snowe.

23. (p. 328) Gérin points out that Charlotte has characteristically suited the climate to the actual period of the year in which she is writing.

24. (p. 328) In other words, she is not like Elizabeth.

25. (p. 329) Jane's shallowness is reflected in her childish speech patterns; Sir William manipulates her with sinister ease, getting all the information he wants without her ever realizing that she is being used.

26. (p. 330) Gérin remarks that the whole of this passage evidently applies to Haworth and the Brontë family.

27. (p. 331) Boulsworth Hill is a landmark on the moors near Haworth. Henry's remark indicates a homesickness reminiscent of that suffered by the Brontë children when away from home.

28. (p. 332) In *Paradise Lost*, the capital of hell.

29. (p. 332) See Revelations xvi, 16 ff. for the final battle between the forces of good and evil.

30. (p. 333) See *OED*, *rate*; to chide, scold.

31. (p. 334) Pattens were a kind of overshoe worn by the Yorkshire villagers as protection against the mud or wet.

32. (p. 335) i.e. Lord Hartford.

33. (p. 335) I omit a subsequent passage in which Sir William procrastinates outrageously, so as to enrage the hated Hartford, though he is equally anxious to capture Hastings.

34. (p. 336) See *OED*, *visnomy*, dialect form of physiognomy.

35. (p. 342) Mary Percy, fully reinstated as Duchess of Zamorna and Queen of Angria, is sister of Sir William. Charlotte's sympathy seems wholly to have turned from Mary, and towards Elizabeth.

36. (p. 346) Day and date are correct by the 1839 calendar. Charles is again the narrator.

37. (p. 347) Another 'northernism' identified by Gérin; piece halls were used in northern wool-manufacturing towns for the display of woven fabrics.

38. (p. 347) The technique – the key scene observed at a distance, by a character who does not know what is going on – perhaps looks forward to that employed in *Shirley*, as Caroline and Shirley watch the attack on Robert's mill in the valley below.

39. (p. 348) See 2 Samuel i, 19, 25.

40. (p. 350) This allusion is, of course, a very painful one; for Branwell, by his obsessive 'private meanness', did finally alienate the affection of his loyal sister.

41. (p. 351) See *OED*, *emmet*, an ant.

42. (p. 351) The dream of securing independence by setting up a school was one cherished by the Brontë sisters, though theirs failed, and by Lucy Snowe, whose school was a success.

43. (p. 351) Elizabeth shares Charlotte's own feelings, who writes in her Roe Head Journal, August 1836: 'am I to spend the best part of my life

in this wretched bondage, forcibly suppressing my rage . . . and of compulsion assuming an air of kindness, patience and assiduity?' (*Charlotte Brontë*, p. 104; cf. also Jane Eyre's dubious response to her new teaching duties at Morton: 'surely I shall find some happiness in discharging that office. Much enjoyment I do not expect . . . I felt desolate to a degree . . . I felt degraded' (chapter 31).

44. (p. 352) Elizabeth's homesickness must parallel that felt by Charlotte for Haworth when she was at Roe Head or the Sidgwicks'.

45. (p. 353) Elizabeth's complaint continues:

> How fruitless then to ponder
> O'er such dreams as chained her now,
> Her heart should cease to wander
> And her tears no more should flow.
> The trance was over – over,
> The spell was scattered far,
> Yet how blest were she whose lover
> Would be Angria's young Hussar!
>
> Earth knew no hope more glorious,
> Heaven gave no nobler boon,
> Than to welcome him victorious
> To a heart he claimed his own.
> How sweet to tell each feeling
> The kindled soul might prove!
> How sad to die concealing
> The anguish born of love!

46. (p. 354) Elizabeth's romantic yearnings for Sir William are reminiscent of Caroline Helstone's for Robert Moore; the way in which she scoots herself up to bed is rather more like Jane Eyre. Elizabeth's feelings for Sir William may at first strike us as odd, but in fact *we* know much more of the unpleasant side of his character than *she* does. Also, he has been kind to her: by allowing her to follow Hartford when Henry was brought to bay at Massinger, and by helping to secure her an audience with his sister the queen. Then, in the missing fragment, he has further shown some feeling for her by attempting to make her a gift of a cross. Finally, the fact that Henry is now out of danger makes his pursuers less frightening.

47. (p. 355) Charlotte's friend Ellen Nussey writes that 'Charlotte had a mortal dread of unknown animals'. 'Reminiscences of CB', *Scribners Magazine*, May 1872.

48. (p. 356) *Continuations*: gaiters continuous with 'shorts'; hence trousers (1825; *OED*).

49. (p. 357) Cf. Mr Rochester's plea: 'You have neither relatives nor acquaintances whom you need fear to offend . . .' and Jane's inner response: 'Who in the world cares for *you*? or who will be injured by what you do?' (chapter 27).

50. (p. 358) This reference to a scene from the missing fragment recalls Jane Eyre's resistance to accepting gifts from Mr Rochester.

51. (p. 360) Cf. Rochester's attempts to make Jane jealous through his supposed attachment to Blanche Ingram.

52. (p. 362) Sir William's jealousy over the conventional good looks of Zamorna, and Elizabeth's amused response, look forward to the scene at Ferndean when Jane teases Rochester with her account of St John's Apollonian appearance (chapter 37).

53. (p. 364) Elizabeth's frankness in confessing her love, and her determination, nonetheless, to preserve her honour, look forward to a similar combination of passion and independence in Jane Eyre.

MORE ABOUT PENGUINS, PELICANS, PEREGRINES AND PUFFINS

For further information about books available from Penguins please write to Dept EP, Penguin Books Ltd, Harmondsworth, Middlesex UB7 0DA.

In the U.S.A.: For a complete list of books available from Penguins in the United States write to Dept DG, Penguin Books, 299 Murray Hill Parkway, East Rutherford, New Jersey 07073.

In Canada: For a complete list of books available from Penguins in Canada write to Penguin Books Canada Ltd, 2801 John Street, Markham, Ontario L3R 1B4.

In Australia: For a complete list of books available from Penguins in Australia write to the Marketing Department, Penguin Books Australia Ltd, P.O. Box 257, Ringwood, Victoria 3134.

In New Zealand: For a complete list of books available from Penguins in New Zealand write to the Marketing Department, Penguin Books (N.Z.) Ltd, Private Bag, Takapuna, Auckland 9.

In India: For a complete list of books available from Penguins in India write to Penguin Overseas Ltd, 706 Eros Apartments, 56 Nehru Place, New Delhi 110019.